F. TENNYSON JESSE

was born at Chislehurst, Kent, in 1888, on her father's side the great-niece of Alfred, Lord Tennyson; on her mother's side descended from Cornish seafarers, until her grandfather made a fortune in coal. After studying art at the Newlyn School of Stanhope and Elizabeth Forbes in Cornwall, in 1911 she began a career as a journalist, writing for *The Times* and the *Daily Mail*, and when war came she was one of the few women journalists to report from the Front.

In 1918 she married the playwright H. M. Harwood, and throughout their long married life they collaborated on several plays. All seven of her own plays were produced in the West End, the most famous of which were the wartime success *Billeted* (1917), and *The Pelican* (1924). Fryniwyd Tennyson Jesse published three collections of short stories and her very first, the famous tale *The Mask* (1912), has been translated and performed dramatically on stage, film and television. She also published poems, belles lettres and a notable history of Burma. She was a brilliant criminologist, editing six volumes of the Notable British Trials series, her *Murder and its Motives* being acclaimed by authorities in this field.

Of the nine novels she wrote, *A Pin to See the Peepshow* (1934) – televised by the BBC in 1972 – is perhaps the best known, whilst *The Lacquer Lady* (1929) is critically considered her greatest work of fiction. Both are published by Virago. F. Tennyson Jesse travelled widely and had dual homes in France and England. She died in London in 1958, leaving behind her a prodigious body of work, the breadth and versatility of which distinguish her as one of the most talented British writers of the inter-war years.

A PIN TO SEE
THE PEEP SHOW

F. Tennyson Jesse

NEW INTRODUCTION
by
Elaine Morgan

Virago

London

To Bobby

Published by VIRAGO Limited 1979
5 Wardour Street, London W1V 3HE

First published in Great Britain
by William Heinemann Ltd 1934

ISBN 0 86068 084 3

Printed in Great Britain by litho at
The Anchor Press Ltd, Tiptree, Essex

INTRODUCTION

By the standards of her day – the story opens in 1913 – Julia Almond, the central figure in *A Pin to See the Peepshow*, lacked most of the old-fashioned virtues that romantic heroines were expected to display; she was selfish, unfaithful, sharp-tongued, and discontented.

On the other hand, she fell just as far short of the standards of integrity and independence expected of the New Woman at that date. She found the question of Women's Suffrage profoundly boring. She did sometimes idly wonder: 'Why did men always think they were in the right, and that they could make women do things?' but in her view the best hope of reversing this ascendancy lay in the fact that she could sometimes catch sight of herself in a mirror and exult: 'It's true. I'm pretty.' What she thought she believed in was love. 'She'd always believed in it. She'd read books about nothing else ever since she could remember anything.'

There is nothing mysterious in the fact that F. Tennyson Jesse chose to write about a woman so far removed from her own cultured and intellectual background. She had a powerful motive for doing so, which emerges dramatically at a late stage in the novel. What is impressive is the skill and artistry with which she re-creates Julia's world, involves us in her problems, and arouses in us by the end of the book a quite passionate wish to defend her.

From the very first chapter, by the rather bossy panache with which she expresses her 'rave' on her English Mistress, Julia reveals herself in her own mind as somebody special, one of the people for whom 'something lovely was waiting to happen'. Possibly we all set out with this conviction. For some, it is strong enough to survive massive repeated doses of discouragement, and in Julia's case it certainly had to. She lived in a seedy London suburb, the only child of two querulous failures. The death of her father, ineffective as he was, nevertheless left her mother and herself financially 'as helpless as a hermit crab denuded of its shell', wide open to a take-over bid from a gruesome set of relatives, so that she escaped in desperation by marrying an older man, a widowed and sexually inept gents' outfitter.

The fact that after several years of this debilitating marriage 'she still knew she was something wonderful' indicated – what? Perhaps it was a symptom of hopeless romanticism, or mental or emotional immaturity; or, alternatively, of an excess of vitality, or of the most démodé of these cardinal virtues, Hope. Perhaps it was just that she was sexy, the possessor – like Marilyn Monroe – of a particular quality 'which, for most men, she carried like a banner'. For Julia, as for Marilyn, it proved lethal.

The trap that closed on her was partly triggered off by her own defects. It used to be a common mistake to imagine that the most passionate women were those most likely to account the world well lost for love; and if Julia had remained true even to her own sentimental tenets she would not have wrecked so many lives. She would have left her husband, defied convention, gone off with her impecunious sailor boy, and all of them might have died in their beds. But the book draws our attention to the Catch 22 bedevilling this escape route. 'Passion and comfort are after all more or less allied, and Julia, who had known passion, couldn't give up comfort.' Or respectability, either. She wanted the lot.

Tennyson Jesse, however, was an historian as well as a dramatist. Without setting out to whitewash Julia, she carefully highlights all those aspects of her social predicament – as a lower-middle-class female in the first half of the twentieth century – which drove her into fantasy and conditioned so many of her responses. In the novel Julia is surrounded by a whole series of vividly drawn minor characters who, besides playing an integral part in her own story, succinctly point the moral that if only she had been upper class – or working class – or better educated – or even French – there would have been simpler solutions to her problems. If she had been male, of course, her particular problems would not have existed at all. Young men with the same powerful belief in an iridescent future were indoctrinated to go out and make it happen; young ladies were expected to sit tight and spin their little webs and wait and dream, and make a decorous grab at anything eligible that happened along.

When I first read the novel I had not been briefed about it, and I was three-quarters through it before I had any suspicion that that portrait of a woman and a society was not going to be the sum total of it – a sort of updated English Madame Bovary. On those terms alone it would have been a memorable book. But then I found that with sickening suddenness the story had moved on to a totally different plane.

Julia becomes no longer the symbol of an unlucky and maladjusted middle-class woman; she is no longer even a symbol of woman. She is the symbol of any human being caught up in a judicial machine where the pretence of administering justice is irrevocably skewed by the prejudices of the people appointed to dispense it. Tennyson Jesse is now writing from the standpoint of her third specialism – as criminologist – and it becomes clear that she has planned the whole book as a long fuse leading up to this particular flashpoint.

Something else becomes clear: she is no longer writing fiction. You can forget that conventional disclaimer: 'Every character in this book is entirely fictitious.' You can remember instead the scathing quotation with which she chooses to preface her story. She is writing about the Thompson and Bywaters murder case.

By any literary criterion I wish I hadn't had to say that. The book works better artistically if the peripety comes for the reader with the same shock of unexpectedness as it came to Julia. But the case was a long time ago. New readers may never have heard of it and might even regard the dénouement as unconvincingly far-fetched.

When I was asked to adapt the book for television I got hold of a transcript of the Thompson and Bywaters trial and made enquiries about Edith Thompson, thinking that conceivably the author of the novel had garnished Julia with a spurious vulnerability and charm to gain our sympathy, and distorted the judicial proceedings to strengthen her case. I learned that most of the people who had known Edith Thompson personally – women as well as men – were hot in her defence, and that the facts which emerged in the trial, except for the substitution of a spanner for a knife, were as described.

In the court case, as in the book, there remained the crowning irony that if the accused woman had not procured an abortion they would not have hanged her; and the even more savage irony that if she could have explained that she was trying to procure an abortion she could have given a plain answer to some of the prosecution's most damaging questions, but 'they had warned her that she must not tell the truth about this'.

The reason was that such an admission would have been fatally damaging to her case. In the existing climate of opinion, abortion would have been considered by the already hostile judge and the gentlemen of the jury to be a more depraved act even than adultery. And whereas adultery was not a criminal offence – let alone a capital one – some of the exchanges in the course of the trial seemed to imply that for her accusers at some subliminal level adultery was the crime for which she was being tried, of which she was found guilty, and for which she was finally put to death.

Arguments about the degree of Edith Thompson's guilt or innocence can never now be finally settled. One thing is incontrovertible, i.e. the aura of sexual prejudice (as palpable as anti-semitism, apartheid or any other form of paranoia) which pervaded the court where she was tried. Even her co-defendant Bywaters may have been an indirect victim of it. He was presented as the helpless prey of an evil woman and in that role attracted some sympathy; but if murder had been done his was undoubtedly the hand that committed it. Thus the people who were determined that Edith should swing for it could not have got her without getting him, too.

The two accused seem to have made little attempt to defend one another or even to communicate. At the first touch of reality the whole fabric of the grand passion they had woven out of words and kisses and a few clandestine meetings dissolved into nothingness. Julia in the novel looks back on it and says: 'It was none of it real.'

A Pin to See the Peepshow when it was first published revived many doubts about the case and about the verdict, but revived them of course too late. You cannot reverse a hanging. So the book's final anger is directed against the whole obscene apparatus of judicial execution. The last chapters should be compulsory reading for anyone who still believes, for whatever high-minded reasons, that the death penalty ought to be reintroduced.

Elaine Morgan, 1978

CONTENTS

"But man, proud man!
Dressed in a little brief authority;
Most ignorant of that he's most assured,
His glassy essence—like an angry ape,
Plays such fantastic tricks before high Heaven,
As make the angels weep. . . ."

DAY PIECE TO JULIA

Morning

THE tram roared and swung down the Goldhawk Road towards Young's Corner. Julia, in the front seat, was pleasurably aware of the feeling of height and authority that such a position seemed to give her, almost as though she were driving the great swaying, clanging thing herself.

There came the grinding of brakes, Julia's body adapted its rhythm to the slowing rhythm of the tram, she peered over the edge at the fat woman slowly descending, while the conductor called loudly: *"Young Scorner, Young Scorner"* . . . How funny if there really had been a young scorner, and if so, what he scorned? Fat old women who climbed slowly off trams, probably. The bell clanged, the driver pushed his shining brass lever, the tram, with a screaming of wheels on the rails, went on round the curve and down the Chiswick High Road, taking up its part again in the orchestra of Greater London.

And what an orchestra—Julia, with no actual thought, was yet aware of it through all her consciousness. It was too insistent all round about her, with its stringed instruments and its brass instruments, its bass notes as of gongs, its sudden sharps both of sound and of colour—in twanging bells and in the thin fine young green leaves of the plane-trees flickering in the sunlight—for anyone as alive as Julia not to be aware of it. She did not think of it as the voice of London, but she did think of it as the voice of life, and she herself was not only part, but the very central core of life. Impossible to imagine any life in which she would not, at some time, share. For Julia did not think of the world as being enclosed in Heronscourt Park and Chiswick; she thought of it as being a great wide splendid place where she and whomsoever elected to be half of herself, could and would roam at will. Thus strange Eastern countries, inhabited by brown men and yellow; Embassies, where the great of the earth walked covered in stars; vast drawing-rooms called "salons" in Paris, where women ruled, and swept about in marvellous dresses, and tapped gentlemen on the arm with fans—all these places so alien from the small red-brick villa off Heronscourt Park, were the world to Julia. The trams were no clearer to her ears than were the cultured accents of the diplomatists of Seton Merriman (whose ancient volumes she obtained from the Free Library in the Park) and the green and gold flicker of the plane-leaves in the sunlight were only the prelude to the day of thrilling emotions that lay before her at the High School.

The "Packhorse and Talbot" (what sort of a dog was a Talbot?) had been left far behind; the thin grey Gothic of Turnham Green Church had faded to the left, so had the sulky, dark-red building that was the Roman Catholic Church at the top of Duke's Avenue (there were some rich houses with very well-off people down that avenue, houses with a window on each side of the door and several black-and-white maids and a garden); and the school was rushing nearer and nearer, with a roar and a clanging. Life was approaching Julia, as it approached her each morning, with a quickening of the orchestra about her and of her own pulses, that chimed in delicately with the whole overture like the thin, fine notes of a flute. Julia, whose appreciation of music had at one time, so she thought, reached its climax with the Indian Love Lyrics, had since absorbed Dvořák's *Humoresque,* and she thought of herself as the light sweet air of it, coming in again and again, with repeated importance, through the blurred shapelessness that all music save a definite "tune" was to her ears. The rhythmic trams, the bright blown plane-trees, the horses' hoofs, the tooting of horns, the grinding of brakes,

4

the clanging of bells, the flicker of colour in gowns and faces, the light tapping of heels, the flutter of curtains at open windows, the tiny contacts with unknown human beings who would remain for ever unknown, as she caught the glint of an eye or the self-absorbed look on a passing face—all these were to Julia at sixteen what they are to anyone at sixteen—the music that set her own life dancing.

Julia Almond was on her daily great adventure, she was going to school. There it was, the grey-porticoed building, with its basement where one had lunch just showing its dark blank eyes about the level of the neglec'ed garden; and the paler patches where the stucco had peeled off, making fantastic faces that grinned from beneath a gutter or a window-sill. An ugly building, but holding all of beauty and excitement to Julia.

She gathered up her books, pushed back her hat so that it should not flop in the wind on this find day and blind her as she alighted, and made her way down the deck of the swaying tram. Arrived at the far end she hit the bell before she started to descend the stairs. The conductor glanced up annoyed—conductors always seemed to think it was an infringement of their privileges if one rang the bell oneself, but how otherwise was the tram to stop by the time one was at the foot of the stairs? This man had his revenge by ringing again before Julia's foot was fairly off the step, and the jerk of the car as it re-started nearly threw her on her nose, but with the easy resilence of youth she steadied herself, and sped across to the pavement.

There was that dull Mary Barnes, who didn't wash enough under the arms but was unaccountably good at Latin, just going in at the varnished wooden gate, her fair, serious face, that somehow was all pointed, like a fox terrier's, poked out in front of her. When Julia arrived at the gate, it was still moving from the earnest passage of Mary Barnes. Julia absorbed the backward swing of the gate into her urgent palm, set it off on its forward journey again, and walked, with that untaught grace that was hers by some miracle or freakishness of nature's, up the path between the dingy laurel bushes.

"The girls" went past the portico, without affronting its majestic steps—those were reserved for parents and mistresses—and Julia followed Mary Barnes round the side of the house to the back, where a glass-house that had once been a Victorian conservatory was now used for hats and coats. Julia had caught up with Mary Barnes by now, and, passing her with a careless nod, went into the glass-house and up to the mirror that hung upon the wall. Mary could either wait or take off her hat without looking at herself, nothing made any difference to her eager pushed-forward face, anyway.

But Julia knew already, with the precocity of the London girl, that hers was a face that needed everything to be just right. She hung up her black cloak—she rather liked that cloak, although it was three years old, being a relic of Aunt Mildred's mourning for King Edward—because it had wide wing-sleeves and she felt she looked like Portia in it. Her black skirt was cut down from one of her mother's, and her scarlet blouse, with its white "Peter Pan" collar, she had bought for herself at a sale, and she had bought as well the scarlet felt hat with the wide brim that made her look, she felt, like an art student. She was to learn fashion-drawing, before going into the dressmaking, and that meant that she would be in a sort of way an art student.

She perched the hat on a peg, a-top of the cloak, and stared at herself in the glass, smoothing the bright wing that lay over her brow. It was nice, that bright brown wing of hair that curved down so low it hid one of her straight brows. Then the soft bright brownness was puffed out a little over each ear by combs, and tied with a big black bow at the nape of her neck. If she hadn't tied it, it would have spread out all over the shoulders and down to her waist. Rather fun, perhaps, for then she could have tossed her head perpetually to get it out of the way, but on the whole more bother than it was worth. She felt freer to turn her head with her hair tied back, and she knew that the curve of her head and the line of her long full neck were the best things about her. Miss Tracey had told one of the other mistresses, who had told one of the other girls, who had told Julia, that Julia Almond had a Chinkwy Chento neck. Julia wasn't quite sure what it was, but she knew it was something to do with pictures painted by the early Italians, and she had had a rapturous afternoon on a half-holiday, with Miss Tracey at the National Gallery, surreptitiously searching for her neck.

Miss Tracey . . . soon she would see her, see that swift

6

distracted smile, that was less distracted for her than any-one else. But at that moment Julia met her own eyes in the glass, and Miss Tracey, for whom she wished to look pretty, was forgotten just because she was looking pretty. Yes, it was a good day. She had felt that it was as she sat on the top of the tram, even the fact that the conductor didn't like her hadn't spoiled that conviction. The air had not been filled with trumpets for nothing. Yes, yes, said Julia's heart at the glance of those narrow grey-blue eyes in the mirror, it's true, I'm pretty.

Julia was wrong: she wasn't pretty, except occasionally. She was very short-sighted, and she saw the pallor of her skin, the narrow brightness of her eyes and the gleam of her hair through a haze that lay like a bloom over every-thing at which she looked. But she was right in believing that there was no other girl in the school who gave back quite that brilliant reflection, a reflection so brilliant that it assaulted the senses even of her who gave it life. She was so young that the hard white light from the roof of the glass-house was becoming to her. There were no pockets beneath the eyes, no lines from nose to chin, and the thick texture of the skin drawn over the rather high cheek-bones, a skin with the matt quality of an eggshell or a white kid glove, defied the searching light to find an impurity. If the modelling of her face had been as good as the spacing of the features she would have been a beauty, but there was a sloppiness in contour, a thickening of the irregular nose, a too great fullness round the lower lip, that only youth could make of no account. On a plain day Julia could look incredibly like a pudding, and she knew it, but she looked lovely to herself that morning, and she turned her glossy head upon her neck like a bird, and smiled for pleasure.

Clang . . . clang . . . clang . . . the school bell crashed in upon her absorption and went on sounding through the classrooms and corridors. Miss Tracey . . . whose presence had power to turn Julia's even pulses into a riot, came beating back into her consciousness on the beats of the bell.

Julia gave a final touch to the gold-brown wing, and, a little late, but unhurried, went towards the classroom. And with her, as part of her, though she was at the moment thinking of nothing but that she would see Miss Tracey, went the small sum of her knowledge of this life. A sense

7

of being clean to the point of freshness, a sense not common enough to her class to be taken as a matter of course (Julia had to bear with the sneers of her family on her habit, caught from Miss Tracey, of a swift morning bath), a sense of her own high-held head, of the fine clear spring morning, of the existence all about her of Chiswick, of the outspread greenness of Heronscourt Park where home was, and where she walked on Sundays with Bobby, the white and chestnut mongrel; of the hundreds of clerks and girls who went to work, and who poured out of the trains and down the wooden stairs to the street like a dark spilled liquid every evening; of the underclothes that lay against her body; serge knickers with batiste lining, and a cambric chemise and a moirette petticoat and black cashmere stockings; of Mary, Queen of Scots and Queen Elizabeth, whom they were "doing" that term; of that tiresome and perpetually moving Saint Paul whom they were also "doing"; of the fact that any day something wonderful might happen that would change the whole of life—someone might leave her a fortune, having admired her silently from afar; or a lord might fall in love with her . . . all this knowledge, of extraordinary little help to her or anyone, brimmed the back of her mind.

She went into the long classroom, the last girl to enter, with her usual calm arrogance, tempered by a smiling politeness, as of one equal to another, towards Miss Tracey, standing in cap and gown by the desk.

Miss Tracey began to read out the short prayers. When they were over, Julia sank back on her bench and opened her desk. There was a scraping of feet and a settling of bodies all about her. The school, with its familiar smells— a mingling of exercise books, clothes, varnished wood, girls, cabbage, roasting meat, and dust—took her by the nostrils and was as savoury as incense.

Recess, and a stroll of twenty minutes up and down the lawn, past the clumps of sickly laurels, whose leaves were blotched with a leprous white. Beneath these leaves the black roots and branches curved like snakes in ambush. Julia hated the garden because of the laurels. While the other girls walked about in couples, heads together, Julia stayed behind in the classroom, pretending to make notes in her notebook. Miss Tracey, her lint-fair head, where the threads of silver hardly showed, sat bent over the marks she was adding up, her pince-nez drooping from her straight little nose. Julia couldn't help wishing that Miss Tracey didn't wear pince-nez, though of course it didn't really make her any less lovable. Only there was always something rather silly about "specs" and she couldn't bear that there should be anything silly about Miss Tracey. Julia herself would never wear "specs," however short-sighted she became. She would only, when she had got on in the world so that it didn't look unsuitable, have one of those hold-up things on a long stem, and gaze at people haughtily.

She would, of course, get on in the world, she never doubted that. She knew, because of the way she was treated here at school, that she was somebody, although she wasn't the prettiest or even the cleverest girl in the school. Julia wasn't going in for "Matric" because she hadn't, till she came to the High School last term, had a good enough education, and because she was soon leaving to go to the Polytechnic for "art." Julia's father was only a clerk in a House and Estate Agency, and though it was better than being Mary Barnes, whose father was a small draper in the Chiswick High Road, it wasn't as good as being Edith Darling, whose father was Something-in-the-City, or Anne Ackroyd, who was a doctor's daughter.

Fathers . . . they were important if it came to crossing swords at school, but they didn't really matter, not if one was enough of a somebody. And Julia was the most dominant girl in the school; somehow—by no means that she could have puzzled out even to herself, except that she was vaguely aware it was just by being herself, and unafraid—she had taken that position. That was how she had established a footing of equality with Miss Tracey. Julia knew that in a way even Miss Tracey looked up to her . . . which, after all, was only natural, for Julia was young, and Miss Tracey was thirty-five-if-a-day. Julia had a sort of dashing assurance, her very adoration for Miss Tracey partook of the gallant swagger of a young man. Sometimes they met in the first-floor bathroom just before lunch, where Miss Tracey was washing her pretty, very white hands, and had put her rings safely on the edge of the basin. Julia, laughing, swaggering, would pick the rings up, and slip them on Miss Tracey's fingers, and drop a kiss on the hand at the finish, feeling like one of the cavaliers out of a Stanley Weyman novel as she did so. Other girls

9

who had a rave on Miss Tracey, would timidly place flowers on her desk. Julia never did that. Once, indeed, she had even taken a bunch of flowers away from a younger girl who had brought them for Miss Tracey, and coolly appropriated them for her own desk. The girl had been keen on Julia, too, and she merely giggled a feeble protest.

Certainly it was thrilling being at school, and in a way Julia could have wished it to go on for ever. As she gazed now at Miss Tracey adding up marks, it seemed to her that nothing more lovely than this friendship could ever happen. Miss Tracey, as though aware of that ardent gaze, lifted her blue eyes, small pretty triangular eyes that even pince-nez couldn't spoil. "Well, Julia, what sonnet have you chosen for to-day's Shakespeare?" asked Miss Tracey pleasantly. Julia blushed. She blushed very easily, and hated herself for it.

"Ah, you'll see," she answered gaily, "it's one I loved directly I read it." Miss Tracey gave her distracted little smile, and her blue eyes wandered to the window. "I always think Dorothy Pepper looks so like a Rossetti," she observed. Julia also turned her eyes towards the garden. There was that dull girl, Dorothy, walking along, her cloud of frizzy red hair bunched out by combs round her pale foxy face.

Bliss to be spoken to in such a way by Miss Tracey, for of course no other girl in the school would have known what a Rossetti was, and Miss Tracey recognised that fact, but tiresome to hear Dorothy Pepper admired. "Father's been making enquiries about the Polytechnic," Julia countered, "he wants me to join next term." "Oh dear, I shall miss you," said Miss Tracey frankly, and Julia's heart sang.

The bell rang again and the girls came pouring in, and settled themselves for the Shakespeare class. Each of the elder girls who cared to do so had learned a sonnet by heart. Not many had so chosen, but of course Mary Barnes had learned "Full many a beauteous morning have I seen," and Dorothy Pepper gabbled through "Let me not to the marriage of true minds." It came to Julia's turn. She looked straight at Miss Tracey and felt she made every word a message as she recited the less popular:

"Being your slave, what should I do but tend,
Upon the time and hour of your desire.
I have no precious time at all to spend,
Nor services to do save you require . . ."

Shakespeare really bored Julia, his turns of phrase
were so difficult and his stories hard to follow. She preferred *Lorna Doone* to anything of Shakespeare's, and at
the moment was reading it in snatches under the half-
opened lid of her desk, feeling very like one of the wilful
warm-hearted girls one read about in school stories, or
like Robert in *The Martian*, reading *Monte Cristo* behind
his desk.

Another bell and Julia gathered up her French dic-
tionary and paper-bound copy of *Jocelyn* and, always
with the hard-working Mary Barnes, whose nose had
grown rather shiny by now with the earnestness of her
scholastic efforts, went up to a tiny room facing north,
cold even upon such a fine day, and settled down to a
special French lesson. Mademoiselle was elderly and always blue with cold, she wore knitted black woollen mit-
tens and her fingers, shiny with chilblains, poked out from
them like sausages. Her face always wore an anxious expression, as well it might, with the supply of younger
teachers always coming on, and the demand for such as
she consequently going down. In the back of her mind
was always present the thought of her mother, who kept a
little hardware shop in a village near Boulogne, and whose
rheumatism grew worse each year. Julia did not know of
the mother and the rheumatism, but her lively young imagination had seized upon the knowledge which her nerves
imparted to her—that the Frenchwoman was unhappy
and poor and worried, and it gave Julia pleasure to be
especially polite to her, to be different from the other
girls, who despised Mademoiselle for all these things, and
in addition despised her for being French. Julia despised
them for insularity, which she thought a splendid word.
And Julia liked her "extra" French lessons, because not
only did the sort of woman she wanted to be know French,
but also she thought *Jocelyn* a most beautiful and touching
poem. That moment when Laurence, whom Jocelyn had
thought a boy, was found to be really a beautiful young
woman, when after the accident Jocelyn tore open Laurence's clothes: *"Je déchire des dents l'habit lent à s'ouvrir.*

. . . Un sein de femme, ô ciel! sous la sanglante toile!"
What a thrilling moment, and what a daring thing to write.
. . . Why, you simply saw it as you read. . . .

Midday

ANOTHER bell. Tidy for lunch. Julia, with her usual
audacity, instead of going to the wash-place for the
day girls, waited and managed to catch just the right moment—the moment when Miss Tracey was washing her
hands before lunch. The little ritual of the rings took
place, but suddenly the luncheon-bell went, and Miss
Tracey took the last ring from her impatiently, saying—
"Don't make me late." Julia stiffened and decided that
Miss Tracey should feel sorry.

Julia waited a moment and then started to go down to
the basement dining-room, the room with the blind eyes
that showed black from the road, white from within,
that her own accustomed eyes had seen that morning.
On her way down one of the older girls, who admired
Julia immensely, caught her by her scarlet sleeve and
whispered: "When are you going to do it?"

Julia suddenly remembered, a few days earlier, she had
betted that she would dare to steal Miss Tracey's cap
and gown after lunch, before she herself resumed them,
and would appear on the stairs, decked out in those sym-
bols of authority, for the whole school to see. No one
had believed that she would do it. Now, with a tingling
of the nerves, she answered, "To-day," and went on
down to the dining-room.

The pudding was spotted dog, pale and shiny, with a
sprinkling of castor sugar that gave it just the right
roughness. Spotted dog was apt to be slimy without gritty
sugar. Julia was greedy; she adored good flavours and was
already aware of the importance of texture in food.
Once, when a little girl at a picnic, she had eaten so much
she was sick on getting home. She had been very
ashamed, and had succeeded in concealing the dreadful
truth. There had been only one occasion when she had
failed to hide her fault, and that, unfortunately, had
been the previous term at school. Jam-puffs were served
and Miss Tracey, a few left before her on the dish, had
asked whether anyone would like another. Julia had
been the only person to answer that she would, and in a

12

deathly and disapproving silence her plate had travelled down the table and back again. Julia, her face burning, had choked the puff down hurriedly. No one would have been more surprised than she to have been told that her greediness was one of her greatest virtues, that it was part of her zest for life, that zest that gave her imaginative sympathy with Mademoiselle, that made her wonder what went on behind lighted windows at night, that made her flinch at the idea that there could be anything absurd about Miss Tracey. She absorbed everything she could, her avid senses appreciated everything that touched them, from spotted dog to a sunset, and her joy in the sunset could not have been as keen if she had not been able to extract the full flavour out of the spotted dog.

She rolled the last morsel upon her tongue now, and, laying down her fork, looked at the people sitting opposite with her narrow eyes, which short sight made her screw up till they were narrower. Everyone looked just the same as usual. Julia liked that; had anyone changed, the background of her exciting life would have been upset.

Right opposite her was Anne Ackroyd, the cleverest girl in the school, who was going to be a doctor. She was two years older than Julia, and she also was leaving at the end of this term. She was very plain, thought Julia for the hundredth time, but her eyes behind her gold-rimmed spectacles were beautiful, stag's eyes, deep and gentle, and she had a sweet smile that at moments redeemed the extraordinary length of her chin. Even the bombiness of her shiny forehead was almost saved by its breadth, and by her beautiful straight dark brows, but her skin was sallow, her hair limp and dull, and her whole face too long and cadaverous. Nevertheless, Julia, the beauty-lover, liked and admired Anne. Partly this was because Anne had an intense admiration for Julia, whom she thought wonderfully alive and dashing, but also it was because Julia recognised something out of the ordinary in Anne, in her really good brain, and her self-deprecatory habit of thought. She had none of Julia's glamour and attack.

Next to her, on the side that was towards the head of the table, was little fair-haired Mignon, "called after the opera." The efforts of her schoolfellows and mistresses

13

to pronounce the name were disastrous. Mignon would have been pretty save for a certain sloppiness about the modelling of her face, not unlike the sloppiness of Julia's own. But Mignon's face would never have the audacity and thrust of Julia's. Nevertheless, little Mignon —she was one of "the little ones"—was quite a personality in her small way. She had heard once that a theatre "up West" was putting on a play for children, and she had gone "up West" and somehow penetrated to the holy of holies. She had been asked what she could do, and she had danced a few little steps and piped a little song and she had been taken on in the chorus of children, all dressed as snowdrops. Envious schoolfellows who went to see her had said she didn't dance as well as the others and looked amateurish, but she hadn't cared. Julia never looked at her without a little pang of envy.

Next to Mignon was sitting Miss Gunther, the music mistress, who sang "Oh! that we two were maying." She only came twice a week, and it was she who had familiarised Julia with the Indian Love Lyrics and the *Humoresque*. She had wild dark hair, a rather pretty gipsy face, and wore a black silk frock, cut square at the neck, without a collar. Dora Hart, one of the big girls, who sat next to her, between her and Miss Tracey, had a rave on her. Julia studied Miss Gunther now. Why wasn't she more exciting? She was certainly prettier than Miss Tracey, whose over-blondness held a bleached and faded quality that her neat little features could not counteract. Also, Miss Gunther was much younger, hardly old at all, only about twenty-two. She wasn't smart, but then neither was Miss Tracey, though in Julia's eyes she dressed very charmingly when off duty, in neat little coats and skirts and soft lace blouses and shady hats with feathers in them. It must be that Miss Gunther wasn't as exciting as Miss Tracey because she wasn't as real . . . thought Julia, in her turn worrying her way to a gleam of reality. Miss Gunther thought she would make herself look somebody by getting herself up as a gipsy with all that wild hair, but she wasn't really enough of a somebody to carry it off. Julia used to tease Dora Hart about her rave on Miss Gunther. . . . "But you say that two terms ago you had a rave on the music mistress that was here then? Well, then, if you have a rave on Miss Gunther now, if you just took her over when the other one left, it's like one does with clothes. You have a Sunday dress, and when it gets shabby, you move it down one to second-best, and buy a new Sunday dress. Miss Gunther is your new Sunday dress, and when you're tired of her, you'll move her down one to second-best and have a rave on someone newer. You'll get a new Sunday dress!"

And poor, nice Dora, who could express herself about as well, and in much the same way, as a big Newfoundland dog, waved her large paws and stuttered and tried to say that no one had ever been quite the same as Miss Gunther, and that she could never, never love anyone else as much, and that when you really suddenly loved someone, you knew that everything that had gone before wasn't real, and that there wasn't anything like Sunday dresses about it. And while she tried to explain all this, Julia would stand and laugh at her. For Julia's instinct told her that if she laughed at other girls who had raves on mistresses, she was concealing her own rave on Miss Tracey. And indeed, she was right. Her laughter and her gallant cavalier swagger, so different from the slavish adoration that was the accepted technique of a rave, did deceive the girls.

Next to Dora, and at the head of the table, sat Miss Tracey. Sweet, intellectual, and completely unaware of the true values of life. Julia knew that, even while her hungry heart had to love her. She knew that Miss Tracey, with all her Latin and Greek, and what-not, didn't really know anything about life. By life, Julia meant men. She didn't know much herself, but a saving crudity in her surroundings, a matter-of-course acceptance of facts in her upbringing (if so casual and haphazard a process could be dignified by the word "upbringing") had taught her a certain amount about the traffic of blind and aching humanity. Next to Miss Tracey came Dorothy Pepper, Mary Barnes, a girl who didn't count, and then came Julia. Nobody else mattered down the whole long table to the far end where Mademoiselle was in charge, and no one mattered at the two tables for "the little ones."

Miss Tracey gave the signal to rise, and there was a scraping back of chairs and a clattering of feet. Everyone poured out of the dim room, with its glimpse of the stems of laurels at the top of the basement windows,

15

stems that stayed still and quiet, instead of perpetually passing on, as feet seen from a basement that gives upon the street pass on and are gone. The laurels, black and snaky as the laurels in the back garden, would always be there. Julia sped up to the first-floor bathroom. There hung Miss Tracey's cap and gown upon the door. Miss Tracey herself had gone into the mistresses' room for coffee. Julia threw on the gown, poised the cap at a jaunty angle over her wing of hair, and looked in the glass. Colour had sprung to life on her cheekbones, a colour that matched her scarlet blouse. She couldn't have been wearing anything that would have looked better with the black cap and gown.

She rushed downstairs. Somehow the news had spread about the school, and every doorway and passage was crammed with eager girls, not a mistress was in sight save Mademoiselle, who smiled sympathetically, though nervously. Julia stayed poised, half-way down the last flight of stairs, laughing and flushed. It was fun, all the girls staring at her, admiring her, even the big girls gaping with awe and admiration, fearful (as Julia herself was) that the door of the mistresses' room might open and Miss Tracey emerge. Not that Julia had committed a crime, but Miss Tracey was quite capable of saying something cutting that might make Julia look small. . . . It would be thrilling if Miss Tracey were angry with her in private, but it wouldn't be a bit funny to be snubbed in public. . . . So Julia laughed and waved her hand and fled upstairs again, and had just hung the gown upon the door and poised the black cap a-top of it, when Miss Tracey arrived, mildly surprised at the flock of girls in the doorways. She gazed at Julia's flushed cheeks in surprise.

"You're not feverish, are you, Julia? Because I was just going to ask you if you would do something for me. Miss Amherst is feeling ill and has gone to lie down, and I wondered if you would take the second form while they're doing their prep. this afternoon? You won't have anything to do but keep order."

"I'd love to," said Julia, glowing still more, "of course I'll do it. I'm only sorry I'll miss grammar with you." Julia never said "Miss Tracey" except when she was speaking in class; she knew how this bright and gay assumption of equality in friendship pleased the older woman.

"Grammar . . . oh, Julia, I don't think you'll mind missing that much. If only you were as good at grammar as you are at history! I can't understand why you aren't. You're so fond of literature. I should have thought *you* would have been good at grammar."

Julia thrilled to the unconscious compliment of that *"you,"* even as she replied smilingly: "Oh, I'm afraid I care more for what people write than the way they write it, and I love history because it's stories about people."

The Little Ones

JULIA sat on the bench that was made in one with the high desk before it, with her notebook open before her, and the Mark Book, symbol of authority, spread out beside it. In front of the desk were three rows of "little ones." They nudged each other, gazed up at her with impish or limpid eyes, pretending to be busy or were openly defiant. Julia felt her heart beating nervously, and remembered Lucy Snowe when she had first been put in charge of an unruly class at the school in Villette. Unfortunately, she felt no such upwelling of power within herself as had visited Lucy for her salvation.

The children "tried it out." Julia spoke sharply, but calmly, and there was a momentary subsidence of the giggling and whispering. Opposite to Julia sat Gladys Pepper, Dorothy's younger sister, a lovely child with red ringlets and a laughing face. Julia was helpless before beauty, and especially she loved the way that this child's mouth opened over her teeth when she smiled. Her lips were too thin in repose, but when she laughed and showed her little pointed teeth, her open mouth was just the right shape. Julia found herself softening towards Gladys, quite the naughtiest child there, because she wanted to see that hard little mouth suddenly transformed into the lovely "square" open mouth that was so satisfying because it was so right.

Next to Gladys sat one of the little boys (they were taken in the first forms, when it was to be presumed they were yet too innocent to corrupt, after the manner of their sex, the little girls).

Leonard Carr was nine years old, already a year too

17

old in age and several years too old in knowledge, had the truth about him been known, for the second form. He was a fine well-grown boy, about to become a pupil at a seedy academy for the Sons of Professional Men that stood behind the main road down Hammersmith way. Leonard's father was really a tradesman, being the manager of a small jeweller's shop in the Strand, but the Academy did not look too closely into such matters. Julia's father had sold the Carrs the little house in which they lived near Heronscourt Park, and there was a slight degree of friendship between the older Carrs and Almonds. Julia and Leonard were too far apart in years to be interested in it. Leonard had bright bold brown eyes, and a full mouth above an abrupt little jaw. He was a young demon, and Julia eyed him nervously. He was giggling and showing Gladys a box he was holding under the desk.

"What have you got there?" said Julia sharply. Leonard looked at her defiantly with his shallow bright eyes.

"You aren't the teacher," he said.

The moment had come, it was necessary to gain ascendancy. "Gladys," said Julia calmly, "show me what you and Leonard have there." As she spoke she looked straight at Gladys, screwing up her short-sighted eyes, but letting what she felt to be a human understanding inform them with a kindly twinkle. Gladys capitulated, and Julia felt a little thrill of triumph. The lovely "square" smile flashed out, and Gladys, taking a long white oblong cardboard box from Leonard, advanced to the desk.

"It's a peepshow, Julia. See, you look in this end." Leonard jumped up. After all, it was his peepshow, and this girl, though ever so old, was not one of the teachers. He called out:—"You can't look without paying! You can't look without paying!"

Julia stopped with the box half-way to her eyes. Something in this vital, grinning little urchin's face touched her quick imagination. "You've got to pay a pin!" he insisted, "You've got to pay a pin!" Julia remembered how all the "little ones" had been parading about for days with boxes of differing shapes and sizes, chanting— "A pin to see the peepshow . . . a pin to see the peepshow!" It was one of those fashions that sweep a school, and each child had firmly clutched a box, unyielding of its joys, till a pin had been forthcoming.

She smiled, a charming elder-sister smile, at the little boy.

"But why a pin?" she said. "What good does a pin do to you?" Leonard looked a little taken aback. The fact was that the collecting of pins was a purely arbitrary rite decreed by fashion, and except that Leonard and a few other daring spirits used them for gambling with, at twelve a penny, they were of no use at all. He thought he had better say nothing about the gambling, and, coming out from his place to stand beside her, he merely answered: "Oh, we collect pins, you know," and laid a grubby hand on the white cardboard show-box. Julia felt in the front of her blouse, and found a relic of last week's dressmaking activities in the form of a pin, and presented it indulgently to Leonard. Then she picked up the box. A round hole was cut at each end, one covered with red transparent paper, one empty. To the empty hole was applied an eye, shutting the other in obedience to eager instructions.

And at once, sixteen-year-old, worldly-wise London Julia ceased to be, and a child—an enchanted child—was looking into fairyland.

The floor of the box was covered with cotton-wool, and a frosting of sugar sprinkled over it. Light came into the box from the red-covered window at the far end, so that a rosy glow as of sunset lay over the sparkling snow. Here and there little brightly-coloured men and women, children and animals of cardboard, conversed or walked about. A cottage, flanked by a couple of fir trees, cut from an advertisement of some pine-derivative cough cure, which Julia saw every day in the newspaper, gave an extraordinary impression of reality and of distance. This little rose-tinted snow scene was at once amazingly real and utterly unearthly. Everything was just the wrong size—a child was larger than a grown man, a duck was larger than a horse; a bird, hanging from the sky on a thread, loomed like a cloud. It was a mad world, compact of insane proportions, but lit by a strange glamour. The walls and lid of the box gave to it the sense of distance that a frame gives to a picture, sending it backwards into another space. Julia stared into the peepshow, and it was as though she gazed into the depths of a complete and self-contained world, where she would go clad in snow-shoes and furs, and be able

19

to tame savage huskies and shoot bears; a world of
chill pallor, of an illimitable white sky, both only saved
from a cruel rigour by the rosy all-pervading light.

It might have been possible for someone less eager and
much older than Julia to apply an eye to that box and
see nothing but cardboard advertisements and cotton-
wool, but it was not possible for her. For the moment
that she gazed into that space of some ten inches by
five, she was lost in a fourth dimension of which she
had never heard. The illusion only lasted for a second,
but time is not to be measured by the clock, any more
than space is to be measured by inches. She felt a
delicious pleasure, was lapped about by it, then withdrew her eye, and was in the schoolroom world again.

"Very pretty," she said primly, "but this is prep. time,
and you must get on with your lessons. I'll keep the box
on my desk. Go back to your place, Leonard."

He gazed at her under scowling brows, and clenched his
grubby fists. Then he took the box, and crouching down,
placed the peepshow between the legs of his own desk.
Julia, staring down at this act of insubordination, saw the
top of his rough dark head, and saw his bare knees, very
square and solid, the skin so tightly stretched across them
that the white light from the tall windows lay across the
modelling of them like water. She was for the first time
in her life struck by the fact that, apart from the obvious
indication over which children might snigger, a little boy
was always unmistakably a little boy. Those chunky
knees could not have belonged to a little girl. The actual
distinct quality of masculinity, insistent from the cradle
to the grave, struck at her mind. She didn't think Leonard an attractive little boy, he was cheeky and dirty, but
she was impressed nevertheless, though her sex-vanity resented the fact. She sharply ordered him back to his seat,
and, having sufficiently shown his independence, he
obeyed.

Julia went on with her own work, and the class subsided into quietness. Presently a squabble arose between
Gladys and the little girl on the other side of her from
Leonard. Julia called them to order, and Gladys looked
up with her flashing smile. The other child, an unpleasant
red-faced little creature with a Cockney voice, continued to mutter to herself. Julia spoke to her, and she
tossed her thin, greasy locks and said something under

20

her breath that Julia rightly guessed must be impertinent.
Julia drew the Mark Book towards her and lifted her
pencil.

"Minnie Tooth, take an Order Mark," she said importantly, and scored the damaging little black line, writing "Minnie Tooth" opposite to it in the approved manner.

The thing was a success . . . the class was impressed.
Only Julia knew that she hadn't really gone into the
ethics of the case. The lovely Gladys might have been
wrong in the initial squabble for all she knew . . . Julia
salved her conscience with the thought that she had giv-
en the Order Mark because of Minnie's impertinence to herself, who stood in the place of a teacher. And, technically speaking, she was correct. Quiet brooded over the
class till the bell sounded, when a mistress arrived, and
Julia gathered up her belongings and went back to her
own classroom.

Arithmetic

THERE it was, just the same as ever, long and low, with
its big window giving upon the back garden, where the
afternoon sunlight lit the neglected turf to brightness.
There was Miss Tracey sitting at her desk, her lint-pale
hair pushed off her brow, her pince-nez glimmering, the
now-famous gown slipping half-off her shoulders; there
was Dorothy Pepper, her puffed red hair and secre-
tive face looking more fox-like than ever; there was the
sentimental puppyish Dora, and earnest Mary Barnes; all
the other pupils who composed the Upper Fifth and the
Sixth, sitting in rows. And suddenly Julia became muddled between this world that she knew so well and which
she knew was the real world, and the peepshow she
had just been living in for a fraction of time. She had
been aware of the peepshow world again just before she
turned the handle of her classroom door, and the warm
light of the classroom gave an impression of unreality to
the familiar scene. The moment of confusion had gone
as quickly as it had come, but it had given a queer little
uncertainty to Julia, who was always so sure about life.

She had forgotten it a moment later, when she opened
her book for the arithmetic lesson. Yet enough of the
uncertainty remained with her to make the arithmetic

21

less of a precise and easy joy than usual, and as the lesson went on, Julia's attention wandered. Her exciting day began to seem flat and dull. It had been gorgeous putting on Miss Tracey's cap and gown, with all the school giggling at her, but now she began to wish that she had let Miss Tracey catch her at the impertinence. What was the use of the dashing gesture if Miss Tracey didn't know of it? Julia had attracted no more notice from the only person who mattered than if she had never done the deed.

Julia began to make swift sketches in her arithmetic book. She had a certain facility with her pencil, though she had neither enough talent nor training for economy of line, but she could "catch a likeness." She drew Mary Barnes, with her terrier face, pursuing Dorothy Pepper with her fox face, towards a goal marked "Top of the School," and the girls on either side of her began to giggle. Julia added balloons coming out of her victims' mouths, with unwitty but extremely characteristic remarks inscribed therein. The girls giggled more loudly. Miss Tracey looked down the room, frowned, raised her fair brows and said: "Quiet there, please." Julia added Dora Hart, with a plumy tail, gambolling far behind, and began to comment on her drawings in a running undertone. Miss Tracey lost patience and said clearly: "Julia Almond, take an Order Mark."

It was the first time such a thing had ever happened to Julia, and all over the room heads were turned towards her. She smiled, and went on drawing. The lesson was just at an end, and there came the sound of a gathering of books, of the opening and shutting of desks, and then the scraping of feet, that was, with the bell, the most characteristic sound of life in the school.

Julia always carried Miss Tracey's books up to the mistresses' room for her when school was over; this was recognised as an honour, and no one ever disputed it with her. Now Julia sat humming to herself, neither moving towards Miss Tracey's desk nor going away towards the cloakroom. "She'll ask me," thought Julia, her heart thumping, hardly daring to look up, lest she saw the books being confided to another girl, "I'm stronger than she is, she'll ask me." And, unacknowledged even to herself, ran the thought that she had wished Miss Tracey to give her that Order Mark, that she had forced her to do it.

"Julia, will you carry my books up for me?" came Miss Tracey's quiet voice, even quieter than usual. Julia rose, went up the room, took the books and stood aside to let Miss Tracey pass through the door before her. They passed in silence up the stairs, and into the mistresses' room, which was empty. Julia bore the books over to the side table and put them down, then turned to face poor, bewildered Miss Tracey.

"Julia ... what on earth was the matter with you? So rude ... so unlike yourself ... you've never been like that before...."

"Oh, I felt like it," said Julia casually. Miss Tracey looked helpless for a moment, then remarked with unexpected dryness: "Well, don't feel like it again."

The scene was fizzling out ... Julia took charge of it. She flung her head back, and with a flash from eyes that for once opened widely, she said: "Well, you shouldn't have done what you did."

"I? Done what I did?"

"Given me that Order Mark."

"I couldn't let you behave as you did without giving you an Order Mark. That was your punishment."

Julia felt her eyes flash again, her head go up still more. "My punishment? How dare you use that word to me?" They stood confronting each other for a moment, the woman and the girl equally ignorant of what the scene was about, of what force was really driving Julia. Mademoiselle drifted into the room, saw the two tense figures against the window, and with a faint murmur of apology drifted out again like a moth. Julia noted with triumph that Miss Tracey hadn't even noticed that futile entry.

Oh, if only Julia were a little girl at a Council School and Miss Tracey could take the cane to her, how thrilling that would be ... to have to hold out her hand, still with those flashing eyes and that proud head, and feel the swift descent and bite of a cane wielded by Miss Tracey! Why wasn't she at the Council School she had attended as a little girl, where there had been nobody she loved? This moment couldn't go any further, it must be changed now, or it would be spoilt. And Julia's eyes suddenly swam with real tears. She began to gulp piteously.

"I'm sorry. It's all my fault. But if you knew what I've been feeling like all day ... at home ... before I came...."

23

Miss Tracey's kind little pansy face lost its primness, seemed to melt and run together at the edges. Something had to be said to meet that sympathy worthily.

"My dog . . . you know . . . I've told you about him . . . Bobby. She's killed him."

"Killed him? My dear, what do you mean?"

"My mother. She's had him chloroformed. . . . He'd got mange. I've not really been able to think of anything else."

"You poor child . . . let's say no more about to-day. I often think about all your difficulties, Julia."

"I know you do . . . I'm a pig . . . I—I'm sorry . . ."

The exquisite emotional luxury of saying "I'm sorry" to Miss Tracey! And yet such was Julia's honesty with herself, however much she might have to lie to others, that she felt guilty and unhappy at having sacrificed Bobby, even though it was only in words, which couldn't hurt him, and though she knew she would find him lively as ever on her return home. She could not have put it into words, but she did have an uneasy feeling that she had betrayed him emotionally, that in some queer way he would suffer hurt, though she knew that to be nonsense.

Homewards

THE tram shrieked and swayed on its way back to the Goldhawk Road. Julia, this time seated snugly on the long plush seat within, remained rapt away from her surroundings. The strong thrill of that day was over, no longer was she leaping towards it with the keen anticipation of morning; rather she felt the acridly-sweet relaxation of fulfilment. The faces of the people in the tram promised no interest to her first quick glance, and she was free to go on with her own secret life.

She had money, she didn't have to work for her living. She was staying with Miss Tracey, who was her companion, at a hotel in Monte Carlo, where they had Table d'Hôte. Miss Tracey was, of course, Julia's chief object in life, and that although she, Julia, had much to do in which Miss Tracey could not share. Expeditions in the surrounding countryside, that was too full of brigands for Miss Tracey's sweet blond timorousness, took Julia most of the day. Then she would come home to the Table d'Hôte and Miss Tracey, to sink into the sweetness of perfect companionship. In her own family circle and all its ramifications, Julia knew only of raucous voices and querulous bickerings, and she dreamed always of a life where no one spoke harshly. With Miss Tracey there could be nothing ugly, only thrilling disagreements and "making-up." They would read every new novel and discuss it, they would be happy just because they were together and could exclude other people. Julia never envisaged a personal relationship that didn't exclude other people—that is to say, they would all love her, but she would love only one—it wouldn't be love if it weren't like that. Until she met Miss Tracey it had always been the image of some wonderful man who had given her the key to this enclosed garden; now, occasionally, she forgot Miss Tracey and drifted off once again to that vision of the perfect hero, but for the most part she was too absorbed in the actual passion of the moment for an imaginary male to obtrude. Julia was not lying to herself, she was caught up, in her last months of innocence, by the purest and sweetest emotion she had yet known.

Now that she was in Monte Carlo she knew how right she had been to risk all on going abroad with Miss Tracey. It was funny, that although she was obviously interested in nobody but Miss Tracey, people, especially gentlemen, would notice her. One—an Italian prince, called Sarasinesca—actually made her acquaintance. He was at first puzzled by her . . . there she was, so young, so beautiful, with such lovely clothes, yet only caring to sit in the sun and read the classics with Miss Tracey. . . . Could it be that he thought Miss Tracey, for all the wonderfulness that Julia knew she possessed, a little dull? Did people like Prince Sarasinesca perhaps marvel at Julia's kindness and self-abnegation? No, no, cried Julia's heart, suddenly speaking genuinely against the egoism of her imagination. But imagination, in the form of Sarasinesca, came back. Yes, he did marvel, though he seemed to respect and admire Julia the more for her oddness. It was Miss Tracey who was jealous of the Italian, who made quite a scene about him. Julia merely replied with simple dignity: "If you can't trust me . . ." Miss Tracey broke down and cried, but not till Julia herself had wept bitterly. And as the dream went on, somehow Miss Tracey was no longer there, never had been there.

Julia, in fact, far from being rich, was the typical

25

Cinderella. She was companion to a rich tyrannical old lady, and she didn't have too good a time, because snobbish people treated her as though she were a servant. Then, one night, when the old lady was giving a dinner-party, one of the guests, a countess, fell ill and couldn't come. Julia was ordered to put in an appearance. She dressed with great trepidation in her only evening frock, a simple black lace. A hush fell on the room as she appeared. The Table d'Hôte was suspended. The Prince, who had not expected to see her, grew pale beneath his tan. All round the room men put up their monocles to gaze at the new beauty.

The tyrannical old lady was suddenly very proud of her, but a lot of the younger women were jealous. Next day she walked out among the white marble palaces of which Monte Carlo is composed, bands were playing, flowers blooming, ruined gamblers, to whom the beauty of their surroundings was as nothing, were creeping away to commit suicide. One of these latter caught sight of her, and throwing away his revolver, he came up to her and took her hand and said: "I can't die while there is someone like you in the world." She saved the gambler, body and soul. Sarasinesca, who up till then had been jealous, said to her that never again could he doubt such an angel of goodness. He fought a duel in her honour, and afterwards went down on his knees to her in the beautiful garden and asked her to be his wife. He spoke English perfectly, but it didn't matter, because Julia spoke every language. She replied in Italian: "But you know I am only a poor companion?" And he answered: "You are the only woman in the world."

Seven Stars . . . Seven Stars . . . hurry off the tram, please. Seven Stars. . . . Julia started to her feet. How maddening, she had gone ever so much too far, and would have to walk back. Her books were scattered over the ridged flooring of the tram. People stared at her as she groped for them, not as the people in Monte Carlo had stared, but derisively. A man in a bowler hat leaned forward and helped her. He was kind, but his face was crimson with embarrassment behind his strawy moustache, at drawing so much attention to himself. At last Julia swung herself into the roadway, her books under the wing-sleeve that made the holding of a parcel a little difficult. She went scurrying back down the road towards

26

Heronscourt Place, which she had to pass through to get into the quiet little cul-de-sac where the villa stood. She walked without thinking, the joy gone out of her. Her day was over.

Not till she found herself in bed at night—when she would probably be too sleepy to imagine anything—could she live either of her real lives again—that which was a projection of her life with Miss Tracey, or that other which was woven purely of reminiscences of novels and her own desires. Now, going down into the Goldhawk Road, she was merely returning to the existence she ignored as much as possible, and daily allowed to slip over the surface of her consciousness like water, remaining unobservant of its tides and currents.

BOOK ONE

1

Home

HOME wasn't so bad, though Julia lived only in escape from the dull and somewhat sordid facts of life as it had to be lived within its confines. The house itself was horrible, a thin wedge like a slice of red-rinded cheese. Built of brick, it was semi-detached, and had a basement. There were only two rooms and a tiny slip that was hardly more than a partitioning-off of the end of a passage on each of its three floors. "Difficult to work," with all these stairs, as Mrs. Almond always complained. In the basement there were the dining-room, kitchen and scullery; on the next floor Mr. Almond's so-called "workroom," where he busied himself with a fret-saw and bits of wood after office hours; the bedroom he and his wife shared, and the sitting-room and hall. On the top, or attic floor, were Julia's own room, which was in front over the sitting-room, the box-room and bathroom. The Almonds did not keep a maid who slept in, nor did they so arrange life as to have visitors. Mrs. Almond's brother, George Beale, and his wife and child came to spend the day every other Sunday, but never to spend the night. No one, after the daily woman had "done" Julia's room in the morning, ever went up there, save Julia herself. It was her own, and she loved it fiercely. It stood for something very special in her life, for decency and freedom, above all for possession.

The house itself was certainly ugly, even to its trimmings, of stone acanthus leaves—which Julia rather liked —but its surroundings were delicious, though she was too used to them to be aware of their charm.

London, is a town of odd corners, but Beresford Villas stood in one of the oddest. To get to them one passed down the side of Heronscourt Place, that quiet spot, giving upon the park, and there stood the two tall, thin red-brick villas, with only their own gardens and the tarred fence, and a field with two cows in it. At the far side of the field a row of plumy elms reared their fountain shapes against the western sky. It was difficult to believe that beyond them again was a row of houses and the roaring trams of the Goldhawk Road where it curved down to Young's Corner. For Beresford Villas were in a quiet green backwater, enclosed on the northern and western sides by the Goldhawk Road, whilst the Hammersmith Road, straight as a ruler, made the southern boundary. To the east was only Heronscourt Park, with its richness of trees. The short strip of road where Beresford Villas stood, ended in a black fence, in which an opening led to a narrow lane known locally as Love Lane, also bordered with tarred fencing and shaded by sycamore trees, that Julia loved above all trees because of the delicate wing-shaped seeds that someone told her, when she was a small child, were the wings sloughed by fairies when they grew a new pair. Love Lane led to one of the old-fashioned roads of small houses with painted iron verandas and French windows that ran between Goldhawk Road and the Park. The very presence of Victoria, of an age when folk were content to be quiet and keep themselves to themselves, to stay in that class of life in which they had been born, seemed to hang over the few acres of small roads and meek houses, and also of rich houses standing in their own gardens, which bordered Heronscourt Park. Not a motor was ever seen, save an occasional taxi with luggage. Till one reached the main roads with their trams, the age of George V never impinged upon the mind.

Day after day, during the rest of the summer term, Julia came back to Two Beresford (as it was always called in the Almond family) feeling that never was there such a place so quiet or a house so dreary. With books under her arm, hope in her mind, and Miss Tracey in her memory, she arrived at Two Beresford, and went up the arch of grey steps that curved over the basement to the front door. The Bridge of Sighs, she had always called it, since Miss Tracey had described to her a Lunn's Tour in Northern Italy.

Julia hated her little Bridge of Sighs, for there had been one dreadful time, soon after going to Two Beresford, when Mr. Almond had been unable to afford a daily woman, and Julia had had to clean those steps. She had done it with indignation burning within her, early in the morning, so that the next-door neighbours could not see her at her degrading task. Mr. Almond had seen many reverses in fortune—hence the sketchiness of Julia's education—but now he was well established, in his quiet, meek little way, as head clerk at the House and Estate Office near Shepherd's Bush.

When Julia let herself into the narrow hall she was greeted by the stored-up smell of all the meals that had ever been cooked in the house, a smell rather like the well-loved one of school, but that gave her no pleasure. Sometimes her mother would hear her and call out to her from the kitchen, sometimes her father's querulous voice would be raised from his "workroom," or, on fine evenings, from the garden in which he took great pride. Julia always tried to come in as quietly as possible, because one or other of her parents, or both, invariably wanted her to do something—to go on an errand, to help with the supper, to weed or to water.

And invariably Julia wanted to go up to her room, just because it was hers, something that belonged exclusively to her—the only thing save Bobby the mongrel, that did. Bobby was rather a rival of the room in Julia's mind. For it was almost impossible for her to slip into the house without his eager heart being aware of that loved entry, and he would come wildly rushing down the hall, leaping up at her and talking in the high tenor that seemed to issue from the top of his brown head. Julia loved him so much that she always forgave him for drawing attention to her arrival.

For the first few evenings after the great day of the Order Mark, Julia had felt a little guilty at meeting Bobby's shining yellow eyes. She still had that odd little feeling that she had betrayed him, which of course was nonsense, as Bobby couldn't know what she had said to Miss Tracey, and it couldn't possibly have hurt him. Nevertheless, Julia now regretted the impulse that had led her to seize upon the only plank that had floated into view on that occasion when all seemed lost. For one thing, how could she now ask Miss Tracey to tea under the elder-tree in the back garden, the lovely heavy tree with discs of creamy blossom? Bobby, shut in the scullery, would yet make his presence known by loud wails, shattering any notion of his premature demise, even if Mr. and Mrs. Almond did not give the whole show away by some innocent but indiscreet remark. And there was another reason—Julia, in spite of the fantastic tales she spun for others, in spite of the day-dreams into which she retreated, had a curious honesty with herself. This honesty seemed tarnished by having made the helpless Bobby a victim of a fantasy.

For, of the whole, Bobby was dearer to her than anything but her room, dearer even than Miss Tracey. Somewhere deep in Julia's mind lay a streak of hard sense, that told her Miss Tracey was of the things that pass, that new interests would come along. Miss Tracey was the vehicle for emotion, all that Julia had; she gave the glimpse of wider horizons save those to be found in novels, but she was not emotion's self.

Already, when she had gone "up West"—a term always used by the Almonds and their kind, although, as a matter of fact, it meant going due east—Julia had been noticed by one or two young men, and by one or two not so young, as she went along the street. Her shining vitality lit up the places where she passed. And this contact of eyes, that swift flicker of knowledge between her and men with whom she did not exchange a word—she even veiled her glance with a sort of glassy impassivity—yet excited Julia. On a day when this fleeting but flame-like admiration of the streets had been hers, Miss Tracey ceased to count. But always she was anxious to meet Bobby—Bobby, with his brown wrinkled forehead, his white jowl tipped with a chocolate-coloured nose that twitched with delight, his white shirt-front and gloves and boots that were all so absurdly neat. Even his tail had a perfectly symmetrical white tip to it, as though

34

it had been dipped in a pot of white paint. Nobody knew to what breed or breeds his parents had belonged, but Bobby was so essentially himself that it seemed unnecessary for him to be of any species, other than that of dog, just dog. And Julia loved him, not so much for himself as because he loved her.

He was a symbol of something that, like her bedroom, was hers entirely, just as Miss Tracey was the symbol of adventure. Bobby was even better than her bedroom, for she could make his ears droop by a slight note of disapproval in her voice, could bring back the resilience to his body and the light to his amber eyes by a lightening of that note. Bobby was an instrument on which she could play, she could always be sure of his reactions. Bobby could never accuse her of lack of honesty, to him she was simply God. His utter trust made something melt in Julia, made her feel warm and protective. That was why she felt guilty on meeting his shining eyes, and she still was nervous lest, to pay her out, whatever Power there was might not cause Bobby to be run over. . . . Julia's idea of the Deity, in so far as she had one at all, was of someone who listened behind doors and tried to trip her up over her own words. She had lied about Bobby, she might be punished through Bobby.

Julia wanted passionately to be honest; she thought wistfully of a sphere in which such a luxury would be possible, where everything was so perfect and people admired her so that she didn't have to lie or even to make-believe. Each day for the rest of the week after the Order Mark she met Bobby with a sense of relief that he was still there. After that, she began to forget, merely remembering in the back of her mind that she couldn't ask Miss Tracey to tea. That was a pity, but she saved up her pocket money and took Miss Tracey to tea one Saturday at Fuller's in Kensington High Street instead. And Miss Tracey actually took her to lunch at her club, full of clever University women like Miss Tracey herself. This was one Saturday before going to a pit, and it was Julia's sixteenth birthday, when she felt herself to be grown-up at last.

Thus Julia's last term passed rapidly enough, and she thrust to the back of her mind the thought that end of term meant farewell to school and to Miss Tracey. Still more did she thrust to the back of her mind the thought that, after all, Miss Tracey couldn't have gone on being the chief thing in her life for ever . . . not now that life was beginning to open out before her like a painted fan. She was sometimes seized with misery that this phase of life she knew and loved was coming to an end, but more often the thought played about the shining future.

One day towards the end of term, Julia let herself into the little hall, sure that her father would be working in the garden, so that, if Bobby did not hear her, and her mother were in the kitchen, she might be able to slip upstairs to her room and give herself a manicure, an art which she had begun to practise. She wanted to have pretty pink nails like Miss Tracey's. Lady's nails.

But Bobby hurled himself, shrieking, out of the sitting-room, and, taking her hand in his mouth, began to lead her, still talking in his high, excited whine, towards the back stairs; not because he particularly wanted to 'go that way, but because it was the easiest direction in which to move in that confined space. Two simultaneous calls of "Juli-er . . ." and "Joo-ool . . ." came from below. Julia sighed as she took her hand from Bobby's mouth and fondled his satiny brown head. She went down the stairs with Bobby, and straight out into the garden by the side door.

Mr. Almond was working in the garden "pinching out" the snapdragons. He lifted an irritated face at her approach. He was a thin, weedy little man, with pale, prominent blue eyes, and a chewed moustache, stained with nicotine. His expression was querulous, but honest and kindly enough. His only legacy to Julia, a brown brightness of fine glossy hair, had all but disappeared, and a few greying wisps, usually trained like feathers across his bald head, now hung limp and damp over his eyes.

"That dog of yours . . . twice he's come galumphing over the antirrhinums while I've bin working. Anyway, you're late, and your mother wants you to go and get something extra for supper."

"He only means it in play. I stayed behind to talk to Miss Tracey. Why do we want anything extra for supper?" Thus Julia replied to all her father's remarks at once, a habit she had acquired as being the best method of dealing with him. If you gave him his due meed of attention in words, you could do what you liked; she had found that out long ago.

"I've a client coming," said Mr. Almond importantly, "a business man in a very good position. Wants a flat or a house in this district for him and his wife."

"Why's he coming to supper?"

"I used to know him at Maldon, when you were a child. When your grandfather was alive and we had a very nice house. He was the son of a friend of mine who was a licensed victualler . . . Starling."

Julia vaguely remembered an old Mr. Starling who had had a public-house in the far-away days before Grandfather had died, before it had been discovered that Grandfather, a retired builder, had sunk all his money in an annuity. . . . Vaguely, too, she remembered a pimply youth who was the son of old Mr. Starling. He had seemed quite old to the little Julia. Her thoughts, which had leaped to a possible romance, at once fell to boredom.

"Oh, well, I suppose I'd better see what Mum wants." Julia went in to the basement dining-room, and flung her books on the table, took a mechanical glance in the mirror, which was framed in beaten copper, with repoussé work, apparently portraying onions at each corner. The room was papered in a dull red which made it dark on the brightest day. "Dignity and Impudence" hung upon one side of the fireplace and "The Stag at Bay" upon the other. Mr. Almond had picked them up cheap at a sale, bird's-eye maple frames and all. The furniture was of fumed oak, with heart-shaped holes cut in it at the most unlikely spots. It was called Art Nouveau, and Julia was one of the few girls whose parents had an Art Nouveau set of furniture. Julia, being artistic, admired it immensely as well as being proud of it. She despised the Landseers and had herself bought, with pocket-money saved up for the purpose, the photogravure of a young woman with her hair down and her bust emerging from cloudy draperies, called "Epanouissement," which hung on the opposite wall. Mrs. Almond had always objected to it, and for a long time could never decide whether to sit where she could not see it herself, thus leaving her husband the seat from which he could, or not. Now it had become to her as the rest of the dining-room trappings, and she would probably no more notice where she placed a strange man in relationship to it than she would where he sat in regard to the cruet.

Julia loved it, she felt a stirring of her own womanhood, something profoundly important and mysterious, when she looked at it.

She passed it now, however, without a glance, and, going into the little passage, called out to her mother. Mrs. Almond answered her from the kitchen, and Julia went into the dingy little room with its old-fashioned stone sink that always smelt slightly of stale vegetables, and its gas-oven that always seemed to smell a little also.

Mrs. Almond was peeling potatoes by the table, her black cashmere gown shielded by a print overall, and her spectacles slipping perpetually down her shiny nose whenever she bent her head. She would push them up impatiently with the end of the knife-handle, and go on with her work. How well Julia knew the gesture . . . she had seen it all her life. Mrs. Almond repeated her husband's account of the supper guest in complaining accents. How could Julia but be aware of her own intense youth and vitality between these two resigned but querulous failures? The only person who equalled her in strength of life was Bobby.

"Something in a glass . . . or a tin. A tongue. Or do you think salmon?"

"Oh, salmon," said Julia enthusiastically.

She whistled to the ecstatic Bobby, and started off on her errand. She went through the top of Heronscourt Park to a "little" grocer's in Lammerswick Road. She liked going that way, because she had to pass the modern Gothic church of St. Michael and All Angels, built in red brick where, occasionally, she went with Miss Tracey. The church was described by Julia's relations as "High." Devoted celibate parsons, who gave their whole lives to the dissemination of the truth as they saw it, made of the church a focus of beauty in a drab neighbourhood. Unfortunately, Miss Tracey knew the rules of the game—the rules that may often be absurd, but that at least have an effect on human conduct—Julia was only aware of the smell of the incense, of the fine thin curves of the

First Pointed Architecture, of the lovely, if at times somewhat sugary, music. Gounod's Sanctus . . . *Holy, Holy, Ho-o-oly, Lord God Almighty* . . . the boy's lovely birdlike voice soaring up and up . . . "And now, oh Father, mindful of the love . . ." only a hymn, but how profoundly moving . . . these were the things that Julia took away with her from Saint Michael and All Angels. No measure by which to live . . . nothing that would make her give up any tempting experience that lay just beyond her nose.

Miss Tracey was not able to envisage such a state of ignorance as was Julia's in matters religious. She saw only Julia's swift response to beauty, and was thrilled by it. Here was a convert! But Julia had no background of dogma which, true or untrue, could at least give bones to her emotion—she was merely appreciative of the unaccustomed loveliness that she met at Saint Michael's. What it all meant she had no idea. And that it did mean something definite to certain people Julia remained sublimely unaware.

The cold, empty, early mornings when Miss Tracey, unquestioningly happy, the tip of her straight little nose red, and her heart quiet and warm with faith, trotted to the seven o'clock service, held no part in Julia's knowledge of life. It was not given to Miss Tracey to realise how completely without what she would have called "groundwork" was Julia's religious sense. Julia understood nothing except the exquisite pleasure given to her imagination.

Julia was technically "Church of England," and that was all she could have told anyone; it was better than being a Dissenter, but perhaps not quite so swagger as being a real Catholic. Beyond this she could have told nothing. On the rare occasions on which she went to church it was because Miss Tracey, instead of going to the little church she usually attended in Chiswick, came to Saint Michael's, and also because, along with Miss Tracey, there were incense and singing and a feeling of something alive all about her. After all, during the sermon, Julia could always dream her own dreams. . . .

And there remained at least the remembrance of these beautiful things whenever Julia passed the grave building, that somehow in its very fabric seemed to stand for something, even if she did not know for what.

So she liked to cast a glance at it on her way to the grocer's.

Julia bought the tinned salmon, and succumbed to a bar of chocolate cream. Then she walked back more slowly, munching as she went. She loved going through the Park at this hour. The air seemed full of a tender greenish light, the grass was dappled with shadow, Bobby tore happily about playing with his kind, children ran hither and thither, young couples walked slowly arm-in-arm or sat close beside each other upon a bench. There was a feeling of life, of life that grew and burgeoned all about.

Julia liked also the sight of the cream-hued house, that was so large and stately, where the rich owners of all the Park, then a private garden, before the District Railway had rattled overhead, had once lived. It was now the Public Library where Julia went to change her novels. What sort of life must it have been, to live in that house, drive out in a carriage and pair, have menservants, dress always in sumptuous silk? Julia only vaguely imagined it. In spite of dreams of Italian Princes and Monte Carlo, culled from books, her longings were more sentimental than ambitious. It crossed her mind that it must be lovely to have a huge place for one's own, to watch the common people staring longingly through the railings, but it did not occur to her as really possible that such a life could ever be hers. At that moment she caught sight of a young couple passing under the trees, arm-in-arm, and foolish absorbed face gazing into foolish absorbed face. Love . . . the thing one read about, that the Sunday papers had "bits" about, that was what mattered. And Julia began to think about love. It must be wonderful even if you only had a tiny house, as long as there was someone to do the rough work so that you didn't have to spoil your hands. To have someone who was entirely her own, as Bobby was hers, who only lived for her . . . that would be wonderful. She arrived at Two Beresford, and, handing in the tin of salmon to her mother, made her escape upstairs too quickly to be asked to stay and help.

Up in her room, Julia drew a deep breath of pleasure. Here she was alone at last, this place was hers. She locked the door, threw off her hat, her blouse and skirt, and sat down in front of the fumed-oak dressing-table. Beyond it she looked out at the field, and the row of fountain shapes that were the elms. The room was papered with a sky-blue paper patterned with sprays of apple-blossom, rather blotchy but distinctly recognisable. The casement-cloth curtains and bedspread were of the same blue, a blue without depth, that was hard and bright, and threw the eye back upon itself. Obliterating the apple-blossom on the wall at the foot of the bed, where she could lie and look at it, was a picture called "Vertige," representing a lady in evening dress upon a sofa, and a gentleman with very well-brushed hair leaning over the back of it and pressing a long and passionate kiss on the lady's upturned mouth. Julia had saved up a long time to buy that picture. On the mantelpiece were half a dozen picture post cards of what were known as "matinée idols," and also one of the Bishop of London, given to her by Miss Tracey.

Julia was not a tidy person, and the dressing-table was a litter of powder (the use of which was forbidden at school and greeted with disapproval at home), combs, odds and ends of ribbon, little boxes, and sample bottles of scent which the chemist, who was a friend of Julia's, used to give her.

She took up a file and set to work on her nails. She was making the acquaintance of her own body this past six months during which she had begun to grow up, and she knew by now the look of her different nails so well that it seemed to her each had an individuality of its own. Her hands were large but well-shaped, and the nails were oval with clear half-moons which gave her pleasure. But the nail on her left thumb was far better than that on her right, the left being almond-shaped and smooth, while the right was much squarer and had a ribbed band up the middle. Nothing she could do would alter that band of ribbing; it grew steadily, always the same pattern, coming like a strip of silk from a loom, out of the mysterious hidden place in her flesh where the nail was perpetually making itself, and being filed away by Julia at the top. Sometimes a white spot would appear, and would be borne further and further up the nail till it could be filed off, but the ribbing was always the same, always would be. It annoyed her, though it

41

was such a faint and intimate detail that no one but herself would ever notice it; yet at the same time it interested her because, though she could not so have phrased it to herself, its perpetual renewal meant an indestructible permanency that was of the essence of her being.

Julia filed, creamed, soaked, polished, happily at rest in the fastnesses of her own body and her own room.

When the nails were finished to her satisfaction, she went to the bathroom, and turning on the geyser, drew off enough hot water to fill the tin basin that stood upon a little spidery stand. She washed to her waist, the lesson of Mary Barnes not having been lost on her receptive mind. Then she combed her shining mane, re-tied it with her Sunday black ribbon, and opening the wardrobe door, looked doubtfully at its contents. The blue? Too stuffy for such a fine evening. It always smelt of cloth, somehow. Then there was only the flowered delaine with the black taffeta waistband and the frill of lace around the base of her throat that made her look like a pierrot. It was schoolgirlish, but, after all, that didn't really matter; the man who had been young Starling was of no importance, he was married, besides being quite old. So the pink delaine with its innocent sprigs of flowers went on over head, and she changed to her beaded slippers, looked in the glass and carefully applied a thin film of powder. A spot of the sample scent on a clean handkerchief, and she was ready. But Julia did not go downstairs. She knew she ought to help her mother lay the table, but the idea bored her, and although always complaining of her daughter's selfishness, Mrs. Almond had never taught her how to become anything different from what she was by nature.

Julia stayed and read *The Forest Lovers*—entranced, if a little bewildered—in her wickerwork armchair, till she heard the creak and slam of the front gate. She was at the window in time to see a stoutish man come up the little path. Twelve years had made of the weedy youth a prematurely gross man. So much was evident, though his face she could not see for the brim of his bowler-hat. Julia waited till she heard the boom of voices from the sitting-room before she went downstairs; at the last moment she scrubbed her cheeks hard with her handkerchief to make them pink. She was the image of spring as she hesitated for a moment, as though in surprise, in the doorway, then went forward and held out her hand in simple dignity. Julia despised giggling misses.

Mr. Starling was as dull as she had imagined he would be, though he was not bad-looking in a florid clean-shaven way. He joked with her about her extreme youth when last he had the pleasure of seeing her, he seemed to think it was funny to recall that she had had jam on her face. Mrs. Almond called up the stairs that supper was ready, and Mr. Almond said: "Lead on, Macduff. We wait on ourselves here, you know, Herbert. The maid goes after dinner. Help yourself . . . it's Liberty Hall here."

Mr. Starling talked a lot about himself at supper. It appeared that he had an invalid wife and wanted a flat so that she would not have stairs to go up and down all day. He was doing well in a business in which he was branch manager—a well-known firm of gentlemen's outfitters—and though it wouldn't hurt her to go up and down once a day when she went out, still she needn't do even that unless she wanted to, for he kept a maid. It was only of importance that she shouldn't be going up and down all day.

Mr. Almond suggested Hamlet Gardens Mansions, but it appeared there was no vacancy there at the moment. Julia admired the mansions very much, they were so big and red and had such lovely elm-trees growing in front of them. Mr. Almond thought again and suggested Saint Clement's Square on the other side of the Chiswick High Road, rather out of the region where his firm operated as a rule, but as a matter of fact, they had a notice-board or two out there. Big old houses that were being turned into "maisonettes." Julia remembered vaguely that Anne Ackroyd lived there. She had once gone back there with her to tea, and Julia had always remembered the plaster lions that sat bolt upright on either side of each flight of white steps. They were really great darlings, those lions, and reminded her of Bobby.

Mr. Starling thought highly of the suggestion of Saint Clement's Square, and the two men made an appointment to meet there the following day. When supper was over, Mr. Almond got out the decanter of whisky, and while Mrs. Almond stayed below to wash up, he led the way to the sitting-room. Julia sat at the table drawing a design for an evening dress, while the two men drank to old times, to each other, to old Mr. Starling, the licensed victualler, who was no more, to the future in Saint Clement's Square, and to each other again. Julia thought men very dull and disgusting. Not thus would her lover be, not thus would her home or her future appear. Poor, dull, middle-aged people—for of course, though Mr. Starling wasn't as old as Dad, yet he must be over thirty—her eager youth felt a pang of pity mingled with her impatience.

She rose and went out into the hall, put on a coat and came back to the sitting-room to call Bobby for his evening run. Mr. Starling looked as though he ought to get to his feet and accompany her. Julia tossed a polite, sketchy refusal over her shoulder.

"It's quite all right, Mr. Starling. I only take him down Love Lane."

The whisky had had its benevolent effect on Mr. Starling. He smiled gallantly. "Love Lane, Miss Julia?" It was rather fun being called "Miss Julia."

"Yes, that's what they call the little lane at the end of the road. I don't know why, you never see anyone in it."

"Ah, some day you'll know why, I expect, won't she, Almond? Too young for anyone to come a-wooing yet, though." And Mr. Starling laughed amiably.

"Joolie's not thinking of anything like that," agreed Mr. Almond; "she's going to learn the fashion-drawing next term. Quite a gift she's got with her pencil, they tell me."

"I believe in young women being able to earn their own living," approved Mr. Starling. "I've no kiddies myself—the wife, you know . . . but if I had they should all learn a trade, however well-off I was."

"That's right," said Mr. Almond. Julia tossed her head disdainfully and went down the Bridge of Sighs with Bobby. It was quiet and cool and fragrant in Love Lane after the smoky room. She smelt the fresh, faint odour of an elder-tree, and looked up at the tall sycamores. To walk here with a lover, some day. . . . Ah, but she wouldn't be here! She would have escaped somehow before love came to her, she hated the half-tones of her dull home, she wanted to meet love in some other place, a place that was fresh and unspoiled.

A young moon, thin and clear as mother-of-pearl, lay upon her back high in the heavens, but the clouds were massing about her. It looked as though the fine weather were over for the time being. Even as she waited for Bobby, pursuing his eager and interested way round the base of the solitary lamp-post, Julia felt the first big lazy drop of rain fall upon her up-lifted face. She called to Bobby, who pretended deafness; she sharpened her tone, and he came towards her with an air of surprise as if to say: "Did you call?" Julia took him straight up to her room, calling out a good night to the rest of the household. Long after she was a-bed, she heard that deep rumble of voices that in a small house means a male visitor. The front door banged as the last lovely page of *The Forest Lovers* was reached, and with a sigh, Julia turned out the gas and settled down to being Isoult la Desirous, roaming the glades of sleep with Prosper.

2

Transition

THE Polytechnic was different from school in every way, it had a different atmosphere, both emotional and actual. It occupied Julia all the autumn and winter, but it was not her life in the way that school had been. Life hung oddly in air, the days were suffused with the feeling of waiting for the approach of something for which all this was but a preparation. She was beginning to learn her trade, which, though not a lofty one, had, or would have, a marketable value, which is more than can be said for education as Julia had known it. Certain values which bore some relationship towards life as it had to be lived, began to make themselves known. For Julia had a receptive mind, its misfortune was that it was too receptive and had, of necessity, absorbed all the useless things. The journeys of Saint Paul are a poor substitute for the discipline of religion; the novels of Marion Crawford, Seton Merriman and Stanley Weyman, may enlarge the horizons of a dweller in Hammersmith, but they narrow down the pattern of life to a romantic assumption that is translated into truth for very few, and those few either exceptionally lucky or—not so exceptionally—undiscerning. Even the sonnets of Shakespeare cease to be of value to one who has merely made use of them to crystallise a passing emotion.

For the love called up by Miss Tracey had passed, slipped naturally into the attic for forgotten things. She herself had accepted the headmistress-ship of a school for daughters of clergy in the Midlands, and, anyway, Julia was now busy at the Polytechnic. A few letters came and went, then the essential unreality of the relationship caused the correspondence to fade away. Another difference between school and the Polytechnic was that at the latter Julia was no longer the most brilliant figure. For the first time she was humbled by the realisation that there were in life ideals, the existence of which had never crossed her mind. "Fashions" were not considered "art" at all by those who drew from the nude and "did oils." Her fashion-drawing did improve; she learned several tricks by which she could always be trusted to give them a professional instead of an amateurish air, but the important thing that happened to her was the realisation of a certain strange something for which a few chosen people strove and which could never be hers; something so different from her own facile cleverness and shrewdness that she could never have part or lot in its attainment. It was a bitter lesson, and the self-love natural to every human being, particularly to the very vital, tried so hard to throw it off that, in a certain measure, she succeeded in forgetting it . . . yet it persisted as a standard, dim but never entirely lost.

"Vertige" came down from the bedroom wall, and its place was taken by a coloured reproduction of Greiffenhagen's "Idyll." Julia liked to lie in bed and look at that glamorous moon, those burning poppies, and the white, swooning face of the girl, languorous beneath the kisses of the young shepherd.

The class she enjoyed most at the Polytechnic was the French class. The teacher, Monsieur Durand, a haggard, elderly, dark-moustached Frenchman, was much more interesting than poor Mademoiselle had been. He had a habit of slipping his arm in a fatherly fashion about the shoulders of the girl pupils while he was overlooking an exercise, which made each girl feel he took a special interest in her as well as in her work. There was never anything you could actually object to or make a fuss about,

47

you were just certain that he was aware that you were a charming young woman.

One warm autumn evening, Julia and her mother were walking through the Park on the way back from the station, when they met Monsieur Durand walking with the rather faded-looking woman who was his wife. Julia was wearing what she called her new "costume," a plain dark blue, with the scarlet blouse and a dark-blue felt hat, with a scarlet quill stuck athwart it. She had natural good taste, and everything she wore she put on after a fashion more often found in a Frenchwoman than in an English-woman. Julia's usually pale skin was flushed with walking, her eyes were bright after the afternoon "up West," her hair, recently knotted on the nape of her neck, gleamed beneath the dark-blue felt. That feeling of being peculiarly alive which was hers after contact with new places and people, had lit her to the illusion of beauty that she could sometimes give. She gave the awkward little bow that was all her inexperience had yet mastered, and Monsieur Durand swept off his romantic-looking black felt hat. But it was quite evident that for the first moment he didn't know whom he was saluting. Then recognition and some-thing else leapt into his eyes—the tribute of an unexpected admiration. Julia felt the colour flood over her face in that absurd way that she could never learn to control. The whole encounter was over in a moment, but it was one of those flashes that imparted fresh life to Julia.

Mrs. Almond looked at her with the quick half-jealous suspicion of the elderly woman who has never been ad-mired by men, and now is not observed at all, and said something sharp to the effect what need was there to go as red as a turkey-cock at meeting a dirty-looking foreigner like that. . . . Julia couldn't explain that it wasn't meeting with Monsieur Durand, but meeting with life for one fleeting moment, that had brought the blood to her cheeks. She was as little interested in Durand as she could be in any human being. He was married, which ruled him off the slate, just as the same condition caused Mr. Starling not to exist as a male. Neither as a human being did he exist. Julia had never even wondered about Durand's private life, he was merely the French teacher, and only existed at all as a touchstone.

How could Julia explain all this when she did not know it herself? Let alone to her mother—because what did

48

mothers know anyway? Or fathers? Julia's sensitive mind shrunk away from the fact that her father and mother had ever had any sexual connection. She knew—if she had let herself think about it—that they must have done so, but that was not anything to do with love. . . . The golden thing, the answer to the great problem of life, which lay in front of Julia, had nothing, could have nothing, to do with anything that occurred between her parents, which must, of necessity, be entirely different. They don't know, they can't ever have known. . . . In the history of the world it is only we—we who are young now—who are going really to know about life.

The Almonds could not afford to go on indefinitely with the education of a daughter. As it was, Julia had had two "extras"—Fashion-drawing and French, which they considered should equip her for the battle of life. Fashion-drawing had an affinity with dressmaking, and so, if you came to think of it, had French, so Julia, at sixteen and a half, began to look about her for a job.

A job. The life of everyone born in Julia's class is of necessity intermingled with the idea of a job. It is at once escape and fulfilment.

She did not want to be apprenticed to an ordinary dressmaker; not the sort who made up "ladies' own materials." Neither did she want to go in a big shop, though she felt sure that if she did so she would eventually become head of her department, or even a Paris buyer. Julia had often and often stood at gaze before the windows of the one or two tiny smart shops that had been started "up West"; shops in which one hat perched rakishly upon a stand, and a necklace and a bottle of scent counterbalanced one wispy frock draped casually in the opposite corner. Now there really was something to a shop like that. . . .

As the spring drew on and the end of her time at the Polytechnic was only a couple of weeks away, Julia often went up West, just as often as she could coax the necessary fares out of her father. She would walk round Hanover Square and down Bond Street, stopping at each shop window, absorbing the curious sense of intimacy that it gave one. Is this where I shall be? Or perhaps this one?

There was a girl at the Polytechnic whose elder sister was in just such a shop, and from her Julia had learned

49

much. There were two ways to attain the desired goal. You could go as a "matcher," which was rather a common thing to do. You ran messages, and went round to the big shops trying to match small bits of material which bored young men cut off for you. You were despised by the other girls, and if by any chance you were a "matcher" to a tailor, you were called a "trotter." In wholesale silk houses where the matchers had a room apart, they often indulged in free fights.

"They are a very rough class indeed," said Miss Clarkson, who was herself very refined, "and of course the pater would never have allowed Lily to be a matcher. She's an apprentice."

Julia gathered that apprentices led a dog's life, nevertheless. Apparently the refined Lily had spent the first few months in floods of tears, but however, the position was a good one and could lead to anything. Of course, you got nothing to begin with, and then only six or eight shillings a week, but it was increased every three months. Then, of course, there were other alternatives—to be a model girl, or a showroom girl—but Julia had an uneasy notion that her father and mother would have deep moral doubts about the profession of a model girl, and one would be extraordinarily lucky and have to have a lot of influence to begin as a showroom girl—you only worked up to that after a long time as apprentice.

Julia followed the adventures of Lily Clarkson as retailed to her sister with breathless interest. Lily was expecting to become a junior showroom girl quite soon. "Tell you what," said Miss Clarkson one day, while they were putting away their pencils and water-colour paints after class, under the blank enquiring eyes of the gods and heroes of Ancient Greece who, white and stately, stood majestic and aloof, down each side of the big classroom, "you'd better come to tea and meet Lily."

Julia was thrilled. How wonderful it would be if the great Lily could somehow find her a job, and she could go home in triumph announcing that her father need not worry any more lest the money he had spent on her education should after all prove wasted, a gloomy notion to which he had given utterance fairly often of late.

The tea-party took place, and Julia was rather impressed by Lily, though at the back of her mind a little voice kept telling her that she herself would have put up a much better show after a year in surroundings such as the elder girl had known. The Clarksons' house was a little bright-red brick villa in West Kensington; Mr. Clarkson was head of a department in a big grocer's store in Piccadilly. His wife was dead, and the eldest girl, Ada, round of face and shiny of complexion, hopelessly dowdy but amiable, ran the house and tried to keep an anxious eye upon her younger sisters. Lily was smart, Julia had to allow that. She wore a little jam-pot hat with an imitation egret in it, and a long fur stole twisted round her and thrown over one shoulder, and such a tight skirt she could hardly put one foot in front of another. Julia wondered how on earth she managed to get on and off buses without being killed, and yet . . . Julia's sure instinct told her that Lily not only was not quite the real thing, but could never become the real thing. She would always say "Moddom," but she was a good-natured girl for all her airs and graces, and she seemed struck by Julia, which was a virtue in her.

"I tell you what, dear," said Lily, "if I hear of anything I'll let you know. I'll take you along to a friend of mine, see? If *I* say you're all right, they'll look twice at you. Don't thank me, dear, it's a pleasure, I'm sure."

And to do her justice, Lily was as good as her word. The day came when she sent a message through the youngest Miss Clarkson to tell Julia to call for her at her shop during the luncheon hour the following day. It was one of those days when Julia should have been at her French class at the Polytechnic, but that did not matter. Half-way during the class when Monsieur Durand, in making his rounds, had come to her and was leaning over her exercise, she glanced up at him. "Monsieur, do you mind if I go now? I've an appointment up in town." He looked at her with his sad, quizzical eyes; she had never observed them so closely before, and now she noted the heavy pouches beneath them. "But certainly, Mademoiselle," he said, still with one long thin hand resting on the exercise book, the other held against his heavy, dark moustache. She could see the tiny lift of amusement, not movement enough to be a smile, behind those fingers. "It is a luncheon appointment, I presume? My felicitations to your companion."

It was not in Julia to deny the implication. An amused look came into her own eyes to meet the quizzical expression in his. "Well, I don't want to be late for it," she said, and then in her best French which would always be hopelessly British, but which was at least fairly fluent: "Les messieurs n'aiment pas qu'on les fait attendre."

"N'aiment pas qu'on les fasse attendre," corrected Monsieur Durand mechanically, and then became intimate again suddenly. "Keep him waiting, Mademoiselle, it does us good."

Julia went off in a little glow of pleasure. Durand had at once jumped to the conclusion that there was some man who wanted to give her lunch! She was, as a matter of fact, a little too early at the shop in Bruton Street, and she had to walk up and down for about ten minutes before the smart form of Lily Clarkson, jam-pot hat, fur stole and all, came briskly out from the door at the side of the shop.

"Ah, there you are, dear," said Lily; "well, come along at once. I know Miss Lestrange doesn't go out to lunch till half-past one. These people very seldom do."

"What people?" Julia, with her free, easy stride, had to restrain herself to keep pace with the puttering steps of Lily in her long tube skirt. "Society people," explained Lily. "I'm taking you to see Miss Lestrange, the Honourable Marian Lestrange. She's a friend of our old woman's. She's starting a shop just off Hanover Square, and I know she wants to get hold of a good class of girl, if you know what I mean, dear. So I spoke up and said: 'There's a young friend of mine, Moddom, whom I think might just suit you. No experience, but what you might call savwar faire,' and she said, 'Well, Miss Clarkson, it will be very kind of you if you will bring her along to see me any day before half-past one.' So I thought I'd let you know at once, because that sort of people so soon forget what they've said."

Julia's heart beat high, and she tried to catch a glimpse of herself in every mirror in the shop windows that they passed. She had on her dark blue whipcord. The skirt was nearly as tight as Lily Clarkson's, though somehow Julia moved in it with a greater effect of ease. She wore her big dark-blue hat and a fresh white blouse, but she wished now that she had borrowed her mother's fur. Her clothes that had looked so right to her on starting out now looked all wrong. Not only the mirrors in the shop windows, but the clothes in the shop windows told her how wrong she looked. As they neared George Street her spirits sank lower and lower. She wondered how she could ever have thought that she looked nice that morning. Even the memory of Durand's sad, admiring monkey eyes failed to cheer her. He probably looked like that at every girl. She had heard that Frenchmen did.

"There it is," said Miss Clarkson. "Doesn't it look smart? Of course, they are still in an awful mess, but it'll look lovely when it's finished, don't you think?"

As a matter of fact it was rather difficult to see the shop at all, because it was still covered, as by a gigantic cat's cradle, with poles, planks and ladders. Further down the road the workmen were lounging and smoking, having finished their midday meal. Large pots of paint still stood about on the planks. Still, it was possible to see that all the woodwork of the shop was being painted a brilliant green, and that above the window was written in flowing letters the word "l'Etrangère." There were, of course, no goods displayed in the window, but it was impossible to see into the shop, for already the curtains of mouse-grey velvet hung upon a rail at the back of the window.

Lily went, with an extraordinary air of importance, up to the shop door and pushed it open. An electric buzzer sounded, and she entered, followed by Julia. The two girls stood there while nothing happened at all. Sounds of talking and laughter came from behind more curtains of grey velvet at the far end of the shop, but Lily, for all her air of importance—which seemed to be becoming less—made no movement towards it.

Julia stood looking about her. Yes, this was the sort of shop she wanted. The walls were painted a paler grey than the curtains, and the ceiling was silver. There were long mirrors in silver frames with garlands of brightly painted fruit, carved in wood, festooned across the top. It was all very modern, far more modern than Art Nouveau, which Julia suddenly realised was out of date. She had heard of this sort of decoration though she had never seen it. Somebody called Poiret did it, so she had heard.

The minutes went on, and Julia whispered, as fresh peals of laughter came from behind the curtains: "Can't you go and tell them we're here?"

Lily looked horrified. "Oh, I shouldn't like to do that," she murmured; "you can never tell with these people." She gave a little refined cough, but it passed unnoticed. Julia suddenly lost patience, and going to the door, opened and shut it rather loudly. The buzzer sounded again. Lily looked at her with round eyes of affright beneath the tiny brim of the jam-pot hat. "You have been and gone and done it!" she whispered, and indeed Julia had.

The laughter ceased. A languid voice called out: "Who's there?" and then remarked perfectly audibly to some unseen person, "Oh, a traveller, I suppose. I'd better see who it is." The grey velvet curtains parted and a young lady, clad in a black frock, so tight that the skirt looked like one trouser leg, and with a sort of black skullcap swathed round her head, came towards them. Julia knew in a moment beyond a doubt that her own clothes were all wrong. Her big full hat, her big knot of hair, everything. The girl was perhaps only twenty-two or three, but she was a woman of the world. She looked oddly like a pierrot, with her perfectly pale face, thin, faint, long eyebrows, and faint, thin, long mouth, slightly curved up at the ends. On each hollow cheek a tiny little curl of ashen fair hair seemed to be pasted—afterwards, Julia found each curl was fastened on a long pin—so closely did it follow the line of the cheek-bone, curving up towards the eyes, as the corners of the mouth and the eyes themselves and the eyebrows all curved up. She had a long graceful neck and an incredibly thin and graceful body, and long thin hands. She was not good-looking but nobody could have passed her without noticing her. She was extremely elegant; the first really elegant person Julia had ever met. She was alarming, too, with the cold, still, terrifying quality of ice or of a steel blade.

"Oh, Moddom," said Lily, "I do hope I'm not intruding. I reely do. You were so very kind the other day and said I might bring my friend along to see you. She is wanting a position as apprentice."

"Oh, yes," said the strange lady in a vague voice. "Let me see, have I seen you before?"

Lily's face went very red. "I'm at Pompilia's. I helped with your fitting the other day—the white satin. When it wanted taking in a bit on the hips."

"Oh, yes, of course, I thought I knew your face. Yes, I shall want an apprentice. I think we shall open in about a couple of weeks now." The narrow, slightly oblique eyes of a very pale grey that could look greenish, considered Julia thoughtfully. "Take off your hat, child," said Miss

54

Lestrange abruptly. Julia blushed deeply and pulled off the offending dark-blue felt.

"You look nice, not that I suppose it matters much in an apprentice, but I hate people round me who don't look nice. What can you do?"

"I—I can draw," stammered Julia. "I've been studying fashion-drawing now for two terms."

The pale eyebrows lifted still higher. "Dear me, I think that's a bit above our station. I hadn't thought of having an apprentice who could draw. Still it might be useful. Wait a minute. I'll ask Mrs. Danvers to come. She knows more about this sort of thing than I do," and raising her voice, Miss Lestrange called out, "Gipsy, come along here for a moment, will you, darling?"

Again the curtains parted and a dark, rather plump, bright-eyed lady appeared, far more brisk and businesslike in manner than Miss Lestrange. Afterwards, Julia learned, Mrs. Danvers had already run a shop which would have been a great success if all her customers had not been her friends, and in consequence, failed to pay her.

"Here is a girl come for the job as apprentice," explained Miss Lestrange. "You talk to her about it, Gipsy."

Matters went very swiftly, for Mrs. Danvers had Julia's age and lack of experience out of her in half a minute. "Seems all right," she said briskly to Miss Lestrange—they both had a curious manner of talking to you, thought Julia, as though you were not there at all—"May as well try her as get in another." She turned back to Julia.

"Very well, we will expect you Monday week. Be here at about a quarter to nine. Of course, you will get no salary while you are an apprentice. You might bring some of your drawings with you. Not that you will have much time to do anything like that when once we get going." She gave a brisk nod and went back between the curtains.

No one asked Julia whether the arrangement had suited her. Lily plucked her nervously by the elbow. "Thank you very much indeed, Moddom," said Lily to Miss Lestrange. "I'm sure you'll find my friend very useful."

"I'm sure I shall," said Miss Lestrange, with a sort of languid impersonal kindness. "Good-bye."

"Good-bye," began Julia, and found her courage failed her at saying "Miss Lestrange." "Good-bye, Madam."

At least, she thought, she would show she knew how to speak, not like Lily with her absurd "moddoms." She picked up her dark-blue felt hat. Miss Lestrange checked her by a gesture. "Your hair," she murmured, looking thoughtfully at her. "It looks too much that way. A lot of girls are bobbing their hair now. You'd better try it. Get it done by a good hairdresser, or it will look a mess."

"All right," murmured Julia. Inwardly she was horrified . . . her precious hair!

Quite calmly, as though she had not suggested anything of overwhelming importance, Miss Lestrange nodded casually and was lost again behind the grey velvet curtains.

"Well," said Lily, when the two girls were out on the pavement again, "aren't you in luck?"

"I thought they were rather rude," said Julia.

"Oh, no," said Lily, shocked, "I thought Miss Lestrange was ever so nice to you. She's the real thing, you know; knows all the slap-up people. She's doing this because she's bored. I don't suppose it'll last long, but it'll give you a good start. I knew she'd take you if I said you were a friend of mine."

Julia felt the least she could do to show her gratitude was to stand lunch to Lily, and indeed with this idea in her head she had stolen half a crown from the vase on the dining-room mantelpiece where her mother kept the current money of the household. They had poached eggs on toast at Lyons', but at least the Lyons' was in Bond Street, and Julia felt that a career in the big world had begun for her at last.

Of course, thought Julia resentfully, Dad and Mum would take it that way, doubtful and critical, throwing cold water, just because she'd found the job for herself and not through them. "It's quite all right, I tell you," she said impatiently, "Miss Lestrange is perfectly wonderful."

"Wonderful is as wonderful does," said Mrs. Almond darkly, and Dad said with an air of importance that sat ludicrously upon him: "I'd better go and see her myself. Can't have people thinking *my* daughter can take a place just anywhere."

In an agonised flash, Julia saw Miss Lestrange's cold clear face, the tilt of brows and lips accentuated to scornfulness, looking at Dad as though he were some odd insect.

"You'll only make a fool of yourself and lose me the job," she cried angrily; "haven't you *any* sense, Dad?"

Mr. Almond looked deeply offended, and Julia felt the hopelessness of trying to get him to understand this entirely different world of which she had caught a glimpse. The words wouldn't come to her, and he wouldn't understand them, anyway. Yet she must, she must, prevent him doing this dreadful thing that would cover her with shame and turn her hot for the rest of her life whenever she thought of it. They were going to supper and whist at Mr. Starling's that evening, and though Julia generally evaded such entertainments—what fun was there in seeing Dad and Mum and the Starlings play whist —she suddenly decided she would accompany them on this occasion. Mr. Starling admired her, she knew, and if she could get him alone for a minute, without that awful stick of a wife hanging around, with a face as long as a wet week, she could tell him of her dilemma. He would breezily assure Dad that everything was all right, and Dad had a great opinion of Mr. Starling as a man of the world. Anyway, the actual supper would be nicer at Saint Clement's Square than at home.

There was the usual squabble about taking Bobby. Mrs. Almond said: "You know quite well Mrs. Starling doesn't like dogs." Julia stood firm. It would be Bobby's first walk that day.

Eventually they all set off, Bobby leaping and whimpering with joy, making rushes at a lamp-post as he remembered the chief business of a walk, and stopping short, turning, and rushing back to Julia again, jumping up at her and saying over and over again how lovely it was to walk with her.

She put him on the lead to cross the High Road, and, panting loudly, he walked beside her with great sobriety to the road opposite that led down to Saint Clement's Square. Then Julia stooped and unfastened the lead, and Bobby shot off, his powerful leg muscles sending him at a terrific pace down the road, the white tip of his tail straight out behind him. "That dog!" complained Mrs. Almond, "he's always so rough."

He was waiting for them when they got into the Square, sitting upright on his haunches and smiling, and looking absurdly like the plaster lions that sat on the pedestals at the foot of the tall white flights of steps. Some of the houses had eagles, but these were not nearly as friendly; the lions had arched backs to their necks just like Bobby, and smiling, upturned mouths.

Julia had always liked Saint Clement's Square. The houses told of a more leisurely and spacious age, even now when they were mostly converted into flats, and all rather shabby and in need of fresh plastering. They had verandas coming out from the first floor, supported by slim, green pillars, and capped with green-painted iron roofs. They were rather like the houses Julia had fallen in love with during one holiday in Brighton, that she had found out were called Regency houses. There were some almond-trees in blossom in the garden of the Square, looking like sunset clouds caught for an enchanted little space of time in the network of dark twigs. A broken statue of Apollo, green with damp, stood in the middle of the Square, the strings of his lyre were made of whitewashed wire and had snapped, and were now curled up aimlessly, his hand poised over them. There were bird-droppings on his shoulder. Julia loved him, he filled her with a pleasing and impersonal melancholy, and he reminded her of the lost world of the Polytechnic, and the white gods who stood blank-eyed down the cast-room. The Starlings' maisonette might be prosaic, but the Square itself was incurably romantic.

Julia managed the minute alone with Herbert Starling. Mrs. Starling was fussing about Bobby, and tying him up to the leg of the kitchen table, to the annoyance of the elderly maid, Emily, who said she would be sure to trip over him, and what harm did the poor dumb animal do, anyway? She was a great one for dumb animals, she was. She persisted in calling Bobby a dumb animal, though all the time he was talking at the top of his voice, explaining that he wasn't used to being tied up to table-legs.

"Mr. Starling . . . I do want to speak to you for a minute alone . . . it's ever so important." His clean-shaven good-natured face flushed, and he said aloud: "Let me take your coat, Julia, and you'll like to get rid of your hat, I expect. Here's the lobby, where I've had the telephone put in."

For a few moments they were in the dim-lit lobby, that smelt of rubber goloshes and overcoats. Julia swiftly told him of her difficulty. He bent his florid face consolingly towards her.

"Don't worry, I'll see to your Dad. Of course you ought to have your chance. I've heard of your Miss Lestrange, she's one of the sort whose photo gets put in the picture papers. 'Society lady starts a shop,' and all that sort of thing. You're a great girl, Julia, you ought to have your chance."

The florid face came nearer, looking like a huge red moon. A brotherly kiss was sketched, rather inexpertly, upon Julia's cheek. She did not like it, but she felt a tiny thrill of triumph all the same.

The next moment Mrs. Starling's voice was heard calling sharply: "Herbert . . . Herbert. . . ."

Julia went out into the passage . . . "and I'll take him back home now if Mrs. Starling doesn't like dogs, I will indeed, Mr. Starling. I'd no idea she didn't. I can easily get myself some supper at home."

Herbert Starling's voice came, grave and pleasant. "That's all right, no need to worry. The missis doesn't really dislike dogs, do you, Missis?"

"I don't like them," said Mrs. Starling fretfully, staring at Herbert and Julia as they came into the dining-room, with annoyance, but no suspicion in her pale eyes.

"She's a great girl, sharp as a needle," thought Mr. Starling gratefully, as he watched Julia's innocent face.

Supper was already laid on the table, but two more guests were expected, Dr. Ackroyd and his daughter, Anne. They were a little late, for, as usual, a clamorous patient had seized on Dr. Ackroyd at the last moment. Even the children would say: "There goes the doctor," as they saw his tall form striding along the streets—he walked whenever possible—his thin, clean-shaven face bent, his long, greying hair lying on his coat collar, and his shabby top-hat tilted a little over one ear. He had a reputation for speaking his mind, and seemed blandly unconscious of the fact that anyone's delicacy could be offended by his so doing.

Once the Ackroyds had arrived, everyone settled down to supper, which was very good; ham and salad, and trifle with brandy in it, and a big chocolate cake. It must be dreadful to be as delicate as Mrs. Starling and not be able to eat what you liked. There was port wine, too, and Julia had a glass and enjoyed it. It was queer, but delightful, that funny sensation of floating, as though you were lighter than air, and yet of being more poised and clear than ever before, that came to her after drinking the port.

Dad seemed to grow mellow, too, at Mr. Starling's. He never looked out for slights, as he was apt to do at his office and in his own house, and when Julia casually introduced the subject of Miss Lestrange's shop, Dad said quite amiably: "Well, now look here, Starling. Don't you think I am in the right of it, as one man of the world to another, to want to go and see this Miss Whatever she calls herself? I can't have my little girl going off just anyhow. Don't *you* think I ought to go and see for myself what I think of the place?"

Julia waited anxiously. Mr. Starling seemed to think the matter over, as though it were entirely news to him, and then gave judgment in his weighty, rather pompous fashion.

"Well, I don't know that I should if I were you, Almond," he said. "Sometimes it's better to let these young people arrange things for themselves. Then if they make mistakes they've nobody but themselves to blame. What did you say the lady's name is, Julia?"

"Miss Lestrange," said Julia; "the Honourable Marian Lestrange."

"Oh, she's all right," said Herbert Starling casually. "Everybody knows her. Why, you can hardly open a picture paper without seeing her photograph. It'll be a very good start for Julia, I shouldn't wonder."

"Well, if you say so . . ." murmured Dad, evidently, as Julia could see, rather glad to get out of a difficult situation. Once his first annoyance at not having been consulted had passed off, he was not very anxious to go and confront a formidable society lady.

"After all," went on Mr. Starling, "we men may consider ourselves lucky nowadays if the ladies want to go in for anything as feminine as dressmaking. Julia might have wanted to be one of these suffragettes and gone about burning churches and hitting policemen."

Mrs. Almond looked shocked. "No daughter of mine," she said with unwonted decision, "would have behaved like that, I should hope. Suffragettes, indeed! I'd suffragette them if I had anything to do with them."

"Oh, I don't know, I don't know," said Herbert Starling,

with an air of large-mindedness; "I daresay they'd be all right if they had husbands and homes of their own."

"Lots of them have," pointed out Julia, rather unkindly, considering the way that Mr. Starling had stood by her. She had no brief for suffragettes—the whole question bored her profoundly—even Miss Tracey had been unable to work her up to the idea that it was important for a woman to have a vote and be what she called "a good citizen." And Miss Tracey herself had always ended her arguments by saying: "But, of course, I don't like this militant business, that's all wrong." Julia had thought to herself that if a thing was worth having at all it was worth fighting for, but she had not been interested enough in the question of the vote to say so.

Herbert Starling's face flushed a little. "Then their husbands should see that they stick to their homes," he said. "Yes, indeed," said Mr. Almond.

Julia glanced curiously from one to the other. Why did men always think they were in the right, and that they could make women do things? Mr. Starling had more sense than Dad, but she could make him do exactly what she wanted, and as for Dad, why, you had only to look at him to see that it was all bluster and no power with him.

"Perhaps they would stay at home," said Mrs. Starling unexpectedly, "if they had good homes and husbands," and she looked with real affection in her pale eyes at her rosy-faced Herbert.

"Some of their husbands agree with them, and want women to have the vote," said Julia, feeling spurred on by some imp of mischief.

"Then all I can say is," said Herbert Starling loudly, "that a man who thinks like that is no man at all. I should not have thought you were one of these shrieking sisterhood, or whatever they call them, Julia."

Julia had a sudden little fear lest she had antagonised Mr. Starling. It only needed another word from him to set Dad off being tiresome.

"I'm not," she said, "not really," and she lifted her long, thick lashes in a swift, shy little glance at Herbert Starling. His own eyes met the glance and again that little understanding of a secret between them leaped to life. Julia was enjoying herself. It was fun having a little understanding with him that no one else in the room knew anything about. He was a kind man, she decided, and it was rotten luck for him to be married to Mrs. Starling. Julia studied her furtively. She sat at the head of the table, like a faintly disapproving ghost. She wore her faded hair in an old-fashioned pompadour, from which the shorter hairs escaped and hung down in straight wisps. A gold-rimmed pince-nez gave her rather the look of a governess, thought Julia, with a fleeting remembrance of Miss Tracey. She must be three or four years older than Mr. Starling, but there was surely no need to make herself look even older than she was by getting herself up in such an old-fashioned manner.

"What I can never understand," remarked Dr. Ackroyd, in the voice that seemed always so unexpectedly deep and booming as it issued from his tall and cadaverous frame, "is why you should imagine that getting the vote should change a woman's nature. Men will be men, and women will be women to the end of time, one imagines. There's really nothing specially awful about going to a polling booth. We men have managed to survive it, and women are a great deal tougher than we are."

"It isn't so much," remarked Mr. Starling, obviously striving to be broad-minded, "that I object to women having the vote, it's the way they're going about things so as to get it."

"Well," said Dr. Ackroyd, "men didn't get the vote till they had torn up a lot of railings, and done a lot of damage. I object very much to women having the vote, but then I object to men having the vote, too. I'd take it away from everybody."

Mrs. Starling breathed a sigh of relief. Obviously the doctor couldn't possibly mean what he was saying. The conversation wasn't serious. She was always nervous when conversation was serious, especially between the gentlemen.

"Now I know you're making fun of us, Doctor," she said. "You believe in the higher education of women and all that. Why, you're sending Miss Ackroyd here to college, and in my young days she'd just have stopped at home and kept house for her father."

"Kept house!" exploded Dr. Ackroyd. "Any intelligent woman with a maid can get rid of the business of a house in half an hour, and in half a day if she's single-handed. If she can't do that she's not fit to have in the house at all. Yes, Anne's going to follow in my footsteps, I'm glad to say, and do you know what I can remember, Starling? I remember when I was a young man listening to a very old and famous surgeon on the platform at a meeting held to discuss the admission of women into the medical profession, and he said: 'Ladies and gentlemen, I would sooner see my daughter dead at my feet than earning her living in such a way.' Funny," continued the doctor, half to himself, and finishing his glass of port, "why daughters always had to be dead at your feet. Never anywhere else."

Anne laughed. She had a very pretty, low laugh, and a pretty, low voice.

"I should hate to be dead at your feet, Daddy, and I'll do the best I can to avoid it, but I think I'd go and learn to be a doctor even if you didn't approve."

"I hope so, I'm sure," said Dr. Ackroyd. "It's no good, Almond, you can't keep young Julia at home doing nothing, even if you could afford to. That's the way to make women husband-hunters and nothing else. Have you ever studied the habits of the common tick?"

"Certainly not," said Mr. Almond, rather startled.

"Well, the tick lives in woods and such places, hanging on to a leaf or a blade of grass, and waiting and hoping for some animal, dog or sheep, to go brushing through the undergrowth, and it falls off and fastens itself on the animal, which unfortunate creature is afterwards called 'the host.' The insects do their mating upon the host, as well as sucking its blood, and when they're swollen with food and young they drop off and lay their eggs. Then the whole business starts all over again when the young are hatched out. They climb up a blade of grass and wait for some animal to pass. Well, that's very like women in the Victorian era, and lots of women now, if it comes to that. I'd sooner Anne learned all about the conduct of the stomach, than that she clung to an aspidistra leaf in the window waiting to drop on some unfortunate man, who would become her host— and worse, for in the human world the host is the mate as well."

Anne laughed again, but Julia thought she understood how some people were shocked by Dr. Ackroyd. Obviously, both Mrs. Starling and Mrs. Almond were feeling outraged.

Herbert Starling cleared his throat: "Well, now, what about a game?" he said with forced cheerfulness.

"Sorry, can't stop," said Dr. Ackroyd. "I'm expecting a baby at any moment. Thanks for my supper, Mrs. Starling. I always say you're one of the best women I know. Can't eat anything yourself, and yet provide good food for others. Good-bye, good-bye," and he talked himself out of the flat.

The four older people began to play whist, but after a while, Anne and Julia went to the kitchen to fetch Bobby. He had been lavishly fed by Emily, and had now climbed on to her steep lap, where he was hanging on precariously, the toes of his white paws curved tightly in the effort to retain his place, though the woman's arms were also occupied in trying to hold his bulky twenty-five pounds or so of weight. It was one of Bobby's most passionate convictions that he was a lap-dog.

He leapt off her lap without so much as a "thank you," and began explaining matters to Julia, who kissed him ardently, and, holding him by the collar, led him through the dining-room to the balcony. There she and Anne settled themselves down under the painted green iron canopy that sloped down like a Chinese roof, and gave a sense of distance to the Square beyond. The sky was a deep night-blue now, but the almond blossom showed pale through the darkness, and in one corner where the light of a street lamp shone upon it, seemed touched by dawn. The air was soft, almost warm; there breathed through the night a feeling of youth and of spring, of country things, that was rather enhanced than spoiled by the clang and roars of the trams from the High Road. Bobby sat down, leaning heavily against Julia's knee, and pressing his head against her, as she played with his velvet ears. Anne produced a cigarette and lit it calmly, to the intense surprise of Julia, who had never seen a girl smoke. But Anne, she knew, never did things for effect. Doubtless, she often sat and smoked and talked with that queer, kind, clever father. Julia, with her intense, imaginative sympathy, suddenly caught a glimpse of their life together. It wouldn't have suited Julia, who wanted to be known and admired, and have love affairs, but it was rather lovely all the same.

Those two odd, clever, ugly beings, so sure of each other, so interested in ideas and the interchange of ideas

. . . it must be lovely to have someone with whom you could exchange ideas. It would never be possible for her to do so with Dad or Mum, or Uncle George, or Aunt Mildred. Perhaps in this new life that was to open out before her, she would find someone to whom she could talk about what lighted windows at night, and glimpses of people in buses or parks, or the fate of characters in a thrilling book, did to her. Certainly the person wouldn't be Miss Lestrange, or Mrs. Danvers, but she would meet heaps of people now. And Julia stared out at the faintly burning cloud of the almond blossom, and breathed the spring and the future into her consciousness.

Bobby stirred a little, and put first one white glove and then the other very gently upon her lap, laying his nose between them; then very slowly as he began to work himself forward, a hind leg came up and rested upon her thigh. Julia didn't move, and, with infinite caution, the fourth leg came slowly up, and Bobby, hunched together and very uncomfortable, had succeeded in becoming a lap-dog once more. Julia laughed and pulled him into a more comfortable position, and with a deep sigh of relief he lay back, his head sentimentally pressed against her shoulder.

"It's funny, isn't it?" said Anne, watching these manoeuvres, "how quietly he goes on and on till he gets his own way. I often wonder what dogs, dogs as clever as Bobby, think about. Whether they really think at all in the way we do."

"I'm sure Bobby thinks," said Julia, as every dog owner has doubtless replied, from the days of the first cave-man to whom a dog was a companion.

"I wonder," said Anne, "whether they know that they belong to a lower order of beings. You see, we're God to them. I wonder if they accept the fact that there are lots of things they cannot understand, or if they wonder about it. The world must seem full of human beings who kick them or pat them, and they go wriggling about and wagging their tails and saying 'thank you.' Do you think they ever want to be us instead of themselves, just as we want to be people greater and more powerful than we are?"

Julia pondered for a moment. "I don't think they mind," she said, "they just look on it all as quite natural.

It must be awfully funny to live in a world where there is quite another race, much taller and bigger and more powerful than you are." And she remembered, though she didn't say so, that sudden feeling of inferiority that had been hers in Miss Lestrange's shop. Miss Lestrange and Mrs. Danvers had seemed such real ladies, but after all, there was no reason why she, Julia, shouldn't become anything she chose.

"Are you really awfully keen on being a doctor, Anne?" she asked.

"Oh, yes," said Anne, with conviction.

"Why?" said Julia curiously.

"I suppose," said Anne mildly, "I want to know things. Real things, facts, I mean, and I want to try and understand people, and Daddy says understanding their bodies is half-way to understanding their minds."

"Don't you want to fall in love and be married?"

"I hadn't thought about it. I suppose I'd like to have children—every woman would—but I don't suppose I ever shall. I'm not a bit attractive like you are, Julia, and I don't want to be the tick on the aspidistra."

"But *love*," persisted Julia, "you must want to be in love," and in Julia's voice there spoke every novel and story she had ever read; every novel and story that her immediate female forebears had ever read.

"Oh, I don't know," said Anne shyly, "it's different for you. You're pretty. At least you're not pretty," she added honestly, "because the bones of your face aren't right, but you look as though you were, and anyway people will think you are. Nobody could ever think me pretty, and I think purely intellectual marriages must be horrible somehow, like religious marriages. I've just read a book; Daddy brought it home and threw it at me as usual: 'This'll amuse you; it's about a saint, quite a new saint, in the Roman Catholic Church, whom they call The Little Flower.' Isn't it a dreadful name? Well, her father and mother wanted to be a monk and a nun, and for some reason or other they couldn't, so they thought the next best thing would be to marry and have children, so as to add to the souls of the saved. Well"— and Julia could somehow feel that Anne was blushing through the darkness—"I think that's dreadful. To mix that sort of thing up with religion makes both horrid."

"Yes, it does," agreed Julia, without really thinking

very much of what she was saying. "I say, Anne, do you know about things, about what happens?"

"Oh, yes, of course," said Anne. "Daddy thinks everyone ought to. Don't you?"

"No," said Julia, "nobody's ever told me anything. I know babies come out of your inside."

"Oh, that!" said Anne, laughing. Julia sat there longing to ask Anne how babies got in, in the first place, but quite unable to do so, and Anne gazed tranquilly out at the Square, and finally ground her cigarette to death against the stone floor of the balcony.

"The people one knows," began Julia at last, "our parents, for instance, they're not good-looking. Why, just look at Dad and Mum, and yet they've been married and had me."

"I know," said Anne. "It seems awfully funny to me somehow. It's as though people ought to do that sort of thing when they're young, and then forget it. It's almost as though it were always wrong, and even impossible, except for now, and except for oneself. I tried to explain that to Daddy once, and he said it was nature's way of making one feel that it was something new, and fresh, and wonderful. He said if young people understood all about it, they'd never do it, and the race would die out."

"Then you do think it's all right for the young," argued Julia, "and yet you say you don't think of it for yourself."

"I don't, not practically, but I suppose I shall want things just the same as most people, only you see I have got a face so dreadfully like a horse that I'm afraid I could only be loved for my mind, and I should hate to be loved only for my mind."

"I think it would be marvellous to be loved for one's mind," said Julia.

"Oh, I don't know, I think it would be very dangerous, and, anyway, all wrong."

"If you're like a horse," said Julia, "what am I like?"

Anne, by the light of a match, from which she was lighting a fresh cigarette, looked at Julia carefully. "You're like a funny mixture of animal and bird," she said, "a soft, furry, slinky sort of animal, with the head and wings of a bird. When you move your head you always look just like a bird to me, just as though your neck could swivel right round."

Julia was pleased. It sounded a nice description.

"You're not altogether like a horse," she said, "your eyes are like deer's eyes, just like the deer in Bushey Park. I went there last summer to spend a day with Uncle George, Aunt Mildred, and that awful little Elsa, and Dad and Mum. They all looked to me ugly except the deer, and their eyes were like velvet, only a sort of wet velvet, if you know what I mean."

Anne threw back her head and laughed. "Wet velvet eyes. Thank you, Julia, that's about the only compliment I'll ever have, and it's a very nice one. Well, I've told you what I want to be. I want to be a doctor, at least I suppose I do; but most of all I want to study biology, and want to find out about thousands of things, specks on butterflies' wings, and why some insects are like leaves, and why things, I mean animals and people, behave as they do. But you, what do you want?"

Julia, pressing Bobby's heavy head against her shoulder, thought for a moment. "I suppose I want everything," she said. "Most women aren't clever like you, Anne, and do want everything. I want lots of people to love and admire me, particularly one person, and I want to love and admire him terribly, too."

"You want to be happy," said Anne.

"I suppose I do," said Julia.

"Well, girls! Well, girls!" said a bright, brisk voice from the open French window, "this won't do. Can't have you stopping here, catching cold, and discussing your love affairs." And Herbert, heavy, big, dark and somehow menacing-looking, when you couldn't see his rosy cheeks, only the black loom of his head and shoulders against the light, stood behind them, a hand on either side of the window.

Bobby thumped his tail heavily, not because he liked Herbert Starling, but because here was one of the gods with a loud voice and the power to turn him out of his comfortable seat.

"Your father's rung," said Herbert Starling to Anne, "from his case. He says not to wait up for him, but go back home."

"Oh," cried Anne, jumping up, "I'll go back. That'll

mean he'll want sandwiches later. Did he say anything about the baby?"

Herbert coughed rather shyly. "I believe he did. A boy——"

"Oh, splendid," said Anne, "I know they wanted a boy this time. It must have been a pretty quick affair. Daddy can only just have got there in time. How much did it weigh?"

Herbert coughed again: "I believe your father said eight and a half pounds."

"Splendid! . . . I'll go and say good-bye to Mrs. Starling. Good-bye, Julia, mind you let me know how you get on in the shop." Anne stooped, kissed Bobby's pink nose and was gone.

Herbert Starling came out on to the little balcony, and Julia suddenly felt she didn't want to talk to him alone. It had been rather nice sitting out there in the warm darkness talking to Anne, and thinking her own thoughts, but she didn't want to have to thank Herbert Starling for what he had done for her at supper. She spilled Bobby off her lap and without a protest he lay brown and limp upon the balcony, and, heaving a heavy sigh, closed his yellow eyes and prepared to go to sleep again.

"They'll be wanting you," said Julia.

Herbert Starling followed her into the house somewhat discontentedly. Julia curled herself up in an armchair, Bobby again on her lap, and tried to read one of the few books the Starlings possessed, a bound volume of *The Quiver*.

The Starlings were not, as they would have said, great readers. Mrs. Starling was one of those women who, with really nothing to do, always say they have no time for reading; and the evening paper after supper and the morning paper in the train going to the City sufficed for Herbert Starling's intellectual needs. Julia derived a certain mild amusement from *The Quiver*, for her own imagination breathed life into any story, however banal, that she read, simply because she could always be the heroine. But she thought it very funny that whole magazines should be written, as this one was, around things like religion and total abstinence. She herself knew nothing of either one or the other. This curious standpoint of things being right and wrong, which somehow informed the rather puerile pages of *The Quiver* meant nothing to Julia's unaffected paganism. Anne and her father had standards, but they were not these. . . . Julia had been taught none.

She was glad when the card-playing came to an end, and she and Bobby could start for Two Beresford through the cool and starlit night. The trees rustled faintly in the Square; the trams clanged and shrieked in the High Road; quietness again lapped her round about when, the Goldhawk Road left behind, Love Lane was reached.

3

The Job

THERE were many days during her first weeks and months at l'Etrangère when Julia wished with all her heart that she had never gone there. She soon learned that the apprentice is always wrong, and many were the tears she shed in secret, and sometimes even before the cool, faintly amused eyes of Miss Lestrange; but when this happened, Julia always turned her head away and tried to pretend that nothing was the matter. She had for Miss Lestrange none of the adoration she had felt for Miss Tracey, but this was not because of any particular quality in either of the two women, it was that she herself had grown past it.

Nevertheless, she liked to stand well in Miss Lestrange's eyes as, for the matter of that, she always liked to do in the eyes of everyone she met. But with Marian Lestrange she was aware of a quality of criticism that was higher and more acute than any she had yet met with, and Julia was desperately anxious in consequence to acquit herself well. Marian Lestrange was not nearly as business-like as Gipsy Danvers. If it had rested entirely with her the shop might have been a failure in the first few weeks; but she certainly did decorate it by her

presence, and she wore her clothes as though they had
fallen upon her from heaven. Gipsy was not smart; she
was pleasant, vital, capable. She could be very quick-
tempered, but nevertheless, Julia soon found that she
had a softer heart then Marian. Marian had a sort of
cool good-nature, and was sometimes taken by a freak-
ish kindliness, but then it was generally for her own
amusement.

One day a tall, clean-shaven, blue-eyed man called in
to take Gipsy to lunch, and he proved to be her husband, Commander Danvers. Gipsy seemed as fluttered
and pleased as a young girl, and after they had left the
shop together, Julia stared after them enviously.

Miss Smythe, who combined the duties of junior showroom girl and junior saleswoman, was taking a last look
at herself in the mirror before going out, and smiled at
Julia.

"It does one good to see them, doesn't it?" she said;
"as poor as church mice. I believe he's got nothing
much but his pay. Of course, you can see he's frightfully
good family and all that. Got a sweet little kid, too; she
brought him in here one day. That's why she works so
hard to try and help things out a bit. They both think
the world of that kid and of each other. It isn't often
you see married people like that, that's what I say."

Julia, whose notions of what she vaguely called "Society" consisted largely of the belief that all the women
had lovers, and all the men mistresses, had to readjust
herself to this new possibility.

A few days later a considerably younger man came
in and asked for Miss Lestrange. He wasn't as good-
looking as Commander Danvers; he had a long, narrow
jaw, and narrow head, but a very delightful smile. Hilda
Smythe was ready with her information when he departed, having failed to get Marian to go to lunch with
him.

"That was Billy Embury," she told Julia, as they
peeped from behind the curtain of the fitting-room and
saw his straight back disappearing down George Street.
"He's mad about Miss Lestrange, but she treats him just
anyhow."

Marian did indeed treat Mr. Embury just anyhow.
Julia, tidying the stock in the shop, once heard what

almost amounted to a quarrel between them in the back room.

"Of course I know," said Marian in a low icy voice, "that you'll do exactly what you choose. If you want to go and join up in Carson's ridiculous army, you will; but I warn you that Father will make a frightful row if I ever have anything to do with you afterwards. Father says if Ulster fights anything may happen. It may be the signal for a European war or civil war. He foams at the mouth if anybody mentions Carson."

"I can't help your father's troubles," said Billy. "I'm an Ulsterman, and I'm not going to be dictated to by Lloyd George and his gang. I'm awfully sorry, Marian, if you feel I've let you down, but there it is, I've got to go now. God knows I've put it off until I'm ashamed, as it is."

Julia could almost hear the shrug of the shoulders in Marian's reply.

"Just as you like, Billy, although it's very tiresome of you just as we've really begun to tango well together. Oh, well I expect I can pick up another partner. Good-bye, Billy, and mind the step, as they say in certain circles, I believe."

Billy banged out of the shop, evidently in a bad temper. What exciting lives these people lead, thought Julia.

Of course, Miss Lestrange was older than she was, and had had more time to collect young men to be in love with her.

Julia took the same sort of intense imaginative interest in the private lives of Marian and Gipsy as she did in the lighted windows of houses that she passed at night. There was nothing more thrilling, thought Julia, than gazing at lighted windows, especially when the curtains were drawn back and you could see into the room; see the angle of a table, perhaps, with people sitting at it. If you knew exactly what the house was like inside, and who the people were, the magic would have been gone. At night Julia could imagine anything about what went on in these strange hollow shells called houses that looked so solid by day; she could feel herself part of every drama played there.

The two work-girls, who sat and stitched in a little back room at the top of the narrow Georgian house of l'Etrangère, interested Julia, too, but not as much as

Marian and Gipsy. She knew their sort before. There wasn't so much to wonder about. They were nice girls enough. Milly Benson, the younger, was stupid except with her fingers, but she was a good worker; and the elder, Meggie Parsons, who had had much more experience, was fitter as well as work-girl. She was rather a grave and serious person whose talk was chiefly of her invalid mother. It seemed odd to Julia that anybody could be so interested in a mother.

The house had only three floors, and the middle one was taken up with the fitting-room in front, which was gaily furnished in modern style with a wide divan covered with cushions, and with odd painted cloth dolls sitting about on it. Behind it was the small room where Mrs. Santley, the hat expert, grey-haired and a veteran at her job, sat and worked.

Like Julia herself, Hilda Smythe, the show-girl, had to be all over the house at once. Hilda's father was an auctioneer, and in the hierarchy of the shop world, being a show-girl, she ranked above Julia, but she was very friendly and pleasant. She was not a pretty girl, but she was very smart and had a beautiful figure, and red-gold hair that was bobbed like Julia's own.

There had been a dreadful row at home when Julia first got back with her bobbed hair, but as a matter of fact it suited her very well. It made her look more than ever as though she came out of an Italian painting, with her long, full neck, her narrow grey-blue eyes. She still did not look pretty, but her moments of beauty were more frequent now that she wore this aspect of a gallant medieval youth. Even her father and mother, who at first said she looked a "sketch" and a "shoot," noticed it, and her cousin Elsa, who came up to spend the day with Aunt Mildred from Dulwich, was frankly envious.

"Mother won't let me bob my hair," she complained. "She says it looks common, but I like it."

Julia, gazing at the thin tight plaits without beauty of colour or texture that hung half-way down Elsa's back, suppressed a smile. The Dulwich relations bored her very much. Almost every Sunday since she could remember, the Almonds had either gone to Dulwich to the house of Uncle George Beale, or Uncle George brought Aunt Mildred and Elsa to whatever house the Almonds were inhabiting at the moment. It was supposed because the

74

girls were cousins they must be good friends, although Julia was six years the elder, and thoroughly bored with Elsa, who was a rather whining, spoilt child. Julia had quite offended Aunt Mildred by refusing to allow her to come and visit her at the shop and bring Elsa with her. Why, they might mistake her for a little matcher, thought Julia. The "matcher," by name Flossie—no one ever knew her surname—was, as Miss Clarkson had predicted, quite a rough little thing, who was put upon by everyone, including the work-girls.

During her first weeks at l'Etrangère, Julia used to come home so tired that she could not even take Bobby for his walk, but used to fall into bed and eat the soup that her mother, with an insufferable air of "I told you so!" would bring to her. It wasn't that the work was so hard; it wasn't that there was so much to do; but that you never knew quite what it was.

Julia had to wait on everyone, and she ran up and down, up and down, the steep winding staircase a hundred times a day. Her first duty when she arrived at the shop was to dust all the furniture, for the charwoman's notions of cleanliness were confined to the scrubbing-brush and pail. She tidied the stock, re-lined the chests of drawers with paper if they needed it, and worked at arranging the window under the directions of Gipsy. Then the real work of the day began; the running up and down stairs, answering the telephone, the waiting on everyone else, and general fetching and carrying.

Miss Smythe, good-natured and generous, paid her sixpence a week for doing her errands for her, and making her the endless cups of tea on which she and the work-room girls seemed to subsist. Nobody's duties were very sharply defined in such a very individual business as l'Etrangère's. Everyone did a little bit of everything. It often fell to Julia to rush out and do the matching, when little Flossie had brought back some particularly unsuitable patterns. As to fashion-drawing, Julia wondered why she had ever bothered to learn it. In fact, nothing she had ever known in her life seemed to be of any use to her now.

All the time she was watching and learning. Quite soon she discovered never to say "costume," but to talk about "a suit," and not to say "the dressmaking," but simply "dressmaking." One didn't even say "bathing

75

costume," no, not even "a fancy costume," everything
had to be "a suit" or "a get-up" or "a frock"; one never
talked of "perfume," but always of "scent." She learned,
too, that "Honourable" was a title never used. You
might almost as well not have it, thought Julia, if the
sight of it on an envelope was all you ever got out of
it. This sort of knowledge Julia picked up with startling
facility. Just as she had learned from Miss Tracey what
were the things to admire in literature, and to be quieter
in her manner than the people with whom her childhood
had been spent, so now she learned all the little shib-
boleths which came so naturally to people like Marian
Lestrange and Gipsy Danvers. How she admired them
. . . their certainty about themselves . . . their calm
conviction of being "all right." For Julia, for all her
swiftness of imitation, and the bold front she put on
things, was always at the mercy of terrible moments of
panic, when she felt common, awkward, and utterly
frightened. Some weakness in Julia made her prefer to
be with the work-room girls, or even with the matcher.
To them she was a superior. She was an apprentice,
and all her vitality, unafraid of criticism, would well
up in her again like a clear spring. But that other thing
in Julia that would not let her be; that thing which always made her reach out for the bright and shining bub-
ble which was beauty, forced her to be as much as possible with Marian and Gipsy, watching them, imitating
them, trying also to appear at her ease.

In sharp distinction from the "staff" were the customers, always spoken of by everyone in the shop as though
they were hardly human beings, but rather a race apart,
just as summer visitors are spoken of by the natives of a
seaside village. Customers and summer visitors are needed
for the money that they bring, but nobody really likes
them.

The opinion in the shop was that customers were always wrong, and the opinion of the customers was that
the shop was always wrong, and Julia could not help
thinking that there was a great deal to be said for both
sides.

She soon learned to classify customers. There were
the great friends of Marian and Gipsy, and then the
shop resounded to the cry of "darling." Some of these
friends paid, and paid at once; some paid after great

pressure (when they invariably said they would never have expected such behaviour from dear Marian or dear Gipsy, as the case might be); some never paid at all, and when they had exhausted their credit, went elsewhere. Some customers were friends of friends. They generally began by saying, "Darling Pamela sent me. She told me you were so cheap, and I do hope you are, because I simply haven't got a bean." Nobody, as far as Julia made out, ever had a bean, and yet, as she put it to herself, they all knew quite well how many beans make five.

Then there were the customers who came in from the street—referred to in the shop as "Women off the street." They came in because they had seen a hat or a frock that took their fancy. These inevitably began by saying: "Will you tell me how much that little hat, or that little frock, is?" as though by using the adjective they could subtly depreciate the hat or frock in question, and suggest that it ought not to cost very much. Very often the answer so staggered them that they drifted out into the street again. Sometimes they stopped and tried on everything in the shop—very occasionally, they bought.

The clothes really were good, and Gipsy really was capable, and so, in her curious, strange way, was Marian Lestrange, but they had a very different way with customers. Gipsy would jolly them along, cheer them up about their figures, and always agree with them. Marian frequently reduced them to tears, and Julia made the discovery that there are customers who like to be bullied and made to cry, even by their dressmaker. When Marian had been particularly brutal to some rather tiresome woman, Julia always expected never to see that particular customer again, but she invariably came back, and meekly accepted Marian's orders as to what she should and should not wear.

It was a queer topsy-turvy world, that of l'Etrangère. A mixture of ruthlessness, unexpected kindliness, hard business and extraordinary amateurishness, and real friendliness. Many of Marian's friends seemed to use the shop very much as a club, and some of them were amazingly good-natured to Julia herself. There was much careless generosity—for Marian would suddenly give a thing away to someone whom she knew was genuinely hard-up at under cost price, and there was also a barefaced exploitation of the rich and disagreeable. And, welding the staff together, with the possible exception of Flossie, there was the feeling that they were all helping each other, all bearing with the customers; all breathing the same sigh of relief when the shop door was closed for the day and the tidying-up had been finished; all sharing in the depression when a large order went wrong, or some customer who had seemed particularly safe, failed to pay.

The same extremes obtained in the matter of food as in the matter of frocks and work. Sometimes Marian and Gipsy would be taken out to lunch by some friend, and come back announcing that they had eaten too much and would never do it again. Sometimes Flossie would be sent out for sandwiches to the nearest public-house, and everyone would nibble hastily while trying to rush an order through in time; and always there were the cups of tea—the endless cups of tea.

Julia had her seventeenth birthday after she had been a few weeks at the shop. It fell this year upon a Sunday, and Mr. Starling asked her to midday dinner, that is to say, that Mrs. Starling wrote a note and asked her, but it was a note obviously dictated by her husband and brought round by him when he knew Julia would be at home.

Julia enjoyed the birthday dinner. At the Starlings' she was able to be a Miss Lestrange, confident and poised, It was obvious that she was admired and looked upon as one who would go far.

Dad and Mr. Starling talked stuff she would have thought dull a few months earlier. They talked about the Irish business, and what Carson was doing in Ulster. Julia had heard so many little bits of political gossip lightly tossed about in the shop that she now knew in a sketchy and superficial way what the men were talking about. Dad said for the thousandth time in his life that he was a Liberal and that the Irish ought to have Home Rule. Herbert Starling announced that he was a Conservative, and that the Irish ought to be kept in their place, or that anyway Ulster ought to be allowed to decide for itself, and that he liked to see a man that was a man and you couldn't deny that Carson was a man, and a strong one. Julia described Marian's angry parting with Billy Embury, and at once both men deferred to her. They evidently thought that anybody really in society like Miss Lestrange must be in the way of hearing things that never found their way into the newspapers. Herbert Starling was obviously pleased that the Honourable Marian Lestrange's favourite tango partner should, like himself, be pro-Ulster. A breath, warm and scented, from the great wicked world, seemed to blow about the Starlings' prosaic dining-table as Julia languidly imitated Marian's disgust. Yes, the birthday dinner was a success, and Julia went back to work next day with something of its glow still about her.

One morning Mr. Almond tut-tutted over his morning paper more than usual. There had been an assassination somewhere—some foreign Archduke—Julia gathered.

"These Servians," said Mr. Almond; "always making trouble. Dear me, I remember as though it was yesterday that awful business when they massacred Queen Draga and her husband, and now, here they are killing an Austrian Archduke. Really I don't know what the world's coming to." However, he soon forgot the place with the strange name of Serajevo, in his worry over Ireland. Julia worried about neither, but she was very sorry when on reading the paper for herself she discovered that the victims of the assassination had been morganatically married. Ever since she had read a novel on the subject of morganatic marriages, Julia had thought such a union the most romantic thing imaginable. You were married all right, and so you were a good woman, and you were also married to a royalty, which was romantic, and yet you weren't married, in a funny sort of fashion; and just that tiny little fact of not being married endowed the whole arrangement with glamour. It was a shame that such people should have been murdered.

Julia agreed with the "bit" that she read in the paper about it. . . . "The assassination of the Archduke Ferdinand and his charming consort has shocked all the world in general, and pained London in particular, for it was only last autumn that they came to England to see a typically English product—the Flower Show."

79

Thus was the arrogant, dead bully sanctified by the Press.

That was a fine July and Julia enjoyed it. She was feeling more at home now in her work. She had even been asked to prepare a water-colour drawing of a frock for a customer. Of course, the customer did not know that it was Julia who had done it, but the thing was a success, which was all that mattered, and Marian flung her a word of praise. Gipsy, more practical, gave her one of her own hats, one that she had only worn twice because it didn't suit her. Julia's mind leaped ahead to a future when she would have a little room of her own, and do many fashion drawings.

But that strange word, Serajevo, kept cropping up and up. More and more Julia caught little scraps of conversation now and then between one of the "Darlings," as the girls used to nickname those customers who were Marian's friends. One day the word "war" was dropped out casually, and startled Julia into an awareness of events.

"Do you think there's going to be a war, darling?" asked one lovely lady, smoothing her hair in front of the mirror, preparatory to putting on her hat.

"Father seems to think so," said Marian. "It'll be an awful bore."

"Frightful," said the Darling, "but I suppose it will have its compensations. I don't really remember much about the Boer War; do you? Except that people mafficked or did something, and nurse wouldn't let us out because she said it wasn't safe."

"That's about all I remember," Marian said. "You ought to wear that hat a little further forward, darling."

"Should I?" The vision looked at her young smooth face, and gave the hat a little tweak.

It seemed odd, thought Julia, that the assassination of anybody might perhaps plunge the whole continent into war. The thing seemed to her practical mind out of all proportion. She read another "bit" in one of the illustrated weeklies: "Bigger issues are involved in this heart-breaking catastrophe of two noble lives and of the fragrant romance which encompassed them." Yes, but why were bigger issues involved? It was all very sad, of course, especially for the poor little children of the romantic couple, but why all this talk of war?

Even at Two Beresford, when Mr. Starling dropped in for a drink, the conversation was serious. Dad and Mr. Starling took different points of view, but both were gloomy.

"The City's in a ghastly mess," Mr. Starling would say. "No movement anywhere. I don't know what's going to happen. It'll be the end of all trade if we go to war."

"We can't go to war," retorted Dad, "the nation won't stand for it. Why, I think there'd be a revolution rather than that. You can't make war without money, and where's the money going to come from? You say yourself that trade will be at a standstill. I pin my faith on the Liberal Government."

"I'm not so sure," said Herbert Starling, gloomily, "and I'll tell you why. We had a Manchester man down at our shop yesterday—the traveller from Marlow & Smith's, where the old man buys his shirts—and he told us that one of the biggest cotton mills in Bolton has stopped the delivery orders of their German customers. He says they mightn't have done that, in spite of feeling uneasy, if the Germans hadn't wired trebling their orders, and that made them sit up and think. The manager was going to comply, but the chairman called a meeting and decided he wouldn't send anything at all, even the original orders. They always had stuff on the water in transit to Germany, but they stopped the stuff that had only got as far as Grimsby. This traveller knew the manager. He said it was pathetic to see him. He went about muttering to himself, couldn't believe that a German cheque might be valueless. But there it is, as I told you, one of the biggest firms in Bolton, and they've stopped delivery."

Dad was a bit shaken, you could see that; newspapers and politics and anecdotes were one thing, but cotton goods were trade, and really meant something.

"You'll see," went on Herbert Starling gloomily, "we shan't be able to keep out of it."

A few days later even Marian was grave and perturbed. It was odd, thought Julia, to come from Two Beres-

81

ford, where Mr. Almond insisted that the English nation had too much sense to go to war, and that Asquith and Lloyd George, to say nothing of Morley and John Burns, wouldn't hear of such a thing, into the feminine, scented little shop where people seemed to talk quite differently, and did not, apparently, get their information from the newspapers.

There was very little business transacted nowadays in the shop, and the only customer who bought anything amounting to a trousseau was a very high-souled lady, who declared war was impossible, because the dear Germans were the most Christian of all the nations. She bought three or four summer frocks to take with her to Germany on her holiday.

"Yes, and you know why," laughed Marian to Gipsy, when the customer had left, "she's having an affair with a German officer she met when her husband was attaché at Berlin. Any nation where you've had your first successful adultery *must* be Christian."

Julia, not for the first time since she had come to l'Etrangère's, was shocked. In her class one didn't talk lightly of adultery. One even had great difficulty in committing it, owing to the exigencies of shallow purses and small houses. This hard compulsion of the respectable poor resulted in a certain standard of morality which Julia had always accepted.

"Winston's all for war," said one of the Darlings a few days later in rather a troubled voice to Marian, and Marian nodded.

"I know, but Father has great hopes of Grey. They say he's doing wonders; but Billy came home from Ulster yesterday and I don't think he'd have done that unless he thought there was more chance of getting into a fight over here. He was full of hints at Pamela's party last night."

The door buzzer sounded, and another Darling entered in a state of high excitement.

"Hello, Marian, darling. I want something I can walk straight into for to-night. I haven't a thing to wear. Hello, Susie, darling. I say, what do you think? They say Asquith went and got the King out of bed in the small hours of this morning, and they sat and talked and talked. Jack says that the thing's a certainty now. Mustn't it have been fun; the King in his dressing-gown, just like Queen Victoria when they fetched her down out of her bed to tell her she was a Queen."

Julia listened to all this talk of "Billys" and "Jacks," and of fathers who were high up in the councils of the nation, and then went home to find life really going on very much as usual, and Mrs. Almond chiefly exercised over the misdeeds of the "half-daily woman."

When Julia reached home on the evening of the third of August, Mr. Almond was moaning over Sir Edward Grey's speech in the House of Commons; but Marian, who went to hear it, had come back to the shop before closing time with her eyes bright, and a colour in her usually pale cheeks. It had been wonderful, she said.

The next day was the fourth of August, and the whole world seemed a little different to Julia as she went to work. People stood about and talked in the streets, and yet there seemed a queer hush over everything. A customer who came in said that Mr. Asquith had told somebody, who had told her, how every day going to the House he was cheered by people in the streets who ran along beside him. It was true they were mostly holiday-makers and unemployed, but it just showed the spirit of the nation.

That morning the groups of people in the streets were larger, it seemed the whole of London was out of doors, marching, or walking about or talking. It was war. . . . Oh, if you'd only seen the crowds outside the Palace last night—and the King coming on to the balcony—and all. And the cheering. . . .

It was most undoubtedly war. The cleaner at l'Etrangère, a Frenchman who had married an English wife, had already left for France, and Julia was horrified to find that one of the girls was expected to clean the brasswork outside the shop. When she saw Gipsy quite calmly go out with her sleeves rolled up and start to do it herself, she thought differently about it. It wasn't, after all, like cleaning the steps at Two Beresford had been, at that awful time when they had had no daily woman. Apparently, people like Marian and Gipsy didn't mind what they did, and so Julia smiled and rolled up her sleeves, and firmly took the polishing rag away from Gipsy.

"I'll do that, Mrs. Danvers," she said brightly. "Your hands matter more than mine." And Gipsy, thanking her, mentally chalked up a good mark against Julia's name.

As a matter of fact, Julia quite enjoyed herself, for at the tiny but smart jeweller's shop opposite, the two elegant young salesmen were employed at exactly the same job, for their cleaners had been men who were on the reserve. The world had apparently gone mad, but it seemed to be an amusing form of madness.

There was no work done in the shop that day; everywhere there was a curious mingling of emotions. Excitement, a strange excitement that could not be denied, held them all together. Business men were in the depths of gloom, youths were exalted, clever young men in newspaper offices sat and wrote like mad the stuff that the great machines were to transmute into that voice of the Press, which is supposed to be the voice of the people. Soldiers and sailors felt that their chance had come at last, men of imagination looked forward with a sickening knowledge of disaster to the time when wife and children would have to be left behind, and everything they had lived for and built up thrown upon a hazard. Wives and mothers, and young women in love, alternated between a knowledge that nothing could happen to their own particular man—God couldn't be so cruel—and the dire knowledge that it was just that one valued life that would be exacted. All over Europe men prayed to God to ensure the victory for the right.

At first it seemed, as Mr. Starling had gloomily predicted, that trade was ruined, especially the luxury trades. People had yet to learn, so long was it since a great war, that nothing stimulates the spending of money as much as the fact of wholesale death. Let us eat and drink for tomorrow we die, was not written by someone who knew nothing of the human heart.

Just as business was at its worst, Marian decided to marry her Ulster enthusiast, Billy Embury, who was always in and out of the shop looking, Julia thought, very fascinating in his khaki, although nobody could have called him handsome. Marian said casually of him one day that he had a streamline head, and it was perfectly true. Everything was narrow, fine, and cut away as though to offer the least wind resistance, and it seemed somehow not at all surprising that he had joined the Royal Flying Corps.

Marian seemed to become less casual about him, and her voice lost the icy quality that had made it cut so coldly when Julia had overheard the quarrel about Carson. When Marian mentioned that she was going to marry him in a fortnight's time, and that everybody would have to hurry up to make her frock, the shop was profoundly excited. Even Flossie ran out for patterns of white satin with some slight show of enthusiasm.

Julia was thrilled, but also slightly surprised. It was so obvious that Billy Embury was a far simpler human being than Marian. Many people were marrying in the intoxication of the moment, but how could one apply such an unbalanced term to Marian Lestrange? My goodness! thought Julia, she's letting herself in for something. After all, marriage is for the rest of your life, unless, of course, he gets killed, which he probably will, because aeroplanes are so dangerous. Julia didn't realise that Marian never envisaged marriage as necessarily being for life. A woman of Marian's class could take divorce in her stride, she would have the "right people" to back her. In Julia's class divorce was as unknown and difficult a luxury as a private aeroplane.

Marian was attracted by Billy, and she was content to let the present pay for itself; the future was unsure enough just now to cease to exist as a definite menace. She was oddly unsettled for one so poised, and having decided to marry Billy one evening when his streamline head looked more attractive than usual, she was determined not to go back on her word. She might as well marry Billy and see how it turned out.

Billy Embury's state of mind was quite different— he simply thought she was the most wonderful girl, what? and that it was up to everyone to go and blot out these beastly Germans who were making such a mess of a perfectly good world, what? and that he was damn lucky if he could get a bit of a good time before they blotted him out, what? Marian, bless her! was prepared to risk it, and at the worst she would have his pension and his small private income.

So Marian became Mrs. Embury at what she called "the shop opposite," by which she meant St. George's, Hanover Square, and Julia went to the wedding and drank champagne for the first time in her life, in company with Miss Smythe, both standing modestly in the shade of a potted palm tree in the hotel where the reception was held.

The actual ceremony was supposed to be "very quiet because of the war," but to Julia it was wonderful. She felt her heart beat as though it would choke when Marian, the oyster satin that Julia had helped to make, swathed round her, drifted up the nave. It didn't seem possible, thought Julia, that Marian could be as cool and unconcerned as she looked, and as a matter of fact she was right. Marian, with a queer little sick feeling, was wondering if she hadn't, after all, made a fool of herself, and dismissing the thought with the comfortable reflection that she could always do something about it even if she had.

There was only a week's honeymoon, as Billy was due to go to the Front, and Marian arrived back at the shop when it was over as though nothing had happened. Julia looked at her furtively; she somehow expected her to look different. Surely marriage, love, whatever you liked to call it, was the greatest experience of life? How could it leave Marian as calm, cool, and amused as before?

However, it did, to all outward seeming, and word went round that it was etiquette in the shop to address her as Miss Lestrange, just as if she had never been married at all.

Poor Billy, thought Julia, loving Marian, thinking of her, yet leaving so little impression upon her body or her mind. Marian would hurt Billy, but Billy would never be able to hurt Marian.

Everyone settled down to the war. Redmond and Carson had agreed to postpone the Irish question; Mrs. Pankhurst had called off her Amazons; and people like Julia and her relations, who could not afford to do war work, struggled to get along with the business of living. "Tipperary" became woven into Julia's mind as the Indian Love Lyrics or *Humoresque* had never succeeded in being. The whole of life seemed set to the tune. Every band played it, it was heard in every cinema. The events of the war were set against this background of sound.

And so the lovely burnished autumn slowly bled to death.

That was a wet and gloomy winter. Julia had a succession of sore throats, and felt that soon her employers would begin to lose patience with her. The first tragedy with which the shop was intimately connected came with the death of Gipsy's husband in H.M.S. *Formidable,* torpedoed in the Channel with the loss of between five and six hundred lives. Gipsy only stayed away two days, but when she came back she was oddly different. She looked, thought Julia, as though a sponge had passed over her, wiping out the bright colours of her personality and leaving only the bare black outlines. She made no reference to what had happened, but worked with a sort of grim intensity. Julia rather wondered that she didn't leave a business which, after all, was a luxury trade, and try and forget herself in war work, but one day she learned why. The first and last customer had gone, and Julia, putting away stock in the shop, heard an unwonted sound from the room behind. She went softly to the curtains and peeped through.

Gipsy was sitting at the brightly painted desk, her dark head buried on her outflung arms, her body shaken by the hard sobs that Julia had heard. Leaning against the wall, looking down at her with a troubled face, was Marian. Presently Marian put out her pale, long hand and touched Gipsy's shoulder tentatively, without speaking. Gipsy made a great effort, and the sobs ceased. She raised her own plump, capable hand and patted Marian's.

"Sorry," she said.

"That's all right," said Marian laconically. Then, after a moment's pause—"Look here, Gipsy, wouldn't it be better for you to clear out of here? Do some war work, or something?"

Gipsy shook her head wearily.

"I can't do that, there wouldn't be enough money in it. I know the business is going through a bad time now, but it'll look up later. People will begin to spend more money than ever, I'm sure of that. And there's little John. I must make all the money I can for him. He's got to go to Dartmouth when the time comes. John would have expected that. They've always been in the Service."

"Of course," assented Marian.

Odd, thought Julia. It seemed to her that if you loved your husband and he was torpedoed, you wouldn't want your only son to go and run the risk of the same thing, but Miss Lestrange evidently accepted the notion as something you'd expect.

Gipsy straightened herself, and blew her funny little turned-up nose till it was pink.

"As long as you can bear with me, Marian, I won't do it again."

"Don't be a fool," said Marian, with a sort of rough gentleness.

Odd people . . . no kisses . . . not even the usual "darlings" . . . neither of them in trouble would have said anything to Julia about it, yet they didn't mind in the least if she saw and heard them. . . . She might have been a piece of the modern painted furniture for all they cared. Julia suddenly felt very lonely. These people all had their place in life ready for them, and it was the sort of place that would enable them to feel at home wherever they went. Julia was at home nowhere. Two Beresford . . . her aunt's house at Dulwich, which was another Two Beresford; her cousin Elsa, who was supposed to be "such a nice little girl," and whom she despised . . . the girls at school whom now she never saw, and never wished to see . . . there was no place for her anywhere. . . . But there should be, there must be. She would make herself invaluable at the shop, and later on there would be love. . . . Some wonderful soldier would come into l'Etrangère's one day with his mother or sister, and would fall in love with the quiet, distinguished girl, who looked so much more interesting than the women she served . . .

Julia often day-dreamed of this remarkable soldier when she went back and forth in bus and train. He was tall and dark, with one of those attractive little moustaches, and hair beginning to go white at the temples, not because he was old, but because of all he had been through. "Your lovely youth has given me back mine," he would say to Julia.

More and more she was, of necessity, beginning to lead two lives. The life that everyone saw, the life that was led by Julia Almond, who left home early in the morning and came back tired in the evening; the same

Miss Almond who ran about London on last-minute errands, dusted and cleaned and answered the telephone with that soft manner that increases the wrath of customers. And the life of this other Julia Almond, the lovely and beloved; a Julia who could hold the gorgeous West End in fee; the Julia who was entirely different from anyone else who had ever lived, because this was the only time in the history of the world that there had been that Julia Almond. This was the Julia who was asked to enter the Secret Service, who won the prize for fancy-dress at big charity balls, who married the wonderful soldier with the hair gone grey at the temples. Everywhere was sorrow, but everywhere there was also that tension that makes people more aware of life. There was something in the air that made life and death better worth while than ever before, and that something was uncertainty.

Gipsy had been right, trade began to look up. The Stock Exchange had reopened, and in February the blockade was declared, which had the effect of throwing English dressmaking back upon itself and stimulating home industry.

Hilda Smythe left to be married, and so efficient had Julia proved herself that she was promoted, long before her time, to show-room girl, at a salary of eight shillings a week. The next event of importance was the opening of the Dardanelles campaign, to a flourish of trumpets and an accelerated heartbeat for the British nation. Soon after the first exploits of H.M.S. *Queen Elizabeth,* Ruby Safford came into the shop.

There was not, at that moment, anything particular about being Ruby Safford, except to the girl herself, who thought it quite as important as Julia thought it to be Julia Almond. Ruby was playing a tiny part in a farce that was dragging on a precarious existence, but it was her first appearance in the West End. Nobody had heard of her, except a few theatrical agencies, managers of No. 2 touring companies, and a Jew named James Gordon, who heard so much of her—and from her—nearly every evening of his life, that he determined to put her on the map and share his responsibilities as soon as possible. Meanwhile, Ruby lived in a little flat in Maida Vale, and Mr. James Gordon, her friend, supported her in a style which, after being the youngest of a small tradesman's large family in the Midlands, she thought very comfortable.

Ruby was very pure. Mr. Gordon was an old friend of the family who was really just like an uncle. Ruby almost believed this herself. She was the type of woman who cherishes perpetual virginity, and has always never loved before. She was capable of marrying, of having several lovers, and two or three children, and of gradually forgetting husbands, lovers and offspring. For Ruby every fresh love affair would be the first time she had ever loved. Every child, since she would never have two by the same man, would be the first child she had ever had. She had the face of an angel, the brain of a hen, the heart of a sentimental barmaid—if there be such a phenomenon—the sexual equipment of a professional, and the attitude towards that equipment of the best amateur. She believed in love, every time.

When Ruby Safford first came into the shop, Marian was away with Billy on a short leave—one of those intensive and intermittent honeymoons which those who married in the war, and those who did not marry, knew so well.

Gipsy, followed at a discreet distance by Julia, who had, since her promotion, learned the art of hovering inconspicuously, went forward to greet her. Ruby was already such a self-assured brilliant creature, draped with furs and jangling with bracelets, that upon meeting her, people at once thought she was "someone"—not just a pretty human being, but a "real" person, the sort of person one reads about in the Sunday newspapers. Ruby had just that poise of the head—slightly thrown backwards—that only women who are very sure of themselves dare assume.

She had seen a pannier frock in the window, a frock with only one pannier and a waggling fish-tail behind, that had attracted her careless notice. She bought the frock, and then tried on everything else in the shop, and, to do her—or Mr. James Gordon—justice, she bought nearly all, and paid cash. She bought frocks, coats, hats, and underwear, and then happened to mention that she wanted a silver fox.

Nothing came amiss to l'Etrangère. Though it was really only a dress shop, Gipsy believed in helping the

customers along as much as possible. l'Etrangère sup-
plied travelling rugs, silk stockings, fitted suitcases, bath
salts, fur coats and even railway tickets from Cook's if
the customer were too busy to see after such things herself. Partly this was policy, but chiefly pure friendliness.
Gipsy had had too scattered an existence herself, and
lived too long from hand to mouth, the hand being her
own as well as the mouth, not to be sympathetic. Frequently she wasted her sympathy on women with plenty
of money and plenty of time, who could quite easily
have paid the full price for goods, and equally easily af-
forded the time to find them for themselves. These were,
indeed, generally the women who were most keen on
being saved trouble and money. Julia, Gipsy and even
Marian spent a large part of their time in rushing round
interviewing that strange race comprehensively known
as "the wholesale." Sometimes the customers repudiated
the debts of which l'Etrangère could bring no proof,
such as railway tickets and travelling rugs. It is easy
to deny those transactions which friendliness has carried
through, not in the ordinary way of business. Very seldom, even when customers paid, did the shop make on
such deals, because the whole object being to get the
goods at wholesale price, Gipsy hadn't—if the customer
were hard up—the heart to charge even a percentage.
Obviously, in the case of railway tickets nothing could
be charged over and above the ordinary price. But it
was this readiness to help which gave l'Etrangère its
peculiar charm, and made it seem like a friendly little
club.

It was also one of the reasons why shopkeepers and
customers felt at once they were on friendly terms with
each other, and also why they hated each other.

Customers were pleased at first when l'Etrangère
would provide them at a moment's notice with a suitcase, or a fox fur, or a pair of dress-preservers, or some
gloves; but when the moment came, as it generally did,
when there was some trouble over a fitting, or the delivery of a frock on time, then the shop people thought:
"And after all the trouble we have taken getting her a
suitcase, dress-preservers, tooth-paste and what-not, with
no profit to ourselves . . ." And the customer thought:
"After all, I daresay I could have got that suitcase,
dress-preservers, tooth-paste, or what-not much better

at a proper shop, and they can't be very real dress-makers or they wouldn't do such a thing, and if they only had been real dressmakers my frock would have fitted." Meanwhile, Marian, Gipsy and Julia would all be sitting up after hours frantically stitching, planning, and even eventually delivering the frock in a taxi so as to meet the requirements of a customer, who, quite unaware that a "little" shop has no particular means of delivery, would remain as calm and unperturbed as though the gown had arrived in the natural course of events from Debenham & Freebody's.

Julia grew to admire Marian and Gipsy more and more as she saw with what real difficulties they struggled, and how any private engagement they might have was considered as nothing compared with the convenience of the customer. She also grew to admire those customers who put up uncomplainingly, because of genuine friend-ship, with frocks that sometimes did not fit, or things that were quite different from those that they had ordered. Friendship worked both ways in a shop, Julia decided. Sometimes the shop people had to put up with unsatisfactory deals, and sometimes the customers; and always, however real the friendship, there was a curious antagonism ready to leap into being, except with the very well-bred.

From the moment Ruby Safford left on that first day, Gipsy declared that she was going to be a tiresome cus-tomer. And Gipsy was right, as she generally was. Ruby was alternately affectionate and very unreasonable. She was wildly admiring, or extremely critical, and she was invariably unpunctual. She sometimes paid cash, and sometimes argued her bills almost out of existence. She was very friendly and embraced in her wide charity Marian, Gipsy, Julia, Mrs. Santley and even the "match-er," to whom, with that wish for universal popularity which makes the successful artist, she invariably flung a kind word if she ran up against her. Ruby was prodigal of kind words—and Julia, in her inexperience, was grate-ful for them, and grateful also for the new world that began to open for her at the touch of Ruby's careless, good-natured hand.

4

Epanouissement

It was Ruby who first admitted Julia to an equality of friendship, and Julia's eager heart responded gratefully. Anne Ackroyd, her chief friend in the old days, was now beyond her ken, immersed in her studies. A mere list of the things she had to study at the Hunter Street School of Medicine made Julia gasp. Whatever did a doctor want with zoology and botany? thought Julia. Anne, lit by an insatiable flame that Julia could never know, seemed not for the ordinary traffic of friendship just now. None of the other girls from the High School had mattered to Julia. Miss Tracey was long outgrown. Julia admired and imitated Marian and Gipsy, but they could not make a friend of her. Marian had often thrown her a kind word, but as a bone is thrown to a puppy. Gipsy had exacted the last ounce of work from her and given her a new hat, now a coat or frock; but Ruby did more—she treated Julia as a human being in whom she was interested. Ruby, of course, was lying, though neither she nor Julia knew it. Ruby was really only interested in Ruby Safford, the theatrical star of the future. But she had a sort of golden graciousness, which spilled over the rim of that lavish cup which was her personality, and the limpid drops were precious to Julia.

For Julia, though she thought she had seen so much of a new world since coming to l'Etrangère, still took people at their own estimate. The strict etiquette of the Almond class, the equally strict lack of etiquette in that of Marian and Gipsy, had not prepared her for this warmth and easy friendship that, to Ruby, was a commonplace of existence.

True, the lives of Marian and Gipsy resounded to the cry of "darling," but only amongst their own kind. It was a password and a shibboleth. Ruby's "dear" at first seemed to Julia more discriminating. Neither Marian nor Gipsy was vain, the admiration and affection of Julia would have held no flattery for them, but Ruby had the vanity that must be fed by love, however easily come by. In "taking notice" of Julia she was not putting herself out at all, she was following the line of least resistance. Difficult and delicate are the approaches of one soul to another if anything worth while is to be created, but to Ruby and Julia all seemed pleasant and easy. Julia was being granted glimpses of an enchanted and uncensorious world that she had never known; Ruby was being the generous, warm-hearted actress, who would as soon be kind to a little girl from a shop as to a duke's daughter. But the kindness was genuine, as far as it went, which was never far enough to alter Ruby's plans or incommode her in any way.

Julia was sufficiently remarkable, especially since she had been promoted to showroom-girl, for people to notice her, but this particular friendliness was something new. Marian's friends were nearly always not only polite but kind. If Julia, as sometimes happened, delivered a dress at the last moment, the customer would almost always say pleasantly: "Thank you, Miss . . . er . . ." And one or two might even give her a glass of wine and a biscuit, realising that she had probably missed some strange hour at which she should have fed.

Several times it happened that not the wife but the husband would see Julia, the wife being in hysterics upstairs lest her dress did not arrive—for, of course, no customer ever had anything to wear if her new frock did not turn up in time.

Once the husband was a grave and kindly man, whose looks thrilled Julia by embodying her idea of a statesman, and who did not seem to know that she crawled upon the surface of the earth; and once it happened that the husband looked at Julia and saw in her that quality which, for most men, she carried like a banner.

On that occasion Julia behaved, as she told herself afterwards, very stupidly. She had not the courage to show that she noticed the arm that had slid about her waist; her heart began to beat rapidly, she liked the arm, the dark head above hers, the careless self-assured manner of a man with a girl whom he thought attractive. She was not insulted by the notion that he thought a dressmaker's girl was his to flirt with if he chose. Julia was not a prude, she had a knack of seeing the essentials, and she passed over such superficial matters. The banality of "I'm not that sort of girl" was never hers, any more than it would have been Marian's; she had that much of natural breeding. But she had a fear that was a weakness—she was fearful, as are most young girls, of seeming to make too much out of trifles and of being laughed at in consequence. While her heart was pounding so that she thought the man must feel it through the cloth of his sleeve, her mind was frantically thinking—I mustn't show I've noticed . . . he'll say I'm thinking things that don't exist if I draw away. He'll say I must have a nasty mind to make such a mistake, that he only thought I was a little girl. . . . I'll just say good-bye and go. And she glanced up at him with a grateful, little-girl look. He at once kissed her on the mouth.

"You're a dear little thing, aren't you. . . ." he said thickly, one hand still at her waist, and the other fumbling at her breast. Julia lost her head and sprang away screaming. It was one thing to imagine things in your own mind—even such things as having a marvellous elderly man in love with you, though he happened to be already married; it was quite another to have this sudden hot breath upon her cheek, to see his face, handsome as it was, looking oddly flushed and coarse so close to her own, to feel this strange hand, impersonal as the paw of a beast, at the opening of her frock. So she screamed, and at once the animal who held her changed to a terrifying gentleman, husband of a customer, in a cold rage.

"You little fool . . ." was all he said, but Julia never

95

forgot it. She had not possessed the knowledge that he had assumed, she had not realised that he expected an easy acceptance of his quite trifling attention, which was not meant to lead to anything. She had, in short, done exactly what she had been afraid of doing, made much too much of something that was really nothing at all. No one, mercifully, had heard her scream and she left the house, knowing that she had been entirely in the right, but having been made to feel entirely in the wrong.

One day Ruby telephoned to the shop, and asked for several dresses to be brought up to her flat on approval, and Julia was packed off with two large cardboard boxes under her arm.

Ruby received her with her usual golden eagerness, that made Julia aware of a warmth in herself that was very like affection. Here, at least, was someone who was kind and human, who would demand nothing unexpected of her.

"You're looking tired to-day, child," said Ruby. "Had a hard day?"

"No, madam," said Julia, demurely.

"Nonsense, I can see you're absolutely fed up. Would you like to come and have a spot of dinner at the flat with me? I can give you a stall afterwards for the show. And you can come round behind afterwards. I'll tell the stage-door-keeper. We could go on and dance later. You're mouldy, that's what's the matter with you. It's not overwork, it's underplay."

"Oh," breathed Julia, "I'd love it." But she began to think of the practical difficulties . . . the dressing . . . and she had no real evening frock . . . the arriving at Maida Vale in time . . . for, of course, Ruby's spot of dinner was early. Gipsy solved the problem.

When Julia arrived back at the shop at about half-past five, with the glad tale that Ruby had bought three of the frocks, she found Gipsy already putting away the stock. It was unlikely that anyone would come in as late as this. Gipsy was very pleased with Julia's success, and this emboldened Julia to ask Gipsy's advice.

"Miss Safford's been very kind, Madam. She's asked me if I'll go to dinner with her and go and see her in her show afterwards. Do you think I can possibly dine, and go to the theatre in blue foulard? It isn't a real evening frock at all, but it has short sleeves."

Gipsy considered her attentively. This was going to be a valuable girl, she told herself, combining a hard business head with the great gift of changing her manner to suit the person to whom she was speaking. And she could look anything she chose.

"I tell you what you had better do, Julia," she said. "You've been working very well lately, and I don't see why you shouldn't have a treat. You know that little black lace frock we've kept entirely for modelling in? Well, I'll give you that. I don't approve of borrowing clothes out of stock. You can have a pair of those sample stockings at cost price. I'll stop them out of your salary. If you hurry away now, you have just time to go to Douglas's and have something done to your hair. It looks as though the moths had been at it. I'll see to shutting up the shop."

How really kind Gipsy was . . . she knew the things one minded about. Julia sent a telegram home—why wouldn't Dad have a telephone?—and rushed out to have a shampoo and wave.

She knew she was looking her best that night. The black lace was slit up to the knee one side, and Julia had lovely legs. Her thin arms, still the arms of a young girl with the pathetic, slightly red elbows of adolescence, showed their pure and lovely line against the soft blackness. Her head looked like that of a lovely debauched boy, but her undeveloped figure with the upward lift of her small pointed breasts was very feminine and young.

That was a wonderful evening. Julia, slightly released by champagne, called Ruby by her Christian name and was not reproved. It was the first time that Julia had ever done that to anyone whom she did not know to be her inferior.

She felt that Ruby's friend, Mr. Gordon, was the kindest and best man she had ever met. Perhaps he did not look very distinguished, but kind hearts were more than coronets, as somebody had said. They all three dined together, and then Ruby went through her little part, while Mr. Gordon prowled about the house like an uneasy leopard, and Julia sat self-consciously in the stalls. "Paper, paper," said Mr. Gordon rapidly, when he came to speak to her during the show, gazing around him with disgust. Julia thought he must want an evening paper, and wondered why he didn't send out for one.

Then there came for Julia the great moment of the evening. Mr. Gordon had already gone through something he called the pass-door, but Julia found her way round to the outside of the theatre to the stage-door, and asked for Miss Safford. The stage-door-keeper, who seemed rather bored, and was picking his teeth with a match, handed her over to a pimply youth, and she was taken along a corridor that smelt like the Tube, and ushered into Ruby's dressing-room, where Mr. Gordon was sitting gloomily and Ruby was dressing behind a curtain. Presently, she came out, clad in a frock of l'Etrangère's, and Mr. Gordon cheered up and had a whisky and soda, while Ruby had a gin and tonic. Julia timidly asked for a little water, which surprised the dresser very much. Just as she was drinking this unusual beverage, a knock came at the door, and a voice said: "Still here, Ruby? It's me."

"Alfie . . ." cried Ruby, "come in. I thought you were going to meet us at Murray's. Julia, this is my cousin, Alfie Safford. This is Miss Almond, Alfie, and we've got to give her a good time this evening."

Alfie smiled and shook hands with Mr. Gordon, who was evidently an old friend, and with Julia, and said "Hello, Ma," to the dresser, who seemed pleased.

Alfie was, as Ruby naïvely put it, "learning to be an officer." Until the war he had been in a stockbroker's office. Ruby was a lovely creature, with dyed red hair, which she wore massed thickly right down to her brows; cow-like brown eyes, and such a full mouth that it seemed almost as deep as it was long—one of those lovely mouths that seem as though they had been put on to the face from the outside. She was absolutely colourless, and had the sense not to use rouge, for her white skin was one of her charms. She had ugly hands, broad in the palm, with short, but very pointed fingers, like talons; and steep little feet that seemed to go straight down into her high-heeled shoes.

Alfie resembled her somewhat, but his figure was far better than hers. It was possible to imagine Ruby becoming dumpy in another ten years, her bust was already threatening; but Alfie had very long legs, and a flat straight back, and a small Roman head, poised with a curious bird-like effect upon a too-long but round young neck. He had just enough good looks for a uniform to translate them into handsomeness. His hair, not being hennaed, was dark; his eyes, like Ruby's, were brown, but they were somewhat slanting; and these narrow, slanting eyes gave an exotic look to his small tightly modelled face. On his high cheek-bones the healthy colour lay in a faint tinge of rosy brown. His teeth were very white and even, and Julia, as she saw him laugh, remembered in a life which she had forgotten, she had liked to see a pretty, red-haired girl called Gladys, laugh; for Alfie's mouth opened square, in just the right shape, as Glady's Pepper's had done. He had an awareness of his own good looks which added oddly to his charm, because it gave certainty to his glance when it meant to catch yours.

At once there was between him and Julia that flamy contact which she now knew so well in the casual meetings of the street and of business, but that up till to-night she had always refused to admit to intimacy. Now she let her own eyes answer, though she still pretended unconsciousness of any understanding in her talk.

Ruby was proud of her cousin, partly because of his charm, and partly because of his uniform, but she was not really interested in him. They had been brought up together in the same Midland town, in a Nonconformist family, as though they had been brother and sister, and each knew exactly when the other was lying.

Nevertheless, Ruby was pleased when Alfie came round to the stage door, and did not bother to contradict anyone who thought he was interested in her "in that way." But only last evening he had announced in her dressing-room that he was tired of being used as a whetstone, and did not intend to come round to the theatre any more; that she never introduced him to a pretty girl; that she had managed without him for a good many months, and that now his time for being sent to France was coming within measurable distance, he felt he could jolly well manage without her. Ruby wanted him about; he was the only male of whom Mr. Gordon was not jealous, and an evening spent alone with her "friend" bored her. It had been partly kindness that had made her ask Julia for the evening, partly the sudden realisation that here was a girl who would "do" for Alfie.

Mr. Gordon, who was the kindest and most amiable of men, danced with Julia once, treading on her toes as he tried to crane his short, thick neck over his shoulder to see what Ruby was up to. After that Julia danced with Alfie. Their steps fitted perfectly, and Julia ceased to worry about what time she would get home; about whether Bobby had had his walk or not, and about what Dad and Mum would say to her to-morrow morning.

"Do you dance a great deal?" asked Alfie, as he steered her in and out amongst the galloping majors of Murray's.

"Hardly at all," said Julia, realising in one of her gifted moments of inspiration that truth was the best policy. "I'm generally too tired by the end of the evening. I work in a shop, you know. Your cousin comes there for her clothes." A year ago Julia would have said "costumes" and "Miss Safford."

"Do you? I was a clerk in a stockbroker's office," said Alfie ingenuously. "I don't think it's a bad old war, not yet, anyway." And he squeezed Julia a little to him in the dance, after the manner of the young men of his particular kind. Julia remained unmoved and rigid; her thick, dark lashes lying upon her cheek. Alfie was young enough and inexperienced enough to think he had made a mistake, which was exactly what Julia had meant him to think. At the end of the evening he asked her rather timidly whether she would come and lunch with him one day soon. Julia shook her head; it was always impossible to say whether you could get off for lunch from l'Etrangère's, but her refusal presented itself quite differently to young Alfie, who plunged further and asked for dinner and dancing. Julia, who would have jumped at the luncheon invitation had she been free to do so, saw that she had done the right thing, and again seemed doubtful, then yielded. They arranged to meet at what Alfie called "The Troc" on the following Saturday evening.

Alfie insisted on seeing her home that night, although Julia warned him it was a very long way. They took the District Railway to Stamford Brook Station, crossed the road to Heronscourt Gardens, and strolled slowly past the sleeping little Victorian cottages, then into Love Lane, and so upwards to Two Beresford.

Julia felt a curious sense of elation as she and Alfie moved together through the quiet little world she knew so well. She had been dancing at Murray's and she was being seen home by a young man, an officer.

She had not fallen in love with Alfie. She knew nothing except the message of her own senses, which said that here was an attractive young man, who, in his turn, thought her attractive. And she was aware also of that strange feeling of the possibility of death which had begun to haunt the world, which permeated the air and which added such a zest to life. For behind her were her schooldays, and the times of weeping at the shop, and far remote from her seemed the sordidness of her home. She was Julia, young and vital; the wonderful world, alive with death and disaster, and strange chances, and amazing marriages, and meals at restaurants, and opportunities of every kind, was within her grasp. She would say to Dad and Mum in the morning: "Oh, it was quite all right. An officer saw me home: Ruby Safford's cousin."

Beresford Villas stood up thin and pointed in the moonlight; about them the skeletons of trees stood darkly. Julia put her finger to her lip, and tiptoed with exaggerated caution up the Bridge of Sighs. She slipped her key into the door, and as she pushed it gently open felt a cold, wet nose thrust into her palm. Bobby added to his other virtues that of knowing her footstep, however light it was, and even when accompanied by that of somebody unknown. Alfie, looking suddenly young, shy, and rather charmingly awkward, stood hesitating on the top step. This, he knew, was where he ought to have claimed a kiss in the best man-of-the-world manner, as practised, or at least described, by his fellow clerks. Yet he did nothing of the sort. He stammered a little as he spoke.

"Next Saturday, then. Can I come here and fetch you?"

Julia thought for a moment. She realised, even accustomed as she was to them, that neither Dad nor Mum was very attractive, and yet if she were to see more of Alfie he would have to know what her people were like—already she called them "her people" even to her-

101

self—whereas a year ago she would have said "her relatives."

"All right," she said. "Come in about seven."

"Right oh!" He clutched at her hand; she smiled at him, and gently closed the door. She waited, her fingers fondling Bobby's head, to hear Alfie's footsteps fading away down the steps of the Bridge of Sighs.

Julia and Alfie went out together a good deal during the weeks that followed, and during the greater part of that time Julia told herself lies. For she was feeling the first stirrings of physical attraction, and in so far as she had been brought up to acknowledge facts at all, it had been to think them not quite nice.

Nothing had ever been explained to Julia—not one adolescent yearning, not one pricking of innocent and natural desire. Mrs. Almond, her own body disappointed by the swift and matter-of-fact assaults of her husband, had early in life come to the conclusion that many of her generation came to—that the whole affair was a song and dance about nothing. Vaguely she thought that the gentlemen enjoyed it, and the women did not. Such had been Mrs. Almond's conclusion, and it did not worry her unduly. When you cooked and washed-up, and "made-over" your old frocks year after year, and coaxed a tired, irritable man into amiability every evening of your life, the failure of certain nerves and pulses to produce a sensation which you did not even know existed, did not affect your daily round or your philosophy of life. The complete failure of the physical relationship had saved Mrs. Almond a lot of trouble. All she had disseminated for Julia's instruction was a certain atmosphere of negation and disgust, which Julia had perforce absorbed to a certain extent. Naturally passionate, her own pulses told her a different story, but her upbringing made her think that she ought to deny, even to herself and most certainly to Alfie, the acknowledgment of her body's desires. For she still was not what she would have called "in love" with Alfie, and she thought such stirrings as were hers ought to be accompanied by sentiment. Alfie was too raw for her, whose imagination had been nourished by much novel-reading, to admire whole-heartedly enough for that state called "being in love." She couldn't talk books with Alfie, couldn't make him see what lighted windows at night did to her. She could only laugh and dance with him and feel these odd new sensations when he touched her, even if he but took her hand.

At first it was easy enough to lie even to herself, and easier to deceive Alfie, when yet his love-making hadn't gone beyond the stage of holding hands in a cinema. He came up to town whenever, as he humorously expressed it, he could wangle a spot of leave. Alfie was by way of being a funny young man. True, he didn't make jokes, long and carefully laid like a train of gunpowder, as did Herbert Starling, but the same silly things amused both him and Julia. Something in Julia told her they were silly, and nothing told Alfie, that was the only difference. Sometimes they would get uproarious giggles at a tea-shop because of some fat old lady at a nearby table who struck them as being a "scream"; sometimes they would stick pins in the tyre of some unattended bicycle. Once, when Alfie had wangled a motor-cycle with a sidecar like a sitz bath, they went to tea at a country inn, and changed all the hats hanging in the lobby to the wrong pegs, so that no coat was with the right hat.

Julia would never have giggled or played practical jokes when out with Marian; on the rare occasions when she had attended a dress show with her and been given tea, she had been as quiet and distinguished as Marian herself, and this she achieved without any difficulty. There was a side of her which responded quite naturally to Marian and her kind, just as there was a side that responded to Ruby and Alfie. And there was something about Alfie . . . not that he was clever, but some charm, something finer than the ex-clerk who liked to make jokes and hold hands in a cinema; a sort of wistful quality, almost a woodland look that in part he owed to his slanting eyes and his brownness, but that was also the gift of his fated generation. Over him, as over all the lovely boys, there lay the menace of perpetual youth.

Alfie hadn't much money, and both he and Julia were simple and unspoiled in their tastes; Murray's was still an exotic spot for the Rubys of the world rather than for them. To walk together through the parks from George Street—down to Green Park, and then through Hyde Park and Kensington Gardens, down to Shepherd's

103

Bush, whence a tram took them to Heronscourt Park—
then they would fetch Bobby and watch him tear about
the green spaces while they sat and talked: this was excitement enough for a long while. Alfie was excited about
Julia, and Julia was excited about the drama of her
relationship with Alfie.

Alfie had not been without his adventures. He had
earned the right in one or two dismal encounters to
consider himself a man. He was Julia's leader and ini-
tiator now. Did he love Julia? Did she love him? That
wasn't the question that very physical young people were
asking each other or themselves, at least these two did
not. Their progress towards the fields of pleasure was
so gradual that in each of them the hypocritical half
that was the result of upbringing could pretend to ignore
it. Julia, if she had paused to consider, would have recognised the weight of all the prohibitions that had been
dinned into her ears since childhood, and which
amounted to the fact that love-making was wrong unless you were married, and rather horrid when you were.
    The idyll, if such it could be called, of Julia and Alfie
had at least this to be said in its favour—it was purely
of the body. The only lies that wrapped it round about—
for the beauty of bodies is that they cannot lie—were
those of their upbringing, and did not affect the matter
long, for Julia's senses were as yet too unspoiled to
succumb to lies.
    This orchestra that was within her, that woke her at
night, that started to tune up an hour or two before she
met Alfie . . . she could not have escaped such a de-
manding music whatever had happened or not happened
in the exterior world of accident. But she had happened
to chime with a period when accident was happy and
easy for such as she . . . when the sight of a young
man in khaki and a girl drew a tolerant smile from a
park-keeper or a policeman. There was nothing to control Julia; neither outside authority nor any imposed by
her own soul, and she was far too ignorant to know that
nature was doing what it chose with her and Alfie.
Her uneducated and undisciplined mind had no control
over her life.
    What standard of judgment could she have. . . ?
She did not know that she would have felt these de-

licious stirrings, whether she had met Alfie or some other young man, whether there had been a war or not. She had no notion that every healthy young girl suffers from a sort of auto-intoxication. All she knew was that she felt alive as never before, and at the same time, unsatisfied. For the first time the thought of another young human body, alive and strong as her own, would not let her rest.

The only morality she had been taught was that of respectability and expediency, but there did lurk a certain amount of fear in her mind. One shouldn't "do things" unless one was safely married. And yet, as Alfie's caresses progressed she found herself, by a pleasant and warm weakness, unable to resist them.

Alfie's strict upbringing had taught him also fear, and he had been encased by far more rigid notions of right and wrong for their own sakes than had Julia. Always at the back of his mind was the feeling that he was doing something which his parents would have known to be wrong. But he and Julia were both entranced by the strange and delicious discovery of pleasure, which neither of them was able to resist.

Julia did not know enough about her body to realise that she might be doing it as much harm as some people might have thought she was doing her soul. She really only knew that when the time came to meet Alfie she was drawn out of the house, and that his caresses excited her, because always just beyond them lay the hope of some bliss which her body imagined, although her mind was still uninformed as to its actual process. That she was finely attuned to love; that she was squandering the talent with which nature had endowed her, she was blindly unaware. She wasted her gifts without even knowing that they existed. They were two ill-educated children fumbling at ecstasy, wandering blindfold down the loveliest glade of life's garden; snatching, tasting, feeling, but seeing nothing.

Usually Julia met Alfie at the corner of Hanover Square. They might go to a cinema, or, as the days grew longer, they would go on the top of a bus to Richmond and wander in the Park, and dine in some little restaurant overlooking the river. Then they would come back and, getting out of the tram at Young's Corner, wander into the quiet side street and up the dark and secret Love Lane.

You couldn't be sure nowadays of having Love Lane to yourself. Every quiet little side street seemed to hold its silent couple, arms locked round each other, quiet as though with a still ecstasy, or with an even quieter misery. Lovers, thought Julia, who were just getting to know each other, or who were parting on the morrow, the man to go out to that dreadful place called the Front, the very existence of which everyone ignored as much as possible, although it was that which gave the sharp savour to life.

Julia was at her happiest in an embrace under the quiet sycamores in Love Lane; sometimes so fiercely happy that she wanted nothing more, for it made her afraid. The first time her still unaccustomed body responded completely to Alfie's caressing hand, and told her of a pleasure that made her feel faint, she was terrified lest this was enough to make her have a baby. It surely couldn't be possible to feel more, was the way she argued it to herself. Alfie was able to laugh her out of that fear, but he was very tender with her afterwards. He had not realised, so eager was the responses of her pulses, the extent of her ignorance.

The fear of having a baby, of "getting caught," as Julia would have phrased it, held her back from going to some hotel with Alfie, although this was an idea which Alfie often turned over in his mind. As a serious proposition it did not occur to Julia—the war was not yet far enough advanced for such things to be a matter of course, and there was no urgent pressure, such as there might have been had Alfie suddenly been ordered to France. She was content to drift along. More and more her parents became to her people who knew nothing, who had never known anything. Mum might complain that she was out far too much, and came in too late at night, but Julia always had an airy, but sufficient answer. She had told them about Ruby, and the stage held a certain glamour for Mr. and Mrs. Almond. They had not the Nonconformist blood which had made the Saffords so angry with Ruby when she first left home for a second-rate touring company. An actress in the West End, even in a tiny part, was quite a personage to the Almonds. It was nice of this Miss Safford to be good to their Julia. Ruby would have been surprised if she had known how often Julia was supposed to be with her. Such a constancy of friendship would have held no place in Ruby's casual social contacts.

Life was lovely for Julia just now. She was not making enough money to be able to leave home, but she had enough ascendancy over her parents to prevent them becoming dictatorial. All the world was loving a lover just then—even at hours when men in uniform were not supposed to be served with intoxicants, a waiter would pour out the drink that had been demanded; not that sex, youthful and unspoiled, often demanded a drink. Young men and girls like Alfie and Julia were too interested in each other to need any further intoxication. Everywhere couples were gazing into each other's eyes over a cup of tea, and feeling the stirrings of desire at any hour of the day without artificial assistance. Julia and Alfie cared not at all if a meal of bacon and eggs was all that they could obtain.

One day Julia received at the shop a wire from Alfie asking her to meet him at Appenrodt's, in the Strand, that evening. She hurried away as soon as she could get free, but he was there before her. He looked, she thought, as she caught sight of him, a little different from usual, more alive, and yet somehow a little unnatural.

She stayed looking at him for a moment while he was still unaware of her presence, feeling as though she were looking at someone in the unconsciousness of sleep; you saw a person quite differently if he didn't know you were there, and her heart said suddenly very gently, over and over, "Alfie, Alfie."

She felt a sudden intense tenderness for his small brown face with the high cheek-bones; his rather too long round neck, his narrow dark eyes. He looked as though he was standing staring out at the future instead of at the crowded Strand, and he seemed young and terribly vulnerable, helpless in the face of what might be coming towards him. She knew suddenly that he was going to tell her that he had been ordered to France.

He did tell her, over the cups of thick chocolate, with whipped cream on the top, which Julia as a rule so particularly loved.

"I can get leave next week, just before we go," he

said, and their eyes met. He paid for their meal and they went to a cinema. They sat silently holding hands —afterwards he saw her home.

It was a damp, warm evening; there had been a shower which brought out the smell of earth and leaves, so that Two Beresford gave the impression of being in the heart of the country. They clung together under the sycamore tree.

"Julia, Julia," murmured Alfie blindly, into the warmth and softness of her neck. "You'll give me that night, won't you? you'll manage it. Surely you can arrange it somehow?"

Julia, heart thumping, all resistance gone, could only say: "How can I? What can I say at home?"

"You can arrange it somehow. It's my last chance, Julia. I'll marry you on my first leave if you want me to. I won't let you down, I swear it, and nothing will happen. I won't let you in for anything."

"Oh, it's not that," murmured Julia, with whom it was most undoubtedly "that," though she would not admit it.

"What is it then? Don't you want to?"

"I don't know. . . . Yes, I do, I suppose I do. But honestly, Alfie, I don't see how I can manage it."

"Say you're going to spend the night with Ruby. I'll tip her the wink, she won't let you down."

"Well . . ." Julia hesitated. Of course, she was afraid of having a baby, what girl wasn't? Your lover told you he would arrange all that, but did he? How was one to know? It was all very well for tarts and girls who had been there before, and even they, she heard, sometimes got caught; but how was she to know whether it was safe or not? Even so far, Alfie had had to explain every step of the way to her, although she felt sure that she did things that her mother and grandmother had never dreamed of doing, even with the men to whom they were married. It seemed to her sometimes that no one could ever have felt the sharp ecstasies that Alfie had taught her. How could the secret fumblings, the half-ashamed realisations of her forebears be weighed against them, or else, why should she have been kept in ignorance, as though there had been a conspiracy to shut off from her the knowledge that there was such a lovely sensation? It was as though love were a secret that had

108

been forgotten, and which, thanks to the genius of Alfie, she had been privileged to recapture.

"Julia, Julia," murmured Alfie again, and he caught her against him, pressing kisses upon her mouth. It seemed to her that her body turned to water within his arms and her strength went out of her. She wanted Alfie more than she wanted anything on earth. Alfie lifted his head, and she looked up at him, dimly discerning the deeper darkness of his eyes through the darkness of the night.

"I'll see," she whispered.

"Promise, promise."

"All right. I'll manage somehow. You're sure nothing could happen?"

"I swear it: nothing."

Julia disengaged herself. Her legs felt weak and she found she was trembling a little.

"I must go now, Alfie, it's ever so late."

He saw her to the gate without speaking, and she let herself in, to meet the querulous enquiries of her mother. Mrs. Almond had the acrid jealousy of the elderly woman who has never been satisfied, who has borne the pains of motherhood without any preliminary ecstasy.

"Where have you been, my girl?"

"Up West," said Julia warily, "to see Ruby's show, if you really want to know, and then I had a little supper with her afterwards."

"Well, I don't like your coming home so late. It isn't right."

"Oh, Mum, what nonsense. Everyone does it. I can't be in by ten if I go to a theatre, can I?"

"That's all very well," grumbled Mrs. Almond, "having a good time's all you think about."

"That's not true," said Julia. "I work like a black, and you know I do. As to enjoying myself, it wasn't very amusing for me playing gooseberry for Ruby and her young man, and the worst of it is, I've promised to do it again. Ruby's got her best boy coming to town for the last night of his leave, and she's giving a party for him. There'll probably only be her dull old uncle for me."

Julia had already explained away Ruby's friend, Mr. Gordon, to Mr. and Mrs. Almond, in an avuncular capacity.

109

She turned to go up to bed, yawning slightly. "I'll probably stay the night with her," she added, "at the flat. Catch me coming all the way back here at about three in the morning and having to be at business at nine."

"Your Dad won't like your being out all night," complained Mrs. Almond, but accepting the suggestion as a truthful one, Julia was glad to notice.

"Dad will have to lump it," said Julia, and went to bed.

But there was a thing called a "Push," and that officer and gentleman, the trusty and well-beloved of King George, known as Second Lieutenant Alfred Safford, was sent off to France at a moment's notice, before he could make an honest woman of Julia. The night that she was to have spent with him in an hotel in Oxford Street, he lay, his peaked face upturned, swept with the green and white of the Verey lights, and then pale with dawn, amidst a tangle of barbed wire. He lay there for many days disintegrating, while Julia, all unknowing that the flesh which had awakened hers breathed no more, walked desperately back and forth across the Park, and her own flesh cried out in frustration.

At last Ruby rang her up at the shop and told her the news, and Julia sat stunned for a while. Luckily no customer came in and Marian was out. Gipsy, noting her pallor, said: "Anything wrong, child?" Julia nodded. "That friend of mine, you know him, Ruby Safford's cousin? He's killed. She rang up to tell me."

Gipsy made her a cup of tea and sent her home, but Julia could not bear to go home. She walked about till she was tired—the walks they had so often taken together, down through Hyde Park and Kensington Gardens, then all the way to Hammersmith Broadway, down the High Road, up through Heronscourt Park, back and forth until suddenly she was so tired she sat upon a seat by the little lake where she and Alfie had often sat, and wondered how she was to manage the short distance to Two Beresford.

She sat quietly through supper, merely telling her parents briefly that her friend Ruby was very upset—her young man had been killed. Yes, the young man who had been going to spend the last night of his leave at

Ruby's party and who had been sent to France instead. She went up to bed early, turned out the light, and tried to sleep. She thought she would be able to cry, but no tears came.

She was sorry for Alfie, dreadfully sorry—it seemed such a shame, but she was not heart-broken, she was shocked. And as she lay in her bed, there suddenly flashed into her mind the realisation that she might at this moment have been in far worse trouble. Alfie might not have gone until after that night they had arranged to have together, and, in spite of his promises, she would now have been feeling very frightened. . . . In that dreadful walk, all the way from George Street to Two Beresford, something finer than this relief had held her mind—the thought that Alfie had gone away without possessing that after which he had lusted, and that now he could never have. During those hours it had seemed to Julia that the only thing that mattered was that she had not been able to give him what he wanted. Alfie, poor Alfie. . . . But now, in the darkness of her own room, she felt relief. She did not realise how she was going to miss him.

Julia remembered Alfie not only with her body, but with her mind. She thought of him in a way that hitherto she had only thought of Bobby, with a mingling of affection and tenderness that made her pitiful. She remembered him more sharply with her senses, where he had lit a fire that smouldered to her great dis-ease. She grew irritable and nervous. The first Zeppelin raid, that took place a few weeks after Alfie's death, was supposed to account for this. As a matter of fact, Julia loved the raid, it was excitement at last, something that could take her out of herself and satisfy her craving for a keener edge of life.

But the raid that stimulated Julia made Mrs. Starling a very sick woman. Her delicacy had never been a pretence; her heart, as well as her digestion, made her life a martyrdom. Herbert showed at his best during the weeks that she was growing more and more ill. He thought for her in little ways that he had not before, tried to make less noise when he came in, and ceased to assure her that she could really manage to eat tinned salmon perfectly well if she chose. Mr. Starling had been one of those who panicked about food supplies at the outbreak of war, and had filled the flat with tinned supplies of every description, which he had been trying to force his friends to eat ever since.

The little supper-parties followed by whist ceased to be held at Saint Clement's Square, though Mr. Starling still sometimes came round of an evening to Two Beresford, and helped Mr. Almond in the garden. It took his thoughts off, he said. Julia hardly noticed when he came. She was working harder than ever at the shop, for Marian had suddenly decided to join a woman friend who was already driving an ambulance at what was called, the Front by people at home, though in reality it was many miles behind the lines. Like Julia, Marian had grown nervy and irritable, though from a different reason. Billy bored her thoroughly when home on leave and now he had added to his sins by being shot down, and taken prisoner. There he would be, in Germany, till the end of the war, and all that was left to Marian was the trouble of sending parcels and writing letters. Better to have him home on leave than that. Why hadn't she waited a little longer before marrying? She couldn't divorce Billy, or get him to divorce her while he was a prisoner, and the war might go on for years. . . . So she went to drive an ambulance and see if she could be more interested "out there" than she succeeded in being on the home front.

Julia worked very well with Gipsy, who promoted her to twelve shillings a week. In addition to being a showroom girl, she now sometimes "modelled" as well, whenever there was a dress show, or an important customer wanted to see a lot of frocks. The wonderful soldier of her dreams never came in, however, and when she turned and swayed down the room head high, hand on hip, presenting her pelvis to the audience in the correct fashion, there were only women to see her. Still, the shop absorbed all her conscious attention. It was only on days off, or in buses and trains, or in the park with Bobby, that her other life, that of her imagination, took charge of her. More and more this dream-life became the chief thing by which she lived; it was more real to her than the commonplace of every day. The dreams varied—sometimes she was in the Secret Service, and did something so wonderful that she was sent for to Buckingham Palace and thanked by the King; sometimes Lord Kitchener fell in love with her—That's the only woman I've seen that I could love, he would say. Sometimes it was just a young lieutenant, with nothing much but his pay, but who was a wonderful lover, whom she married secretly, and who would come back and claim her after the war, and meanwhile wrote her the sort of love-letters that became famous, the sort you read about in history.

Meanwhile the summer dragged on, autumn came, and with it an air-raid in which forty-one civilians were killed—and if you counted Mrs. Starling, who died a few days later of shock, forty-two. Hers was the first funeral Julia had ever attended, and in its way it was as thrilling as Marian's wedding. Gipsy gave her a black frock out of stock, a frock which had failed to sell. It was rather romantic to be in black, to drive to the cemetery behind the hearse, and to know that for the passers-by you had the importance of being a mourner.

In sober truth, few people can have been less mourned than poor Mrs. Starling. She had been an invalid since her marriage, and what faint attractiveness might once have been hers had vanished early. Herbert thought he was sorrow-struck, because he was a bereaved husband, and so sorrow was a matter of common decency. Herbert's sister, Bertha Starling, whom Julia met for the first time at the funeral, made very little pretence at regret. For the Almonds, it had always been the bluff, friendly Herbert and not the pallid Mrs. Starling who had been the attraction.

After the funeral everyone went to Saint Clement's Square for what Mr. Starling called "a cold collation." There was a ghostly quality about the function that impressed Julia to the point of excitement. For one thing, she discovered she had never been so hungry in her life, although she had had a good breakfast, and no hard morning's work. At the shop often she didn't manage to get lunch at all, and the fact never worried her. Now, in spite of a shamed feeling that it oughtn't to be so, she ate and ate, only hoping that no one observed the fact. She ate cold chicken and ham and tongue and potato salad and chutney and bread and cheese and cake, and the more she ate the hungrier she seemed to be. The sherry was rich and dark and she drank it in sips after satisfying her thirst with water. And everything, food, water, and sherry, seemed so good to her palate and that hungry void within her, that only the fact that it was a funeral and she was Julia Almond, prevented her asking for more, and from picking up the chicken-bones in her fingers as everyone did at Two Beresford on the rare occasions when they could have chicken.

And, in spite of her avidity, there was to Julia something ghostly and odd about this feast. She had only been to this house for parties. The parties had sometimes bored her, and sometimes amused her, but always the occasion had been, officially at least, a party. This, too, was a party, but with a dead presence at the head of the board. Strange that someone who in life had been so unnoticeable that she hardly seemed to be in the room, should now make herself felt so insistently. Was it perhaps the fact that nobody really mourned her which made conscience uneasy?

"Well," said Herbert Starling, with a sort of melancholy satisfaction, as he wiped his lips, "there's one comfort at least, and that is the doctor says she'd have got much worse if she'd lived; there was a growth, he said, but he didn't tell her about it, because with the state of her heart he really hoped that she'd pass away without ever knowing."

Julia glanced up from her coffee, intercepting a glance that Bertha Starling was just giving Herbert, who remained all unconscious of it, but in one of those sharp moments of clarity that flash across the consciousness, Julia could read the thought behind Bertha's hard little eyes, that were like flecks of steel in her long bony countenance. Julia knew, as plainly as if Bertha had spoken aloud, exactly what was her opinion of her brother's late wife; tiresome, inefficient, a drag upon poor Herbert.

Bertha was ten years older than her brother, and after the death of their mother, when Herbert was only eight, had superintended his life until the pale girl, daughter of the local minister, had ensnared him. Bertha had lost Herbert then, now it would not be her fault if she did not recapture him.

Suddenly Julia ceased to hunger, and felt she had really eaten too much. She yawned a little and wished she were at home—for she had the day off—to go up to her room and sleep. She hadn't been sleeping very well at night lately, but the older people were still talking together, sympathising with Herbert in his loss, discussing symptoms—his symptoms, he'd been having indigestion lately—and advising remedies. Herbert, for the first time for years, was able to feel a little ill himself, no longer being overshadowed by a professional invalid. Like many healthy persons, he was by nature inclined to be nervous about his condition, but it had been no good indulging in this luxury up till now.

Julia went to the window, and sat down in an armchair with a high back that shut her off from the rest of the room. She was wanting Alfie as she had not wanted him for months. This death which had brought them all together to-day was so unimportant compared with his, and yet who had there been to give even this semblance of mourning to Alfie? His parents were dead. He had no brothers or sisters. Ruby had been sorry after her easy fashion. But it was really only Julia, though she hadn't, after all, loved him, who was the poorer for his loss. Alfie was dead before, thought Julia, he had never had the chance to be alive, but at least he had left her with this legacy of unrest, and that was more than poor Constance Starling had been able to leave to anyone.

Julia ached for what Alfie's hands had promised her, as she stared out through the autumn mistiness at the trees in the Square. Their yellow leaves drooped, and beneath them the mute Apollo seemed to droop also, his hand vainly striving to touch the unresponsive air to music.

5

Two Beresford and Saint Clement's Square

NOTHING, as Mrs. Almond always declared, ever came singly, and although the death of Mr. Almond occurred eighteen months later than the death of Mrs. Starling, yet Mrs. Almond kept on repeating this remark, with the air of a fatalist pronouncing an inevitable law.

Poor Mr. Almond hadn't put up much of a fight for his life. The weather was cold and wet, and he went off, as most elderly people go off, with pneumonia. He had been a querulous and rather ineffectual man, but a good man according to his lights; that is to say, whenever he made money he had spent it on his wife and daughter, and now they were left as helpless as a hermit crab denuded of its shell.

Julia was now earning fifteen shillings a week, of which she gave seven to her mother; but Two Beresford couldn't be run on seven shillings a week, and eight shillings was very little for her fares and clothes, now there was no Dad to help her out when she needed a new coat or shoes. There were some two hundred pounds to come in from his life insurance, and that would be all.

Again Julia went to a funeral, wearing the same black

frock, but not savouring as much the importance of being a mourner as she had at the funeral of Mrs. Starling, for this, after all, was serious. She knew she couldn't expect much help from Mum, who sat and cried, and said, what were they going to do now?

The problem was solved in a manner that was practical enough, but to Julia, very unsatisfactory—Uncle George, Aunt Mildred, and Elsa of the plaits were to give up the house at Dulwich and come and share expenses at Two Beresford. The house at Dulwich had been too expensive anyway, since the son, Albert, had got married and set up on his own, and Uncle George and Aunt Mildred were only too glad of an excuse to be rid of it.

Julia knew that and resented all the more that the Beale family should pretend that an arrangement which was highly satisfactory to them should be entirely an act of charity on their part.

The rent of Two Beresford was only thirty pounds a year; that of the Dulwich house had been double. Uncle George, too, had lately been transferred to another office—he had been made manager of the office where Dad had been chief clerk. It was Uncle George who had got Dad the job in the first place, that was the worst of it; it was always Uncle George who succeeded in doing things, and Dad who had always failed, until this last job of all, which had been of Uncle George's finding. Further, by coming to live at Two Beresford, Uncle George would save train fares from Dulwich. Mrs. Almond would do most of the cooking, so the Beales would be able to do with only a day woman, and Julia, of course, was expected to turn in her seven shillings a week. Oh yes, thought Julia, it was all very pleasant for everyone but herself. Mr. Almond's "workroom" was now to be turned into Mum's room, and Uncle George and Aunt Mildred were to have the conjugal chamber. Julia supposed that the box-room would be turned into a room for Elsa, though what would happen to all the boxes of the two families she couldn't imagine. Some of the Almonds' furniture was sold, and some of the Beales', and everyone except Julia, and perhaps poor Mrs. Almond, seemed pleased with the arrangement. She, Julia knew, was not pleased, but what could she do, an elderly and tired woman with no resources? It wasn't much fun for her, thought Julia, having to become a sort of general servant in her own house, even if it was her own brother and sister-in-law who were to share it with her. Besides, Uncle George bullied women. He bullied his sister, and bullied his wife, and it was only pert little Elsa, with her turned-up nose and her ready tongue, who was able to keep him in his place at all.

Julia was sorry for her mother; although she didn't really love her, she had always been sorry for her—she was such a helpless little withered leaf of a woman, blown about by circumstance, but Julia could not but be sorry for herself as well. She was getting on so well at the shop. There was talk of another rise in her pay, but power was more important to Julia than pay, and she knew already that she had power. Marian was often away; workgirls came and went, only Gipsy and Mrs. Santley, the hat expert, were always at the shop on time, and, of course, Julia herself.

Julia loved business. She loved the planning and contriving, she loved being clever with the customers, and the travellers, and she loved the beauty of the fabrics with which she had to deal. Already she knew Gipsy looked on her as her chief prop and stay, and Julia was passionately determined never to let her or the business down. The business had saved Julia in the dreadful months that had followed since Alfie had been killed. It had not allowed her time to think too much about herself, or to listen too much to the insistent memories of the body, those reverberating echoes of the pulses. Of course, there had been times when she had suffered, still without admitting to herself what it was she wanted. She had made friends here and there, gone out dining and dancing, as every attractive young woman went out dining and dancing, but no one had yet taken Alfie's place, chiefly because the demands of the shop had made it too difficult. Julia did a lot of the buying now, and a lot of the interviewing. Customers who knew the shop, not those who came in from the street, would always ask for Miss Almond if Gipsy was not available; some of them even asked for Miss Almond straight away.

Julia had one flirtation with a young man of about her own age, and one with a colonel, whom she afterwards discovered to be married, and whose wife wished to divorce him, but with neither of the men did she go to the lengths to which she had gone with Alfie. She couldn't resist flirting with them, but she didn't really want them, not as she had wanted Alfie. With her body she still wanted passion, but not with any one human being; with her imagination she still wanted the sentiment of love, and it evaded her, as it had evaded her even with Alfie.

After all, if she wanted an admirer, there was always Herbert Starling at hand—good-natured, masculine, attracted by her, as she had always known him to be through those sensitive nerves of hers, which hardly ever told her wrongly. Herbert also was different nowadays. He had enlisted under the Derby scheme—his firm had promised to keep his job open for him—and at the moment he was expecting to get his commission and to be a real officer and wear a soft collar and tie, instead of one of those up-and-down tunic collars that Julia hated.

Yes, the world was interesting, what with the war, and these changes always going on in people, although it wasn't the glamorous excitement now that Julia had dreamt of in Heronscourt Park, or that her flesh had told her of in the days of Alfie. The war—it affected Julia probably as little as it affected any human being, and yet she was intensely conscious of a difference, as was everyone else. It was the background of her life, a background splashed with brilliant colours and by strange gleams, and clamorous with the sounds of an awful orchestra. She herself might have no one out there in all the mud and misery, but she knew many people who had. Life was penetrated by the excitement of vicarious sorrows. Julia sometimes wished that she had been free to go out to France, to be a W.A.A.C. or a Wren, but in the first place, she wasn't old enough, and in the second place, she thought the uniforms very unbecoming, and in the third place, she didn't really want to go. She loved her life at the shop; she loved her rare evenings of gaiety, generally with Ruby or Ruby's friends. She was becoming a person of importance where she was, she might be nobody out there. Men might fight and curse and agonise in the mud of France and Flanders, but in London trade was booming, people had money to spend upon clothes who had never had money before—wives of clerks were now wives of officers, whose pay accumulated at Cox's and was spent in one glorious burst when leave-time came.

Most of the people Julia knew in her shop-life had lives utterly distinct from the sort that was known at Two Beresford. Dances every night, and that meant frocks and silk stockings. Nearly every woman she met in her shop-life was having a love-affair, or a hasty marriage, and these meant *crêpe de Chine* underclothes, which had replaced the embroidered lawn threaded with pink or blue ribbon, that it had once been Julia's highest ambition to possess. Many of the wives, and many unmarried girls, were working in various ministries, and drawing good pay, and this good pay meant clothes, and still more clothes. What was the good of saving in a world gone mad? True, the customers were not of the class which during the first months of existence had come to l'Etrangère's, but what did that matter? They paid better than the Darlings had ever paid. Some of the Darlings still came, but they still didn't pay.

Everyone was leading, in a new sense of the term, a double life. Some were working harder than ever before, but playing harder also. Some—those who loved—felt as though half their lives were going on at the Front, because of the under-current of dread that was always theirs. Julia, though she continued to lead the double life of her imagination which she had always known, which all children know, and which had persisted with her beyond childhood, because of the lack of satisfaction in her actual life, yet led it less vividly than ever before. She was too tired most nights, or even at the week-ends, to indulge much in that youthful habit of day-dreaming. The world had got her, the world of the shop, and what she saw of London after hours, though it was not often spread before her.

For Julia took her work very seriously; she was satisfied by it, as every capable person is satisfied by the knowledge of a job well done. And Julia was very capable. There were two Julias, although for the first time they were only leading one life. There was the intensely practical Julia, with a good head for figures and a talent for organisation; and there was the dreaming Julia, who had been loved by Lewis Waller, and an Italian Prince, and Lord Kitchener, and Dennis Eadie, and by a wonderful warrior yet unmet. He was fading away, that man yet unmet, simply because Julia hadn't the time or the energy left for him. She wanted him as badly, but she no longer believed in him as completely as she had. More and more she was becoming aware that life wasn't like the story-books after all . . . the practical Julia was overlaying the dreamer, who was by now almost unaware of her own existence. Even day-dreaming cannot exist if it is crowded out by hard work, and the would-be dreamer is exhausted physically.

One day Julia arrived home later than usual from the shop. One of the most difficult of the customers, "the Brand woman," had returned a frock, after having worn it at a party for which she had ordered it, on the grounds that it didn't fit. Gipsy was determined not to let her off as lightly as that. She had happened to be at the party herself, and had seen the customer, triumphant and pleased with herself, in the gown which she now returned. Her mouth grimly set, Gipsy had insisted on the customer putting the frock on, and had shown her how easily it could be altered in the one or two places where, it was true, the fit was not yet perfect.

"I don't think I'll have it," Mrs. Brand kept saying; "once a thing's altered, it's never really satisfactory. It isn't as if I had worn it. It can't make any difference to you."

But Gipsy, with Julia's assistance, had gone on pinning and cutting, until the customer's resistance had been worn out. If the worst came to the worst, Gipsy had determined to say that she had caught sight of Mrs. Brand at the party the night before, but that would mean losing her for good; and although she occasionally did those unforgivable things, yet, on the whole, she was a fairly decent customer and paid her bills promptly. She was, to everyone in the shop, "that Brand woman." Only the very nicest customers were spoken of, even by Marian and Gipsy, as "Mrs." It would generally be: "Is that Brand woman's dress ready?" "That Smith woman's coming for her fitting to-day." "That Lucas woman has rung up to say her hat's too tight."

Julia was tired when she arrived at Two Beresford, almost too tired to caress Bobby, and she went straight up to her room to lie down until her mother should call up that supper was ready. She didn't really care if she had any supper or not, she almost thought she'd go to bed instead. Her room ... for the last hour she had been looking forward to it, to the quietness of its privacy, to the familiar fumed oak, the familiar blue hangings, though she no longer liked that blue—to the Greiffenhagen "Idyll" that seemed to her now like the vague memory of a dream. With Bobby pressing against her, she opened the door of her room and went in. How odd, the gas was lit already. Julia stood and looked about her, and her heart seemed to miss a beat. Her writing-table had been taken away and instead of it, along the wall, there was another bed. The bed wasn't made up, a roll of blankets lay on the top of it, and the pillows, indecent in their striped nakedness, were without pillowslips; but evidently the bed had come to stay. A deep red colour of anger flooded Julia's face. For a moment she stood still, unable to trust her voice. Then she went out on to the landing and called over the stairs: "Mum, where are you? Mum."

There was no answer, only a distant clattering from the kitchen. She hears me all right, thought Julia, she knows; and, her exhaustion forgotten, she went swiftly down the stairs and out into the kitchen. Mrs. Almond, busy at the stove, didn't look round.

"Mum, what's that bed doing in my room?"

"That bed?" said Mrs. Almond, with would-be deceptive vagueness, and as though all houses were full of strange beds that ran about at their own volition.

"Yes, that bed. Where's my writing-desk gone, and what's that bed doing there?"

"Oh, that'll be Elsa's bed," said Mrs. Almond. "You know your Uncle George and Aunt Mildred and Elsa are coming next week. That's Elsa's bed."

"I won't have her to sleep with me," cried Julia.

Mrs. Almond fiddled with the taps of the gas-stove and adjusted them to her liking, then turned round and faced her daughter.

"Julia, you've got to have her to sleep with you. There's nowhere else for her to sleep."

"She could have the box-room."

"And where do we put the boxes, and all the spare bits of furniture that your Uncle George doesn't like?"

"Sell them," said Julia. "We don't want them. We never go anywhere. Why should we have boxes?"

"Julia, how can you talk that way, and why should you mind having your little cousin in your room? She'll be pleasant company for you."

"Company for me! A child like that! I tell you I won't have it, Mum. I can't work as I do at the shop, and then come home to find someone in my room. I've got to have it to myself."

Mrs. Almond began to cry. "Oh, Julia, I was afraid you'd hate it. I knew you'd make a fuss. What can I do? We can't go on living unless George and Mildred come here. You know we can't live on what you make."

"Let's take a lodger," said Julia. "We can let the room you and Dad used to have to a business man, bed and breakfast; we'd get a pound a week for that."

"A pound a week! How could we live, both of us, and pay rates and taxes and rent and everything, on a pound a week, and the fifteen shillings you're earning?"

"Well, then, let's move somewhere else. I'm not set on this house, and I don't see why you should be. Let's take a tiny flat somewhere."

Mrs. Almond began to cry again, and murmured something about being turned out of her home.

"Oh, Mum, what nonsense, you've had heaps of homes. We've been moving round ever since I can remember."

Julia's heart sank. She knew how rock-like was her mother's obstinacy, and she guessed, too, that her mother was looking forward to having blustering Uncle George to live in the house. Uncle George would take all responsibilities off her shoulders, even if she had to work for him like a general servant. Mrs. Almond had no faith in her own sex. If Julia were making enough to support the whole household, Mrs. Almond would always expect the money to vanish mysteriously like fairy gold. It was always the gentlemen to whom one looked for the solid things of life.

"When are they coming in?" asked Julia.

"Next week, Tuesday, I think your aunt said. They've had a great stroke of luck getting rid of their house so quickly."

Tuesday . . . five days more in which to possess her soul.

"I don't want any supper, Mum. No, please don't bother

123

me. I don't want anything," and Julia went back to her room, Bobby at her heels. She undressed and got into bed, neglecting for once the usual careful creaming of her skin, neglecting even to clean her teeth. She tried to read, but as long as the light was on she could not avoid seeing that horrible little bed with its pillows, over which, next week, she would see the scrawny plaits of Elsa lying spread out.

Julia stretched up her arm to the gas bracket and turned out the light. Bobby heaved a deep sigh, and laid his face across her feet. He swallowed once or twice, and she could feel the movement of his lower jaw on her instep, then he lay quiet. It's too bad, it's too bad, thought Julia. She could not yet cope with the thought of how she was to meet this disaster, and what she was to do. If only she were earning more, if only she could afford to take a high hand. She wasn't earning enough upon which to support herself away from home, yet she must, she must, have her own room. She lay awake hour after hour thinking of the preciousness of her own room. Here she had always been able to take refuge. Here she had lain and thought about the wonderful future; here she had lain and ached for Alfie; here she had imagined herself in turn every heroine of whom she had read. This wasn't a mere room, it was her own soul. Whatever had happened at the shop during the day, however tiresome customers had been; if Marian and Gipsy had spoken sharply, if Dad and Mum had been more than usually uncomprehending and annoying, all those tiresome things had fallen off her like an outdoor garment when she came to her own room. Only Bobby had ever shared it with her.

She wondered desperately if it would be any good if she took Gipsy and Marian into her confidence—if she asked them for a rise. She was worth more than she was getting, she knew; she was the one treasure who is always being looked for in a little shop, and is so seldom found. If she could get two pounds a week, perhaps she could manage to live on that somewhere; get a room and boil herself eggs. Anne . . . would she let her a room in the house, which must be much too big for Dr. Ackroyd and herself at the corner of Saint Clement's Square? But she didn't really want to live with Dr. Ackroyd and Anne. She admired them, but they somehow weren't comfortable people. They looked too clearly at things to be quite comfortable.

Her great friend was still Ruby, who was always kind to her, but in a desperate case like this Julia ceased to romance, and faced facts. She knew she couldn't live with Ruby; that she would degenerate into a mixture of maid and dresser and unpaid companion if she were to do so, and there would be perpetual scenes about Ruby's lovers, and Ruby would always be wanting to discuss the lovers. Nobody but Ruby could exist as a personality in Ruby's flat. If only one of the men Julia had met had been marriageable, even mildly marriageable! But no one had been any good to her except Alfie, and he had only been physically right. Still, if there had been an Alfie now she'd have married him all right.

Julia fell asleep at last, to dream that Elsa was sitting up in the bed opposite, looking at her with impish glee, and repeating over and over again: "I'm here for life. I'm here for life." Towards dawn Bobby crept up the bed and placed his head beside hers on the pillow. She stirred a little in her sleep, and suddenly woke with a cry, pushing him away from her. It hadn't been Bobby . . . ridiculously enough, it had been Herbert Starling whose head had been upon the pillow, his large florid cheek almost touching hers.

She sat up in bed, still shaking, to see Bobby gazing at her reproachfully in the wan light. She stared round the room, and the sense of where she was and what had happened came suddenly back to her. There was the horrible little bed, with the striped ticking on its pillows, and here was Bobby's reproachful face close to her own. What a relief!

She stroked his head and settled down to sleep again, but sleep would not come, and eventually she got up, lit the geyser and ran a hot bath. Then she went down to the kitchen, made herself some tea, and cooked some eggs and bacon, for she felt ravenous by now. After all, there were still four more days. Something would happen. Perhaps Elsa would fall off an omnibus and get run over. Something surely must happen. She couldn't give up her room.

But when Julia came home next day, most of the Beales' furniture had arrived, and on the Friday the

Beales themselves turned up to see that everything was to their liking. What impossible people, thought Julia, her ears far more attuned by now to the light gay voices of the Darlings, and the quick, rich tones of Gipsy's voice, and the cool drawl of Marian's.

There was Uncle George booming and blustering. There was Aunt Mildred, oddly dominating through all the booming and blustering. Perhaps, thought Julia, that was why Uncle George was always so noisy, he knew that really Aunt Mildred was far stronger than he was, and had never been frightened by him. Aunt Mildred looked as though she had been cut out of wood. She was rather of the same type as Bertha Starling, except that no one could ever have mistaken Aunt Mildred for anything but a matron, or Bertha Starling for anything but a virgin. Where Aunt Mildred's hard contours were rounded, Miss Starling's were concave. Aunt Mildred had a high colour exactly in the middle of each solid cheek, and Miss Starling's thin face was pale, but they both looked as though they would be hard to the touch. Their eyes were close together, their mouths were thin. Both knew what they wanted in life, but Aunt Mildred had got it, and Miss Starling never had, until now. She was keeping Herbert's flat for him; she was saving money, but the unfortunate Herbert didn't want, at the moment, to save money, though no one had been more "careful" than he all his life till now. Aunt Mildred would save money too, but it would always be to her own advantage; Bertha saved money to Herbert's advantage, although he didn't want her to. Herbert wanted to be cutting a gallant figure just now. Look at this move, thought Julia; Uncle George appeared to have blustered his way into it, but she didn't doubt that the irresistible force of Aunt Mildred, relentless as one of those tanks the papers were full of, was behind him. Look what they were getting—a nice house, Mum to do most of the work, and all of that for nothing except paying cheaper rent than they had been paying before, and giving Mum the little bit of food she ate. The eight shillings a week Julia contributed to the housekeeping would pay for her own breakfast and supper all right.

Elsa seemed insufferable that evening to Julia. For Elsa was being the gay, spoilt, little much-loved daughter. She ran up and down the stairs, sang at the top of her rather pleasing little voice, played with Bobby, and managed, Julia noticed, to get hold of the best things to eat.

"I've great plans for Elsa," Uncle George boomed from the hearth-rug, "great plans. Her teacher says she's never seen a child so advanced for her age."

Julia suffered in stony silence till supper-time, when Herbert Starling walked in unexpectedly. He looked a fine figure of a man in his uniform. He was an officer now, and he had come to show himself off. He did so good-naturedly, while Elsa asked bright, childish questions about his various buttons and badges. He looked, thought Julia, suddenly seeing him anew, very much nicer than he had ever looked before. His field-boots were beautifully polished—trust Bertha to see to that—his buttons were bright, he carried himself with great dignity, and the drill had taken at least four inches off his stomach. But at tea-time she decided despairingly that he was as stupid as ever.

"Well, well, Julia," he said, "so you're going to be quite a happy little family party here. That's right. I don't like to think of you and your mother alone here, thinking about the old days."

What a fool, Julia thought, resentfully. The old days—as though Dad had ever amounted to anything particular. What was the good, when people were dead, of talking as though they had been perfect? Why was it always done? She remembered Mrs. Starling's funeral, nearly two years ago now, everybody had spoken then as though they had lost somebody irreplaceable, and now they were doing the same thing over poor, ineffectual Dad.

Julia had been fond of her father in a sort of way. When she had been a very little girl and things hadn't been going too badly with them, he had liked to play with her sometimes on a Saturday afternoon, but she had never known quite where she was with him. His own affairs had always preoccupied him to the extent of making his relationship with other human beings very immature and slight. Little Julia had never known how her advances would be received. In company, who was more fond of children than Mr. Almond, who more playful? And yet, when the visitors had left, and Julia expected him to finish the game with her, he would often turn and snap at her and tell her to be quiet. Even her infant sense of justice had realised that he hadn't meant to be a hypocrite. He was just trying to be the sort of person that he wanted to be in front of visitors, a family man who was fond of children and clever with children. When the visitors had gone and he was tired, and his nerves were ragged, he didn't want to be bothered with children. When one of his schemes for making money had gone wrong, he didn't want to be bothered with anyone. When he had managed to land a good job, Eldorado opened before his eyes, when the job dwindled into nothing and disappeared, the whole horizon was black to him. Julia had been accustomed ever since she remembered anything, to the opening of the black side of the fan or the white, at a flick of fortune's wrist. The poor little man who had, by chance, caused her mother to conceive her and had through all her adolescent years caused these fluttering fortunes in the daily life, had died, and that was all there was to be said about it.

Poor Dad. . . . Julia was sorry for him, as she was sorry for all helpless things, or rather she was pitiful for the mess he had made of her life. She wasn't sorry for him personally, because he didn't exist any more. She was sorry for the pity of it all. Poor Dad, he had kept together this little house, and now Uncle George had entered it like a north wind, and was blowing about in its once-sheltered corners—Uncle George, who had got Dad his best job—how Julia hated him for that.

"Half-past nine . . ." Herbert Starling interrupted all Julia's sequence of thoughts by standing up and announcing that he must be getting home, Bertha would be expecting him. He stood looking expectantly at Julia across the dining-room table, still covered with the litter of the solid Sunday supper-tea, and it suddenly dawned upon Julia that he was expecting her to see him off at the front door. She couldn't have told how this knowledge came to her nerves, whether it was by a curious stillness in the elderly people around her, a certain muffled eagerness, in Uncle George and Aunt Mildred and Mum, or a pert, precocious interest on Elsa's part, but suddenly she was aware of the fact. For a moment it seemed to her so absurd that she remained sitting, her elbows upon the table, her chin upon her hands.

Mr. Starling . . . he had always admired her, an instinct in her had told her that, and admired her in what she called to herself "that way," but that it could be taken seriously by people other than herself seemed suddenly amazing. Herbert Starling . . . why! he was years and years and years old, and though it was true that he looked much younger now in his officer's uniform, and his stomach was flatter, you couldn't make a figure of romance out of poor old Herbert Starling, not if you tried to ever so. Nevertheless, the thing that would never let Julia be, the wish to be attractive to men, and her own interest in herself whenever they were attracted, rose within her now, and even in her misery she felt a faint stirring of interest.

"Must you go?" she said mechanically, as she pushed back her chair and rose to her feet. "Got a coat?—not that it's not a warm evening for the time of year," and, still talking what she felt to be utter banalities, she did what was expected of her. She went out to the hall, picked up Herbert's British-warm, and held it for him. Herbert wriggled into it, and turned towards her.

"When are you coming to see me, Julia—Bertha and me, I mean, of course? You know I'll be going off to France in a few days." He didn't add that he would be busy sitting on a stool at a mysterious place called Railhead.

"Oh, I don't know," said Julia vaguely, "we're very busy at the shop, you know."

"You're not busy on Saturday afternoons, my girl. What about to-morrow afternoon? I know I can manage that. Look here, Julia, I'll tell you what I'll do, I'll call for you, and we'll dine, and go to the pictures or a theatre. It's too early in the year for the country or I'd suggest going to the country for the day; but I'll get a box somewhere, say the Coliseum, just for us two. What about it?"

Julia hesitated—a box, the Coliseum—she and Alfie. Alfie . . . she had no longer the smallest sentiment regarding him, but the effect he had had upon her lingered. He represented the sole intimacy she had had with the male sex until now. Herbert . . . if she went out with him it would be admitting in a way that she knew what he wanted. She looked at him. He did look rather splendid, after all. He was so very much of a man, or so it seemed to Julia; his rosy, clean-shaven cheeks, the essentially masculine odour of tobacco and soap lingered about him . . . he wasn't so bad, poor old Herbert. After all, an evening with Herbert wouldn't kill her.

Julia enjoyed her evening with Herbert. He was respectful though hungry-looking, and she found herself regretting that it would be the last time she would see him for some months. Yet, at the same time, she didn't wish him to propose to her, although marriage with him would have solved all her problems; that is to say, she didn't wish him to propose yet. He'd have to go away anyhow, so there was no point in it. She'd see what she was feeling like when he came back on his first leave, and it would be fun to refuse him, kindly and respectfully. She might have met someone simply wonderful by then; that person whom she always expected round each corner.

Meanwhile, she enjoyed the dinner. She enjoyed the admiration in Herbert's eyes; his clumsy attempts at gallantry. He made a fuss of her, and nobody had made a fuss of her for a long time.

On Tuesday the Beale family moved into Two Beresford. Julia was spared that great event, but she came in for the full horror of the accomplished fact.

Julia had accepted an invitation to see Ruby in her new play that had only been running for a couple of days, and whose fate was still hanging in the balance. She had the notion that if she got back to her room after Elsa was asleep it would at least be better than enduring the childish conversation which went on ceaselessly from the hope of Uncle George's house.

So Julia danced the whole evening through; danced, she was quite well aware, not nearly as well as she usually did, and of the men she met, two out of the three were already in love with Ruby; the third was sixty years old, and did nothing to encourage a cheerful view of the future as regarded herself.

Ruby was at her most distracted, full of her debts, of the way her friends had failed her, of the way the other actors stole her laughs, of the way Mr. Gordon had behaved since he had wanted more of her than a good woman could give, and since she had, of course, refused him. . . . And what was she to do about the two young men, one in the Flying Corps and one in the

130

Submarine Service, who at the moment wished to marry her?

And the odd thing was, thought Julia, watching them, they did both wish to marry her. There sat Ruby, with her red hair, her big sleepy brown eyes, her dark deeply-modelled mouth, and her full white cheeks; obviously not a virgin, obviously not what she said, a clergyman's daughter; quite obvious to anybody who had seen her on the stage not a very good actress; and yet here were two ardent, earnest young men, only too anxious to endow her with their very good family names and their pay, in the touching confidence that, if she accepted, it would be because it was the love of a lifetime, and that she would be a good and faithful wife. Is it, thought Julia to herself in humorous despair, being on the stage that makes people able to believe these things, so that they are able to make other people believe them too? Yes—that was it, she decided, in one of her flashes of insight. It was because Ruby believed it herself that these young men believed it. What luck, to be able to cheat yourself like that. . . . And Julia's thoughts flew back to Herbert, in his tent or his billet, or wherever it was that people like Herbert were sleeping. She knew by now that Herbert wanted her. She couldn't cheat herself about that. Ruby could always label any emotion love, but Julia couldn't. She hadn't, even in the first flush of a young girl's awakening desire, been able to call her feelings for Alfie, love; how much less then could she thus label this feeling that she had for Herbert, and that he had for her? He had begun to interest her, that was true; it was so obvious that he wanted her, and to be wanted by a man could never leave Julia quite unmoved. As to what Herbert felt for her . . . that was unmistakable. Julia thought of last Saturday. After all, he wasn't so bad, poor old Herbert.

She was very tired when she got home, so tired that, oddly enough, for the time being she had forgotten Elsa. Bobby didn't meet her in the hall, and she concluded that he was already up in her bedroom. She went up the short flight from the front door and stopped short as she heard the sound of a masculine snore from the back bedroom. Of course, Uncle George and Aunt Mildred . . . there they were, snoring away in that ghastly manner, inside the room where Dad and Mum had snored in the same fashion. Somehow it was worse, more indecent, because it was Uncle George and Aunt Mildred. Upstairs there would be Bobby on her bed, and Elsa tucked away in the little bed, her nose pointed to the ceiling, her plaits pointed right and left over the pillow.

Julia went very quietly and slowly up the stairs, crept quietly into the room, and saw the tap of the incandescent gas had been turned down, and a faint glow only lit the room. Yes, Elsa was asleep, thank God, sound asleep, her mouth a little open, her nose a little shiny, her plaits right and left, just as Julia had imagined them. But Bobby, where was Bobby? Julia looked everywhere; no Bobby. Then she guessed—of course—Uncle George and Aunt Mildred would think it unhealthy for Bobby to sleep in the same room as their precious Elsa. Again the hot, burning tide, as when first she had seen Elsa's bed in her room, invaded her. She slipped out of the room again and down the stairs to the sitting-room, calling Bobby's name softly. There was no answer. She opened the dining-room door; no, he wasn't there; the kitchen; no, he wasn't there. She went through to the scullery, and was greeted with a sudden whimpering that rose to a wild scream of joy. There was her precious Bobby, lying on an old sack; Bobby, who had always slept on her bed. Julia went down on her knees on the stone floor and gathered him into her arms against her only evening-dress.

"Mother's darling," she murmured. "Did they put him to sleep in the scullery?"

"Wow-oo, wow-oo, wow-oo," said Bobby.

Julia set her jaw. She might have to have that awful little rat of a girl to sleep in her room, but at least she would have Bobby also. Whispering to him to be quiet, she led the way upstairs again, Bobby creeping very quietly behind her without speaking. He realised perfectly well that this was a dangerous adventure. Julia took him into the bathroom with her while she made ready for the night, and then he crept quietly into the bedroom and on to her bed, without even thumping his tail as usual.

Of course, there was an awful row next morning—a breakfast-table row. Uncle George, Aunt Mildred, the would-be placatory voice of Mum, and the shrill piping of Elsa. Disgustingly insanitary habits—dirty habits—a dog to sleep in your room, on your bed, taking up all the oxygen—give you all his fleas. Had Julia ever observed what dogs did when they were out? Think of the things they licked, and then came home and licked her. The things they ate, the places they put their feet in. Dogs weren't even clean as cats were clean. They were thoroughly dirty.

Julia sat, white and still, through breakfast, but when it was over she pushed back her chair.

"Well, you can do exactly what you like," she said, "but either Bobby sleeps with me or Elsa doesn't. I don't want Elsa, and I do want Bobby, and after all, it's my room. I'll sleep in the sitting-room on the sofa, but Bobby shall sleep with me. Elsa can have my room to herself; after all, why not? Uncle George is paying the rent now."

As she was leaving the house a sudden thought struck her. How could she leave Bobby to these angry people? She went back, fastened his lead to his collar, and started out with him. Bobby, enchanted, jumped all about her. Laboriously Julia lugged his elephantine weight on to the top, first of a tramcar and then of an omnibus. It was a wet day, and she was chilled to the bone by the time she reached the shop. Bobby, who had never been up and down the stairs of a moving vehicle before, was extremely alarmed, and held on with all his claws at each step. Julia took him straight through to the back of the house in George Street and tied him up to the runaway basin in the lavatory, and went to find Gipsy.

"Mrs. Danvers," she said, "I'm in the most dreadful trouble. May I tell you about it?"

Gipsy looked at her out of her bright, rather sweet eyes. Julia had been with them for nearly three years now, and had never troubled them with anything personal. Gipsy felt she owed Julia something, and nodded her head. "Tell me all about it."

"It's this way," said Julia. "You know father died a couple of months ago? Well, our only way of keeping on living, mother and me, was to have Uncle George and his wife and their horrid little girl to live with us, and they've come. And the little girl, Elsa her name is, shares my room. I don't want to bother you, Mrs. Danvers, but you can't think what that means to me. Whenever I get home tired, or whenever things haven't been right at

133

home, I've always had my room. When I was a little girl I won a scripture prize once, and the only thing I remember about it is that I wrote a long answer to the question, 'What were the Cities of Refuge?' Well, my room was my city of refuge, and now I've got to share it with Elsa. Well, I don't want to bother you with all that, but they've taken my dog away. You don't know Bobby, but he's always slept with me. I've always taken him out for a walk when I've got home, however tired I was"—this wasn't strictly true, but it seemed true to Julia at the moment—"and now he's been put to sleep in the scullery. I brought him up here to-day. I hope you don't mind. He'll be as good as gold. What I wanted to ask you is this, if they still won't listen to me, may I sleep here on the divan in the fitting-room to-night with Bobby, until I can find somewhere to go to? I'll try and find a lodging-house, or something. I don't know much about these things, but I can't go on at home if it's going to be like this," and to Julia's horror, the slow tears began to fall from her eyes.

"You poor child," said Gipsy unexpectedly, "how perfectly horrible for you to have to share your room. Where's Bobby, I'd like to see him?"

"He—he's in the lavatory," said Julia, between her sobs.

The thing, of course, was as good as done. Bobby practically told Gipsy that she was his long-lost mother. He at once tried to be a lap-dog, and he shook hands at least twenty times.

Gipsy gazed at him entranced. It seemed to her incredible that there should be a dog so vulgar, so plain, and so fascinating. If Julia had come to her complaining that she had had a baby from which she had been separated, or a mother, or sister, or a little crippled brother, or a husband, she might have had very little sympathy; but a dog, even a dog like Bobby, with a cocoa-coloured nose and the most amazing lack of shape, was a sure pass to the heart of anyone of Gipsy's or Marian's kind. A dog was a dog.

At lunch-time Julia went out and sent a prepaid telegram to Two Beresford. She addressed it to Almond, and not to Beale. *Will come back to-night if can have Bobby otherwise will not return.—Julia.*

134

Just before the shop closed at six the answer came: *Expect you both supper.—Beale.*

Julia and Gipsy studied the telegram solemnly together. "Does he mean Bobby can sleep with me?" said Julia. "You see, he only says supper. Still, after all, I sent the telegram to mother, and Uncle George has answered it."

"From what you have told me," said Gipsy, "I imagine your Uncle George would have answered it, whoever you had sent it to." She fumbled in her bag and produced a Yale key. "Look here, Julia, if you find after supper that they won't let you have your own way, come back here. Here's the key; the first time I've ever let you have it. It's a spare one and you can keep it. Bring some sheets with you and make up your bed on the divan in the fitting-room, and you can bath somehow in the runaway basin in the morning."

Very slowly Julia put out her hand and took the key. "Mrs. Danvers," her voice shook a little, "I can't tell you what I think of you for this."

"Nonsense, Julia, of course, you know I trust you by now. Why, you're part of the firm. If you can't have the key, who can? and by the way, your salary goes up to thirty shillings. You can't really live on it, but it'll enable you to pay them enough to keep them a bit quiet. Perhaps you can get the box-room cleared out after all, and stick your little cousin in it."

Julia and Gipsy stood looking at each other. Julia realised for a moment how good Gipsy really was, though she was nothing like as kind and gushing as Ruby. Gipsy had her own troubles; she had never got over the loss of her husband, she had the boy to educate, she had masses of bad debts; but she really cared about Julia because Julia had given of her very best work to the shop.

Once again Julia fastened the lead on to Bobby's collar. This time she took him home by the District Railway, and bought a ticket for him. Bobby ate half the ticket before they arrived at Stamford Brook Green, and the chewed remains had to be rescued from his mouth and presented to the ticket-collector.

Rather to Julia's disappointment everything was peaceful at Two Beresford. Her announcement of her rise in salary was greeted with awe and admiration. Certainly Bobby could sleep with her; nobody had meant to be unkind. Julia, who had pictured herself going back for the night, with a tooth-brush and a roll of sheets and blankets, to the shop in George Street, was disappointed.

But she had to sleep again with the little pert face of Elsa present to her consciousness. Even after the light had been put out in her room, even with Bobby's head pressing against her feet, she remained conscious of this intrusion. Her room had gone, it was no longer hers. Why had she made the mistake of basing her ultimatum on Bobby's presence rather than Elsa's absence?

Gipsy gave Julia the thirty shillings a week, and still Julia didn't go away and live "on her own." Soft living had taken hold of Julia by now. How could she live anywhere on thirty shillings a week, and have Bobby with her—and how could she leave Bobby in the disgruntled household of Two Beresford? Thirty shillings a week! A room and breakfast at a Bloomsbury boarding-house; nobody to fill her hot-water bottle when she came in each night. After all, Mum might not be much good at running a house, but she did get Julia's supper when she came in dead tired, and Two Beresford had been run more or less to suit Julia. She simply couldn't face going off into the void and slaving for herself; doing her own bits of mending, that Mum did at present, and living in squalor. The weakness of the flesh that had always pursued her, was hers now. Passion and comfort are, after all, more or less allied, and Julia, who had known passion, couldn't give up comfort. It was weakness rather than strength that enabled her to go on day after day at Two Beresford.

No one ever knew, except Julia herself, how the presence of Elsa in her bedroom pressed upon her in the weeks that followed. It wasn't that Elsa was inconsiderate —she was only too careful not to give offence.

"Of course, Julia, I know this is your room really, do you mind if I put my brush down here? Did I wake you, Julia, in the night when I had to get up? I'm so sorry if I did. I know you work so hard."

Julia's instinct told her, although she could never have made either Mum or the Beales understand it, that Elsa was just pretending all that consideration, that she was pretending everything. She knew how seldom Elsa was

136

really asleep when she came up at night after an evening out. She knew quite well that through those golden up-curled eyelashes, Elsa's light-blue eyes were watching her. Always there would be a different reception. As the nights grew warmer, Elsa would be the innocent young girl who thought no ill, and would be lying practically nude upon her bed, arms outflung, sleeping with the innocent smile of a child upon her pretty, insipid little mouth. Sometimes on a cooler night she would be curled up like a dormouse, looking younger than ever. Once she had even fallen asleep upon Julia's bed, as though slumber had overtaken her while waiting for the elder girl's arrival, half undressed, book fallen from her hand. Julia knew perfectly well that she wasn't really asleep, that she had put down the book just as she heard her coming, but she couldn't possibly say so.

It began to get upon Julia's nerves, this wondering how she was going to find her cousin when she came in late at night. Sometimes Elsa was sprightly, anxious to know whether Julia had been enjoying herself, sometimes studious and martyr-like, doing some work, not able to get to sleep because she was expecting Julia. And then the time came when Bobby's heavy breathing began to disturb Elsa.

"It's the hot weather, I suppose," she'd say, with a wan little smile. "He can't help it, poor dog, he just has to get off Julia's bed and fling himself down on the floor. He can't help the noise it makes."

Julia, also, would have been glad if Bobby had not insisted on sleeping on her bed during the summer weather, but she simply just hadn't dared to do it.

She let herself in quietly, and went upstairs and into her room. The gas was burning full on, and Elsa was lying asleep in bed with Bobby in her arms, his face on her shoulder, his pink mouth half open, his pink eyelids tightly closed. A few crumbs of sweet biscuit lying on the floor told their own story. Elsa had been coaxing Bobby to sleep on her bed. Julia laughed, and snapped her fingers loudly, regardless of whether she woke Elsa or not. Bobby opened one sleepy, yellow eye, gave a few perfunctory thumps with the white tip of his tail, closed the eye and went to sleep again. Julia sat quite still, with murder in her heart. She went towards the bed to pull Bobby off it by the collar, and then suddenly realised

137

that if Elsa woke up and saw her, or if Elsa was already awake, which was quite likely, she would be playing right into her hands. With the greatest self-control she had yet exercised in her life, she got into bed and turned out the light. Her reward came in the morning, when Bobby, who had plumped, as usual, on to the linoleum in the small hours, crept on to her bed at about six.

Neither Julia nor Elsa said anything to each other about his defection, but when next night Julia found the same state of affairs obtaining, Boby once again asleep in Elsa's arms, she knew that the whole arrangement was a deliberate scheme. She had refused to sleep without Bobby, had she? Well, now she should see that Bobby loved Elsa more than he loved her. She was out all day, Elsa attended a school near-by, came home to lunch, took him out for a walk afterwards, fed him at mealtimes, and made a fuss of him without cease. Bobby, at first languid under these attentions, became rather struck by them. Here was a pleasant person who would give him everything he wanted. Why should he lie in the hall waiting for Julia, when he could be on Elsa's bed, stuffed with sweet biscuits, until he fell asleep?

Julia bore it for a few days, and then, just as she was feeling she could do something desperate, Herbert Starling telephoned her at the shop. He wanted to take her out to dinner, and to see the new play at the Haymarket, *The Freedom of the Seas,* the following night.

"Oh dear," lamented Julia on the telephone, "and I've promised to go out with Ruby, you know Ruby Safford, the actress?"

"Oh yes," came Herbert's voice, "you've told me about her. Well, look here, why couldn't she come, too, and bring a friend, of course. I'd like to give a dinner-party for a friend of yours, Julia."

Julia's cheeks began to burn with pleasure as she sat with the receiver in her hand. How wonderful, she could produce a friend, a man friend, an officer, who would give a party for her and her friends. It was the first time such a thing had ever happened to Julia.

"Well, what do you say?" came Herbert's voice impatiently over the telephone.

"Yes, I think that'll be all right. I'll telephone Ruby. I don't think she'd made any special plans."

"Right oh," said Herbert Starling. "If you don't let me know, I'll conclude it's O.K. We'll dine at the Pall Mall, it's next door to the Haymarket. Where shall I call for you?"

"Oh," Julia said, thinking for a moment. She had better dress at the shop. She'd never have time to get out to Heronscourt Park and back, and besides, there'd be the usual endless questions to answer.

"Call for me here," she said, "I'll change here. The shop door will be shut, but knock at the house door, I'll be ready."

"Right oh," said Herbert. "Seven o'clock, then, so as to give us plenty of time for dinner."

"That'll be lovely," said Julia, hanging up the receiver.

It was the luncheon-hour, and there was no one in the lower part of the shop but herself. She rang up Ruby, who was still in bed, and told her the change of plans. Ruby was charmed. She'd bring the flying boy, such a dear boy, as Julia knew, and Ruby really thought that he really did love her. Didn't Julia think so, too? The Pall Mall at seven-thirty, that would be lovely. And again Julia hung up the telephone.

She was determined to put all her troubles out of her mind for the time being and enjoy the dinner and theatre. Thank heaven, he had the sense not to bring that gloompots of a sister with him; and she could forget her existence, and the existence of the Beale family as well. As a matter of fact, Aunt Mildred, not without guile, had asked Miss Starling to supper that night. Julia, laughing to herself, could guess at Bertha's fears when she discovered Julia was out . . . and at Aunt Mildred's reassurances. Of course, nothing would suit Aunt Mildred's book better than that Julia should marry Herbert Starling, and the Beale family would have Two Beresford to themselves—for no one counted Mum. Marry Herbert Starling . . . it was the first time Julia had put the possibility into words even to herself, and her heart began to beat faster. She thought of Herbert as she had seen him the other night, jovial, masculine, authoritative, very much of a man in his uniform. He'd always been interested in her; she'd known that even in the days when he had been married, and when, anyway, she'd thought him too old to be worth considering. Julia had lived in the world since then, she no longer thought a man of thirty-five old, and after all, she herself was twenty, nearly twenty-one . . .

She had always had an extraordinary terror of age. Though when she was a child she had wished to be grown up, simply because she thought to be grown up meant freedom, she had yet felt the fear of age as soon as she had got into her 'teens, and on her twentieth birthday had had a gloomy feeling that she had left youth behind her.

She dressed with care at the shop after closing hours, putting on the black lace frock, which she had brought up to date by shortening it and adding a transparent hem. Then she put on a black and silver cloak, given her by Ruby.

It flashed across her mind now that if she married somebody—say, Herbert, for the sake of argument—she would be able to "buy in" more clothes, for, of course, she would still go on working at the shop—catch her giving up her independence! and there would be an allowance from her husband as well. Come to that, it would almost be worth marrying Herbert to see the face of that old cat, Bertha, who thought she'd got her claws into him for good.

The years of overhearing the conversation of the Darlings, and watching how they lived, had not been without their effect on Julia; she no longer had the notion of marriage as necessarily being for life, that had been hers in an uninstructed youth. You could always get out of it somehow or other if it turned out too badly. Economic independence, that was the thing that mattered for women, more and more she saw that. Look at Mum, who now had to have the Beale family in her house for the rest of her days, simply because Uncle George could support her and she couldn't support herself. Look at Anne, she got on with her father, but she would be independent of him once she was through her training, and if she chose to go, she could. Look at Marian, everyone knew she was only waiting for the end of the war to get a divorce. Billy wouldn't want it, but he'd have to agree, and just because she had private means she could get on quite all right without him, and could choose someone who amused her more next time. Tired of "the Front," Marian was back again at the shop, and having an affair with an "indispensable" young man who was in the Foreign Office. Even Gipsy, hard-up as she was, had her husband's pension and earned enough extra by the shop to support herself, and would send her boy into the Navy, though she had to work like a nigger to do it. Soon she, Julia, would be economically independent, too, but with nothing put by . . . how could she put by? She would always be at the mercy of an extra bad go of flu, of any long illness. . . . That was where a husband would come in so useful, it gave you a sort of background, something other than yourself to depend on. . . . She wondered just how much she could have depended on Alfie . . . not much, perhaps, but, anyway, what was the good of thinking of Alfie? Herbert wasn't Alfie, but he had come on wonderfully this past year, in spite of Bertha. Being a widower, and then going into training, had done marvels for him, thought Julia, not realising how much was due to his uniform.

Was that his taxi stopping in George Street now? She dusted a little rouge over her cheeks—the use of rouge, begun when she "modelled," had made all the difference to Julia's looks—and gathering her cloak about her, went downstairs just as a knock came on the house door. Herbert was standing on the pavement; he came quickly inside the passage before she could step out.

"I've told the man to turn the taxi," he said, speaking rather thickly, so that for a horrified moment she imagined he had been drinking. Then, with a little thrill of triumph, she realised it was sight of her which had affected him. She held the cloak wide for him to see the black lace frock, and her bare arms against the silver lining.

"Do you like me?" she asked.

"You know I like you all right, Julia. . . ."

"I'd better turn out the light before we open the door again, or we shall be arrested for signalling to the enemy or something," Julia interrupted hurriedly. She had seen the flame that lit in his eyes, and she felt she didn't want him to speak, not yet, anyway. She clicked out the electric light, and put her hand out to the door-handle. The same moment she knew she had done a foolish thing. Herbert had caught her roughly, both arms about her, and was holding her hard against him. In the darkness his lips settled on hers. He kissed her long and hungrily till she felt she could hardly breathe, and began

141

to struggle. He still held her, she could make no impression against that solidity and strength. She hadn't minded it at first; it was pleasant to be kissed, even if it did not send through her body the thrills which she had known, but the feeling of choking terrified her. At last the grip of his arms slackened, and with a little sob Julia switched on the light. Herbert looked very ashamed, his face was red. Julia's composure grew as she noted the loss of his.

"A nice mess you've made of me," she observed coldly, and opening her evening bag, took out a little mirror and a pocket-comb. Herbert watched her dumbly while she put herself to rights.

"I didn't know I was dining out with someone from the Zoo," went on Julia, reddening her bruised lips with her lipstick.

"Julia . . . I don't know what came over me, I'm sure. . . ."

"Don't you? That's not very nice of you, Herbert." And she laughed up at him as she shut her bag.

"You mean you're not angry . . . ? Oh, Julia. . . ."

"I won't say I'm not angry; you'll have to behave yourself very well all the evening to make up. I'll have to risk the police and open the door with the light on. . . ."

And Julia threw the door open and then switched off the light. Herbert followed her out and closed the door behind him. The taxi was ticking away by the pavement, Julia stepped into it as calmly as though nothing had happened to disturb her. Still looking rather sheepish, Herbert ordered the man to drive to the Pall Mall Restaurant, and sat down in the taxi beside her. Julia smiled a little to herself in the darkness of the taxi. Thus should he see her home, but it would be Julia and not Herbert who set the pace.

The evening was a success. Ruby took Herbert for a very nice gentleman indeed, though the young "flying boy" stressed his "sirs" rather impudently when he spoke to him. Herbert knew how to order a dinner and how to treat a waiter. Julia had dined once or twice with temporary gentlemen, who thought it was the correct thing to bully the waiter, and Julia had hated them passionately. Herbert made no such mistake. He was, if anything, a little too cordial, but not slavish.

Ruby looked lovely, far lovelier than Julia, though not

142

with Julia's fine, pure beauty of bone in limbs and body. But Ruby's face was, so Julia always told herself enviously, a real face. It didn't vary from day to day and hour to hour as Julia's did. Julia watched Herbert a little anxiously . . . it seemed to her that any man must prefer Ruby to herself. But Herbert came as well out of the Ruby test as out of the waiter test.

He admired Ruby, that was evident, and Julia knew him well enough to know that he must be pleased and flattered at being seen out with an actress, but he didn't lose his head, or, for a moment, let Ruby absorb the chief place in his thoughts. That, all through the evening, was quite obviously held by Julia.

The play was very interesting, Julia thought, although Ruby criticised most of the performances.

"My dear, they could have got a laugh there. You agree, don't you, Mr. Starling? You see how easily one could have got a laugh? Why, if I'd been playing it, I'd have put in quite a different inflection," and Ruby imitated what Billie Carleton had just said upon the stage. "You see? If she'd said it that way, she'd have got a laugh."

Got a laugh . . . got a laugh. . . . How often had Julia heard it. It seemed to be the great ambition of actors and actresses to get a laugh, the other ambition was that nobody should steal your own particular laugh. How often she had heard Ruby say: "You see, dear, what a mean thing she does there? She won't wait for my laugh," or, "You see what he does? Goes right down centre, and with that bit of business steals my laugh. That was really *my* laugh there."

Julia sometimes thought that if Ruby had played Lady Macbeth, she would have tried to get a laugh. She might get a laugh, too, thought Julia grimly, but it wouldn't be the sort she wanted.

However, this evening, Julia rather agreed that Billie Carleton did nothing much save look pretty, but after all, there was Dennis Eadie, who had taken the place in Julia's heart held in her childhood by Lewis Waller. He played the lawyer's clerk—Alfie had been a lawyer's clerk—called George Smith, who fell in love with his employer's daughter and was sacked, but the war was the saving of him, for he got a commission in the Navy, and then, three years later, in command of a tramp steamer, he found his employer and daughter torpedoed, and saved them. Julia felt her heart beat harder and faster; and as always from her childhood when she was at the theatre for a few entranced hours, she passed into what seemed for the time being to be the real world.

When she had been a little girl of seven, Mr. Almond happened for the moment to be better off than usual, and he had taken her to the pantomime. It was *Little Red Riding Hood*. Julia had never forgotten the thrill of admiration that had passed through her when she had first seen the chorus of fairies, lovely creatures in pink tights and high-heeled slippers, glittering with spangles, with gauzy wings springing from their shoulders. Just at the moment when she was most entranced, leaning over the Upper Circle, Mr. Almond had remarked: "Pretty solid fairies," and for a queer moment two thoughts had existed side by side in Julia's brain. There was the Julia, there still was the Julia, who saw these lovely beings from another world, and believed in them without a doubt; and there was the other Julia, who suddenly, with a sense of shock amounting to horror, realised that these weren't fairies, that perhaps they weren't even beautiful, that they were creatures whom her father saw as solid young women. Young as she was, at that moment she had felt a resentment against him for destroying her illusion.

A few months later she was taken to see *Henry V*. The excitement she felt was far profounder than anything she had been aware of at the pantomime. The beauty of the words beat through her like a rhythmic pulse; she went nearly wild with excitement, and when Henry V had recited:

"*I see you stand like grehounds in the slips,*
Straining upon the start. The game's afoot;
Follow your spirit: and, upon this charge,
Cry—God for Harry! England! and Saint George!"

Julia had leaned forward wanting to cry out: "I'll go! I'll go!" . . . Only a tiny little thing at the back of her brain prevented her, a tiny little thing that said: "Although this is the loveliest and most exciting thing you have ever met, it isn't quite real. You'll make yourself noticeable if you call out, the grown-ups will be angry with you. This isn't real life." But for years there had persisted with Julia the memory of *Henry V*. It had, in a way, been more real to her than things like meals and washing-up and the quarrels of her parents, and the discussions as to what should be done for the best.

Now, of course, she was grown-up and critical, and yet always the glamour of the theatre captured her. Even the sense that Herbert was by her side; that he was an officer, and was standing dinner and the theatre to Ruby, who was a real actress, even the knowledge that Herbert desired her, and that his and her future were in her hands, ceased to exist for her as she watched the stage. She was Billie Carleton, or at least, she was half the part that Billie Carleton played, and the other half of her was Billie Carleton playing it.

Only after the play was over did Julia start to apply certain things in it to her own circumstances.

"A squirrel will not keep to the ground." That was a phrase used in the play, and Julia felt its truth. She wouldn't keep to the ground for ever, she was made for the tree-tops, as Smith for the freedom of the seas. No Uncle Georges should stand in her way. Oh, it was time she broke away from home, thought Julia, with a sudden definite conviction. How could she ever have any peace or freedom at Two Beresford? How could she ever become the self that she felt she had it in her to become?

She glanced up under her dark, straight lashes at Herbert Starling. He was gazing entranced at the stage, his lips were parted, and his solid pleasant face gave the curious effect of being open, like a window with a blind up to the top. As though he felt her eyes upon him, he looked down at her, his lips closed, but the shutter of caution which most people wear ordinarily over their eyes did not, for once, close down over his. For the first time they looked at Julia simply and frankly, and told a very simple story. He could never be again the man who had tried to persuade himself that he felt a paternal interest in the daughter of a friend, nor could he be the business man pretending that he wished to help an attractive girl to make the best of her career. He could not even be the widower who had joined up and was doing his best for his country, and liked taking a pretty girl out for the evening; he was just Herbert Starling looking at Julia Almond, and candidly admitting that he desired her. For the first time with him, Julia felt a flutter of that stirring she had known so well with Alfie, and she felt it merely at the meeting of their eyes.

Later when he was helping her on with her coat, and ran his hand down her bare arm as he did so, she felt no response at all, but her mind was still lit with excitement. She said good-bye to Ruby and the young man, and only protested feebly when Herbert said he was going to drive her all the way back in a taxi.

"It'll cost the earth," she protested.

"I don't care if it does," said Herbert. "You're worth the earth, aren't you?"

He chose the best taxi he could find, in which they started out together on the long drive to Heronscourt Park. Herbert, remembering the terrible thing he had done at the shop, remained seated firmly in his corner of the cab, with his hands locked between his knees. Julia yawned and murmured: "I'm sorry, but I'm so dreadfully sleepy."

"Poor little girl," said Herbert clumsily, but still attempted no further measure of comfort. Julia's eyelids dropped and closed, and a few moments later she had sagged gently towards him, and her head was resting against his arm. Herbert clenched his hands more firmly than ever. Julia stirred a little, half woke, stretched, and sleepily laid one bare arm across his knee. Gently Herbert's big fingers closed over it. Julia's fingers made no movement to withdraw, she just seemed to lean against him a little more heavily, and to go to sleep like a tired child. Stealthily Herbert's arm came round behind her, and then, as a jerk of the taxi threatened almost to dislodge her from her seat, gathered her more firmly to him. Julia slept peacefully. Herbert, his very forehead pink with emotion, continued to hold her. This was what he had missed by marrying, when he was still a boy, a girl several years older than himself, who was a minister's daughter. This was life, this warm, lovely, breathing thing he held in his arms. There'd be trouble with Bertha, of course, but that couldn't be helped, a man couldn't regulate his life by his sister's. She didn't like Julia . . . well, what plain, elderly woman would like Julia? It wasn't to be expected. Get a real good-looker and high-stepper like Ruby Safford, and she liked Julia all right; thought no end of her, anybody could see that. "A squirrel will not keep to the ground," the same phrase had struck the prosaic Herbert as the imaginative Julia. Well, this squirrel shouldn't be kept to the ground. He'd make a nest for her wherever it was that squirrels had their nests, high up in the trees. Not literally, of course, because there was the flat in Saint Clement's Square, and very good solid furniture he wouldn't dream of getting rid of, but she should re-decorate the place as she wished.

Through war-time London the taxi drove, and Julia slept, or so Herbert thought. As the taxi began the long run down Holland Park Avenue, for it had taken the road north of the Park, Julia stirred, awoke, yawned, stretched, and found herself in Herbert's arms. She tried to sit up, with a little apologetic laugh, but he held her firmly.

"No, you don't, my girl," he said, and stooping over her he picked her up, although she was no feather-weight, and held her on his knees.

"Give me my answer now, Julia. Will you marry me before I go out to France again? There's just time."

"Will I what? Oh . . . Herbert, put me down, suppose the taxi-driver looks round."

"Can't see if he does," said Herbert. "That's the best of London nowadays. I shan't put you down till you give me your answer."

Julia, lying across Herbert's solid thighs, with his solid arm holding her firmly against him, allowed herself the luxury of complete relaxation. How strong he seemed. . . . This would be the solution of all her troubles. She could get away from Two Beresford at last. She could go on working at the shop. Herbert would mostly be away at the war, and she would have that lovely flat in Saint Clement's Square, and Bobby to keep her company. What would it be like, though, to be married to Herbert? She supposed it would be as all right as being married to most people. Her body didn't thrill like a harp when he touched her, as it had thrilled to Alfie, but then he hadn't caressed her as Alfie had caressed her. Doubtless when you were married all that followed. Julia had not the slightest idea how personal and how much a matter of chance success in this thing could be. It had been so dreadful lately at Two Beresford; the horror of going home to share a room with Elsa quite prevented Julia from thinking that it might be even worse to share a

147

room with Herbert. After all, he was a man, and it was much more natural to share a room with a man than with someone of your own sex; besides, people like Marian didn't share a room, so why should she? She could start a new order of things at Saint Clement's Square; be the little queen of the flat, and Herbert should knock at her door when he wanted to come in. Besides, the war wasn't over yet. There was heaps of time to think of really settling down.

The taxi hesitated, and came to a stop. Julia slipped off Herbert's knee to the seat beside him. The driver leaned back and shouted: "Which turning did you say it was? I don't know the place."

Julia put her head out of the window. "The next to the left. Don't go all the way down. Just stop at the corner."

The taxi came to a stop again at the corner of Herons-court Place.

"Shall you keep him?" asked Julia, as she got out.

"No," said Herbert. "It's a fine night. It won't take me any time to walk down and across the High Road. Besides, I want to speak to you."

He paid the man and she noted he was lavish, as he had been with the waiters. That pleased her, and she didn't realise that it was Herbert, the officer in his uniform, who was being generous, not Herbert Starling, the ordinary business man.

The taxi drove off, and they started to walk down to Two Beresford, Herbert, with his big, careful hand taking a firm grip of her upper arm lest she should stumble. It was very dark, and the precaution was not unwarranted. As they reached the gate of Two Beresford and stood there for a moment, the great white pencil of a searchlight slowly swung its way across the night, making a pool of brightness against the surface of the sky. Julia followed it with her eyes. How lovely it was, in spite of the air-raids, which, as a matter of fact, she never minded. Searchlights always thrilled her, strange, bright enquirers into space, bringing the sky so much nearer by holding that pool of light pressed against it.

"A fine night for a raid," said Herbert. He glanced up at Two Beresford, which, of course, was shrouded in darkness, like all the other houses in London; no faintest thin thread of light showed down the edge of curtain or shutter at Two Beresford; the whole household was asleep, perhaps even Elsa.

"Julia," said Herbert thickly, "Julia, you know how I feel. You must answer me. I shall have to make arrangements. There's not much time. I'll be good to you, I swear I will," and again his arms went about her.

She peered at him through the darkness. It was good to be held like that, and her body began faintly to respond to his, as though from a long distance away. She felt very tired after the weeks of conflict with the Beales, and the worry over Bobby, and the nervous fret of always having Elsa in her room.

"I'm not in love with you, Herbert," she said.

"Have you ever been in love with anybody?"

"No," said Julia truthfully, and realising how hopeless it would be to try and explain the exact place of Alfie to Herbert.

"That's all right then. Why, you don't know you're born yet, my girl. It's yes, then?"

"Oh, I suppose so," said Julia, and this time she held up her face. Herbert kissed her differently, clumsily and gently, and she liked him better than she ever had before.

"We won't wait long," he murmured. "You're not set on marriage in church, are you, or anything like that?"

"I'm not, but Mum might be."

"Oh, that doesn't matter. When can I see you tomorrow?"

"I don't know. I can't tell you. We're dreadfully busy just now."

"Well, can't you lunch?"

"Oh no, I never can say about lunch. Sometimes we never get any."

"Well, I'll ring you up then."

"No, you mustn't do that. They don't really like me being rung up at the shop. Call for me after six, and I'll come away with you if I can. Don't come in. I'll look out of the window about six."

Herbert grumbled a little . . . keeping him hanging about all day, and then standing in the street like an errand-boy . . . but there it was, she would have her way.

She fitted her key into the front door, and there on the top of the Bridge of Sighs, Herbert kissed her again,

149

more greedily this time. Julia nodded at him, and pushed him gently back with her outspread fingers against his face. His breath felt hot against her palm. She shut the door between them, and went upstairs to find Bobby sunk in sleep on Elsa's bed.

There were, of course, things to be talked over, and Julia found herself as business-like as she was at the shop. She wouldn't, she said quite frankly, marry Herbert if Bertha were to live with them, neither would she—and here Herbert was terribly shocked—share a bedroom with him. She didn't tell him it was a room to herself that was beckoning her, particularly that lovely room in Saint Clement's Square, with the tall windows, cut into large square panes, and the window-boxes, and the view of the drooping trees and the broken statue of Apollo striking his dumb lyre in the midst of them.

"You can come and see me when you want to," said Julia firmly, "but I'm a very light sleeper"—this was totally untrue—"and men snore, at least Dad did, and I'm sure you do. After all, you slept in your present room all the last months you were. . . ." She stopped. She didn't like to say: "All the last months you were married to your wife."

Herbert looked down at her, his expression a mingling of indulgence and irritation. "Oh, well," he said, "I suppose you'll have to have it your own way."

In spite of Mrs. Almond's tearful objections, the marriage took place at the Registrar's, much to Julia's relief after she had read the wedding service. The things they wanted you to say. . . .

She felt funny enough the morning of her marriage as it was. She awoke in a state of panic, feeling that she couldn't go through with it. She sat up in bed and stared across her room at the saucy little face upon the pillow opposite, a face purged now of its impertinence by unconsciousness, the face of a child. Lucky Elsa, not having to be married this morning. . . . And yet, she supposed, lucky Julia, to be going to be married to what Dad had always called a good solid man, who loved her, and was taking her away from this dreadful Two Beresford; where Uncle George boomed, and Aunt Mildred organised everyone almost out of existence, and Elsa was always altering her performances and being a different sort of little girl, none of them real, and Mum was tearful and sycophantish by turns.

And as to marriage itself . . . well, Julia had picked up fragments of knowledge here and there, and had no reason to believe, taught as she had been by her own and Alfie's youth and ardour, that it would be anything dreadful. True, she hadn't had those exquisite and almost terrifying physical sensations she had had while yet a virgin with Alfie, but then there was no reason why she should have had; Herbert's hands had been respectful. Marriage would bring those. And she did want them; she admitted that to herself at last. She had wanted them, had ached for them, ever since Alfie had taught her. Only lack of any strong temptation, combined with hard work, and the interest and exhaustion of hard work, had kept her what was called "straight." Marriage would satisfy all that. It wasn't as though Herbert repulsed her in any way; he didn't. So when he started to make love to her, all would be well.

Julia was given a week's holiday for the honeymoon. Miss Lestrange and Mrs. Danvers had both been ever so nice about it, and had given her quite a little trousseau out of stock—a set of *crêpe de Chine* underclothes and a night-gown and a pink charmeuse wrapper and pink mules with ostrich-feathers curling all about them, that tickled her ankles but looked lovely. Her simple grey satin frock had been made in the workroom, and Mrs. Santley herself had made the little grey felt hat with the imitation ospreys curving like prawns round about it. The work-girls had given her a grey bag to match the get-up. Mum had given her her going-away coat, of squirrel-dyed coney, that looked almost like real. Mum had bought it out of Dad's insurance, and had explained between her tears that it made it seem partly like a present from Dad, too. Uncle George and Aunt Mildred, in their relief, had stumped up a good cheque—twenty-five pounds. Even Bertha, furious and full of forebodings, had at last been prevailed upon by Herbert to behave decently and give an electro-plate and glass epergne of great hideousness. Julia laughed to herself whenever she thought of the ejection of Bertha from Saint Clement's Square.

Julia bathed and dressed herself with care, adding the touch of rouge that made all the difference to her looks, which were those of gleam and glow, not the true beauty of bone that remains as a beautiful mask throughout life. Elsa watched her protestingly. Rouge! She was sure Mummy wouldn't like it, nor Auntie either. Julia laughed. What did she care? She felt better about the marriage now she was dressed.

Uncle George did things well, she had to hand him that. A car had been hired for the occasion, and he himself wore his best suit, with a white slip in his waistcoat. At the Registrar's, however, he was outshone by Herbert in uniform. Elsa carried a bouquet, a smaller replica of Julia's, and looked exceedingly pleased with herself, and pretty in her unexciting way, in the pale blue that Julia's education at l'Etrangère's had taught her to dislike, but which Aunt Mildred thought so sweet for a young girl. The Registrar's office was a bleak place, with walls painted dark brown below and a dingy cream above.

It was rather terrifying, the swiftness with which the ceremony was over, there seemed to be no one point at which she could have arrested it if she had suddenly been overtaken by panic. Almost before she knew it was over, the Registrar was shaking her by the hand and saying: "Allow me to wish you the best of luck, Mrs. Starling." Mrs. Starling! . . . that had been the thin, pale-faced woman with the pompadour of faded hair and the gold pince-nez. . . . It surely couldn't be Julia. . . . She looked down at the ring on her finger and up at the flushing face of Herbert. Mrs. Starling . . . no longer Julia Almond. It was as though, in some curious way, she had ceased to exist.

6

Marriage

JULIA sat 'in the train opposite Herbert, who had fallen asleep. As they were no longer starting for a honeymoon, but returning from one, Herbert hadn't tipped the guard so as to ensure privacy, and a fat, elderly gentleman, with respectable-looking side-whiskers, shared her compartment, rather to Julia's relief. The journey from Hampshire to London alone with Herbert would have seemed longer had they been alone together; people who had been on supposedly intimate terms for a week would have felt the necessity to try and make the time pass pleasantly. As it was, she could read *Home Chat* and *Home Notes,* and the rest of the ephemeral literature with which Herbert had provided her, without the uneasy consciousness that she ought to be paying attention to her husband.

Her husband. . . . That was funny, to look at Herbert and reflect that he was her husband. What did it mean exactly, this thing that had happened to her by means of the person called Herbert Starling? What did it all amount to? What was the sum of the past week?

It hadn't been wholly dullness, though she had often felt dull enough to scream. It certainly hadn't been pleasure, or even excitement. Not even peace, although she thought she might have expected peace in marrying a kind, well-to-do man like Herbert. He possessed the power, so she had thought, to solve all her problems for her. Now it seemed to her he had solved none, but only presented her with a different set. Was it possible that, to avoid sleeping with Elsa, she had agreed to sleep with Herbert? He swore he would stick by the pact they had made of separate bedrooms at Saint Clement's Square, but had jovially insisted that the honeymoon was different.

It had, indeed, been different. The only time she had felt at peace had been after lunch, when Herbert liked to have a little sleep, and she had been free to walk over the sand-dunes, past the little bungalows and along the edge of Poole Harbour.

Not that Herbert hadn't been kind. He had. But her body still felt battered as well as her soul. Apparently a man didn't necessarily give a woman the sensations she craved, although he attained them for himself. That pleasant, rather dull-looking man opposite, with that slight air of foolishness that everyone has who sleeps with his mouth slightly open, was the strange man with whom she had passed that first devastating night, who had assaulted her, apparently without any thought of her own sensations.

Julia glanced away from Herbert to the fat old gentleman with the side-whiskers who was reading the *Financial Times*. Had he, too, been a wild beast in his day, and mixed the whole thing up with a sort of sentimental possessiveness? She supposed so. One looked at people in buses and trains, when their bodies were quiescent and their minds somewhere else, in a book or a newspaper, or behind them at the place they had left, or before them at the place they were going to, and they seemed harmless enough, and so they were while you were looking at them—but what hadn't those apparently tranquil bodies harboured? Souls that had been jealous and angry and afraid and envious, even murderous, and the bodies themselves had been passionate, intemperate, greedy, agonised. People you saw in the buses and trains weren't really themselves at all, only the quiescent ghosts of what they had been, and what they might still be again.

Perhaps Alfie would have proved unsatisfactory. She

knew he would have been selfish, probably unfaithful. But she thought of his expert caressing hands, and of Herbert's uncompromising attack, and wished that she had known more about the art of love.

Oh well, it wasn't any good bothering now. Herbert would be leaving her to-morrow, anyway. She supposed she'd have to go through it again to-night, and then there'd be the peace and comfort of Saint Clement's Square. She'd be her own mistress in her own flat. She could take Bobby for a little walk, leave him with Emily the maid, who adored him, go back to l'Etrangère's, and take up her work as though it had never been interrupted. She would be Miss Almond again; how heavenly that would be.

Julia leaned back in her corner and opened *Home Notes*, studied the fashions, read the short story. There were a man and a girl in the story. They were in love . . . there were difficulties which came right in the end. Love . . . this sort of thing she read about. Did it exist? Ought she to have waited and given it another chance? After all, she'd always believed in it. She's read books about nothing else since she could remember anything. It was really Alfie who had spoiled her certainty, Alfie who had given her such divine sensations, but whom she knew she hadn't loved in the story-book acceptance of the term. Julia turned to the correspondence column. Someone called Daisy had written to ask "Isabel's" advice, and "Isabel" gave it to her with her usual sound measure of common sense.

"Ask him why he has suddenly become so casual in his manner when other people are present," wrote "Isabel." "Possibly someone has been making mischief. Whatever the trouble, there is no remedy as satisfactory as a good friendly talk, but be very careful not to let it degenerate into a 'scene.' "

Could she have a good, friendly talk with Herbert? Quite impossible. Herbert, except when he wished to ask for the fulfilment of certain simple needs, was very inarticulate. If Julia tried to explain herself to him, he would only laugh and pat her on the shoulder, and suggest a nice bit of dinner and bed. That had been Herbert's recipe for happiness all this week, varied by a nice bit of lunch and bed. She supposed she was lucky that he had consented to have the after-luncheon bed to himself.

Julia returned to *Home Notes.* Here was "Mopsa." "Isabel" advised her not to wait too long for marriage, but the winter was always an expensive time, and winter would soon be coming on, and, after all, fifty shillings a week wasn't much to marry on. What about just waiting for the spring, when "Mopsa's" boy might be making more? There were so many good jobs nowadays for men who were too delicate to get into the army, and what about "Mopsa" herself trying to make something, most girls worked nowadays, so that she could put a bit by to help furnish the nest?

If Julia had waited. . . . Well, she supposed she could have lived on thirty shillings a week, though how she would have arranged for Bobby she didn't know. Anyway, her nest was already furnished with the rather dreadful furniture that had been Herbert Starling's and Mrs. Starling's, but at least it was solid, and there was something in Julia that appreciated the solid things of life—security, mahogany, good insurance, a regular salary, an assured position. The other half of Julia wanted danger and excitement and romance.

Well, she reflected, gazing at Herbert as his own snoring woke him up with a sudden jerk, she was done with these last three things for ever, except, perhaps, the danger implicit in child-bearing, and Herbert had promised her that till the war was over this should not be hers. Besides, Julia had asked Anne how to prevent "anything happening," just in case Herbert was careless or deliberately dishonest. For some men, Julia knew, thought they had got hold of you for life if you had a baby.

"Judging from what you tell me," wrote "Mrs. Jim" of *Home Chat,* "I would say that you and this widower are particularly well-suited to each other, and stand every chance of happiness. If you are sure there is sufficient trust, respect and affection between you, why worry? As you were born in August, your lucky day is Sunday, your colours green, orange and brown, your stone the sardonyx, and your number thirty-four."

Well, she hadn't been born in August, her birthday was in July, and, anyway, she'd look awful in brown and orange, and what was a sardonyx? But otherwise it did seem to apply to her and Herbert. Only what exactly was trust, respect and affection? She supposed she was fond of Herbert, and he was greedy for her. Affection . . . that was something that grew; perhaps it would grow between them. Trust and respect. . . . Here she was more lost even than with affection. Herbert was a decent sort. He was honest about money. She knew they thought a great deal of him at his place of business. He had been kind and, Julia thought, probably faithful, to the dull, ailing Constance, so it was presumed he would be kind and faithful to her. But trust and respect. . . . Respect for what? Trust to do what? She didn't really know how Herbert would behave in any crisis, any more than Julia knew how she would behave.

She had to let Herbert sleep with her that night, but he sank to sleep at last, pleased with life. And to-morrow she would be Julia Almond again.

7

End of an Era

It was very pleasant being Julia Almond during the weeks that followed. Herbert was away. Bertha had retired to the dry bosom of that family where she had been a "P.G." until her brother had become a widower, and Julia lived through what were, perhaps, the happiest weeks of her life. She had Bobby, she had a maid, she was busy and appreciated at the shop, and on Sundays she could either go to Two Beresford in the character of a prosperous young bride, or Two Beresford could come to her with obvious envy in its eyes. And there were even better things. There were evenings spent talking with Dr. Ackroyd and Anne, evenings when again Julia caught glimpses of those unattainable ideals which she had first realised at the Polytechnic, and which still had the power to stimulate her.

Sometimes she and Anne would go to the pit of a theatre, and then Julia tasted again of the romantic life which, whenever she met it, absorbed her utterly.

Julia's life, through those last months of the war, seemed to her exquisitely arranged. She had given up any notion of the war ever coming to an end. Like most other people, she seemed to be suspended in a space where time was not. Nobody thought in terms of time any longer. This was life as they had always known it. It seemed to be life as it always would be. Marian, Gipsy, Mrs. Santley, the work-girls, the wholesale people, the travellers, the customers, Darlings and otherwise, Ruby and Ruby's affairs, Mum, Uncle George, Aunt Mildred and Elsa, Dr. Ackroyd and Anne, and Herbert, in so far as she was aware of him in his chatty and rather dull letters, made up the personal element of her life.

Not a very exciting life, perhaps, for a young woman of twenty, but marriage had not taken away from Julia that sub-conscious hope of a glory yet to come. She didn't put it to herself in plain terms, she didn't say: After all, I may still fall in love, everything may change. She was simply content to go on as she was because, far ahead, perhaps, or perhaps only round the next corner, something lovely was waiting to happen. A letter might come, the telephone might ring, there were infinite potentialities in these two mundane happenings. In spite of the feeling that she had arranged her life, there still remained the possibility of something exciting, though quite what it might be, she didn't envisage.

For the first time in her life her surroundings didn't jar on her. . . . She heard no quarrelling, no utterances of discontent. The autumn evenings when she came back to the yellowing leaves and the mute Apollo pleased her senses, the mellow light that filled the Square, the evenings at the theatre with Anne, filled her imagination with the same glow. During the day-time, the hard work and successful deals done at business, stimulated and excited her. Her body, under the impression that, after all, there was very little in this business of making love, left her alone, her mind was fully occupied, and her imagination was free to project itself into those fields peopled by the characters that walked upon the stage or across the pages of novels. She was content.

"The Armistice is going to be signed to-morrow," said Marian one day, just as Julia was hanging up some models which a traveller had just brought in.

Julia stood, the frock in one hand and the hanger in the other, wondering whether she had heard aright.

"That's what I was told," answered Gipsy soberly. "Is it really true?"

"Oh yes. They're expected to sign it some time tomorrow. It'll be funny, won't it, Gipsy?"

"Yes," said Gipsy, after a moment's pause. "It'll be funny."

Yes, thought Julia, fitting the frock to its hanger, and hooking the whole thing into place on the rod, it would be funny. What would it be like? She didn't know, nobody knew. It would be wonderful, of course, people would leave off killing each other, the train-loads of wounded would cease, the terrible lists in the papers, the orders for mourning. Everything would be lovely, the war was won. Would it be lovely? Julia tried to remember what it had been like before the war. What she could remember didn't help her. She had been too young and life had been too different. Why, there'd still be hansoms in London, although, of course, even then there had been far more taxis. Still, hansoms hadn't been museum pieces as they were now. Frocks were ever so much shorter now, and everybody spent heaps of money, and people went everywhere by car, and nobody thought flying anything out of the ordinary. Little shops like l'Etrangère's, instead of being rarities, were springing up all over the West End. Money, that was the thing that you always came back to. Everybody spent money in a way that only four and a half years ago would have seemed incredible.

Why, Herbert would come back. Julia's heart seemed to miss a beat as she picked up the next frock. Herbert would come back and he wouldn't any longer be an officer. He'd just be Herbert Starling, as she had known him originally, only older, balder, fatter, duller. The Herbert Starling she had married, in the polished field-boots, the Herbert Starling who tipped waiters so munificently, and took her everywhere in a taxi, would become again the Herbert Starling in plain dark clothes, who went to the City every day. He'd be a tradesman once more. And Herbert wasn't a tradesman as she was a shop-girl. It didn't matter in the least selling women's clothes in a little shop such as l'Etrangère's, you could be anybody's friend, and still do that, but you couldn't be a manager in a branch of gentlemen's outfitter's and be an officer and a gentleman.

Frantically, Julia tried to search in her memory for the Herbert Starling she had first known, and could only find him in glimpses that made him all the more terrifying. She had not thought him wonderful even then, though, of course, he had been streets ahead of Dad; but he hadn't been the Herbert Starling she had married. He hadn't belonged in the world as she knew it now, as she had known it ever since the war began, which, after all, was the only world she knew. What had all the years of her drifting childhood meant until that time? Nothing, except a confused movement from place to place, a confused sense of unreality and change, in matters of money, even, and food and clothing. Life had begun for Julia with the war. She knew nothing else, and its upheaval of values had been to her simply a normal progression.

She bought an evening paper on her way home, which told her nothing as definite as the few sentences she had heard interchanged between Marian and Gipsy.

That evening she went to bed early, with the idea persisting in the back of her mind that if she didn't think about the news, perhaps there wouldn't be so much truth in it, that if she slept through the hours, she was bound to awake to the world as she had known it.

She went to the shop as usual next morning. There was nothing out of the ordinary about the streets. People weren't standing talking in groups, as they had done at the outbreak of war. If peace were going to be declared to-day, it was a secret that had been well kept from the common people.

The charwoman, who arrived a few minutes after Julia, snorted at the mere notion of peace and, plunging her rag into the bucket of water, slapped it down briskly on the linoleum of the passage.

"Ho," she said, "I'll believe it when I see it. Peace, indeed! They've kept on telling us about it, and when 'ave we 'ad it?" And she started to swirl her cleaning-rag round and round vigorously.

But at half-past nine Gipsy arrived, her face flushed, her eyes bright and, Julia thought, suspiciously moist, as though tears were very near.

"Julia, it's true. It's peace. Eleven o'clock this morning. It's all arranged."

Gipsy didn't wait to see the result of her news. She threw off her hat and coat and went out to stand at the street door. The feeling of news was already in the air.

At the shop-fronts the cleaners had stopped their work. The postman was standing at the street corner; loafers had sprung up as though from the ground. At the hat-shop at the corner all the girls were crowded together at the windows looking out. At a house a few doors down, which was let out in service flats, the housekeeper was at the door, her wispy grey hair untidily bundled up, her plump, inquisitive face moving quickly from side to side.

"It's peace," Gipsy called out to her. "It's being signed this morning."

"Oh," said the housekeeper. She didn't seem to think it very wonderful or interesting news, she seemed rather embarrassed by Gipsy's enthusiasm. Gipsy turned and came back into the shop.

"I don't suppose we'll sell much to-day," she said, "but you never know. Anything may happen."

She and Julia busied themselves arranging the window and seeing to the stock generally. Marian didn't turn up.

Suddenly there came a clashing sound, and the air became full of bells. Like birds, the beat of the bells flew about London. Man was giving tongue through his creations.

Gipsy turned, and going into the back of the shop, drew the curtains together with a rattle of rings along the pole. Julia didn't look through. She knew that she would see Gipsy with her dark head upon her plump arms, sitting at the painted desk, as she had sat over four years ago. There were thousands of women like Gipsy in England and France, in Belgium and Italy, and America and Germany, in little European countries and great dominions overseas. Probably, thought Julia, even in Turkey and those funny places, if one only knew, all saying to themselves, Why couldn't this happen earlier? Why did *he* have to go first? Gipsy wouldn't grudge any other woman the salvation of her husband or son, but she would be unable to avoid the bitter reflection, and she would be unable to avoid, too, the thought that Marian must be wishing it had been Billy Embury who had died; whereas Billy was alive, and well, and coming home to go through the farce of a divorce, while John Danvers's bones still lay on the bed of the Channel, his flesh eaten away long ago, his soul no one knew where. And Alfie? Julia hadn't thought of him for ages now. Where were those scattered bones? One with the earth upon which the life had been stricken out of them; and his soul, if such things there were, where was it? Who could say? Alfie had had such very little soul, even in life. He had been so graceful, so woodland, so beautifully animal. And Herbert? He was sitting somewhere in his office, wondering how soon he would be free to get back to Saint Clement's Square and his wife.

And the bells went on clanging and beating, and suddenly the telephone-bell went. Gipsy lifted her head from her arms, picked up the receiver and said "Hello" in a curiously dead, flat voice.

"Oh, all right," Julia heard her say. "Yes, I think that'll be best. Obviously there's nothing doing. Right. Goodbye." And the receiver was clicked back into place.

"That was Miss Lestrange," Gipsy told Julia. "She says we'd better shut up the shop. There'll be nothing doing to-day. Tell the girls, will you?"

Julia sped upstairs and told the rest of the staff, who were already wriggling into their hats and coats. When she came down again it was to find Ruby had flowed into the shop like a golden tide.

"Isn't it wonderful," she said, "isn't it just too wonderful? After all we've suffered all these years! I've got a table at the Carlton Grill. As a matter of fact, I was told about this yesterday, so I rang up Ventura and told him to engage me a table. Mrs. Danvers, you'll come, won't you?"

Gipsy, busy pulling her hat over her eyes, shook her head. "No, Miss Safford, though it's very kind of you. They'll be expecting me at home."

"You'll come, won't you, Julia?" said Ruby, hardly noticing Gipsy's refusal, which she had expected. "You must come. We can easily squeeze in one or two more. Jimmy's coming to the party, you know—Lord James Heighton?"

Julia did, indeed, know . . . Jimmy had been in Ruby's dressing-room every night for weeks.

"I'd love to come," she said; "they won't be expecting me at home. In fact, there isn't anybody who could expect me, only Bobby, and he won't know anything about peace having been signed."

Ruby had a taxi waiting for her. Already the streets were crowded with frantic, singing, shouting throngs. Ruby said: "The Carlton Grill," and they started off.

They soon got caught in a block. Two young men leaped up on the step of their taxi and started blowing horns and waving their hats. A middle-aged woman, looking very frightened, was borne up to the taxi by a sudden surge of the crowd. Julia opened the door and called out: "Which way are you going? Can we take you anywhere?"

"Charing Cross," said the woman.

"Well, we're going to the Carlton Grill. We can take you quite near. Jump in."

The woman got in thankfully, and sat down on one of the little seats. She was a quiet, reserved person, dressed in very good taste, though rather shabbily. Ruby turned a glowing face towards her. "Isn't it wonderful?" she said. "Listen, it's all London speaking. It's London's heart beating. It's the Empire's heart beating. Did you ever hear anything so marvellous?"

The lady gave her a little, pale smile. "Yes," she said, "it's marvellous. I'm very thankful it's happened. I wish it could have happened before."

"Oh, so do I," said Ruby, with sincere enthusiasm, and with a note in her voice which implied that she had lost everyone near and dear to her. "What we've all had to go through. Have you anyone out there?"

"My husband was killed at Gallipoli," said the lady quietly.

Ruby said nothing, but Julia said: "My husband's in France," and almost believed for a moment that Herbert was in danger at his rail-head.

The taxi moved on, and they all three sat enclosed in the little artificial intimacy that it made, Julia wondering about the stranger, and aware, without consciously thinking of it, how warm-hearted and unconventional she had been in opening the door to an unknown woman; and Ruby thinking of the forthcoming meeting with Jimmy, and how wonderful it was to be alive in such a wonderful world and to be Ruby Safford. The strange lady was thinking of Gallipoli, and hoped that nothing had happened to Julia's husband in the last few hours of the war, when it seemed so wicked and ironical for anything to happen to anyone.

The taxi drew up at the Carlton Grill. Ruby paid the fare, and pressed an extra ten shillings upon the driver, who said: "God bless you, lidy, I'll drink death and damnation to the Kaiser with this," and Ruby waved her hand to him and laughed, and started to go down the stairs to the Grill Room.

Julia turned to say good-bye to the strange lady, but she had already gone. Julia could see her neat, self-contained back, and her high-held head, disappearing down the Haymarket.

That was a marvellous lunch. The Carlton Grill was crowded to overflowing, total strangers called out to each other from table to table. Ruby was asked by Ventura to make a speech. She stood up, and lifting her champagne glass, cried: "Here's to us. Who's like us? Damned few!" and everyone drank the toast with roars of applause.

The rest of the day was like a kaleidoscope that Julia had had in her childhood, masses of sparkling, bright, moving colours, that changed and shifted and fell into different positions. As the hours went by it became impossible to move about London. She and Ruby and Jimmy, and another young man called Tommy, who apparently was a friend of Jimmy's, whom they ran into in the course of the afternoon, managed to get something to eat at a restaurant in Baker Street, where they had finally struck in their attempt to get back to Ruby's flat.

Julia enjoyed that dinner. The confusion was indescribable. Signor Canuto was rushing hither and thither, and had far more clients than could be waited on, and Julia sprang up, and herself found the table where the dishes were deposited, and Jimmy and Tommy, obeying her orders, managed to collect their whole dinner while it was still hot and excellent. That was fun; Julia liked arranging things, and being a success, and the two young men enjoyed doing what she told them. Ruby seemed quite to sink into the background.

Then Jimmy (or Tommy) succeeded in getting a taxi and guarded it, while Ruby and Julia were hustled in, and they all went round to the theatre. Every seat was sold out, and Julia sat on the stairs of the dress circle and watched the play, in which Ruby was playing lead —a successful little comedy of war manners.

Afterwards Julia went round behind, and they all drank champagne in Ruby's dressing-room, she still dressed as a land-girl and with the make-up on her face.

Finally Tommy announced that he must see Julia home. It wasn't safe for a girl to go through such crowds alone, and see her home he did. They fought their way somehow through the yelling, dancing crowds to Charing Cross Station, where Julia would have been swept right down the stairs had it not been for Tommy's arm round her. Out at Hammersmith the world was still boiling and seething like a stew in a pot, but it was comparatively quiet once Stamford Brook Station was reached. But even in the sacred garden of Saint Clement's Square a bonfire had been lit. It was blazing all about the Apollo; he drooped, cynical and unmoved, amidst the leaping flames, an ancient unknown god martyred by exultant Christians. Against the firelight the children of the neighbourhood looked like little black imps. The world had gone mad to celebrate the fact that the world had ceased to be mad.

"Won't you come up and have a drink?" asked Julia, as she fitted her key into the lock.

"I don't mind if I do," said Tommy. "All that champagne makes a fellow beastly dry. It's a horrible drink. I can't think why women like it. Have you got any beer?"

"Plenty," said Julia gaily.

She opened the door of the dining-room, where Bobby always awaited her arrival, and was met by the usual chestnut-and-white whirlwind. Tommy approved highly of Bobby, and said he was a splendid fellow, what? and he had had a dog just like him, picked up in the trenches, but a beastly shell got him.

Tommy was not a very intelligent young man, but he was a very pleasant one, and he was a gentleman. He shook Julia's hand cordially when he said good-bye, and went whistling down the stairs. Julia felt a little disappointed. Why couldn't it have been a marvellous romantic young man who had seen her home on the night of all nights, not just a pleasant young creature who, but for the war, might still have been a public schoolboy? Could it be that she wasn't attractive any longer? She studied herself in the glass. No, she didn't have to worry about that, and, after all, nobody is attractive to everybody. Tommy had just been one of those few men who said nothing to Julia, and to whom she said nothing. But she was very tired. Too tired to think about the world, or Herbert, or herself, or the shop.

She felt dirty after so much contact with sweaty bodies pressing her all around, and so, exhausted as she was, she lit the geyser and ran a hot bath. She emptied half a bottle of bath-salts into it, and lay back cosily in the warm water. Vaguely there came to her the sounds of shouting and cheering. She lay thinking about nothing, neither happy nor unhappy, merely utterly relaxed.

BOOK TWO

"They order, said I, this matter better in France——"
A Sentimental Journey,
by Laurence Sterne.

Beginning of an Era

THE ragged ends of the war took a long time to tidy up, and at first nothing seemed to be very much changed, except that people were happier. Trade continued to increase and people danced more than ever. Even the soldiers didn't all come pouring back home as Julia had expected, and it was Christmas before Herbert arrived back at Saint Clement's Square.

His job had been kept open for him, and he went back with great relief to being manager of the Strand branch of Dick Dash's. He had enjoyed swanking round London in his field-boots and breeches all right, but it had been an interruption to serious business, and the rest of his life stretched pleasantly before him—a rise in salary soon at Dick Dash's, for, with the expenses of living going up like this, he'd no longer be comfortably off on five hundred a year. Of course, Julia was earning, but he wanted Julia to give up the shop. He wasn't, he told himself, the sort of man whose wife had to work.

The very day he came back, Julia wasn't there to receive him. She had been kept at the shop, and Herbert sat at a substantial tea with a sense of injury. Still, she'd made the flat look very nice. There were big clusters of chrysanthemums in the sitting-room—a pretty penny they must have cost, he thought—and Emily, the maid, and Bobby, both seemed pleased to see him. Emily had always liked him. She was the old-fashioned sort who preferred to wait on a man than on a woman, and he had been rather nervous lest Julia shouldn't hit it off with her, but everything seemed to be all right. Julia was a clever kid, you had to give her that. Just at the moment, until he could see how things were going to shape in the business world, it might be as well to let her have her head and go on playing at being a shopkeeper. After all, it meant that she was really no expense to him at all. She dressed herself, got her clothes much more cheaply through the shop than she could have done otherwise, paid for her own midday meal and her tea, and could do her share towards paying for amusements. All that was worth considering. Still, it would have been nice to have seen her glowing face and have been able to put his arms round her and give her a good kiss.

Herbert went up to the top floor of the flat when he had finished his tea, lugging his heavy kit-bag with him. He put it down on the top landing, and sat for a moment looking about him, then he opened the door of the front room, Julia's room, and went in. It was quite dark and he switched on the light. The curtains were not drawn, and outside the night suddenly turned a deep, soft blue. Herbert stood looking about him. The furniture was just the same as it had been in poor Constance's day, but how different Julia had made it all look. . . . There were more chrysanthemums on the dressing-table, and the curtains were a shiny chintz, covered all over with Chinese pagodas, and funny little men, and humped bridges and flowers. Curious things, he thought, all green and bright red on a shiny white ground. The legs of the dressing-table were covered with skirts of the same stuff, and the old grey carpet had been dyed vermilion. The greatest change was in the bed. Herbert stood staring at it suspiciously. He had always liked that bed, it had looked so cheerful with its round, shiny, brass knobs that winked in the light. Now Julia had covered both ends of it with the same material as the curtains; pretty cleverly too, he had to admit, quite a tailor-made sort of job, fitting very neatly and bound with green, so that the ends of the bed looked more like painted wood than

172

anything else, with all those little trees and Chinamen and pagodas and God knows what, upon the stiff, stretched, shiny white background. The coverlet was vermilion, and a panel of the chintz; a whole little pagoda, with a Chinaman sitting beneath it, and a tree bending over it, had been cut out and appliquéd just where the coverlet rose up over the single pillow.

Yes, it was a single pillow. Herbert stretched forward and turned the coverlet down. Well, he wasn't going to keep up that nonsense about sleeping in the other room. He'd bring his pillow in now, and he went firmly into the other room. That was just as he had known it, and he couldn't tell whether he was disappointed or relieved. She might, he thought, have put herself out a bit for him. On the other hand, he certainly did like things as they had always been. The single bedstead twinkled at him brassily, the coverlet was a clean white honeycomb one, the curtains were the dark red curtains that used to be in the front bedroom, cut down to fit this window.

Herbert went up to the bed, lugged out the pillow, moved Julia's pillow to one side of the double bed and planted his firmly beside it. There, he reflected with a grim humour, she can have all the damned Chinamen sitting in pagodas that she likes, but she'll damn well have to have me along with them.

He looked at the wrist-watch that he had worn since he became an officer and a gentleman. Nearly seven o'clock. Surely she must be in any minute now? Should he have a bath? He had been travelling all day from that beastly rail-head. Or should he wait and have one before he went to bed? Better have it now. He had found out during their honeymoon that Julia was funny about those things, and was horrified that he just shaved and washed his neck and hands in the morning.

He went into the bathroom. That looked different too. There was a jar of bath-salts on a glass shelf that had been put up behind the bath. Herbert hesitated, then could not resist the temptation to take a handful and throw them into the hot water. He sniffed critically. Pleasant, he couldn't deny it, but he'd smell like a tart if he got into that. However, he did get into it, and found that the smell soon wore off. He scrubbed himself well, reflecting that that would do for two or three days anyway, whatever Julia might say, and then dressed himself in a pre-war suit of dark blue, which, he was pleased to see, was a couple of inches too big round the waist.

He was downstairs in the sitting-room again, and was having time to wonder rather discontentedly why Julia had hidden all his family photographs, good silver frames and all, when he heard her key in the lock. Bobby had already recognised her step in the Square, and was standing against the front door of the flat, his chocolate nose pressed against it, trembling with excitement.

Julia's greeting to Herbert got rather mixed up with her greeting to Bobby, who would talk and jump up at her, and Herbert felt the moment had come to assert himself. He pushed Bobby out of the way and took Julia firmly in his arms.

"Well, now, let's have a look at you, my girl. You're a nice one to be so late when you knew I was coming back."

He tilted her face up under the white glare of the bell-shaped electric light in the little hall. Julia was very pale, and there were dark shadows under her eyes.

"I'm sorry, Herbert, but we're having such an awful rush. People will come in and buy things at the last minute at Christmas time. We've got a special line of novelties over from Paris as Christmas presents, and I couldn't get away."

"Well, you'll get away to-morrow all right, or I'll come and fetch you. I'm novelty enough for you this Christmas."

"Emily got you your tea all right, didn't she?" asked Julia, disengaging herself and pulling off her hat wearily.

"Oh yes, and I've had a bath because I guessed that would be the first thing you would ask me. Put some of those scented things of yours into it, just to see what they were like."

"I must go and wash," said Julia. "I'll tell Emily supper for half-past seven—liver and bacon, because I remembered you liked it. I won't be long. I'll tell her to put it on now," and Julia escaped from his arms and ran upstairs.

She washed quickly, and changed into a little black frock with a lacquer-red belt, and slipped a long string of red beads round her neck. She leaned forward and stared at herself in the glass on the dressing-table. She was looking rotten. She quickly made up her face, and combed out the shining wing of her hair across her forehead. That was a bit better. Her short-sighted eyes didn't observe the bigger lump the two pillows made at the end of the bed.

"Come on, my girl," roared the voice of Herbert from below, "supper's in and I shall have eaten it all if you don't hurry up."

"You can," said Julia, languidly, as she came downstairs. "I'm much too tired to eat."

However, she forced herself to be cheerful, as she felt it was rather a shame that poor old Herbert should come home and find her so unresponsive. The fact of the matter was she was not feeling tired, so much as spiritually exhausted. Ever since Herbert had written to her saying he would be back in a week's time, she had been trying to face the thought of a life spent with Herbert as its central figure. That morning when his wire had arrived, she had felt quite sick and faint for a few minutes. It was absurd, she told herself angrily. After all, she knew Herbert. She had managed to get through the honeymoon, and that last time hadn't been so bad. She'd be away all day, there'd only be the week-ends to get through somehow. Yes, but how? She'd be happy enough with a book, just resting and reading, but Herbert didn't read. He didn't even converse, as Julia by now understood the term. She had been happy these last few months alone in Saint Clement's Square. She loved her new surroundings, she loved the sanctuary that the whole quiet place had been to her. She had loved being mistress of the little establishment, and sometimes having Dr. Ackroyd and Anne in for coffee. She had liked being a refuge to poor little Mrs. Almond, who would blow in like a leaf, and subside with a faint rustling sound in a corner of the room, when she could get away from Uncle George and Aunt Mildred. She had even loved pouring out tea for the Beale family in this spacious room that belonged to an older age, where she was the mistress, and where the Beales had to behave themselves.

Now all this was to be invaded by Herbert, rather as a quiet flowery meadow might be invaded by a bull, and yet she couldn't have had it without Herbert. She must be grateful to him for that.

Julia sat and watched him enjoying his liver and bacon, and had a curious little feeling that she must be dreaming, that she couldn't be going to live here with that strange man. He didn't seem somehow the same Herbert Starling who had given dinner to her and Ruby and the young flying man at the "Pall Mall," who had tipped the waiters, and taken them all to the theatre. "A squirrel cannot keep to the ground." Well, Herbert would keep to the ground all right, there wasn't any doubt about that. You might as soon expect him to alter as to expect him to leave this warm room and go out into the cold, blustery Square and start climbing one of the trees that swayed in the wind. Julia couldn't help laughing a little to herself at the mental picture of Herbert perched on the topmost bough for the night.

Herbert leaned back in his chair and wiped his mouth with a deep sigh of content.

"Pretty good, that," he said, "only you might tell her to cut the bacon a bit thicker. It's all fried to nothing. Where do you get it?"

"Palmer's Stores. I have it cut on number three on the machine on purpose. I can't bear it unless it's crisp like that. I'll have mine cut on number three, and yours cut thicker."

"That's a good girl," he approved; "where's the whisky?"

Julia got up and fetched it, and put it beside him with a syphon. He helped himself lavishly and took a long drink.

"You look as though you wouldn't be the worse for a drink of this," he said kindly. "Here, give me your glass."

He was right. Julia did feel better after she had drunk half a tumbler of the fairly stiff whisky and soda he mixed her.

After supper had been cleared away Herbert sat down in the best and biggest arm-chair, and stretched his legs out to the gas-fire. That had been Julia's chair until now, but she saw him take it without any resentment. She had been brought up to expect, as a matter of course, that the best chair was for the man of the house, but she made a vow to make him get another one equally comfortable as soon as she could.

Emily appeared at the door and announced that she had come for Bobby. Emily was devoted to him, and whatever the weather, always took him out for his little run, a fact for which Julia was very grateful, for she was often so tired herself that she hardly knew how she could have faced the stairs down to the front door and back. Bobby, always pleased at any suggestion, bounded off with Emily.

Herbert emptied his glass of whisky and soda, drew his feet in from the gas-fire and sat forward, knees apart, and hands clasped between them. He looked at Julia with little eyes that were rather like Bertha's, set flush with his face like chips of steel, but more kindly than his sister's could ever be.

"She won't be long," he said. "Ready for bed, my girl? Drink up the rest of that whisky and soda, it won't hurt you."

Julia picked the glass up and began to drink. As the fluid became less she found she was staring at Herbert through the bottom of the tumbler. Like all short-sighted and astigmatic people, she could see better even when looking through the bottom of a tumbler, or between two finger-tips held close together against her eyes, or between the chinks in the brim of a coarsely-woven straw-hat, than she could without anything to narrow down and focus the field of her vision. Now she stared at Herbert and saw him distorted through the curved glass at the bottom of the tumbler, but much more clearly and sharply than she could have if she had been look-ing at him in the ordinary manner. There was a little flaw in the bottom of the glass, and she sipped very slowly so as to be able to see his face as it changed, as the flaw caught it now at one place, now at another. Quite suddenly the whole of his lower jaw would swell out till his face looked like that of a hippopotamus, a tiny tilt of the tumbler, and he would have practically no jaw at all, only a thin little slit of a mouth, and a bulbous forehead. Another little swing and he would have eyes set up under his hair, a long thin nose, a long upper lip and practically nothing below it.

What with being very tired, not having eaten much, and having taken a strong whisky and soda, and also being very nervous about Herbert's reappearance at Saint Clement's Square, Julia began to giggle a little. There was Herbert's face, as she put down the tumbler, just as she had always known it, pink, healthy, clean-

177

shaven, obstinate, kindly, and oddly blank; but she had only to put up the tumbler and this amazing fantasy of faces, of which each was Herbert's face, was hers for the asking.

Herbert looked sharply across at her and sat up.

"What are you smiling at?" he asked. "Pleased to have the old man back, after all; is that it, Julia?"

"Yes, I suppose so," said Julia lightly, standing up and stretching to show how tired she was. "You're not such a bad old thing, Herbert."

"I should say I'm not," he agreed; "it's not such a bad little home either, is it, or such a bad girl to come back to?" And without warning, his big arms closed about her.

Julia let herself go limp within them, she merely yawned in his face and said:

"Oh, Herbert, I'm so dreadfully sleepy."

"Ready for bed then," said Herbert. "Up you go."

Julia went up to the bathroom, and through the noise she made cleaning her teeth, she heard the bang of the street door as Emily and Bobby returned, and the low sound of conversation. She creamed her face, wiped the cream off, and then, instead of, as usual, going straight to bed, lightly-powdered her face again. After all, if you *were* married, you couldn't go to bed all shiny.

She went into her bedroom and looked round for Bobby, but he was not there. She called downstairs to Emily, whose room was between the kitchen and the sitting-room, below Herbert's dressing-room. "Emily, Emily, where's Bobby? Send him up, will you?"

Emily's own door opened, and she began to speak, but was interrupted by Bobby himself, who, escaping from her hold on his collar, came flying up the stairs. Herbert, who was in the sitting-room, must have heard all this, for he came out, slammed the sitting-room door, and said to Emily, who seemed uncertain what to do for the best—"Oh, that'll be all right," and came up the stairs, turning out the light on the downstairs landing as he came. He came into Julia's bedroom and shut the door.

"We can't have Bobby sleeping with us," he said, "it's not healthy."

"With us?" Julia stared at him, and something in his

178

gaze made her turn and look at the bed, and for the first time she saw the two pillows.

"Oh, Herbert, I can't have you here all night. I'm much too tired; beside, you know what you promised me."

"That! Oh, rats! I'd have promised you anything. This is different. I'm home now. Home for good."

"But you promised," said Julia, "you promised. You know you did."

"I tell you that doesn't matter," said Herbert, getting suddenly angry; "this is my house, isn't it? I'm not going to sleep in a beastly back bedroom, and besides, we're married, aren't we? I tell you what, Bobby shall sleep in my room if you like, if you don't like him to be downstairs, though I don't approve of it, but there it is, you can't say I'm unreasonable." And, seizing the surprised Bobby by his collar, he pulled him along into the back bedroom. Bobby set his four white paws against the floor, his collar rumpled his skin in a chestnut roll round his surprised face as he turned a protesting, yellow eye back at Julia. But Julia wasn't noticing what happened to Bobby, she was gazing at her bed. She had known that Herbert would make love to her that night, she was prepared for that, she wasn't unreasonable; but he had promised always to go away afterwards. She had looked forward to being able to forget all about it, to lie along in the bed that would once again be hers, in the room that would once again be hers, as she had always thought of it. She had never worried about poor Constance, she had never cared enough about Herbert to suffer any retrospective jealousy on that account.

She heard Herbert walking about in his bedroom, heard him going into the bathroom, heard him come out again. When he opened the door of her room without knocking, and came in and shut it behind him, she was still standing where he had left her.

"Not in bed yet?" he said cheerfully.

"Herbert, I don't want to send you away, it isn't that, but I can't sleep with you all night. I'm too tired. I do want to be alone. You do understand, don't you?"

"No, I'm damned if I do," said Herbert, and his face altered, thickened and swelled somehow, as it had when she looked at it through the flaw in the bottom of the glass. "Come on, Julia."

Julia got into bed. It wasn't this she minded; even if

179

she didn't love Herbert, at least she didn't love anyone else, and he was clean, and smelled of soap, and he wanted her, although he didn't know how to make her want him. It wasn't this, it was afterwards; and, long after Herbert had fallen asleep and—true to her fears, was snoring lightly—Julia lay awake, loathing him for his sleeping person, as she hadn't loathed him while he held her in his arms.

At about three in the morning a solution of the problem came to her. She slipped out of bed very cautiously without awakening him, and out of the room, opening and shutting the door with infinite caution, carrying her pillow with her. When the astounded Emily called them with tea in the morning, she found Herbert, pink and snoring, alone in the double-bedroom, and Julia sleeping heavily in the back bedroom, Bobby across her feet.

"Of course," said Julia desperately, across the breakfast-table to Herbert, "I knew there'd be a row. You can't say I didn't warn you. If you want to stay with me you shouldn't snore."

"You're my wife, aren't you?" was all Herbert could think of, as he contemptuously tried to gather together on his fork the thin, brittle curls of bacon cut on number three.

"Yes, I'm your wife," said Julia, "but I'm not deaf, and I'm not a peasant woman who can sleep through anything, and I'm not a street-walker to be paid to sleep with you."

Herbert blushed with genuine, offended modesty. He was not used to the conversation that was a commonplace among the Darlings.

"If you don't let me alone to go to sleep," said Julia —"and when I say 'sleep' I don't mean anything else— then I'll have to go away and leave you."

"Now you're talking tripe," said Herbert, "you can't go away and leave me, not just like that, and you know it."

Julia did know it, she realised it couldn't be done. There'd be Mum and Uncle George and Aunt Mildred and the piping questions of Elsa, and perhaps, most horrible thought of all, Herbert coming round to the shop and making her life there impossible.

"Oh, you're miles behind the times, Herbert," she

said, "nobody sleeps in the same room now, and besides you know you did promise me."

"Beastly bacon," muttered Herbert, "might as well try and eat shavings. Well, we'll see. I've got to go now or I shall be late. Are you coming too, Julia?"

"No, I go by 'bus."

He stood shrugging himself into his overcoat in the hall, and suddenly looked pathetic to Julia, and she felt very sorry for him. She took down his bowler hat and gave it a little rub with the cuff of her frock, feeling terribly like a little wife out of *Home Chat* as she did so.

"I'm sorry, Herbert," she said softly, "I didn't mean to be a beast. It isn't that, you saw that last night, didn't you? It's just that I must get my sleep."

Herbert's face softened, and yet there was something greedy in his eyes as he stared down at her.

"All right, Julia," he said, "I'm a bit of a blundering ass, I expect. Is it all right, old girl?"

"Of course it's all right, Herbert." She raised her lips to his, and he kissed them hungrily. Oh yes, he thought, he had been a bit of an ass. After all, if she cared to play the fine lady a bit, why shouldn't she? She was good enough, heaven knew, and it wasn't, as she said, as though she'd refused him anything that mattered. He wouldn't stand for any nonsense like that, and she knew it. He ran lumberingly down the stairs. With a feeling of exquisite relief, Julia heard the front door slam.

They accommodated themselves, as any two human beings, forced by pressure of circumstances to share a life together, must accommodate themselves.

Herbert told himself that all was well, that he had a fine wife, that business was going splendidly; and if sometimes he regretted the yielding, glamourous girl who had once been beyond his reach, he soon forgot about it in the solid satisfaction of those things which he did possess. Julia didn't forget love, although she had never met it, but instead of imagining it as waiting round the corner for herself, as she had been wont to do in the days when she had first gone out into the world, she reverted more and more to the childish habit of identifying herself with the heroines of the books she read, and of the plays and cinemas that she saw.

Gradually, without observing it, she came to use Saint Clement's Square as she had used Two Beresford, as a place in which she died to all save her dreams. Her actual daily life was at the shop, her life at Saint Clement's Square was an opportunity for carrying on her second life, that of her imagination. Herbert, of course, was there, but she had won the great battle of the bedroom, and his love-making, although it didn't interest her, she bore with patiently. After all, that apparently was what love-making was like. She had been right when she had imagined, as a young girl with Alfie, that this was a wonderful secret, forgotten for generations, rediscovered by him, and that other people, apparently, didn't seem to know.

The shop was becoming more and more interesting, for Marian hardly ever came and Gipsy was now the head and Julia her second-in-command. She was now earning fifty shillings a week, and commission, and Herbert was still only making his five hundred. This put her definitely on an equality with him, for though he was responsible for the rent and the ordinary housekeeping, Julia paid all her own expenses and all the extras such as flowers and fruit, to which Herbert objected, and this gave her a certain authority in the household, which would not otherwise have been hers.

Marian, in her cool, casual, easy fashion, was divorcing Billy Embury who, lean and haggard, more streamlike than ever, had consented to pass a night at a hotel with a woman who made her living after this fashion. Marian had met somebody else who amused her a great deal more than poor Billy had ever amused her. He was, to the horror of her parents, an actor, but there was no holding Marian once she had set her mind on anything; and Julia watched with admiring envy, and yet with a touch of distaste for such heartlessness, the easy progression of Marian Embury towards the state of being Marian Bellingham. Frank Bellingham came once or twice to the shop—tense, dark and eager. Julia liked him, and felt oddly sorry for him. There was somebody who believed in Marian, and who believed in his job, and he was going to have great difficulty in running the two together. Marian, for the moment, was interested in the stage, but Julia knew by now that Marian would never really be interested in anything but herself.

She had never really cared about the shop. She didn't understand now when Frank Bellingham talked the jargon of his profession, but it amused her for the time being. He would be one of the sequence of men whom she would take and discard. Meanwhile, he thought her wonderful, as Billy Embury had thought her wonderful, and looking more of a Mona Lisa than ever with her up-curled mouth, and her long eyes, Marian proceeded, with that languor of hers which seemed half boredom and half pleasure, on her way. She married Frank Bellingham as soon as her decree was made absolute, and enthusiastically took up life in Bloomsbury.

Ruby was frankly contemptuous of the whole affair.

"I know that sort of woman, my dear," she said to Julia. "She'll amuse herself with poor Frank for as long as she chooses, then she'll throw him away, and Frank will go to the dogs, and that'll be the end of his career. You'll see if I'm not right."

Later Julia discovered that Ruby was not altogether unbiassed. She had lived with Frank Bellingham herself long ago on tour in the days before even Mr. Gordon, whom Julia had always looked upon as Ruby's pioneer, and Ruby had thrown Frank away—as Julia had learned to express it—for Mr. Gordon and his flat in Maida Vale. Now Frank Bellingham had set up in management. He had done well in the war, had come back with a good deal of glamour attached to his name, played lead in a play where he had made a great hit, and his star was for the moment in the ascendant.

How unfair life was, thought Julia. If she had been in Marian's position she felt sure she could have made Frank fall in love with her. If she had been free to drift in and out of the theatre in beautiful clothes, and ask him to parties, and show him how really interested she was in the stage, he might have fallen in love with her instead of Marian. That sort of half-world of the theatre she had occasionally touched with Ruby wasn't the real thing. She could see that now.

Julia liked working with Gipsy. She felt more at ease with her than she ever had with Marian. They had become really friendly, though Gipsy always knew how to keep a little touch of dignity in their relations.

One of the great moments in Julia's life came when Gipsy first told her she was going to send her to Paris.

During the war it had not been possible to buy from Paris, and London wholesale model-houses had done their own designing. But now Paris was once again supreme.

"I'd go myself," said Gipsy, "but I'm just getting my boy ready for Dartmouth, and I want his last week in London to be as nice as I can make it."

Julia was thrilled. Paris. . . . At once life sprung into bright colours for her again. It was nearly time for Herbert's holiday, but she wouldn't let that disturb her.

"Oh, Mrs. Danvers, I'd love to go. But shall I be able to do it all right? I should hate to let you down."

"You may make some mistakes," said Gipsy cheerfully, "but after all you've got to learn sooner or later. I'll send you to a little hotel I know of, and tell them to look after you. The commission agent will come along to you in the morning, and you can tell him the sort of things you want to look at. I'll make a list out for you before you go, then he'll take you to the dress shows and various wholesale houses. He pays your taxi-cabs, lunches, and all that sort of thing and keeps an expense account. If you do all right this time you shall go again. I'm not particularly keen on leaving England, and you've really more flair for clothes than I have. I'm better at this end of it. I'll give you a list of the wholesale places to go to for wools and silks. When you have chosen your models, then you can go to the wholesale houses for materials. They all keep books of the patterns chosen by the model-houses. Now look at this suit," and Gipsy, rapidly turning over the pages of a fashion paper, pointed out a little tailor-made street-suit with a bright-striped scarf round the neck. "I think we ought to do that one. You see it's called 'Petite Chose.' Just tell them you want that model, and they'll produce materials for it at once. Now when can you go?"

"Whenever you like," said Julia.

"Well, the new models are just out, so if we're going to get them ready for the autumn you'd better go now. What about next Sunday? and then you can start right in on Monday morning."

Julia went home on wings. Paris . . . freedom, adventure. She would make a success of it, she must. If she made a success of it she'd be sent again to Paris. It meant escape for a few lovely days.

Herbert sulked when she told him the news. He didn't think a married woman ought to go gadding about as though she were single, and what did she know of Paris anyway? Anything might happen to her. Men had no respect for a decent woman over there.

"I have respect for myself," said Julia; "that ought to be enough, I should imagine."

"I've a good mind not to let you go," fumed Herbert.

"Let?" Julia's soft, short-sighted eyes looked dangerous for a moment.

"I don't like it at all," went on Herbert, "and I've a good mind to go and tell your Mrs. What's-her-name so."

How history repeated itself, thought Julia! It seemed such a short time since she had coaxed Herbert into the lobby of his flat to tell him that Dad insisted on going to l'Etrangère's, and had begged him to help her. . . . Now here was Herbert, who had been so sporting then, threatening to do the same thing. It was maddening work being a woman, if you had to be a daughter or a wife.

She sat down on the arm of his chair—they still had only the one big arm-chair—and did what she very seldom did—began to coax him.

"Do be reasonable, darling," she said. "I've got to go if it's my job, haven't I? And it's such a chance, too. If I'm a success at this my salary will go up again. I promise you I can look after myself. Why, I've been going about London now for over five years, and I don't suppose Paris is very different, and I speak French quite well, you know, or did once, so I shall understand what anybody is saying to me. Oh, Herbert, don't you see? It's the chance of a lifetime. Emily will look after you beautifully while I'm away."

"It isn't that," said Herbert, "I don't like your going to Paris alone."

She knew perfectly well the thoughts that were going on behind his slightly-flushed forehead. He could see her in his mind's eye, at a little restaurant-table having a meal with some attractive Frenchman in the trade, being taken to the theatre, enjoying herself, exercising all those arts she'd once used on him, and which now she was too tired most days to employ. She would be out of his ken. He couldn't keep track of her. She might be unfaithful to him, who could say? He realised suddenly how little he knew of her, after all, how secret and hidden away from him was her life, although they lived in the same house and he paid for the food she ate. What, after all, he asked himself angrily, did she do for him? She was out all day, either very tired when she got back at night or eager to go out to a theatre or picture palace, or even dancing at this new place at Hammersmith, and then he was always too tired for any such nonsense. That wasn't his idea of home. He wanted a nice, warm, loving wife ready for him when he came back in the evening, willing to sit opposite him and listen when he read bits out of the paper, and willing to lie by his side all night, so that if he flung out his arm he could feel her there beside him. But he couldn't make Julia become this sort of wife. He had been weak with her, that's what it was. He ought to have taken up a stronger line from the start, but when, as now, she leaned her cheek against his head, and the scent she used came to his nostrils, he found himself unable to deal with her as he ought; for one thing he was only too afraid he wouldn't win. This Paris business, he supposed she'd have to go, but next time he'd manage to go over with her. He couldn't at this short notice, but, after all, they appreciated him pretty well at Dick Dash's, and if he gave them plenty of warning, they wouldn't grudge him a couple of days, but he wouldn't tell Julia of his plan beforehand.

"All right," he said aloud, "you can try just this once."

"That's sweet of you, Herbert," she slipped off the arm of his chair, "I do hope Emily's got something nice for your supper, because you deserve it. I'll go and see."

Julia approached Paris with a far stronger sense of adventure than she had approached her marriage. It was stronger even than that with which she had faced going to an hotel with Alfie. Both these things had seemed so inevitable, so to grow out of circumstances, that she had felt as though a current were bearing her along, and all she could do was to go with it. But Paris broke into her life from without, sharp and clear as a wedge of sunlight cutting through shutters.

Calais she adored; the red, fluted roofs, the old grey houses, the French porters in the blue blouses, shouting their numbers. She was "abroad," that was what mattered. It wasn't England. She was going abroad at last. Even the low platform, and having to climb up high to get into the train was a delightful change.

She forgot everything to do with her life in England. She forgot Two Beresford, and Saint Clement's Square, and the only thing she remembered about the shop was that she was going to do her best for it. It was always going to be a success, and always she'd be sent over to Paris.

The little hotel in Paris to which Gipsy had sent Julia was a quiet, modest, flat-faced house, tall and thin, with green shutters. It was larger than it looked from the street, for it was built round a courtyard, where there were a few wicker-work chairs and tables and trees in tubs. To Julia's delight her room looked out on this courtyard. Accustomed only to the boarding-houses of England, whenever she and her parents had been able to take a holiday, it seemed to her a paradise. Dinner was delicious—all sorts of odd lovely dishes and white wine out of a carafe. The wine made her feel exquisitely clear in her mind, sure of herself and of life, although at the same time it gave her a floating feeling, as though she were light as a balloon. The dining-room was dark, but she could look through the big windows and see the slant of the evening sunlight in the courtyard. It must be lovely to live in France, this sunlight set life to music, just as the wine set the meals to sunlight.

Julia enjoyed that solitary dinner, though for the thousandth time she bitterly regretted her short sight and astigmatism. She couldn't watch her fellow guests and wonder about them, because she would have had to put on her spectacles to see them, neither could she read a book at dinner without wearing her glasses, because of her astigmatism. It was tiresome being a woman if there were anything wrong with your sight; you had to choose between seeing and being seen. Julia chose to be seen.

There was running water, hot and cold, in her bedroom, though for the same price in England she would only have had a heavy china toilet set, and been obliged to ring for a small can of hot water. Julia, who had always thought that the French were a dirty race, was surprised at this.

The sun was still shining next morning, and Julia went down to the rather gloomy little lounge with the dusty palms, in a state of excitement and exhilaration. She felt quite impatient waiting for the agent who was to take her the rounds, and she kept looking at herself in a big dark mirror with a curly gilt frame, that hung at the end of the lounge, to make sure that she looked all right. It would be dreadful if she were considered dowdy in Paris. She thought she looked all right. Gipsy had given her a little thin black frock with a lacquer-red sash, and a little black turban that she wore pulled down over one eye, trimmed with a swirl of greeny-black cock's feathers, tipped with red; the feathers swept down past her cheek, one lying softly against her cheek-bone, and the others curving down the side of the long thick neck, which was her only claim to classic beauty. Yes, her clothes were all right, and she thought she wore them well; of course, Gipsy had given them to her in the way of business, because the representative of l'Etrangère must look well-dressed, but Julia was grateful to Gipsy all the same.

As she studied herself in the dark glass, which was rather like trying to look at yourself in the depths of the sea—for you discovered in its depths, by careful peering, a drowned Julia deep in green water—she heard the roundabout door revolve and she turned to see a thin, pale young man, dressed in grey, enter, limping slightly. He caught her eye at the same moment, and they stood hesitant, each guessing who the other was. Julia took a step forward, the young man swept off his pale-grey felt hat.

"Mademoiselle Almond?" he asked.

"Yes," said Julia, smiling at him. Of course, she thought to herself, that is how they would write about me from the shop. I suppose they've not thought about passports. A nice thing. I've given my name as Mrs. Starling at this hotel, and he might easily have asked for me as Miss Almond. What would they have thought then? But she was pleased. It was part of this new freedom in the new world, that she should be Miss Almond.

"I," said the young man, "am René Imbert. Mrs. Danvers has written to me about you. I will call a taxi."

He bowed and passed out again through the revolving door, and Julia heard the taxi arrive. She went out and joined him on the pavement. She jumped briskly into the taxi, and noticed that Monsieur Imbert climbed in with a certain difficulty, dragging one leg behind him. This soon passed from her mind.

The morning was taken up with strenuous work. Monsieur Imbert took her to various model-houses and she chose her models, including one of the new trousered evening-frocks. The first house they arrived at was, like most of those to which she went afterwards, beautiful, but decrepit and dirty, with a lovely staircase, painted ceilings and beautiful panellings. Monsieur Imbert paid off the taxi in the street, and stood aside to allow Julia to precede him through the big doors at the entrance of the courtyard, at the far end of which was an old house that looked as though it might fall to pieces at any moment. Julia hesitated a moment in its dark doorway. Could it be possible that all the things which she had heard about Paris were true? Was it possible that Herbert had been right when he had darkly hinted about the white slave traffic and all that sort of thing? She shook herself impatiently. Yet she had never imagined it was to such places that one came to buy models. For one awful moment she hesitated in the hall, Monsieur Imbert behind her, and a flight of rather dark and evil-smelling stairs before her. Then her fear of being ridiculous triumphed, and she started to go upstairs. All the way up the four flights she heard the heavy, dragging step of René Imbert, oddly ominous in that strange place. A light step and then a heavy one, a light step and then a heavy one; the repetition hit upon her mind with a curious sense of doom. At the top of the house she found a pleasant little Frenchwoman with an egg-shaped bust, and a dark moustache, who displayed for her the most lovely model underclothing.

Julia had been used to pretty underclothing in the war, when *crêpe de Chine* had come into fashion, and young women had had their chemises and drawers embroidered with the regimental badges of their young men. But these "undies," in the language of the shop, were lovelier still. Julia bought enthusiastically, but with caution. By the time they had left that particular house she was free of her fear of the white slave traffic, and she and Imbert lunched together in amity.

René Imbert looked very pale, and Julia wondered whether his leg, which obviously had something wrong with it, was paining him. She asked him timidly, for she was afraid lest reference to his disability might hurt his feelings: "Ought you to go up all these stairs—I mean, doesn't it hurt?"

He laughed and shook his head. "Not a bit. It sounds worse than it is; at first I thought I would never get used to it, but now they have made me a splendid new one."

"A new one?" She stared at him.

"Yes, a new one. This fellow," and he slapped his right thigh resoundingly, "never grew on me."

"Oh," said Julia, her face crimsoning, "I'm sorry. How dreadful for you!"

"Ah," he said, and unable to express himself fully in English, he broke into French: *"Ah, mademoiselle, pour ma jambe—je m'en fiche de ma jambe. Elle reste en Alsace regagnée, où elle se trouve fort bien."*

Julia stared at him and then her eyes suddenly filled with tears. He wasn't boasting. He wasn't even being dramatic. It was as natural to him to say such a thing as it would have been unnatural to an Englishman. He was unfolding for her the fine flower of his thought without any self-consciousness.

"Oh," said Julia, "that's beautiful . . . the way you said it . . . I mean, the way you think about it."

"Thank you," he said. "I'm glad that you should feel it so," and turned the subject as shyly as any Englishman might have done.

After lunch he signalled another taxi and took her to a couple of dress shows; and though Julia was at first bewildered by the stage setting, the clever lighting, the luminous grey walls, the beautiful creatures who swung forward in dress after dress, yet she kept her head, and noted down the models that she thought would be best for l'Etrangère's. She was exhausted by the time the two dress shows were over, and went back to her hotel.

The next morning young Imbert arrived punctually, and spent the morning in taking her round the wholesale model-houses. She found that the houses themselves were nearly all dirty and ill-kept, but that the models were exquisite.

They spent the afternoon at René's office. He had already taken the references of the models she had chosen at the dress shows for her, and telephoned the various wholesalers for the materials and trimmings that she wanted. It was a queer, stuffy little office, with black linen-covered boxes arranged one upon the other almost up to the ceiling. It was eminently businesslike and, as ever, René Imbert was extremely correct. He took her back to her hotel at about six o'clock in the evening.

"How long are you going to be here, mademoiselle?" he asked.

"One more whole day," said Julia. "Mrs. Danvers wanted me to look at the novelties, the new bags and things like that."

"Yes, I can manage that, and then perhaps you will dine with me, as it will be the last evening, and business will be over?"

"I'd love to," said Julia, and wondered to herself whether he was going to be what she called a "real Frenchman" at last.

The next day dawned clear and exquisite, and Julia put on a lavender-coloured frock and a wide summery hat of the same colour. She saw René Imbert's eyes light up as he caught sight of her.

"You look like summer," he said. "Do you know that colour takes the English grey out of your eyes, and makes them lilac? Your eyes are French to-day."

Julia laughed gaily.

"That's splendid," she said, "as I'm in France I'll try and keep them French as long as I'm here."

"I was thinking," observed Imbert at lunch, "that it would be a pity if you went away without seeing something of Paris. Would you perhaps be kind enough to come to the theatre with me to-night? It will at least be a good French lesson for you."

"Oh, I'd love to," said Julia, "if you'll explain all the bits I don't understand. What shall we go to?"

He studied her thoughtfully. "You are very young," he said unexpectedly, "although you are an English miss, and I know they have much freedom; I must be careful where I take you."

Again that too ready colour, which Julia felt was her curse, burned in her cheeks. This was the moment to tell him that she wasn't really a "miss" at all.

"Oh, but you know," she said, "Miss Almond is my name at the shop, because I went there when I *was* Miss Almond. I'm really Mrs. Starling. I've been married for ages and ages, nearly a year."

A curious expression flitted across his face. He seemed, she felt, to look at her differently, though quite where the difference lay she could not have told.

"Even so," he said, "there are things to which I should not take you. Places where your husband wouldn't like you to go, except perhaps in his company. You are still very young, even if you are a married woman. With us it makes all the difference when a woman is married, but Englishwomen seem to remain the same, sometimes all their lives."

"Do you know many Englishwomen?" said Julia; "you seem to know a lot about us. Where did you learn English so well?"

"I was in a family for two years at Hampstead, but then came the war and I had to go and fight."

Julia, looking at him, wondered.

"Were you," she hesitated, "were you a liaison officer?"

Such funny people were officers nowadays; after all, look at Herbert, and she knew so little of the French, and anyway Monsieur Imbert seemed to be such a perfect gentleman that she didn't like to assume he had been a private.

He threw back his head and laughed, and she noticed how white and even his teeth were.

"Oh, Lord, no," he said in his easy English, tinged with a slight French accent. "I didn't want to be anything different from the others. No, I was just called up with my class, and eventually I became a lieutenant as everyone else was killed. I got through for so long without what you would call a scratch, and then one day a shell got me. These things are fate. No man can avoid his fate. Now, if you will excuse me, I will read down the list of theatres and see what I can take you to."

He ran his finger thoughtfully up and down the amusements list in the newspaper, eyebrows raised, and mouth pursed, so that he looked, with his pallor and the dark, close-cropped cap of his hair, oddly like a pierrot. Finally, he decided on a fairly innocuous little comedy, which still seemed to Julia when she saw it, very daring. Nobody seemed to pretend anything in it, and the happy

192

ending consisted of the husband being left in a contented state of deception, and the wife equally contented in her lover's arms. Beds were mentioned freely; at one point the lovers were discovered in bed.

Julia was a little shocked, because she was so used to the habit of thought which knows that such things exist, but which pretends that they do not. She had seen many plays that centred round adultery in England, but it was always taken seriously, which somehow made it seem all right. Yet there was something restful about this point of view, and she couldn't help enjoying herself. René seemed to notice nothing odd about the piece, it neither made him goatish nor puritan, and it would have made Herbert both. René saw her back to her hotel and, since he knew that she was a married woman, bent down and kissed her hand when he said good-bye. Nobody had ever kissed Julia's hand before.

"Oh," breathed Julia, "I do hope I've done everything all right. I hope Mrs. Danvers will be pleased."

"You have done splendidly. You see when I tried to show you the models for England and America you wouldn't look at them more than once. And you did not buy any 'Fords'! Everything you have chosen, you have chosen well. You have a sense of clothes in a way that is rare in an Englishwoman, if you will forgive my saying so."

The next day René saw Julia off at the station. They lunched together first. She felt that he was interested in in her, and yet his eyes were not passionate; they were quizzical and kind and disconcertingly intelligent, as usual.

"You have not been in France before? You are—if I may say so—not usual, not the young lady one would have expected. And you are married. Has that been long?"

Julia found herself describing her life, Two Beresford, Dad's death, Uncle George, Saint Clement's Square. . . . Herbert. . . . Not Alfie.

Julia had never before been out with anyone who wanted her to talk about herself. The men on leave had wanted to make love, or to say how their wives misunderstood them, or how lonely they were. Herbert had never been interested, she could see now, in her as a person apart from herself, and her relationship with him.

Alfie had been a flame that might have consumed her, but never a mind that wanted to know hers. At the shop she was that capable Miss Almond, but no one was interested in what her life was like day by day, although everyone had been kind about her wedding. Ruby would say to her: "Darling, now you simply must tell me everything you've been doing. I'm dying to know. Did I tell you what an awful time I've been having with young Carruthers? My dear, too awful. He swore he'd shoot himself, and I said . . ." At home Julia had always been accepted as a matter of course.

The exquisite and stimulating flattery of René's interest flowed over her like sunlight, flowed into her like wine. She was, after all, the person she had imagined herself being when she was at school, an interesting, thrilling person.

She knew she was talking well. She wasn't explaining too much, she wasn't indulging in self-pity, but her eagerness about life brimmed in her eyes and on her lips. She felt twice as alive as she felt in London.

"You should have been a Frenchwoman," said René, at last, as they sipped their coffee.

"Oh, why?"

"I don't think I will tell you, not this time anyway. Perhaps next time you come over to Paris. Perhaps then we will become really friends. You must not forget that now you are still Miss Almond to me. I have only just begun to know you, although I think already I know the woman in you better perhaps than anyone else has ever done."

" 'The woman in me?' What do you mean?"

"I mean the thing that makes you interesting and attractive to a Frenchman."

"Just because I'm a woman, do you mean? Would you be interested in any woman?"

"To a certain degree, of course. But not as much as in you. You have a quality that is appreciated and recognised with us more than it is in England."

"It's funny," said Julia, "that you wanted me to talk about myself, and do you know, I never even realised I was doing it? I've always found men wanted to talk about themselves."

He threw back his head and laughed.

"To take you out and talk about oneself! What a waste! A Frenchman would naturally want a woman like you to tell him all she could about her heart and her mind. I know that you thought Frenchmen are bold, bad men, who only want one thing from a woman. Is that not so?"

"Of course not," said Julia violently, but her blush betrayed her.

"We may want that one thing, but we don't want it without knowledge. Woman to us is the most precious thing in the world, the most interesting."

"Oh," said Julia naïvely, "I do wish I had been born a Frenchwoman."

"I too wish it for your sake. You would have had quite a different sort of life. I think a better life. You might not think so."

He signalled to the waiter, and after carefully scrutinising the bill, paid it. Julia stood up, and he helped her into her coat. They drove to the station, and Julia wondered whether he would put an arm round her and kiss her; but he seemed to have become quite impersonal, and Julia felt vaguely disappointed. He bought her a *Daily Mail* and saw her into the train.

"I won't wait to see the train go. There is nothing more stupid than standing about trying to think of things to say."

"Good-bye," said Julia, "you've been so kind. It's made such a difference."

"It is I who thank you. It has been most charming."

She couldn't hear his limping footfall this morning, because of the noise on the platform, porters with trolleys shouting to people to get out of the way, the banging of trucks and the babble of voices, but she watched his slim, grey back till it disappeared through the barrier. He didn't look round.

Herbert seemed very dull that night. He asked her about her trip, but his question seemed prompted by suspicion. What had this agent fellow been like?

"Oh, a little man," said Julia vaguely, "pale, with a wooden leg."

Herbert seemed pleased, though he said: "Poor fellow, I suppose that's the best sort of job he can get, even

195

though I must say it doesn't seem a man's work dealing with women's clothes."

"I don't see that it isn't just as good as dealing with men's clothes," said Julia unkindly.

"Of course it's different. Obviously it's different. One's a man's job and the other isn't."

Julia yawned. "I'm frightfully tired, Herbert. I must be at the shop early to-morrow. I'll go to bed. Don't come in and disturb me, will you?"

Herbert stared at her, his mouth and eyes fallen open with dismay. Julia kissed him lightly on one cheek and went upstairs to bed.

Gipsy was very pleased with Julia. All the models proved a success, and were copied for l'Etrangère by the wholesale house, Coppinger's, with which Gipsy dealt. Mr. Coppinger was rather a friend of Julia's, and he was an obliging little man who flattered himself he was something of a dog and took a keen interest in racing. His tips were followed by the staff at l'Etrangère's, from Gipsy downwards. The bets were generally laid with the milkman who served the shop, and Mr. Coppinger might say to Julia: "Like to have half a crown on the Lincoln? I'm putting a quid to win on 'Blushing Bride,' and you shall have half a crown of it." He always paid up when she won, and Julia always paid up when she lost; but Mr. Coppinger would sometimes put on half a crown for her without asking, and on these occasions he never told her if she lost.

"You know, Mr. Coppinger," said Julia one day, "when you put on money for me without asking me, the horse always seems to win."

His little kindly eyes twinkled at her out of his weather-beaten face—somehow he always contrived to look a countryman. Julia almost suspected him of using that liquid advertised as giving a sunburned complexion, for his harmless vanity was to be taken for a horsy character.

"Don't you worry, Miss Almond. If I put on a horse for you without your authority it's only right I should stand the racket if it loses."

He was friendly and respectful, and sometimes when she had finished transacting business with him he would take her into the Regent Palace Hotel, which was near his place of business, and they would have cocktails together, or even split what he called "a half-bottle of the boy." Julia had the knack of getting on well with her business associates, and though there was nothing to stimulate her mind or her curiosity about her relationship with Mr. Coppinger, as there was about this new friendship with René Imbert, she was always pleased to see the pleasant, capable little man.

He was as pleased as Gipsy with her choice of models, and took her cheerfully round to the Regent Palace, and ordered sandwiches and the "half-bottle of the boy" that marked a successful deal. Julia watched him curiously, she felt quite different about him since she had been to Paris. She liked him as much, but she no longer felt he was on an equality with her, though he was a prosperous man with his own business. He didn't realise what she was really like, at least he only realised what one side of her was like, the side that was a good sort and put on no frills and knew how to do a job of work. It was all very nice and pleasant. She was glad after a hard day's work of the champagne and the sandwiches, but that was all. It was not in his twinkling eyes that she could find mirrored the Julia that she wished to be.

Herbert's holiday, which was arranged to be at the same time as her own, was an anti-climax after Paris, though they went to quite a good boarding-house at Southsea, almost a private hotel, for trade was booming more than ever—the peace seemed even better than the war. Bertha joined them, for as Herbert very reasonably said, it was bad enough for the poor old girl to have lost him again just when she had thought she had got him back; and if Julia wouldn't have her to live with them at Saint Clement's Square, which would have been much the most economical arrangement, then she must jolly well make the best of her during the holidays. Julia countered by paying for Mrs. Almond to go also. It was high time, she said, that poor Mum had a bit of a rest from slaving for the Beales and listening to Uncle George blustering away at her.

Julia hated Bertha by the time the fortnight had come to an end, and Bertha certainly disapproved of Julia. Indeed, Julia herself felt she was being a different person from the girl at l'Etrangère's who could seem so quiet and distinguished, and different again from the glowing girl of Paris. With Herbert's family and her own she became once more the Julia who was sometimes rowdy, who liked scandalising people, and drawing attention to herself in public in a way that she would have died sooner than do with Mrs. Danvers or René Imbert.

But what was she to do at this stuffy boarding-house, full of old people like Mum and Bertha . . . and Herbert? For Herbert did seem old, though he was only thirty-six. It had only been desiring Julia that had made him seem more alive, and now that she was married to him he no longer felt it incumbent on him to seem young or even considerate. His desire was of a different quality now; it no longer flamed, it smouldered with a domestic heat. He liked to be warmed, but not to be burned. Yes, he seemed to go better with Mum and that awful Bertha than with Julia, and she seemed to go better with the two young men in the boarding-house who taught her to play tennis, and used to take her on the pier. One of them even took her out in his side-car, much to Herbert's annoyance.

Herbert and Julia had to share a bedroom at Southsea, because Herbert said he wasn't going to pay for two rooms, and anyway people would think it funny if they didn't share a room. Every night Herbert would scold Julia for her frivolous behaviour during the day, and Julia flared back at him.

"You make me tired the way you go on, Herbert; you're stuffy, that's what's the matter with you, stuffy as that old sister of yours. I suppose she's been putting you up to this?"

"I don't know what you mean by 'putting me up' to anything. I can see for myself that you don't know how to behave."

"And you always do, I suppose? What about that time you came to fetch me out to dinner from the shop? Behaved more like a bear than a man."

"And you liked it all right."

"That's not true. I hated it."

Herbert laughed. "I know all about just how much you hated it. What did you marry me for?"

198

"Not for that."

"I don't know what you mean by 'not for that,' but I married you for what any man who is a man marries for, and for a well-run home and peace and quiet. Not to foot the bill for someone who rushes round all day with a couple of young bounders."

"They're no more bounders than you are, and they both fought in the war; didn't just sit in an office miles behind the lines."

"Oh, shut up. I'm sick of this. Get into bed."

And sometimes he would turn his stout back on her, and without saying god night, go to sleep; sometimes he would perform that rite which, if ever they quarrelled about it, he called exercising his rights as a husband.

Winter came again, and Julia, as usual, had two terribly bad colds, and a slight one that went on and on. She was hardly recovered when she had to go to Paris again to buy the spring models.

Herbert couldn't get leave from the Company. For one thing, trade showed signs of faltering, and it was far too soon for him to hope for another holiday. He didn't worry, as he had worried the first time. That dark, domestic winter in Saint Clement's Square, the ordinariness of colds and sore throats, and familiar surroundings, had all combined to make him less nervous. Besides, always in the back of his mind there was Julia's description of the Paris agent, as small, pale and with a wooden leg.

She went with rather a sinking of the heart, for no one knew better than she that unless the weather were fine in Paris, she would no longer give the impression of the warm, vital Julia of the preceding summer. Also she found it more difficult to see, without the sharp shadows and bright contrasts of sunlight with which summer made the world more or less clear to her. Everything was a uniform shade of grey. She found it far more difficult to get about without glasses.

René was not waiting for her at the station. She felt a little twinge of disappointment. He was not at the hotel either, but there was a large bunch of flowers already arranged in water in her room, with a card bearing his name laid beside it.

She had hardly unpacked before the telephone rang.

"Is that Mademoiselle Almond?" said René's voice.

"Yes."

"Good evening, madame. It's René Imbert speaking. Did you have a good journey? Would you be able to come out to dinner to-night?"

"Oh yes," said Julia, feeling at once less tired and less plain than she had hitherto. "I'd love to if I shan't have to dress."

"Oh no, we will just go to some quiet little place. I will call for you at half-past seven. Is that all right?"

"Yes."

"*Au revoir* till then."

"*Au revoir.*"

They dined at a little restaurant in the Rue Blanche, and at once Julia felt herself, without any difficulty, becoming again the attractive young woman she had been before in René's eyes. Even her cold cleared up and she ceased to have to blow her nose. For the first time she began to let flow towards René that quality of sex which was in her a gift. On her previous visit she had been too puzzled by him, and too interested in the new Julia he presented for her view. Now she felt self-confident and very much mistress of the situation. She could not know that to René's logical mind she was giving him every reason to believe she meant to fulfill what her eyes promised; and, although his two years in England had given him a good deal of experience of the "respectable flirt," he placed Julia above that order of chilly voluptuaries. Her excitement, which in reality was all about the dream Julia, and not at all about him, yet communicated itself to him. He kissed both her hands with more fervour than correctitude when he left her at the hotel.

The next day he was ill, with a sharp attack of the fever which had attacked him intermittently since the war, and Julia, though disappointed, soon forgot him in the thrill of exploring for herself and buying successfully alone. She found one or two smaller, cheaper, and more individual houses than those to which he had taken her. That night, alone and bored, suffering from a reaction from the exaltation of successful buying, she felt disturbed and unhappy. She wished to do her best by the shop, and still she hated to do René out of his commission. She could already see that by the time she got to know Paris a bit better it would be far more economical if she went about by herself, finding out places where even the wholesale people bought their goods, the places where everything was started. She could get the models, the hand-bags, and the underclothes more cheaply, and she wouldn't have to pay an agent's commission. But it would mean breaking with René—and somehow she knew he could have been a friend of a quality hitherto unknown to her . . . oh well, what was the good of worrying. Things would work out some way.

She was glad that her time in Paris was so short, and that on the last day there was nothing to do but finish up the business she had already transacted with René.

The last evening was very different from the first. René, well again, had looked forward to that dinner with interest and pleasure, but Julia was *distraite*. Not till the wine and the flattery of his interest had begun to bring her to life did he catch a glimpse of the Julia of that earlier evening. And that glimpse was short-lived.

Julia glanced round the little room and noticed that she and René were the only two people who were not obviously lovers, for here were midinettes with their heads leaning against the shoulders of their best boys. Here people quite simply and naturally stooped to kiss; here the man's arm was always round the waist of the girl dining with him, unless he actually needed that arm for using his knife and fork, when, with strict Latin logic, he removed it, cut his meat up into small pieces, replaced the arm round the waist of the loved one, and fed himself with the fork.

René followed her eyes, and with what seemed to Julia his uncanny knowledge, followed the processes of her mind as well.

"You see," he said, "they're all lovers here. It is quiet. There is no music. Who in heaven's name first started the idea of music at meals? It must have been someone who knew nothing about music, still less about food, and least of all about conversation."

"I thought music was supposed to . . ." Julia hesitated, "to sort of help when you were in love?" she continued lamely.

René laughed. "Oh, that is the English idea. In France you don't even need wine. You need nothing. The beauty

201

of making love is that it is what you call in England 'a standing jump.' We can do it from nothing. It is quite enough in itself."

"But . . ." began Julia, and then stopped. She couldn't go on in the English manner about "being in love." Her mind clarified by the Vouvray they had drunk, she realised that René did not use the word "love" sentimentally. Yet the English mingling of the romantic and the respectable in her, which she owed to her upbringing and not to her own nature, made her unable to accept that nature's true conclusion—the logical acceptance of passing pleasure which was René's heritage.

"Now you, Mademoiselle Julia," said René, "—pardon me the 'mademoiselle,' because here in Paris you are 'Mademoiselle,' apart from the fact that it seems to me that you have not been married at all—for you, love is not easy. As I told you before, you should have been born a Frenchwoman."

"Yes, I remember," said Julia, overcome by the interest of discussing herself, "and I remember that you said you couldn't tell me why. But surely you can tell me now? We know each other well enough," and she narrowed her short-sighted eyes at him, really so as to see him the better, though it looked to René as though at last she were beginning to play the game as he knew it.

"Because you were made for love," said René. "That is a bad thing for an Englishwoman. To become a professional in that one thing is not well looked on in England. Here it is a different affair."

Julia stared at him. "To become a professional? What do you mean?"

"Well," continued René, rushing upon his fate, "in France you would have started, I hope, by having an *amant de coeur* . . . which is a part for which many men would have worked hard, believe me, mademoiselle. And that quality you have could not have gone unnoticed here in Paris. There would have been . . . whom shall we say? . . . a rich wine merchant, and then a millionaire. Yes, there would certainly have been a millionaire, and no more work for charming Mademoiselle Almond."

Julia blushed slowly, but with intense violence. She felt the blood creep over her neck and face, and yet all the time in her mind there ran the thought: Now I can be

202

offended. Now I can make an excuse not to deal with him any more, and that will be for the good of the shop. How lucky that I blush so easily. And something else, something truer and more honest within her was sorry for René, because she knew he was justified in what he had said. Because she knew that, shocked as her English middle-class blood had been at this matter-of-fact portrayal of her life, yet had she been French she knew that she would not have taken offence had it not been in her business interests to do so. She could be free now, free of René Imbert or any other agent. She could range Paris at will, going to the little places she had discovered, buying the very best things and paying no commission. l'Etrangère would profit as never before.

"You're . . . you're insulting me," said Julia. "How dare you!" And then her sense of humour warned her that "how dare you" was a stupid thing to say—and more important still, that neither Marian nor Gipsy would ever have said it.

She opened her eyes wide, and René's face swam like a large surprised balloon in front of her.

"I think it's beastly," she said energetically, flogging herself with her own words into belief of what she said. "All that you say about love. You don't really mean loving, you only mean sleeping with someone. It's horrible, all that!"

Her blush had told René where he had been mistaken. She was too encased in her upbringing to accept herself. Always the two would be at war, and this time, for some reason he did not comprehend, it was the upbringing that won. He bent his head politely.

"I'm very sorry," he said. "I thought one could discuss anything with you. I was mistaken. Forgive me. Perhaps it is all in that little difference of phrasing. The English say 'sleeping with' when they mean they don't sleep. We French say *coucher avec*, and we mean it. I ought to have known."

"Yes, you ought to have known," said Julia angrily, with the thought of l'Etrangère, and l'Etrangère's benefit, held firmly in her mind; and yet in her innermost being feeling very ashamed of herself. "You ought to have known. Of course, I can't have anything more to do with you; you understand that?"

"I understand, madame," said René.

He called for the bill and sent her home in a taxi, paying the driver beforehand, and thus putting himself in a curious manner, thought Julia, in the right.

Julia went back triumphant to l'Etrangère. She was able to tell them that for the future she could manage without an agent, and she brought back with her better models and novelties than they had ever had before.

When after her first day's work at the shop she returned to Saint Clement's Square, she was able with more truth than usual to tell the sulky Herbert that she was too tired to have anything to do with him.

She took Bobby into her room with her and then she slept as she had not slept for years. It seemed to her that her life was laid out clearly before her at last. Saint Clement's Square was just a place to sleep in. She must deal with Herbert somehow or other. Love, certainly not in the sense that René Imbert used it, was not for her. She wanted romance with her love. She wanted what she had read about in all the story-books ever since she could read at all. If she could not have that, she had, as a solid fact, l'Etrangère. She, and she alone, far better than even Gipsy, could build up the business until it was the most important dressmaking business in London. She loved even the business troubles that they had, because she had to fling herself into them and use her ingenuity and work hard. As for the rest of her life, it would continue to be in books and in the dream life that she imagined—and, after all, she would be so drugged with fatigue that that surely would be enough.

So the pattern of the days and months persisted; the damp pallors of spring, the uncertain gold of English summers, of which the chief interest to the Starlings, and thousands like them, was the probability of it being fair for "the holidays"; dim, burning autumn, that touched even Saint Clement's Square to fire, through the evening mists; and the cold and wet of winter that seemed always like a dark tunnel which had to be traversed. In winter Julia's sore throats and the rheumatism from which the ageing Bobby suffered were her chief worries. There were, of course, bright flashes, the sudden pleasures of little successes, visits to Paris . . . vague regrets. The tension of battling with the first slump, the pride in survival. Occasional theatres, lovely fabrics draped by her pleased fingers, fine sunny days. And always the feeling that life was all about her, and still more strongly the belief, not yet faded, that round the corner of the next little period of time, life, as she had always imagined it, still lay in wait for her.

BOOK THREE

"The trouble with the present generation is that it has lost its sense of sin."
MR. GLADSTONE, *circa* 1870

The Dream

TIME, felt rather than seen by Julia, as a pattern flying swiftly past her, went more slowly for Herbert. Julia had her creative work at the shop. Herbert had only the hum-drum round to which he had been accustomed. Julia was given a rise in salary; Herbert asked for one, but very nearly got what he described to Julia as "the noble order of the sack" instead. Julia had her limited, but highly coloured, imagination as a field into which she could stray when she disliked the outer world of fact; Herbert had no such solace.

Thus all the time, two human beings, never at the best very close to each other, grew further and further apart, and in them both worked those strange and unknown ferments to which everyone is subject. Outwardly they were a respectable married couple; a husband consider-ably older than his wife, who both went to work every morning, and kept going a cosy little maisonette for home hours. Yet inwardly neither Herbert nor Julia corre-sponded to the description of them that their immediate friends—with the exception of Dr. Ackroyd and his daughter—would have given of them. Julia was a differ-ent person "up West," and at home she withdrew into a book, or her own imagination. She never thought for a moment that she was just an ordinary, respectable wife and wage-earner. She still knew she was something wonderful.

Herbert only wanted to be an ordinary, decent husband and wage-earner; he distrusted the wonderful, and he only knew that his life had turned to nothing in his hands, like withered leaves. He had no joy in his wife, for whom he had once lusted so violently, and for whom he occasionally lusted still. He had anxieties in business, and he was jealous, perpetually jealous, of the strange thing in Julia that he couldn't catch and pin down, but which he knew was there. He was jealous also, more simply and plainly, of her greater success, of her few years, and he was angered by the way she could always make him feel common and vulgar when she chose.

Julia had always kept the habit of going home, when possible, on the top of the bus, when she could slip on a pair of spectacles under the brim of her little felt hat, and the world would leap into sharp reality for her—a reality of edges and contours such as she seldom knew. Then she could study the faces of the people in lighted windows, the faces of the other people on the top of the bus, and always she would think of them in relation to herself, wondering what she would have been like, married to such and such a man; pondering on the differences there evidently were between her and some strange woman.

In winter-time, if it were wet weather and she had to go inside the bus, she would notice, with the glow that beauty always gave her, how the reflection of the bus would run alongside through the wet and lighted streets. Like a ghost bus, she thought, with ghost people sitting inside it. Fragments of ghost bus, and fragments of ghost people, cut into strangely by sharp lines and shadows, by passing traffic, by corners of houses, but always there, always keeping up alongside.

Herbert had no interest in his fellow-humans, and winter and summer he came home by the Underground, behind an evening paper.

One day in spring, a wet day, but with gleams in the sky, and a fine thin promise of misty green upon the twigs and branches of the trees, Julia arrived home rather exhilarated by the soft rain upon her face, and

the uncertain gusty weather, than tired by it. She had had
a successful day at the shop, too; had coaxed a difficult
customer into buying a couple of frocks, and had succeeded in selling a hat to a "woman off the street," as
the shop parlance had it, when describing new customers
who, struck by something in the window, came for the
first time into l'Etrangère.

Success was vital to Julia's well-being. She glowed
with it. It always enabled her to triumph over fatigue.
She put her key into the latch and found Herbert had
arrived home before her, and had had his tea; but as she
patted him gaily on the shoulder—an unwonted attention
for her—and even fetched his slippers and his pipe, he
looked at her with the ever-ready sullen suspicion at work
in his little steel-coloured eyes.

"You seem very pleased with yourself," he observed
shortly.

"I am pleased with myself," said Julia. "I've been very
clever to-day. If you like, I'll make you some toasted
cheese for supper."

"You know perfectly well my stomach won't stand that
sort of thing any more," complained Herbert. "Besides,
there are going to be people here."

"People, what people?" Julia turned to stare at him,
as she was leaving the room.

"Oh, only those relations of yours, as usual. But Elsa
has got hold of a young man—first time and last, I should
think. Anyway, they want to amuse him playing cards, so
they are bringing him along."

"Oh, well," said Julia pacifically. "You like cards, too,
don't you? I expect it'll cheer you up."

She ran upstairs, and as she changed into a clever little
black frock that she knew would make Elsa look extremely undistinguished, she herself felt quite a little glow
of interest at the thought of meeting anybody new. Life
had been the same for such a long time now.

Elsa arrived with her father and mother and Mrs. Almond. That night Julia had to admit, with a little shock,
that the kid wasn't bad-looking, after all. Her hair, which
she still refused to cut, was arranged in a new way; the
long, colourless plaits were bound in whorls, like snails'
shells, over each ear, and Elsa had a little colour in her
cheeks. That's probably because of the young man,
thought Julia wickedly.

211

Elsa introduced him, with some giggling, with the remark: "You'll never remember when you must have seen him last, will she, Leonard?"

Julia screwed up her short-sighted eyes and gazed at him in an effort to remember. No, she couldn't have met him on any of her business trips. There was something swaggering and carefree in his walk. Could he have been a sailor perhaps, of course an officer, she added hastily to herself, on one of the cross-Channel steamers? But then she had never talked to any.

She looked back at the war years, her years of experimenting, so unsatisfactorily, save with Alfie, and realised with a sudden shock that this man was too young to have been in the war, that he was younger than she was.

"You won't remember me," said the young man, "and I suppose I can't rightly say I remember you. But we were at school together—must have been, so Elsa says, when we get on to dates."

"Of course, he'd be much younger than you, Julia," said Elsa, "but I know you said there were little boys at school when you were there."

"I left when I wasn't sixteen myself," said Julia, "and, of course, as Elsa says, you'd be in a different class."

"My name's Leonard Carr. And I do seem to remember hearing about a Julia when I was there. You must have made a splash in that school!"

Leonard Carr? . . . Julia seemed to remember something also. She "thought back" with a violent effort to those days that seemed not so much far away, as in a different life. And suddenly a memory swam up in her mind, the memory of that day at school when she had taken the "little ones." Yes, this boy must be several years younger than she was, and yet he didn't seem it, somehow.

Though she could look plain enough on her bad days, she could still look radiant as a bride. This young man was strong, self-assertive, with a high-held head and thick curly hair, and bright brown eyes. She remembered the peepshow, with its fairy effect, and she remembered a sturdy assertive boy. The peepshow had been in a cardboard box. She told him about it, and he laughed pleasantly.

"I don't remember that. Done too much since, I expect! I went to that other school—the Academy for

212

Young Gentlemen—or whatever they called it, but the dad's business didn't do so well, and, anyway, I don't think I was cut out for an Academy for Young Gentlemen, so I ran away to sea."

"You ran away to sea!" echoed Julia delightedly, all the romance of the world ringing for her in that one phrase, losing her faint feeling of disappointment that he should have forgotten the peepshow.

"Yes, I'd a pretty bad time in what's called a Geordie, a collier in the coastwise trade. But it was aeroplanes that I was always keen on, and I got into Halton."

"Halton?" said Julia.

"Yes, an aircraft apprentice, you know. I'm a leading aircraftsman now, an L.A.C. I'm a fitter-mechanic, but I'm back at sea because I was posted on an aircraft-carrier."

Julia felt hopelessly ignorant. What on earth was an aircraft-carrier? He saw her vague look, and laughed.

"H.M.S. *Thunderous,* that's my ship; she belongs to the Atlantic Fleet. It's a great life. We go to the Mediterranean, and round Scotland, and all over the place." He put both his hands on his hips, and stared down at her with his bright, shallow eyes. "Have you ever been up?" he asked.

"No, I'd love to. I thought I'd fly to Paris next time I went over."

"Oh, *that!*" He dismissed it with scorn. "You might as well go in a motor-bus. That's not flying."

"It's quite flying enough for her, and too much to my mind," said Herbert.

She knew in another moment Herbert would say that if we had been meant to fly we should have been given wings, and she felt that was more than she could bear.

"I do envy you," she said. "I'm sure it's a much better life for a man than going into business."

"You bet it is," said young Carr. "Why, I'm only twenty now, and look at all the places I've seen—Gib., and France, and Italy and Malta."

"How lovely," said Julia. But to herself she was thinking: Only twenty—and she was twenty-six and a bit, almost seven years older than this man who had been about the world, and who knew about things of which she had never heard.

Twenty! Julia thought it out rapidly. She knew a lot of things, that he didn't know either, but it all seemed to her very useless. What would a man like this think of her triumphs in getting lingerie, or bead-bags more cheaply than anyone else in Paris, and getting hold of a so-called "exclusive" model? Why, he'd laugh at the whole thing; and who could blame him? He was a man; not like Herbert, who was just in the gents' tailoring.

"We've made great friends," said Elsa, in her sharp little voice. "His dad's still living here, you see, and, of course, he knew daddy . . . and your mother," she threw in as an afterthought, "so we've been going to the pictures together."

"That must be very nice for you," said Julia mechanically. "Beer or whisky and soda?"

"Beer for me," said the new-comer robustly, "anyway, to begin with. Fellows who don't go a bit slow at first when they're on shore are asking for trouble. Mind you, I don't say I'll say 'no' to a whisky and soda later."

Julia laughed. "You're hedging, like all men," she accused him. "Herbert?"

Herbert was already unscrewing bottles, his face more cheerful. Obviously, this rather forthcoming young man was attached to Elsa. Besides, he must be years younger than Julia, poor old girl, though he must admit that she could still put up as good a show as anybody else. And without all that muck on her face that the customers at the shop used.

They played whist, and as usual Uncle George conducted a post-mortem, and Mrs. Almond cried a little, very gently. Herbert argued that every card he had played was perfectly right, and Leonard Carr laughed and said it was only a game, anyway, so what did it matter?

This Herbert was not prepared to concede. Anything, according to Herbert, that was worth doing was worth doing well; and he stated emphatically this remarkably original aphorism.

Julia, who did not play whist, and who would not read because it meant wearing glasses, sat by the fire with Bobby until it was time to hand round sandwiches and offer whiskies and sodas. Mrs. Almond had her usual glass of stout. Elsa girlishly remarked that she never could bear anything to drink, and might she have a little milk, perhaps a cup of tea?

At last they all left, with many hand-shakings and remarks on the weather and hopes that they would meet again soon.

Julia felt the added vitality that young Carr's presence had given her, tingling through her as she tidied up the sitting-room and made ready for bed. Unfortunately, this touch of brilliance about her, rare in this last hard-working year or so, always awoke Herbert to the desire which she detested in him. On this evening, by the time she had quarrelled with him, refused him what he called his rights, not even giving in for the sake of peace, all glow had left her. She felt depressed, even saddened. What was the use of anything? If she was not attractive, nobody looked at her, and she couldn't do her job at the shop. If she was, then there was this perpetual struggle with Herbert. To think of all the people who had been torpedoed in the war; and all the people that had bombs dropped on them, just as far behind the lines as Herbert—why could not a bomb have dropped on Herbert? Why, she knew women who had lost two or sometimes even three husbands, and all had died; none of that nasty divorce business. And here was Herbert looking as solid as Saint Paul's.

Julia gazed round the room for which she had given up so much, and for the freedom of which she still had to fight. How sick she was of it. The little glazed chintz Chinaman which had so excited her when first she clad the room in its new trappings. . . . Everything now had the blurred and hazy look that fabrics cannot avoid after years in London air.

What a fool she had been to marry Herbert. Why couldn't she have trusted life a little longer? Why hadn't she had the energy and the courage to break with her mother and the whole of the rest of the household at Two Beresford? But how would she have lived if she had? Girls earning as little as she had been earning simply had to live at home. Oh, well, it was no good going into that sort of thing now, but it was bitter to see Anne Ackroyd, see her content in her chosen profession, watch the play of her brilliant but accurate mind. It was bitter to see Marian's progression from affair to affair with no one thinking any the worse of her. . . . It was bitter to see Ruby still talking respectability and virginity, and still always in love for the first time. It was bitter this evening to see Elsa suddenly grown attractive—in a commonplace little way enough—but still she had those lovely years of the early twenties in front of her, the years that Julia felt she herself had wasted.

The shop? After all, if she died to-morrow, what would it matter to the shop? They would miss her at first, yes, for she was good at her job, she knew, but no one was indispensable; and it was for that last and most pathetic delusion of human egoism that Julia still hankered. To be all in all to somebody. Just like the people she read about when she was a young girl, in the books she had taken out of Heronscourt Park library. To be to somebody what Gipsy had been to her sailor husband, and what, if rumour were true, Gipsy was being now to an elderly married man, whose wife refused to divorce him, but who had lived apart from him for years. Oh yes, Gipsy, in whom she had so believed, thought Julia bitterly, had not been able to stay the course. Her son was in the navy, and she was always alone in her flat when he came home on leave; but everyone knew that Gipsy had given up the unequal struggle of trying to make a comfortable living honestly at last; and that why one always saw her on first nights was because she had someone to pay; someone who liked to be seen with her, who had given her a lovely car driven by a chauffeur.

Not that Julia grudged Gipsy any of it. What she felt was the unfairness that she herself could not behave in the same way. Just because Gipsy belonged to the class of life where a liaison was taken as a matter of course, she was able to indulge in one. Nobody imagined that she loved her elderly banker much, but she was fond of him and he was devoted to her—finding peace in her presence after years of stormy matrimony.

At least, the banker's wife would never dream of turning up at the shop and insulting Gipsy; always when goaded too far Herbert held this threat over Julia's head. She was his wife, wasn't she? Well, one of these fine days he would teach her that a wife's place was the home. He would come into that blooming bandbox of hers and give her a bit of his mind. That's what he'd do. Oh, Julia knew with a sick certainty that if pushed far enough he would do it, and that all her years would go for nothing. There could be no scandal, no rows at the shop.

Julia, her victory over Herbert won, went to bed

gloomily enough, but next evening all was changed for her again. As she was leaving l'Etrangère's—she had stayed behind wrestling with the accounts—Julia became aware that someone was pacing to and fro a little farther down the street. She put the key into her bag, as she pulled the door after her, and started to walk briskly in the opposite direction.

"Evening," said Leonard Carr's voice. "Elsa told me that was where your place was, so I thought as I was coming back this way . . ." The voice trailed off a little, and Julia looked at him severely. To herself she said: He might have thought of a better one than that! And what cheek, anyway! He needed taking down a peg or two. But directly she found herself meeting the glance of his bright shallow eyes, seeing the light of the street lamp upon his curling hair, and on his smiling mouth, as he stood hesitating before her, severity vanished.

"I thought you'd be out half an hour ago," said Leonard, dropping into easy step beside her. "I hoped you'd come and have some tea with me."

"Oh, I can't," said Julia quickly. "I'm late as it is. Herbert doesn't like it if I'm not back."

"You're too good to him," said Leonard, "you spoil him. Why shouldn't you have a little amusement? It seems to me you work hard enough!"

"Herbert doesn't like going out at night," murmured Julia.

"Well, that's no reason why you shouldn't like it. Look! Ring him up. Make an excuse, and come and have something to eat with me, and we'll go to the early house at the pictures. It won't make you really late. There's someone to give him his supper, isn't there?"

"Oh yes, there's the maid."

Julia hesitated. It was very tempting. It was so long since she had had such an offer made to her, except in the cheery impersonal fashion of Mr. Coppinger. Again she was struck by a strange likeness to Alfie in this young man, although Alfie had had something about his whole aspect that Leonard lacked. And yet Leonard, in spite of his youth, was very much of a man. Her instincts told her that. And suddenly she remembered Alfie, and a little note of warning sounded in her mind like a bell, and was gone.

"I don't think I'll come to-night, thank you," she said

217

quickly. "Why don't you ask Elsa? I'm sure she'd love to go."

"I will," he said easily. "Let me see, we go back on the same bus, don't we?"

Julia had the poor satisfaction of sitting beside him during that long homeward ride along the north side of the Park, and down through Shepherd's Bush to Heronscourt Park and Young's Corner; knowing that through her own fault he was going to take that silly, giggling little Elsa out, while she herself was going back to the usual dreary evening with Herbert.

The next night the family came in from Two Beresford, Leonard Carr with them, as before.

Leonard had brought a lot of snapshots of the Mediterranean with him, and he sat between Elsa and Julia on the sofa displaying them.

"Oh, I like the one of Naples best, Leonard," said Elsa. "Show her the one you showed me the other night. Or where is that funny one with the nigger in it?"

Elsa was, in fact, determined to show Julia that she was a great friend of Leonard's, and that the snapshots were not new to her. This plan had its drawback because it enabled Leonard to devote most of his time to Julia and to spend longer over the photographs with her. When Elsa got up to get herself some lemonade, he said to her in a low voice:

"I haven't got much longer this leave. Can't you make it to-morrow evening to come out with me? What about dancing? I'm sure you like dancing?"

Julia's eyes glowed. It seemed as though an earlier and a brighter world was swinging into her orbit once again.

"I'm afraid I couldn't," she said in a low voice.

"Not if we made a party of it? Let's all go to the Hammersmith Palais de Danse—your husband, your cousin and all of us."

"That might be possible," said Julia, with a little sinking feeling of disappointment.

"Of course it's possible. And then the next night you shall come to the pictures with me to make up for my having been a good boy."

He jumped up and walked over to the table, where Herbert and Uncle George and Bertha and Mrs. Almond were playing cards.

How sure he looked of himself, thought Julia, narrowing her short-sighted eyes to gaze at him as he stood hands in his jacket pockets, his feet slightly apart, as he broke in a little upon the older folks' game. Fantastic, but true, such was his vitality that the complaining Herbert and the delighted Elsa had promised to make up a party of four with himself and Julia.

"You can hire young men out for sixpence there," Julia told him, laughing, her spirits rising in the old familiar fashion which she thought to have left behind. "I shall take one of them if I don't like your dancing."

"You can hire young ladies, too," he retorted, "and if you and Elsa don't behave, Mr. Starling and I will do just that; we will hire ourselves two beautiful blondes."

Herbert murmured something about dancing being a stupid business—never could do with it, even in the war, and hadn't danced since. But Julia laughed gaily, and tweaked his ear with more affection than she had shown him for a long time past.

"You're getting stuffy, Herbert," she said. "That'll never do, will it, Mr. Carr?"

"Oh, what do we wear?" cried Elsa. "What about my pale blue glacé?"

Elsa would want to wear pale blue, she always did, thought Julia viciously.

"I shall go in a little black turban hat. It's much smarter," she said, "and a black frock. You always look well dressed if you're in black. That's one of the things you learn in Paris."

"Oh, Paris," said Elsa viciously, with a sudden sharp little snap of her pointed teeth. "You think of nothing but your precious Paris."

"You see, I know it very well," replied Julia tranquilly.

And for the moment this appeared to her to be true. She forgot that all her time there was taken up in rushing from wholesale house to wholesale house, in seeing model after model. It seemed to her she really knew Paris well, and she thought sentimentally of the past when she had lunched and dined with René Imbert. What a fool she had been about him. What a fool she had been about everything. But she wasn't going to be again. She was going to enjoy herself for a bit now.

The dance next night was a great success, at least,

219

Julia thought so, and Leonard thought so; but whether Herbert and Elsa thought so was quite another matter.

The following evening was a Friday, so she could tell Herbert she had to stay late and see to the accounts, and might even go back with Mrs. Danvers to her flat to "do the books" with her. This last was a stroke of genius. She knew Herbert would not dare to ring her up and follow her to Gipsy's. After the other girls had all gone, after Gipsy herself had wished her a pleasant good night, and taken her departure, Julia stood for a moment in the fitting-room of l'Etrangère's looking about her.

She had helped to decorate that room during the slack season of 1922, when the first slump had lain heavy upon the land. She had painted the frieze of dancing figures, harlequins and columbines and clowns that ran round the top of the room above the glittering silver wallpaper. That "amusing" doll, with the bright red hair and the scarlet mouth and white face, which lolled back in the corner of the divan amongst the coloured cushions, was one she had brought back from Paris on her last trip. Everywhere she looked there was some trace of her handiwork. This is mine, she thought passionately. This could not go on without me. Couldn't ever be the same. This is much more mine that Saint Clement's Square can ever be.

She stood for a moment while the evening light brimmed the room like the last of a high tide; and it seemed to her that she had at least achieved something. It wasn't everybody who could work hard and get a good business together, especially when they had started as an apprentice as she had done. Yes, she had made all this, and she had made the new Julia that stood looking at her from the full-length mirror. This Julia in the smart little black suit, with the little black lace hat—a "Russian hat" that came down to her blind, but lovely, eyes—she had made this elegant thing called Miss Almond. She could always create her again at any moment with the right clothes and the right stimulus, however tired and shabby Mrs. Starling might look back in Saint Clement's Square.

Julia swept the little soft black satin coat about her, and went from the narrow winding stairs. She knew that she looked her best, as she hadn't looked for several years, when she stepped out of the house door and found Leonard Carr waiting for her.

They had a delightful little dinner at Frascati's, a place which Julia knew Marian and Gipsy despised, but which seemed to her wonderful, when she was with someone like Leonard, to whom it was also wonderful.

"Posh place this," said Leonard contentedly, and Julia at once accepted his standards, and found herself furiously resenting the thought that Marian and Gipsy might have laughed at him.

"You know I can't believe it," he said, at the end of the dinner, during which they drank Asti Spumante. "I can't believe that we haven't met all these years."

"Nor can I," said Julia. "It seems as though we had met somehow, or as though they weren't there. I don't quite know how to put it."

"I'm no good at words," he said. "They're not my strong suit, but you're pretty clever with them. You're pretty clever in everything you do, dresses and everything. I can see that all right."

"Oh, I don't know," said Julia, laughing. "I spend most of my time thinking what an awful fool I've been."

Leonard's eyes met hers very quickly, and then looked away again.

"We all make bad breaks sometimes, I suppose," he said.

"You don't seem to have," said Julia. "You've chosen the sort of life you like."

"Oh, that. Yes, that's a great life."

He suddenly seemed withdrawn, living in his own past, and Julia found herself invaded by a swift, sudden aching, like jealousy, of that strange and many-coloured life he had lived without her. Strange ports. Strange women. Everything one always thought of connected with the life of a migrant such as a sailor or a flying man. Why, nowadays, she had heard that women—even real ladies with money—were not above having a bit of fun with a good-looking man, even if he was not quite an officer. And although she, of course, could refer to Leonard as an officer, she knew he wasn't that, and never would be unless another war came along.

"Anyway, you're not married," she said suddenly, "not made a fool of yourself that way?"

"No, not yet," he agreed; and at once Julia thought of Elsa, smug little Elsa.

221

"Well, don't hurry," she urged him. "It's a frightful mistake to marry very young, as I did."

"I expect you're right," he said. "But, after all, it's very much a case of whom you marry, isn't it? Lots of fellows I know are much happier married. I suppose everyone comes to it!"

"Not you," said Julia, flattering him with her attentive eyes. "You seem so free, somehow. It would be like. . . ." She paused for a moment, and went on: "rather like putting a lion in a cage. Do you know, I can't think of you as Leonard. It seems too soft a name for you, somehow. Since you first came to Saint Clement's Square, I've thought you looked much more like a Leo. Has nobody ever called you Leo?"

"Nobody ever has, but you will, won't you? I like it."

"Leo . . ." She paused for a moment. "Yes, I will if you like, at least sometimes. I don't think Elsa would like it if she heard me call you Leo."

A shadow passed over his handsome face. He thrust his full under-lip out with a little air of sullenness that already she had noticed to be frequent with him.

"What has Elsa got to do with it?" he said. "She's only a kid."

"She's your age. Much better suited to you than I am."

"Well, I don't think so, and that's that. Age is experience. I'm years older than Elsa. She doesn't know she's born yet. I bet I'm older than you, if it comes to that. Do you know, you seem awfully like a kid yourself sometimes. I was a bit afraid of you when I met you the other day, but now you seem like a girl. You seemed so important, and talked of such a lot of grand people I know nothing about."

"Oh, well," said Julia lightly, "that's my job. I mix with a lot of them. But you must see what you call grand people, too, when you go to sea—the Riviera, for instance. Lots of rich people go there."

She watched him as he spoke, screwing up her eyes to see him better.

"Oh, I suppose so," he said, "but I don't have anything much to do with them. Of coure, there are silly women everywhere, if that's what you mean," and for a moment a little self-conscious smile touched his full lips. "But that's nothing."

"I expect you think we're all silly," said Julia, with a

222

sudden despair that struck even herself as out of all proportion. Why should she care so much what this young man thought, or said, or did?

"Oh no," he said softly, "not you, for instance. I knew you were different directly I saw you."

The eternal theme had begun. Julia leaned her elbows on the table and cupped her face in her hands.

"How do you mean—'different'?" she asked.

Herbert was up and waiting for her when she got home that night, his heavy face set in lines of anger.

"Where have you been, Julia? Don't pretend you've been at Mrs. Danvers's all the time, doing accounts."

"No, I haven't," said Julia calmly. "I ran into Leonard Carr and we went to the movies. Now don't make a fuss, Herbert, because I can't be bothered to listen to it. I have been to the movies alone with a man. Think of that. Isn't it dreadful?" And she went into her bedroom and banged and locked the door.

Herbert was furious and gave her such an unpleasant week-end that she decided her candour had been, perhaps, a trifle foolish. He accused her of "carrying on"; of trying to take Elsa's young man from her—both of which accusations were true, which did not improve matters. And yet if she were to go on meeting Leo, it seemed safer to make as little mystery of it as possible. Elsa would hear of it and be wild, of course, but she didn't give twopence for Elsa.

On Monday night she was alarmed to see Herbert waiting for her outside the shop when she came out, and she spoke to him shortly.

"Herbert, you know this is the one thing I can't have. You mustn't call at the shop for me. How often have I told you that!"

"I used to come, before we were married," he said.

"Oh, then. Besides, it was the war, and everything was different."

"Well, didn't young Carr call for you on Friday?"

"No, he didn't," said Julia.

Herbert glared at her, but she knew that he had no knowledge to go upon, and refused to let herself be flustered into any admission.

There were only two more evenings that she could see Leo before his leave was up. One of these was taken up by a family party at Two Beresford, to which Leo had brought his father and mother. His father was a thin, harsh, dyspeptic-looking man, but Julia felt her heart go out towards his mother. She was an old countrywoman, out of place in London, withered like a russet apple, with hands whose knotty joints were enlarged by rheumatism and hard work; but she had the same bright eyes as Leo, only they seemed less on guard than his. They had more of the twinkling brightness of a robin's.

At the party he gave out that he had to be down at Portsmouth next evening ready to go on board. He had warned Julia what he would say, and although she at once felt Herbert turn and stare at her, she went on calmly sorting her cards for a game of rummy they were playing, without the smallest sign of interest flickering across her face.

In the evening of the following day, when she was left alone at the shop, she rang up Herbert at Saint Clement's Square. He had just come in, tired and hungry, as she had guessed.

"Ruby has given me two seats for her show to-night," she told him. "Can you come?"

"But we've seen the show," complained Herbert.

"I know, but this is business. We've done her new dresses, and she wants someone from the shop to go and see what they look like."

"Well, I don't care a damn what they look like. I can't come all that way back."

"Oh, do come, Herbert. I shall have to get one of the girls to go with me if you don't."

She had bluffed him, and bluffed him successfully. Herbert was quite satisfied. He didn't really mind being left alone in the evening so long as she was not out with some other man. He announced sulkily that he would stay at home, and Emily would give him his supper.

"I shan't be late," Julia told him. "It wouldn't be worth going on anywhere after the show if you're not there."

She hung up the receiver, extremely pleased with herself. It was true that l'Etrangère had made Ruby's new dresses, but Julia knew them by heart and wouldn't have to pretend anything she didn't know.

So, when work was over, she stayed and changed in the wash-room of the shop, pulled on a little hat, and slipped out into the darkening streets. She took a taxi to the

Pall Mall entrance of the Carlton, paid it off, walked quickly through the foyer and out by the Grill Room door, and then up the street to Piccadilly Circus, where she entered the maze of the Criterion Restaurant and went upstairs. Leo was waiting for her, looking so handsome, though his dress-clothes were hired. He had a figure that set off any clothes. He had already, with that decisiveness which Julia felt was so masculine and so thrilling, engaged a table, not on the edge of the dancing-floor, but back in one corner where the lights were soft, and where they were as far away from the orchestra as possible. Julia remembered for a moment René Imbert's remarks about music and food. Perhaps Leo was not very grand, perhaps he would not have passed in the world of l'Etrangère, but he was a man all right—a man who knew what he wanted and how to get it. He had, she noticed, the air of authority that comes from discipline, and she felt, as she sat down at the table, a sudden little pang that life should be so badly arranged. Why couldn't he have been the same age as Alfie? Why couldn't she have met him in the war when she had met Alfie, and married him? Of course, unlike Alfie, he wouldn't have been killed. He would have stayed in the Air Service and become a fully-fledged officer, and she would have had a decent place in the world, instead of having her life cut up into three distinct fields as it was: her life at the shop; her mere existence at Saint Clement's Square, and her life of the imagination which, for the first time, seemed to be taking on flesh and actuality in front of her. If only it hadn't just one or two things wrong with it; if only she had been free. . . Oh, well, what was the use of "only"?

It was their very last evening. He hadn't yet even kissed her, hadn't made love to her except by the tacit assumption that she was prepared to join him in a little lying and scheming so that they could be together. He really didn't care twopence about Elsa, or he would have wanted to have his last evening with her. Julia's spirits rose. She put repining behind her and set herself to enjoy the evening.

They danced and they talked. Talked of life, Julia would have said, because they talked about themselves—and they were young and alive, and felt the rest of the world as a mere background to themselves.

"Do you believe a man and a woman can be friends?" he asked her, and Julia gave the correct answer.

"Of course I do. Why shouldn't they?"

"Oh, I don't know," said Leo. "Only two reasons, I suppose—that the man is a man, and the woman is a woman."

"There needn't be anything like that," said Julia primly, at once establishing her defences as much against herself as against him. Even with this delightful new note in her life, she must remember to keep herself respected, and being respected meant not being found out, not even by the other person.

"I shall miss you," he said as they danced. "I'll think of you when I'm up in the cold and rainy North."

"Oh, you'll be thinking of a girl in some port."

"I shan't. I shall be thinking of you, and you know it. You're not like anyone I've ever met, but I told you that the first day, didn't I? You're different."

"You're different, too, if it comes to that," she told him.

Here they were, back at it again—this essential difference that set them apart from the rest of the world, which somehow made it right that they should have their chance of happiness.

Julia looked at the little silver wrist-watch that had been Gipsy's Christmas present to her—"a reward for a good girl," Gipsy called it.

"I must get back," she said. "I mustn't be a minute late to-night. Herbert knows to a sec. how long it would take me to get back from the theatre." They were sitting at their little table again. He leaned forward and put both his hands on her knees under the table.

"We can't say good-bye like this," he said. "It's absurd. Can't I see you alone? We've never really been alone."

"I know," said Julia. "But how can we?"

"You don't understand," said Leo. His face was flushed after the wine he had drunk, and he seemed to Julia a creature of the light, from the wave of his thick hair—which her fingers longed to touch—to the brightness of his eyes and mouth, and the warm pressure of his hands.

"We can't," she repeated dully. "We can't."

"I don't believe in 'can't.' Wait until I get back again."

"You'll have forgotten about me by then."

"Oh no, I shan't," he said. "I'm going to write to you for one thing, and you're going to write to me."

"Herbert would see the letters."

"Oh, I'll just write a polite and friendly one to Saint Clement's Square; but there must be somewhere else I can write? What about the shop?"

"No." Julia shook her head. "Mrs. Danvers doesn't like us to have private letters there. Besides, it might be opened; they might think it was business."

"What's the best post-office for you?" he asked. "I can write *poste restante*."

Julia's eyes shone. This was romance indeed. She thought it over for a minute.

"Wimpole Street's the nearest," she said, "but it's the wrong way of the stuff for me, so to speak. Wigmore Street would be the best. You see, I could take it on my way home, or on my way to work."

"What shall I write to you . . . what name?"

"I don't know, my own name, I suppose. It's uncommon enough; nobody else would get it—Miss J. Almond."

"Very well. . . . Miss J. Almond," he said, rising to his feet and looking down at her. "Now we're going to have this last dance together before we go home."

Before we go home, echoed Julia's heart as they danced. If only it could be true. Already she was seeing Leo less as the wild and free young man that she had described him at Frascati's. Already she was wishing that they were, indeed, going home together. But then she, Julia, was different. She wouldn't have made home a cage. She would have made it a place that Leo loved to come to. She shook her head a little impatiently. It's no good; no one can rearrange life; there was always something just wrong somewhere. She must just enjoy this while she had it. It was fun, and had lifted her out of the dull rut of her days, and given her back some of the old uplift of the spirit.

"Where shall I write to you?" she asked, as they sat down again at their table and Leo called for his bill.

"To my ship, care of the G.P.O.," he said, "that always finds me."

"I wonder what sort of letters you want," said Julia, as she wrapped her cloak about her.

"I want the sort you'll write," he told her, grinning like a schoolboy.

"Oh, you're hopeless," said Julia. "You've an answer for everything."

They went back by Underground because of the time. Leo saw her safely across the road to the corner of Saint Clement's Square, then he withdrew her into the dark shadow of a tree.

"Julia," he said, "I shan't see you again till. . . . Julia. . . ."

She lifted her face to his, and for the first time since the far-off days of Alfie she felt her body respond naturally and swiftly. Her fingers tightened on his arms.

"Oh, Leo, why are you going?"

"I don't know. We ought to have done this before. I'll let you know directly I get back. I must hurry now, Julia. I have to get down to Portsmouth."

"Is there a train so late?"

"I expect so; if not I'll jump a lorry. So long as I'm there by the morning it's all right."

"Wait a minute." She clung to him. "You'll write me before your ship sails? To Wigmore Street?"

"Yes, I'll write."

"I'll send you a wire," she promised him. "You might not get a letter. Oh, Leo. . . ." They kissed again, more deeply, then parted, and she saw his figure with its easy, swinging walk become one with the shadows and the blurred lines towards the main road.

She went slowly down to her house. Her legs felt strangely weak, and yet her body was clamorously alive. If Herbert tried any of that funny stuff to-night, she would murder him.

She went up between the grinning plaster lions, let herself in softly at the outer door, and then went quietly up the stairs to her own door. She put the key very gently into the lock and crept into the darkened hall. The steady thump, thump, thump of the tail against the floor told her that Bobby lay there waiting for her. He could no longer jump all over her with the old excitement, but she never came into the flat, or, indeed, into a room where he was, without that thump, thump thump greeting her ears even if it were in the dark.

She turned on the light, and went down on her knees beside him as he whimpered, and waved his white paw in the air to her. She kissed him between the shining yellow eyes and led him upstairs. On the outer landing she paused and listened. Herbert's snores, long and rhythmic, came from the back bedroom. He knew, by now, that if he went to sleep in Julia's room she would simply take the back bedroom for herself; and he had learnt that it was better to make his demands of her when he really wanted them satisfied rather than to irritate her by his sleeping presence.

Julia and Bobby passed into the front bedroom. She shut the door quietly, and as quietly bolted it, to be on the safe side. She lay awake most of the night, her hungry pulses clamorous as she had not known them for a long time. Then towards dawn she fell asleep and dreamed uneasily a dream in which the blind Apollo in the Square and Alfie and Leo were all somehow inextricably mixed together. Somehow they kept changing from one to another, and yet always maintained a continuity of personality.

Julia entered upon a new phase of existence, a phase of building up the most dangerous relationship in the world —that spun of words and, worse still, of words put on paper. As the weeks went by she lived more and more for her letters to Leo and his answers to them. They were getting to know each other, she felt, in a far more real and true way than they would have had they been together. This, she felt convinced, was the right way to begin a relationship.

Her hair, her skin, even her eyes, seemed to take on an added brightness as the summer months drew on. Herbert used to stare at her suspiciously sometimes. She was so obviously a woman with a secret happiness, and yet what could it be? That young Leonard Carr was tossing about somewhere off Scotland, he knew that much. She had only had one polite letter, and a picture postcard, as far as Herbert knew; and yet he felt more than ever before that Julia was escaping him, that she had escaped; that her brightness, that glow about her, which was what had always enchanted him, had slipped hopelessly through his grasp. He couldn't put it into words, but he was dimly aware of the fact.

Nevertheless, thank goodness, that young Carr had joined his ship again. An unsatisfactory sort of young fellow; played fast and loose with all women as far as Herbert could see. Was supposed to be courting Elsa.

Then, apparently, got an infatuation for Julia, and though he laughed and joked with Elsa, he never bothered about being alone with her at all. And now, apparently, he had gone off and bothered just as little about Julia. Probably he had seen that he, Herbert would stand no nonsense. Good riddance, too, thought Herbert. Probably Julia had flirted with him a little, because she was always down on that kid Elsa, and wanted to show her that she could take her young man away from her. Women were like that—such was Herbert's honest conviction.

Perhaps he did get jealous for nothing, made too much of a few dances and cinemas. Julia seemed as happy now that the fellow had gone, anyway, and it was a consolation to Herbert that if the happiness had nothing to do with himself, it at least had nothing to do with Leonard.

And Julia went on her way in a dream, more vivid than she had ever known. Even the shop had lost some of its objective reality for her, and no longer did she stare at the lighted windows at night, or wonder about the other people in the bus. She lived in her letters, as much in those she wrote as in those she received; yet neither her letters, nor Leo's, could really be called love-letters. They were still, she felt, exploring, getting to know each other, although she was sure he would tell her he loved her when next he came home.

Meanwhile, her life at the shop, even her life at Saint Clement's Square, became more vivid for her as she crystallised them in her letters. She never talked about the shop to Herbert. Now, at last, she was able to put down all she thought and felt about it; describing the customers, the funny ones, the tiresome ones, those who paid and those who didn't. She described her visit to Paris, dwelling a little perhaps on the politeness and attentiveness of Frenchmen.

But they really are wonderful, Leo, she wrote. *I don't mean that agent we had, who tried to make love to me, the one I had to give up, but all of them. It seems so funny to be back in England and to the downrightness, if there is such a word, of Mr. Coppinger. We have put through quite a big deal with him, though, and he stood me some champagne at the Regent Palace, and actually backed a winner for me. I have no luck racing, as a* rule. *I have no luck even when we play rummy at home; but don't they always say—lucky at cards, unlucky in love? but after all, love's more important than cards, isn't it? Not that I seem to have been very lucky at either, but one can't help always hoping and wishing. What are you doing, I wonder? I think about you such a lot. There's none of the men I meet in business who can be a friend to me the way I feel you are. It's funny, isn't it, because we didn't meet very often. Oh, I had another bit of luck with Mr. Coppinger that I forgot to tell you about, besides the champagne. He ordered copies of the original models he bought, and let us have the real Paris labels from them without extra charge. This makes a lot of difference when it comes to selling a frock. Americans will pay twelve or fifteen guineas for something with a Paris label, when they will only pay seven or eight for an English one; and that's important for me, Leo, because you see I get a percentage now, and that is the way I hope to make really important money some day soon.*

Another day she wrote: *We have had a spell of warm weather and I couldn't help thinking of you somewhere in the grey and the wet . . . doesn't it always rain in Scotland? I've not much news—life just goes on from day to day, but none of it's very funny. We have a fairly nice lot of girls in the workroom now, and that makes an awful lot of difference to Mrs. Danvers and me; and we have got a new apprentice who cries all day, of course; I used to myself. The workroom girls are rather rowdy, and Mrs. Danvers went up the other day and found them all sitting along the floor sucking oranges, and seeing who could spit the pips out the furthest at a line of new model dresses hanging on the opposite wall!*

A letter like that amused Julia to write. She loved the life at the shop, and to build it up like this, touch by touch, for Leo's eyes, seemed to make it more important to her even than before. More and more she escaped into her letters as Herbert became grumpier and grumpier. It was all very well, he thought angrily, for Julia to seem happy. Her salary had been raised, and she was getting a percentage on sales—but he was still stuck at the £500 he was making before the war, and it

231

was hardly worth more than half what it had been. He scowled at each new frock or hat that he saw Julia wearing.

"I should think you might be thinking of saving," he said to her one day, "with things beginning to crumble as they are."

"Dick Dash's may be crumbling, but l'Etrangère's isn't," retorted Julia. "We've weathered the slump. Why, we've got five more girls now, and give real dress-shows. If people only paid, we'd be on velvet; and as it is, our credit's as good as anyone's."

He has been grousing again, she wrote to Leo during her luncheon-hour the next day. *He says everything is crumbling, and the world is going to the dogs, I suppose, as usual. Of course, we aren't too flourishing, even here, because the customers won't pay their bills; but what's the good of worrying. I do think society women can be pretty awful, though. Just fancy, last month we did the whole of a trousseau for a young bride, very rich people, and she never paid. So at last we had to bring an action against her, and would you believe it, we lost it. Her father said he wasn't responsible because she was now a married woman, her husband said he wasn't responsible because she contracted the debt before her marriage, and she said she wasn't responsible because she was under age. I know Mrs. Danvers was awfully worried, and you would think you couldn't lose a case like that, wouldn't you? Makes you wonder whether there really is any justice at all. However, we've managed to get round the corner again.*

Herbert had followed the case in the papers, and commented on it acidly to Julia.

"Lose a few more like that, my girl, and your precious shop will be on the rocks," he said to her. He was suffering again from jealousy, not a personal jealousy of her so much as a jealousy because life seemed to be treating her better than it had been treating him. Poor Herbert, thought Julia suddenly, looking at his despondent face with an impulsive pity. Gents' outfitters during the war had done a roaring trade because all the temporary gents had two uniforms as well as greatcoats, hold-alls, kit-bags and the rest. But now the temporary gents were back from the war, finding they had lost several inches round the waist, and could get into their pre-war mufti comfortably, Dick Dash was not selling as much as he had, either off the peg or bespoke tailoring.

I'm really very sorry for him, she wrote to Leo. *It must be dreadful caring about nothing but money, though, of course money is important. What one could do with it! I look at all our customers, they are all divorced about three deep, and it doesn't seem to make any difference. Everybody knows them just the same, and if they hadn't money they couldn't do it.*

Leo's letters differed from Julia's. His were more simple. He thought not at all of the problems of the world around him. He only knew that in spite of the good times he managed to have, the personality of Julia was always in some queer way present in his mind. He wrote to her, telling her of any funny things that had happened on board, or in port, and then with the naïveté of his class plunged straight into the personal, instead of weaving it into the fabric of his letters as Julia did even when she was not, apparently, writing about herself. Julia managed to build up for him her whole life so that he began to feel that something more definite and real was existing hundreds of miles away without him than the world he was actually in. This was an entirely new sensation to Leo, to whom the world ended with the present, and with his own immediate surroundings. He began to feel rather proud of himself that he had engaged the interest of such an "out-of-the-ordinary" woman as Julia; and directly he felt that he began to be more interested in her than ever.

This was a new game for him, this funny game of trying to capture thoughts and put them upon paper, so funny that they created another world for him. The letters were not all joy, though, and sometimes he seemed to feel a little drag at him as of a chain; and once he told himself, impatiently, that when he was back he would get her out of all these ifs and buts and whens and whys—all this wondering about life as she saw it going on around her. *She won't think of anything else, once I've got hold of her,* he said to himself, *but I suppose all women are like that. She's clever, but I bet I could* teach her a thing or two. I didn't rush her enough, that was the trouble.

For Leo's simple gospel was that you could always stop a woman's mouth with kisses, and when that failed, and you were sick of each other, you could go away; "you," of course, being Leo, and not the woman.

Julia loved his letters. She loved their matter-of-factness. Still more she loved the impatient note that began to sound through their pages. He would be back soon; it was July.

She realised the great annual problem of the holidays would be upon her. What would Leo do? Would he sink back into that sketchy position known at Two Beresford as "Elsa's young man"? or would he go where she and Herbert went? Was Herbert going to insist on the usual family party? In that case, she would see Leo; but it would be almost worse than not seeing him at all.

As a matter of fact, the holiday question was unexpectedly settled by a quarrel with Herbert. Julia came back one evening full of the news that Marian had grown tired of Frank Bellingham, and had gone off with someone called Hugh Carruthers. This time she was going to let her husband divorce her; it was less trouble. As the guilty party, she did not have to turn up in court, and more important still, you didn't have, as Marian had very practically remarked, to live like a nun for the next six months. Herbert, who had been irritable for some time, now exploded angrily. He told Julia exactly what he thought of her fine friends, as he termed them. At first Julia tried to speak reasonably.

"After all, Herbert it's her own affair, isn't it? Everybody doesn't look at divorce the way we do, you know. After all, it's more sensible, if you don't get on, to leave each other, isn't it?"

Herbert raved. He dragged in not only his mother, but his late wife, who, he said, would have been incapable of making such a remark. Julia suddenly lost her temper, and told him that he was crude, stupid, and, what was far worse, thoroughly common.

"You didn't think so when you married me, my girl. You were glad enough to do that."

"More fool I," said Julia. "I didn't know what it would be like. Do you think if I could get away from you now, I wouldn't?"

234

"Well, you can't," said Herbert. "Understand that. I've got you, and I'm going to keep you."

"Unfortunately," said Julia, "you don't keep me. I keep myself."

Herbert's face crimsoned, and Julia, for a moment, was afraid. He took her by the shoulders, and she felt his strong fingers digging into her flesh.

"I'm willing to keep you, you know that perfectly well. Leave that damn shop of yours, and come home and be a decent wife, and I'll keep you all right."

At the touch of his hands Julia lost her fear. She stared at him icily.

"Oh yes, you'd keep me like a general servant, because that's what it would be. No, thank you. And take your hands off me."

Herbert, who had been borne along by the strength of his own anger, dropped his hands sheepishly.

"As to not being able to get away from you," went on Julia, "you've said enough about that, and I'm going to get away from you for my holiday, if I can't get away from you for good. You can make what arrangements you like; I shall go away alone."

"Oh, you will, will you?" said Herbert. "And where will you go?"

"That's my business," said Julia.

She sat down and wrote that night to a Mrs. Rainbird, who owned a farm-house in Essex. At one time, in his drifting career as a house-agent's clerk, Mr. Almond had worked for nearly a year with a Colchester firm who had been responsible for the selling of "Brown's Farm" to Mr. and Mrs. Rainbird; and several times during the summer that followed, Mrs. Almond and Julia had visited the pleasant, low, white house. They had even spent a week's holiday there, and Julia had always remembered the place with joy. It had been one of the few enchanted weeks of her childhood. Most of it had been spent in such dreary places. A letter of condolence, and one of acknowledgment, had passed at the time of Mr. Almond's death. Mrs. Almond was too colourless to have made many friends in her passage through life, but the robust farmer's wife had always kept a pitying remembrance of her, and of the eager child that had been Julia.

It would give Herbert such a fright, reflected Julia, if she took Bobby and went away without him. Of course,

235

there was always Leo. It might mean not seeing him; still, she needn't commit herself definitely to Mrs. Rainbird's as yet; but if she did go, and if Leo couldn't see her, well, then, it was fate.

Three days later she was able to announce casually to Herbert that Mrs. Rainbird had asked her to spend the holiday as a paying guest at Brown's Farm. Herbert stared at her. He didn't expect her to carry out her threat.

"You can't," he said, "I've taken rooms."

"Well, you shouldn't have done it without consulting me."

"You weren't here. As a matter of fact, your Uncle George rang me up at business. They're all going to Torquay, and it was a question of making up my mind on the spot. You've got to book your rooms beforehand at these boarding-houses."

"When did you take the rooms from?"

"From the 11th of July." He was watching her carefully as she spoke.

Julia stared at him in honest bewilderment. "What on earth do you all want your holidays then for? Anyway, that settles it as far as I'm concerned. Mrs. Danvers has asked me to take the first half of August, and I have to fit in with other people in my business just as you have. I shall go to Brown's Farm, and you can all manage quite well without me. I'd rather be alone with Bobby. It'll be much more of a rest."

But something happened to make Julia change her mind. The next day she came out of l'Etrangère, in the glow of a summer evening. Thanks to the Daylight Saving Bill there had been no ghost buses for a long time now, and she was going back to the rather dreary prospect of a daylight supper, and a walk with Bobby. She came out this evening, blinking a little in the soft evening radiance, the last, as usual, to leave the shop. The staff, of course, got off as soon as they could. Even that tower of strength, Gipsy, since the acquisition of the gentleman known behind her back as "the boy friend," had other interests than the shop. She no longer devoted long stretches of time, after work-hours were over, to the interests of l'Etrangère, although she was as capable as ever between ten in the morning and six in the evening, interviewing customers, choosing models, and generally keeping the reins of government in her hands. Still, the fact remained that it was Julia alone who looked upon the shop as an essential part of her life; and Gipsy had long known and recognised this fact, not only in the latch-key that she had given her, but in the complete confidence she reposed in her as well.

There are times in the lives of two human beings whose ways converge, when either may become suddenly aware, with an awareness not in the ordinary course of everyday life, of the nearness of the other.

Julia had that sense, as she stepped out into George Street, on this summer evening. She knew that Leo was far nearer to her than he had been, that there would be a letter waiting for her at Wigmore Street. She knew it with some strange knowledge of the nerves, and she was right.

The letter began in the ordinary way. It thanked her for her last one, and asked her whether any more orange-pip-spitting competitions had taken place. Julia read the beginning quickly. He very seldom said anything that mattered at the beginning of his letters. It was as though the exercise of words was something alien in his experience.

There are a pretty good-looking lot of girls in Scotland, read Julia, with a sudden leaping of the heart that almost hurt her, *and yet no one has interested me. I wonder if you know why? I don't quite know myself; just because they weren't you, I suppose.* Julia's heart settled down again, and she glowed and dimpled as she read. *We are on our way south now, bound for Torbay for the regatta. I've had a letter from Elsa. It seems your Uncle George is fixing up for a joint holiday with my people to go to Torquay. Did you know this? I don't think so, or you would have mentioned it, wouldn't you, Julia? Anyway, the family party is bound to include you, and though I would rather have you alone, we ought to have a good time, and be able to arrange something. You would enjoy the regatta. The Air Force puts up a very good show. We have our own boat crews from the Carrier, and we are all very keen. I get ten days' leave after the regatta, so if we can have ten days as a family-party first, it ought not to be too bad. What do you think? We'll have to talk it over when we meet.*

The rest of the letter was unimportant, and Julia folded it up and put it in her bag. Nobody at Two Beresford had mentioned the regatta to her, or the plans for a holiday, and neither had Herbert. Yet Herbert must know, that was obvious. That was why he had made his plans to join the family party, for Herbert hated doing anything peculiar, and he would tell himself that he was quite able to look after his own wife. He would, in fact, do anything sooner than let either Leo's family or the family at Two Beresford think that he was in the least jealous of Leonard. All that was understandable. Julia followed the processes of Herbert's mind very quickly. What annoyed her was that she had already agreed with Gipsy to take her holiday at the beginning of August. Would Gipsy consent to an alteration? While she was still at the post-office, Julia went to a call-box and telephoned Gipsy.

"Would it be possible," she asked, "without throwing everything out at the shop, for me to alter the date of my holiday? I find my husband has already taken rooms at Torquay with the rest of the family from the 11th of July."

"The 11th of July!" came in Gipsy's soft, rich voice, somewhat sharpened by surprise. "Oh, but Julia, that's impossible. Why, it's one of the heaviest months."

"Oh, I know," said Julia, quickly, "I wasn't asking for that. I thought if I could get off by about the 16th or 17th." There was a silence, during which Julia pictured to herself Gipsy rapidly making calculations.

"Well, I think that might be managed, Julia, a fortnight from then. You know it's the last half of August I want to get away, and we both can't be way at once. If you can take over from me by the tenth, I think that will be all right."

"It's awfully good of you, Mrs. Danvers. I'm frightfully grateful. I'd no idea all these arrangements had been made."

"Oh, that's all right," said Gipsy.

Julia boarded the bus in a state of mingled excitement and anger. Herbert had evidently thought to catch her out. He had expected her to know about the regatta. Well, she hadn't known, but she knew now and she would announce that Mrs. Danvers had allowed her to change her dates, with the most innocent air in the world.

For, after all, there was no reason why Herbert should suspect that she had heard from Leo to-day, since she obviously had not heard yesterday. How pleased Herbert must have been, thought Julia, when she said she couldn't go. He must have realised that while he had saved his face with the family, yet Julia had committed herself to being alone in Essex. Julia smiled to herself. She was going to enjoy watching Herbert's face while she told him of her change of plans. She did tell him that evening.

"Oh, by the way, Herbert," she said airily, "I've managed to change my plans—about the holidays, I mean."

"Oh," said Herbert, looking at her suspiciously. "Been seeing Elsa?"

"Seeing Elsa?" Julia stared at him innocently. "No, why should I? I don't see Elsa any more than I can help —you ought to know that."

"I thought she might have told you the reason they are going to Torquay is that young Carr will be there for the yearly regatta and, of course, he and Elsa want to see as much as they can of each other."

"Oh, that's why, is it?" said Julia. "Well, the regatta will be rather fun. When does it begin?"

"The 11th of July, and it lasts for ten days," said Herbert.

"Then I shall miss most of it. I can't get down until the end of the first week. I expect Elsa is getting all excited again. I wish I could persuade her not to wear pale blue. She'd have a much better chance of getting a young man, and of keeping him."

"I suppose that's one of your clever remarks," said Herbert. "I don't know what's wrong with pale blue, myself. It was my mother's favourite colour, and there's nothing like a nice pale blue for shirts."

Herbert was not a sensitive or observant man, and yet during the days that followed it was impossible, even for him, to ignore the fact that Julia had changed. The old glow came back to her, that quality she had carried when first he knew her, that had attracted him while the first pale dyspeptic Mrs. Starling sat at his table. But in those days it had been a glow that shed its light upon everyone. He himself had had his snatched kisses in the hall, but now this self-same quality enwrapped Julia like a burning bush; and though she was less irritable with him than she had been for some time, it was simply because she hardly knew he was there. The glassy and unmoved front she presented was a better protection for her than all her physical shrinking and her frantic refusals of him. Many a night Herbert told himself, as he sat sulking over his whisky and soda, that this time he would stand no nonsense; that this time he was going into her room; but those bright unseeing eyes kept him out more effectually than anything else had been able to do.

Julia arrived at the boarding-house at Torquay after the others had already been there a week. She arrived confident, and armoured all about with what Leo had written her. Elsa was nothing, merely an excuse for him to see her. It was worth not coming down for the first part of the regatta, if they could arrange to meet for part of his ten days' leave afterwards.

Julia did not flatter herself that it would be easy. She had a fortnight's holiday. This would see them beyond the end of the regatta, and Herbert would expect her to spend the rest of the time at Torquay. She and Leo would have the greatest difficulty in seeing each other alone, but Julia's blood rose to the challenge. She felt the same excitement, only intensified, that she felt when she smuggled dutiable goods in from France. That little act of smuggling was always as good as a cocktail to Julia. Once she had decided upon her course, something happened to her mind that made everything she said seem true to her. When the Customs official at Dover or Folkestone asked if she had anything to declare, she would gaze at him with limpid eyes and, handing over her keys, say, "Nothing, here are my keys . . ." and would remain calm and unworried while the official opened her suitcase to be confronted with a very limp, innocent and spinsterish-looking hot-water-bottle lying on a rather faded dressing-gown.

Julia fell in love with Torquay at first sight. There were palm-trees just as she had seen them in photographs of the Riviera. The bay itself had a lovely curve. The water was brilliantly blue to someone accustomed only to the waters off the south-eastern shores. The boarding-house didn't seem too bad either—full of stuffy old things, of course, as boarding-houses always were, but there was a certain excitement in meeting even her family

240

and Herbert; an excitement engendered by the fact that she knew she was carrying a secret which made her feel very much cleverer, and more alive, than any of them.

It was fun to be kind to Mrs. Carr, whose bright eyes studied her distrustfully, and who seemed frightened by the imitation elegance of the boarding-house. It was fun to be politely rude to Bertha, grimmer and more inarticulate than ever. It was not fun to have to share a room with Herbert, but she went drearily through the performance that might keep him quiet for the rest of the holidays; and drearily went through the accustomed routine of making that performance safe as far as results went. This was still part of her life. It had to occur occasionally, or else Herbert's quarrels would become unbearable. But as she lay in sick disgust, she told herself that something must happen, something would be bound to happen which would free her of this tyranny for ever.

The four remaining days of the regatta passed in a dream for her. There were boats rowed quickly across the water, the blades of the oars flashing in the sun; but with her short sight she could not, even with binoculars, be quite sure which of the rowers was Leo. The little white sails leaned over to the wind, fluttering, leaned over again on the other side—or as Leo had tried to teach her to say "on the other tack." Guns went off, and she never knew the result of anything until she had been told.

The ships lay grey and imposing upon the blue waters, but Julia had not, on the whole, enjoyed the regatta, except for an afternoon spent on the aircraft-carrier, being shown over it by Leo. Of course all the family was there too, and Elsa, who had been over H.M.S. *Thunderous* before, was insufferably superior; but the afternoon was worth while for the quick little pressure of Leo's hand as he helped her about the ship. She longed to take back with her a more accurate picture of where he lived, and ate and slept, but that was impossible. She could not wear her spectacles when with Leo; and a blur of polished brass, grey paint, scrubbed decks, shining mahogany and cast erections of steel were all that Julia could have told about the aircraft-carrier—save for the amazing fact of one big deck, built like a lift, which rose up at, apparently, great expense to the Admiralty;

with the aeroplanes, ready for taking off, drawn up up-on it.

Leo managed to tell her, in an undertone, that he would be free the day after the regatta, in the afternoon. He was not telling anybody but her, and could she say she wanted to go for a walk alone, and meet him at Bab-bacombe for tea?

It was easy to make excuses to walk alone. Elsa was a lazy little thing, and preferred wearing high-heeled shoes, and dawdling about looking in the Torquay shops, to taking a country walk. Julia knew, with knowledge obtained at l'Etrangère's, what to wear and what to do in the country. She had neat brogues and heavy stock-ings, a smart little tweed suit and a pull-on hat in which she could have passed for any one of the Darlings. She paused on her way out to ask Herbert whether he would not come with her. This moment gave her the same little exquisite fear that smuggling was wont to do. She knew there was no real danger of Herbert coming too. He would be much better if only he took more exercise, as Dr. Ackroyd always told him, but he did not seem to mind putting on fat, and feeling livery—although, direct-ly anything was the matter, there was no one more frightened than Herbert. However, Julia had always heard that men were like that, and she accepted it as normal.

Her gambler's gesture was justified. Herbert, replete with a heavy midday meal of the boarding-house, stared at her stonily from his wicker-chair at the front door.

"If only you had given me warning," he grumbled.

"I did," said Julia. "We talked about my walk this morning; if only you'd listen to me, but you never do. Try and get out before tea, Herbert, because you really ought to take more exercise, you know."

She nodded as though she had been a complete strang-er, he told himself angrily, took up her stick and was off, leaving him without any ground for complaint, and yet feeling vaguely angry.

Leo overtook Julia as she was walking down the steep, winding road to Babbacombe. He glanced quickly in both directions—there was no one to be seen. He caught her in his arms and kissed her passionately, but did not speak at all. Julia hung in his arms. She felt more than excited, she felt actually happy, wildly happy, for the first time in her life. They still did not speak, except to stammer out each other's name when he released her, but, hand-in-hand like children, went on down the road to the edge of the sea. There they sat down on the sand and talked.

Julia hated the first thing she heard her voice say:

"You must have seen lots of pretty women: you told me so in your letter. I expected you to have forgotten me."

"They weren't you," he said, repeating what he had written. "They weren't you; that's all that matters."

Julia glanced up at him, and again felt happiness flooding her whole being. Each was a little shy of the other, and each had built up an entirely different personality out of the letters, and now, with that curious feeling that everyone knows on waking from a dream, they had to adjust the world of spun fancy to the world as it lay about them. Julia, of course, was quicker at this fusion than Leo, because there was only one Julia for him; the Julia who sat opposite to him in London, who had written him the letters, and who was lying pressed against him on the sands at Babbacombe now.

They did not kiss again. It was curious really, thought Julia, as she felt the rough cloth of his coat up against her cheek. You couldn't even call their parting kiss in London "making love." It was such an isolated act in their relationship; and yet now that they met again, after months of being apart, they knew that they would be lovers.

"You talk about my meeting girls," said Leo at last. "What about all the men you meet? What about What's-his-name, who stands you champagne at the Regent Palace?"

"Oh. . . . Mr. Coppinger. He's a dear old thing. Besides, that's business. That doesn't count."

"Well, what about your husband?" said Leo. "He counts, I suppose?"

"Not really, not at all," said Julia, and suddenly she had a curious sensation of feeling light and free as air. Herbert had always seemed to matter such a lot, to be such a dead weight, and now she suddenly realised that he didn't matter at all.

"What I mean is . . ." She stopped.

243

"Oh, you can't get round it, say what you like," said Leo. "After all, he is your husband, isn't he?"

Julia put her hands to her ears. "For heaven's sake don't say that. It's his favourite remark—'after all, I am your husband.' He always says it when. . . ." She stopped, and a deep burning colour spread over her face and neck. It was the first time Leo had seen her blush, and he gazed at her fascinated.

Into his shrewd, matter-of-fact mind, there came at once the end of the sentence that she had not uttered—"when he wants to make love to me." That had been the thought in her mind. Unimaginative as he was, he could almost hear Herbert saying it. He changed the subject abruptly.

"How's business?" he asked.

"Oh well! Work-girls come, and work-girls go, but, like matchers, they're all very much the same. We have a good apprentice, thank God, which is the chief thing. Customers don't pay, but still we survive."

They were back on the facts of everyday life, where Leo was at home; and the more they stayed in that world the easier he found it to play the urgent, masterful young man. While he had been away from Julia she had seemed in an odd way to control his movements, as she had certainly his thoughts. Now they were together he took his place as leader.

"I suppose," said Julia, "you'll stay here for your leave so as to be with Elsa?"

"Not if I can arrange anything different, I shan't. Mum'll be a difficult person to manage, but I'll do it somehow."

Julia felt a little quickening of triumph. Easy enough to steal someone from insipid Elsa, but not so easy to steal from that old, tenacious country woman, with her bright robin's eyes.

"Well, I don't know how you'll explain it to Elsa either," she said.

He thrust her head back against the sand, and sat looking down at her.

"I've never kissed Elsa the way I did you," he said. "Never wanted to. Do you remember that night in Saint Clement's Square, Julia?"

Julia remembered it; she felt faint with desire as she lay there.

"You've got to love me, you know, Julia, you've got to."

"Leo, I'm married."

"Well, what's that? What about all your fine friends that you tell me about—the Honourable What's-her-name? Dishonourable, I should think, from what I hear of her. We've a pretty plain name for her sort at sea, I can tell you."

"I don't suppose you've any peculiar words at sea, you probably only mean 'bitch.' It's said quite a lot in business circles, believe me, especially with customers who are troublesome. Besides, you see, Leo, I'm not that sort. I want to be happy, of course, who doesn't? But I'm not like that, I'm not easy. I've never let anybody make love to me, not really, and Herbert's so difficult," ended Julia, in a burst of truthfulness.

"He needn't know. Why should he?"

"Of course he will. Elsa will suspect, for one thing, if you aren't hanging round her all the time; and Herbert likes me to account for every minute of my time I spend away from him. Goodness knows what I shall say I've been doing when I get back this evening."

"Well, you haven't been doing anything," said Leo ruefully. "I wish you had. Julia, what are we going to do?"

"I don't know, you'll have to think of something. Oh, Leo, it's funny. I've never felt anyone was stronger than me before. I've never waited for them to plan and arrange things. You're different somehow. . . . It's all very well," she said, after five minutes had been spent in the ever-delightful exercise of discussing just how they both were different from the rest of the world, "but what are we to do? We'll never be alone together for a moment, not without . . ." she corrected herself, "not unless I stay in the boarding-house and pretend to have a headache, and then you can pretend to sprain your ankle and come back after you have all set out for an excursion. And, believe me, that wouldn't be much good, for Elsa would come back with you. And, anyhow, the boarding-house is filled with stuffy old cats. Boarding houses always are."

"I can't go on like this. Either we'll have to fix something or I'll have to give you up."

Julia's eyes dilated, and it seemed to her in the pain

of the moment as though she could actually feel the blood drain from her heart.

"Leo," was all she could say, "Leo. . . ." She was inarticulate in the face of the first profound emotion of her life.

"Well, I'm only flesh and blood," said Leo, as his underlip thrust out, and his eyes became surly. "I'm not getting much out of this, am I? You know I'm crazy about you, and I've got to have you; and you don't do anything to make it easy."

"What can I do?" said Julia, hopelessly. "Don't you see how impossible it is?"

Leo leaned forward towards her, and spoke in a low voice.

"Julia," he said, "there are rooms in that house of yours—where the shop is . . . isn't there a room where we could? . . . You've got the key, haven't you, if we could get back to London . . . ?"

"Oh no, Leo, no, I couldn't do that. The shop . . . you don't understand. The shop's quite different. Mrs. Danvers trusts me. I couldn't do that."

"Well, if your precious Mrs. Danvers is more to you than I am . . . I thought she did a bit in that line herself?"

"It isn't that," said Julia. "You don't understand. It's the shop," yet even as she spoke the vision of the fitting-room, as she had often seen it when she had turned out the light and left it, floated before her mind's eye. All dark, except the faint light from the street-lamp below; darker than the world outside, so that you could move about in it safely without being seen, and yet see your way quite well; even see the glitter of the different-coloured tinsel cushions on the wide divan, and the pale face, and dark mouth, of the red-haired doll. She put the vision from her hastily. The shop was sacred.

"We'll have to think of something. We'll arrange something, we must," she said. "Leo, don't talk of leaving me, you can't."

"Well, I can't go on like this," said Leo.

Julia gazed at him despairingly, realising for the first time how the poor live. She couldn't stay away for a night, and go to an hotel. What could she possibly say to Herbert? Besides, what sort of hotel did one go to for that sort of thing? She hadn't the faintest idea. Perhaps

Leo had, she thought, with a little jealous pain. She had heard stories of quite a big hotel near Paddington, but that would be horrible, sordid and dreadful. And there probably wouldn't be such a place at Torquay, and anyway, she and Leo couldn't be missing at the same time.

It came over her, with a dreadful pang of certainty, that she would have to give Leo up. It was too difficult, too impossible. She wanted love as much as he did, but failing the fulfilment of their desire, she still could have found happiness, she told herself, in just seeing him, talking to him, meeting him. It wasn't enough for him. He would sooner have nothing, if he could not have everything he wanted. She stared at him hopelessly, and her mouth began to quiver, and her eyes filled with tears. He looked at her:

"That's all you can do, is it——cry. Isn't that like a woman. You work me up to this, and then you can't think what to do about it."

"But how can I, Leo, how can I? What's there to think of?"

"There must be something. I've only got ten days from to-morrow. Come out with me for the day on a motor-bike?"

"Oh, Leo, think of the trouble there'd be. Think of Herbert, think of Elsa. It would be simply ghastly. Everybody in the boarding-house would hear about it."

"Well, if they do . . . You're not there for life."

"No, but I'm with Herbert for life, at least he seems to think so. Oh, Leo, if only we had money. I could always support myself. I make plenty at the shop, but Herbert is always threatening, if I leave him, to come and make trouble, and that would be the end of everything. Oh, Leo, it isn't possible. What can I do, what can I do?"

He stood up and helped her to her feet, and started mechanically to brush the sand from her shoulders and skirt. He looked sulky and incredibly young. How difficult men were, thought Julia; Herbert in his way, and now Leo in his.

They walked back together, only separating in the outskirts of Torquay. Julia clung to him at parting, speechless from the sense of loss. She went back to the boarding-house, bitterly unhappy. It was much later than she thought, and the whole party, excepting Bertha, was already gathered in the gloomy little lounge, where the wicker-chairs and cheap cretonne curtains tried to give an impression of alfresco gaiety.

Julia looked about her. Everybody seemed to be there except Bertha . . .

"I say, I had no idea it was so late," she said. "I'll run up and change. Don't wait for me, any of you."

To herself she thought: I don't care if I miss their beastly supper. There's never enough to eat anyway, and they look shocked at the mere thought of a drink. What a life!

But the party, with the tenacity peculiar to families that go about in herds, waited for her. Indeed, when she came down again some ten minutes later in the afternoon frock that was considered suitable for the occasion, Bertha had joined them. Bertha looked flushed, as though she had been walking fast. She was dressed in her outdoor things. She turned and stared at Julia.

"So you got back before me," she said. "Young legs walks faster than old ones. You've changed too, I see."

"I don't know what you mean," said Julia. "I always change."

"I mean I saw you coming down the hill from Babbacombe with young Carr. As a matter of fact, I saw you going up the hill from the beach, too. I've been having tea there. That's a nice thing, I must say, to leave your husband and go out and spend the afternoon flirting with your little cousin's young man."

"Oh," cried Elsa, jumping up, "he told me he couldn't get on shore this afternoon. It can't be true."

"What's this?" said Herbert. "Julia, what's the truth of this?"

"For heaven's sake keep your voice down," said Julia. "D'you want the whole boarding-house to know that you don't know how to behave? All right, since Bertha has, apparently, been spending the afternoon spying, I did go out with Leonard. I did meet him at Babbacombe; he asked me to yesterday when we went over the ship, and if you don't like it," she ended with more force than elegance, "you can lump it."

"Oh, Julia," came in a feeble little cry from Mrs. Almond, but nobody paid any attention to her.

Dinner was eaten somehow. Nobody spoke much. Herbert reserved what he had to say for the bedroom.

Julia had come back from her walk feeling unhappy, but virtuous, because she had decided that there was nothing to be done about Leo, felt the genuine indignation that everyone feels when only half an accusation is true. The half that was untrue seemed to her far the more important. She put her hands over her ears at last and sat wearily down on the edge of the bed.

"What's the good of going on?" she said; "you know I saw him—well, what about it? As a matter of fact, I told him I couldn't see him any more. That it wasn't possible, he must give up thinking about me. Now what have you got to say?"

"I don't believe you," said Herbert.

"Very well, then, don't believe me, but I can prove it to you. I'm sick to death of you, of the whole lot of you. Nothing comes into my life that is at all different, or beautiful, that you do not try to spoil. I'll leave tomorrow. I'll go back to London.",

"You can't," said Herbert, "I've paid for your first week here."

"Well, you can ask them to give you double portions. It won't hurt them: they nearly starve us. But I'm going back. I shall probably go down to Essex after all. I've another week of my holiday."

Herbert began to be alarmed. It would look very odd if Julia left suddenly the next day. Besides, there had been something in her voice which had made him believe her when she said she had been telling Leonard that he couldn't see her again alone.

"There's no need to do anything in a hurry," he mumbled shamefacedly.

Julia got into bed and lay with her back to him without answering. Herbert followed her into bed and tried to "make it up," which led to another quarrel. There were two things, Julia reflected ruefully, that she and Herbert invariably had rows about: one was bed and the other was bacon. Since they were in a boarding-house, where bacon was never cut on number three of the machine, this particular row was about bed. Julia would give Herbert no solace; she felt exalted, dedicated. If she could not be for Leo, she would not be for anyone. She was no longer for Herbert.

Her box was packed before breakfast next morning.

Elsa's eyes looked very red and swollen at the break-fast-table, and so did her nose, Julia saw with pleasure.

"Don't worry, Elsa," she said, "I'm leaving to-day." Elsa only sniffed miserably, and did not reply.

It was all very well, reflected Julia, to talk so glibly about leaving, but she must see Leo first. It all depended whether he turned up that morning or not. She sat turning the pages of the railway time-table in the lounge, pointedly ignored by the rest of the party, when the sallow youth who carried the luggage up and down, and in the afternoon donned a sort of hotel livery, came up to her and told her that she was wanted on the telephone.

Julia went quickly to the office where the telephone was situated, and shut herself in the little glass box. Her heart beat as though it would suffocate her. Yes, it was Leo. She had known it from the moment she had seen the sallow youth approaching her. Quickly she told him what had happened.

"I'm on shore now," he told her, "and must see you. Julia, can you meet me in the Rock Walk, right away past the Torbay Hotel, in half an hour?"

"I'll be there," she promised him. She put on her hat and walked quickly out of the house down to the sea front. She strolled into a shop, bought some picture-post-cards, and putting on her glasses watched carefully to see if anyone came after her. No, she had managed it all right. She paid for the postcards and left the shop. A taxi was cruising slowly along; she jumped into it and gave her order. That'll throw them off anyway, she told herself. I don't see old Bertha, or Herbert for that matter, running to a taxi.

Leo was already there waiting for her. They sat down in a sheltered seat, and Julia, who hadn't cried, felt her eyes filling with tears again as they had on the beach at Babbacombe, as she looked at Leo's face and then at the palm trees, which dropped their graceful heads against the brilliant sky.

She told her story quickly.

"So you see, Leo, we shan't see each other again," she ended, "except perhaps at yours and Elsa's wedding. I'm going this afternoon."

"But you can't go. You *know*, I've got my ten days' leave now. It's all I shall get till Christmas."

250

"I can't help it. Bertha seeing us has absolutely torn it."

"Where are you going?"

"Back to Saint Clement's Square at first, and then I shall probably go on to this farmhouse in Essex."

"Can't you wait at Saint Clement's Square? I could come up there somehow."

"Leo, I couldn't. They're dreadfully nosy people in the flat below. Besides, I should hate it to be like that. I can't explain it to you, but I should. I want it to be somewhere you've never been before, somewhere just for us. Besides, I should be frightened all the time of Herbert coming back, even if the people below didn't see us. It would spoil it all."

"That's all very well," said Leo, his under-lip stuck out in the sulky way she had begun to dread, that made her heart soften over him; it made him look so absurdly like a little boy. "But I can't give you up like this, Julia. I can get away for the end of my leave, if I spend a few days here now."

"They'll want to know where you're going," said Julia. "You'll have to write every day. They'll be full of suspicions now, you know."

"Damn that old woman," said Leo, angrily. "I bet she followed you on purpose, directly she heard you were going for a walk."

"I expect she did. She has always hated me. She doesn't think I'm good enough for Herbert. She wants him to get rid of me. I wish to goodness he would. I don't ask anything better."

"Let me think a few minutes," said Leo. "There must be some plan."

Julia's spirits rose. She had done all she could. She had practically given Leo up; she was leaving. If he insisted on following her, what could she do about it? Accustomed as she was to living in a world of make-believe, it was very difficult for her to think of practical plans. All that side of her went into the business, none of it into her own life. But Leo, for whom nothing was a dream, would surely manage somehow.

"You can't get recalled to Portsmouth?" she suggested timidly; "they couldn't cut short your leave for anything, I suppose; I mean, you couldn't pretend they did—that you were wanted?"

He shook his head. "No, that's impossible. It'd be too easy for people to find out it wasn't true."

"Haven't you got a sick relation who could send for you?" asked Julia, "that's what they always do in books. They have telegrams calling them away, saying somebody is ill, or something."

"Not a relation, but I tell you what I've got—a pal who'd do anything for me."

"Oh, that's an idea," cried Julia, "men are always supposed to be such good friends to each other. Where is he?"

Leo was thinking it over. "It's old Hopkinson," he said at last, "he was a captain's steward. He's retired now. Started a chicken farm New Forest way. If I write to him, and tell him to wire me saying he is ill or something, he will. Look, this's his address." He took out a note-book, scribbled down the address, tore out the page and gave it to Julia. "When I'm fixed up, I'll stay with him a day, give him all his instructions about letters, and get across to this farmhouse of yours."

Julia gazed at him admiringly. Directly a plan of action had been thought of, Leo became the dominant partner. It was wonderful to have everything decided for her like this; to see his bright and eager face, and his intent eyes.

"You'll have to write a lot of picture-postcards," she said gaily, "and date them different days, and your friend Hopkinson can post them for you."

"Oh, I'll do that all right," said Leo, with a grin, as he remembered what good cause Hopkinson had to be grateful to him.

"I suppose he'll have to open your letters," said Julia, "and wire you if there's anything important in them. You don't mind your letters being opened, do you?"

"Not a bit," said Leo.

That means he isn't hiding anything from me, said Julia's heart. That means he isn't keen on Elsa, not even the tiniest little bit. Aloud she said:

"It's worth separating and even losing those precious days of your leave, if we can have three or four days together. It doesn't seem possible, Leo. It's too good to be true."

"It's going to be possible," said Leo. "You've only just got to do what I say."

How lovely it was, thought Julia, just to let herself go, and to have life arranged for her by this eager lover. For that was what he was. Somehow, without any open declaration, without ever saying the words, "I love you," she knew it for a truth. She, like other women, was going to have her lover at last.

A lover, thought Julia, and savoured the word upon her tongue. It made her feel free, and splendid, merely to think of it. And her lover was coming to her because he wanted her, because she wanted him, because she loved him. Not because, like Gipsy, she had tired of battling for a living, and was content to give gratitude and affection. Not because, like Marian, she was hungering, questing and unsatisfied. But because she knew what she wanted, and she was going to have it; because Leo wanted it too.

She left Torquay that afternoon, and her mother saw her off, anxious, and half weeping. Julia knew her mother thought it was a pity that she could not get on with Herbert. After all, once you were married, you *were* married, and there it was. That gentlemen were odd, Mrs. Almond was the first to admit, but then she had always told Julia so. Julia ought to know that gentlemen must be humoured.

"All that's stuff and out of date," said Julia, when Mrs. Almond tried to give faltering expression to these convictions upon the platform of Torquay station. "Don't you worry about me," she added, putting her head out of the window. "I shall enjoy a little peace at Saint Clement's Square. Besides, it means I can send Emily off for her holiday at once. I'll look after Bobby. As a matter of fact, one of the girls at the shop wanted to spend her holidays with me. We may go off to Mrs. Rainbird's, or we may not. I'll let you know. Tell Bertha to look after Herbert, she likes doing it," and with that the train began to draw out of the station, and Mrs. Almond was left upon the platform.

Julia wired to Mrs. Rainbird that she would be coming after all, gave Emily a present of an extra pound to help with her holidays, and then departed to Essex, taking with her Bobby, his brush and comb, his chamois leather and his blanket, all of which paraphernalia excited him profoundly.

The farm was all Julia had remembered it. A simple

253

white two-storeyed house, made pleasant by its simple and unsuspicious occupants, who thought it would be very nice for Julia when her "cousin who is on leave from the navy" could come and see her. Mrs. Rainbird knew a lot of people who were officers now who wouldn't have been before the war, and was not surprised. Besides, now Julia had got on in the world, Mrs. Rainbird was never tired of exclaiming at her elegance.

She only had from the Saturday to the Monday alone with Bobby, just long enough to explore, to find again the great circle of the mere, a deep olive-green lying in the cup of thickly-wooded hills that rimmed it all about. Ancient trees hung their branches over the edge, dripping their leaves into its tranquil waters. A little stream, in which movement was hardly perceptible, led into it from the river. A gentle little river that ran between flat meadows and lines of willows; while in the distance were the shapes of big curving fields, pale with oats, or golden with corn, or patterned with haycocks. Fields divided by dark hedges and dark plumy elms, whose spreading tops drooped over against the sky.

Julia, rather alarmed, launched herself and Bobby in the punt and paddled gently round the mere, keeping in under the overhanging branches; and then as she grew bolder, and Bobby ceased barking distrustfully, and showed signs of settling down, taking the punt through the outlet into the river. The river, at least, was shallow, whereas they told her at the farm that the mere was bottomless, and if you fell in, and couldn't swim, you were drowned and your body never came up again.

They were full of information at the farm about Constable, of whom Julia remembered hearing before. This was "Constable country" and the Rainbirds seemed proud of it.

Julia received a very practical letter from Leo. He had managed it. Hopkinson had duly sent him a wire saying that he was ill and asking him to come and help him as Leo had instructed him. He showed the wire, and the letter that followed it, to Elsa. Leo had helped the obliging Hopkinson more than once out of a bad place, and the little steward was doing his best to repay him now. Twice when he had got drunk, when the aircraft-carrier had been in the Mediterranean, and once when he had over-slept at the Maison Tolérée at Ste. Maxime, Leo had managed to save him. Hopkinson asked no questions, and repaid his debt.

Therefore, the "cousin from the navy" arrived, and found rooms at the village inn, strolled over, and was casually introduced by Julia, and approved of. A very nice young gentleman; he would be company for her. Mrs. Rainbird did not like to ask Julia whether she had lost her husband—she had merely stated that she married in the war when writing from Saint Clement's Square —but somehow she had received that impression. There was no photograph of him in Julia's bedroom, and the few picture-postcards she sent off she posted herself.

On Julia and Leo's first day together Mrs. Rainbird gave them a picnic lunch of sandwiches, hard-boiled eggs and home-cured ham, and mustard and cress; and Leo brought beer from the inn.

They went down to explore the river and the mere. It was one of those days, rare in England, that are hazy with heat. There was a little hut at the mere's edge where the punt was moored, and there Julia changed into her bathing-suit. Leo was ready for her when she came out. Each avoided meeting the other's eyes, the old taboo of class and custom strong upon them for the first few minutes. They were alone together, and they were almost naked.

Julia was pleased, as never before, that she had a lovely figure. Even on the days when her face was plain, she knew that her neck, and the way her head was set upon it, her sloping shoulders, and her small firm bosom, her slim hips and long straight legs were lovely. Thanks to poverty, which had always caused Mum to buy her shoes a size too large while she was growing up, her feet were not misshapen in any way. Like this, in her skin-tight green suit, she felt at least equal to Marian, and to all the Darlings that came into the shop.

After the first minute she moved forward, putting her feet timidly on the grassy edge, full of tiny stones and twigs. Leo looked splendid, she thought, stealing a glance at him. Yes, as splendid as she did.

"I hate cold water, you know," she said at last. "I can only swim a very little. They say it's awfully deep."

"I'll keep in here by the edge," he promised her, "and I won't let go of the back of your belt. I'll take care of you. Just let yourself go, and don't be a bit frightened."

Julia obeyed him with a voluptuous sense of pleasure. The almost stagnant water was fairly warm. Leo swam strongly and easily, with his one hand, holding her up with the other. Julia had left Bobby with Mrs. Rainbird, who already loved him; for he didn't like things he didn't understand, and he was no dog for the water. It was only with the greatest coaxing that he had trusted himself the day before in the punt—a nasty contraption that had the habit of sliding away as soon as his front paws were on it.

"Not too much, Leo, not too much. Oh, I'm out of breath, and I don't want to get cold. Oh, Leo, I've put down my feet and I can't feel the bottom. Take me in."

Leo laughed and turned her head to the shore. "Hang on to this bough," he said, "like this."

He made her clasp both her hands round the overhanging bough of a big tree. They hung on to it, side by side, letting their feet trail down into the depths of the water.

"Isn't it lovely? Look up," said Julia, "look, layers of leaves, and leaves and leaves ever so far up to the sky. It's like being in a room, a lovely green room."

"Does nobody come here?" asked Leo.

"One other family has the key to the gate at the top of the meadow, but they're not here yet. There's nobody but you and me. The farm people don't do this sort of thing."

She swung herself along to the shore, her hands on the bough. She had never known the enjoyment of good physical exercise. She had been brought up in surroundings where games held no place, and in a family which had never heard of them. This was almost the first time she had felt a healthy tingling through her body. Dancing was the only thing she had learned to do. It would be lovely, she thought enviously, to be a good swimmer, and to play tennis and golf, and do those things the Darlings did. But then, being so short-sighted, she would have to wear her specs, though she could manage without for swimming, thank goodness.

Everything was all dapple sun and shadow, gleaming water and green leaves. She ran into the hut and rubbed herself down, feeling glowing and alive as never in her life before. It had always been cold when she had bathed in the sea on her holidays; besides she wasn't a good swimmer, and waves frightened her. This deep, cool, secret greenness was the place for her. It was a magic place, thought Julia excitedly, as she slipped on her one simple under-garment, and her white cotton frock, and passed over her head the green beads that Leo had brought her from his last voyage.

They lounged in the punt, lying half in and half out of the sun, opposite to each other, suddenly silent, although they had talked rather more than usual during the meal.

In the circle of the mere there was nothing but silence and peace. The trees dipped their heavy branches into the water over which they skimmed, to Julia's delight, strange fugitive insects that progressed rapidly, but with immense determination, in many directions, all of which were apparently important, since they seemed to be making such a fuss about the exact course they took over what was, apparently, a featureless stretch of glossy, olive-brown water.

Odd little things, thought Julia, skimming here and there so eagerly, as though it mattered where they went. Swallows dipped and curved into the sunlight, their glossy blue-black backs and creamy throats, and sharp-forked tails, seeming to flicker like flames about the air. Brilliant peacock-blue dragon-flies, with large heads, darted hither and thither. Two were clasped in a nuptial embrace, and fell blindly about the air, always recovering themselves before hitting the water or the branch of a tree. It looked and sounded more like anger than love, thought Julia, as they buzzed past in their quick erratic course.

Leo leaned forward and taking up a paddle, with a few quick strokes drove the punt into an immense bed of rushes. The rushes parted to meet them, and then closed on them again. Leo shipped his paddle beside the gunwale, where it would be out of the way.

"Comfy?" and the simple little childish word knocked at Julia's heart. She nodded and looked at him.

"These cushions are lovely and soft."

"They always say," said Leo, "that you should never change places in a boat, but I'm going to, all the same. I'm coming there beside you, Julia." She moved a little to one side to make room for him. Leo lay down beside her and threw one arm across her breast.

She looked up into his face, seeing it really clearly for the first time as he bent over her. He looked a very lovely,

257

human animal, as lovely as someone called Alfie had looked, for there had been someone called Alfie who had taught her something of the joys she should have been having for years; and now she was going to have complete joy, and love also. For what was love if it was not this quickening of the pulses at a footfall, this deep contentment at a mere presence? This exquisite weakness that was coming over her as his hand began to slip down her and his mouth to come nearer to hers. Oh yes, this was love. It must be. And then fierce pleasure took hold of them, and even Julia forgot for a while whether it was "love" or not.

Julia was completely happy. She ceased to worry about Herbert, about Elsa, even about how she and Leo were one day to get married—for, of course, they must get married. She knew that much even while she was so happy in the possession of her lover. Life wasn't all like this holiday. It had to be lived somehow, on the lines that society had laid down; and for young people like Julia, with a living to earn, and a family who thought divorce disgraceful, the problem was a difficult one. Besides, still further back in her mind, or tucked away in the very bottom of her heart, was the knowledge that she wanted to keep Leo always, and that Leo might not be so very easy to keep. He was young, full of animal health, and his profession took him away. She had little of glamour and excitement to offer in London. Stolen meals, for which they had to lie and plan, stolen visits to the pictures, stolen walks—what were these for someone like Leo? But she let none of this worry her on this magic holiday.

Herbert could not be unreasonable for ever. He must agree to a divorce eventually, and she would just have to steel herself to meet the inevitable rows before he gave way. All that lay in the future, but for the first time in her life Julia was not worrying about the future. The present was a golden cup, full to the brim with wine, and she laid her mouth to it and drank in slow and completely-realised sips of ecstasy. The deep woods knew their love, which had seemed so essentially a thing of London streets; the mere knew of it, and Julia's own body, appeased at last, held, during waking and sleeping hours, the knowledge of that appeasement.

On the fourth and last day, when they went down to the mere to bathe, Julia had a sudden inspiration, and when she came out of the hut where she had undressed, and stood in the green, light-filled air chequered with dapplings of sun and shade, she was naked. She stood there smiling, confident, happy. Leo was a little shocked. In his experience of love, and he had only known bought love, he had seen a naked woman, but he had imagined always that nice women did not care for that sort of thing. Julia was always surprising him. He did not realise that years at l'Etrangère's, and mixing with Marian and Gipsy, and the Darlings, had taught Julia a greater freedom then would ordinarily have been hers. But as he stood looking at her, his moment of criticism was lost in excitement. Even her changing face held to-day a brightness that was beauty, and her body had a changeless quality even in clothes; its assertion was always complete.

She slipped, laughing, into the water, and he put his hands round her. Then, glancing about, he lifted her into his arms and carried her up to the grassy edge of the mere. She lay looking up at him, and laughing. He rubbed her down gently with the towel she had dropped, and then forgot everything—even the fear of some wandering onlooker. They both surrendered themselves completely, and though when they were dressed, and at lunch in the punt, Leo might with any other woman have felt again a return of his moment's embarrassed criticism, with Julia it was impossible to do so. She had been free for the first time to give full play to the greatest of her gifts, and at last she knew what that gift was, and she was completely happy.

Later Leo fell asleep in the punt, his head resting on her knees, and looking down at him she felt her mood change, not suddenly, but with a natural and inevitable gradation. It was as if her child, instead of her lover, lay asleep. She felt the melting pity that every imaginative human being feels on looking at the helplessness of sleep. "Sleep, the little death." Where had she heard that? It was true, anyway. How helpless, and oddly innocent he looked, his young full mouth slightly open and his thick lashes upon his cheeks. No, it was not in the expression of his face that his helplessness lay. It lay, thought Julia—blindly groping after her thoughts—in the with-

259

drawing of his mind; of the safeguard, when awake, the mind exercises over the body. It was as though he lay there helpless, at the mercy of anyone who saw him. Not physically, of course, his alert senses would always bring him to full consciousness in a flash; but it was as though everyone were helpless in sleep, without the majesty of death. Death was majestic. Julia knew that much; even her ineffectual little father, even the over-fretful Mrs. Starling, had struck her, when she saw them dead, with a sense of awe and of her own inferiority. Because nothing she, or anyone else, could do, could hurt a dead person any more. But a sleeping person lay inviting wounds, ready to be chilled by a breath, yielding, infinitely pathetic.

Julia felt the tears come into her eyes, and an absurd thought of Bobby to her mind. How dependent, how sweetly and happily dependent were men and dogs. A child must be very like that too. Herbert wasn't like that, because he snored. Besides, he looked even more completely Herbert when he was asleep, not oddly different as Leo did.

That night Leo went back to Portsmouth, where his mother, and Elsa, who had joined forces with her, arrived to find him. The four wonderful days had been worth everything to both Julia and Leo. He looked curiously at Elsa's little, pretty face, and wondered why he had taken her to the movies. He was all the time absorbed in the thought of Julia.

Julia was already installed at Saint Clement's Square when Herbert came back, and he found nothing at which he could complain. His bacon was cut thick, his flat was spotlessly clean, and he had no suspicion of how Julia had been passing her time; and yet he was somehow aware that she was changed. And he could not tell where the danger lay. She spoke amiably to him, even during the first week when, Emily not yet being back, she had to do the housework. She ignored their quarrel at Torquay, and its cause. This made him hope at first that she had repented; but when he tried to go into her bedroom he found out his mistake. She slammed the door in his face and bolted it. If the damned door, thought Herbert, had simply had a key, he would have taken it away; but he was helpless in face of the bolt.

A few nights later he went up to bed before her and installed himself in the front bedroom. Julia took one look and went straight into the back bedroom, and slept there. Even Herbert thought it would be ridiculous to go after her. He was deeply, burningly angry with the intense anger of the frustrated male, or, indeed, of the frustrated female. The very currents of his blood would never forgive Julia, just as her blood would never forgive him for his violation of her, that had been, for her, unattended by any pleasure. However sorry she might sometimes be for him—and having imagination she was far more sorry for him, in spite of her greater ruthlessness, than he was for her—her body would never forgive him, any more than his would forgive her.

When he was not being actively angry he felt suddenly desolate and a little afraid. He thought longingly of the days before the war that would never come again, when money had gone so much further, when Mrs. Starling, even if she did not attract him violently, was uncomplaining and submissive; when he had been in his own little circle a somebody, and the only prop of his household.

A sort of peace had been patched up between Julia and the Beales. Young Carr was with his ship in northern waters, outwardly all was peace; and yet Herbert was aware that this was a very different Julia. Julia was aware of it herself.

She was still the triumphant and fulfilled woman of the days in Essex, but although she herself was not aware of it she had changed even since Essex. As René Imbert had told her long ago, her talent was for love, and in France she would have enjoyed her talent happily; but in England such was the force of her upbringing, and the social sphere in which she had been born, that even her association with the shop had been unable to rid her of an intense instinct for respectability. Knowledge of the Darlings had loosened her moral code, but not her social one, and already the pagan goddess of the mere was being transformed into a passionate and possessive woman, who wished to enjoy her love openly and without criticism from the world. The woodland spirit that had been hers changed to the actual; it was as though the laurel tree had become a city Daphne, and the reed had taken on the flesh of Syrinx.

261

Julia did not deny, even to herself, the beauty and the wildness of those days by the mere. She did not reflect that perhaps to go back there, and try to recapture the same emotions with a Leo whom she had succeeded in marrying, might be to find those emotions changed like fairy gold into a handful of rubbish. She only knew, what most women know, that life is an affair of compromise; that the dream had somehow to be welded with the facts of living, and, like most women, desiring this compromise, she insisted that the dream would gain and not lose by it.

It had been all very well, she told herself, during those few idyllic days in Essex, to think that this was all she asked of life; but now that she had love, she had begun to ask a great deal more instead of a great deal less of life.

Nothing is as voracious as a woman who, for the first time in her life, has had physical satisfaction. She must go on having it—and Julia was not as one of the Darlings —she wanted respectability with her romance, and this was not, in Julia's case, from the base desire for safety. But unless she had respectability, how could she have any romance at all? Leo had nothing but his pay, which was only 5s. 6d. a day, though when he was twenty-one, which he would be shortly, he would be getting more. Julia always made over £5 a week at the shop, but they couldn't keep her if Herbert came and made "scenes" there. With her capabilities, and the reference Gipsy would give her, she would certainly get another job; but Herbert would probably pursue her there as well. If even Gipsy, who was fond of her, and respected the work she had done, couldn't keep her, because of the "scenes," a strange firm certainly would not do so. And romance could not live in sordid poverty.

She and Leo might never find it as easy again to snatch a few days together. It could not be, she told herself passionately, that already she had experienced both the beginning and the end. She, too, must have her happiness; other women did. Why should the mere accident of money, and of class, make it impossible for her? Herbert must be made to see reason; he must.

A day or two after Leo's ship had arrived in Northern waters, she found a letter from him awaiting her at l'Etrangère's; for an added difficulty in their lives was that she could no longer call for letters at Wigmore Street. You were supposed, she discovered, only to use a *poste restante* when you were travelling and had no London address, and then only for three months. She had been so often that she had been recognised, and the clerk, on the last occasion she had called for letters, had been a surly man and had made trouble.

However, Julia was always the first at the shop, and her fine susceptibilities as to the sacredness of the shop were wearing off. Leo marked his letters "Personal," and Julia had enough authority now to be sure that no one would open her letters. If she were away Gipsy might do so, imagining the letter to be on business, but Julia knew that directly Gipsy was confronted by a personal letter she would seal it up again without reading it. That was one thing you knew about with people like Gipsy, although she was no longer what was called a "moral woman." She had, Julia supposed, lost her honour, and yet Gipsy would never be dishonourable.

Well, she herself was like that too, Julia thought defiantly; she asked nothing better than to be honourable. Armed with this conviction, she attacked Herbert again after reading Leo's letter, for it was the first passionate love-letter he had ever written her. It was as though he had become articulate. Fire had touched him with the gift of tongues. It was the sort of letter that looks ordinary enough when read in the unsympathetic atmosphere of the divorce court, or printed in the more sensational papers. It was full of "darlings" and "dearests" and the word "love," but to Julia it was wonderful. It was not only the most ardent love-letter he had written her, although she had had several of those since he rejoined his ship; but it was the first one in which he had touched on the subject that lay deepest in her heart— the subject of marriage.

I must have you for myself always, he wrote. *What is the good of my thinking I can marry anyone ordinary after you; and as I told you before I'm only flesh and blood. I can't live a life of just seeing you at tea-shops, or taking Bobby for a walk in the Park. I used to be sorry for the men who had to stick in little homes when when they were on leave, who had wives and children, while I could go out and enjoy myself. Well, I don't think I want the children, in fact, I know I don't; but it's you I want to go out and enjoy myself with, and it's you I want to go home with. Herbert will just have to consent to a divorce.*

She wrote a short answering letter before she left the shop.

Leo, my darling, your letter has come, and I am so happy. I could sing, if only I could sing in tune—which I can't! You've never heard me try to sing, have you? It would make you laugh. Some day when we're quite alone I may do it for you, if you are very good, because I don't mind you laughing at me.

Darling, do you know the thing that pleased me most about your letter? It was the last sentence, when you say, "I wish you belonged to me really, darling." Of course, I know you do, and I want everyone else to know it, too! Leo, that's how I feel. Everything is changed since I belonged to you. I thought I could be quite happy just meeting whenever we could, and making love, but now I don't want to have to hide it. I hate the thought of having to plan and scheme, and perhaps not being able to manage it. That's the worst thought of all, isn't it, darling? You and I must belong to each other, because we were made for that. You know at first I used to mind being a few years older than you. Now I don't. All that's unimportant. It's only you and me that matter, darling. I'm going to talk to him again to-night. He must agree to something. After all, everyone divorces nowadays, and if I don't want any money, I don't see that it matters to him. Oh, Leo, I'm going to put your letter next to my heart, like a sort of magic armour, then he won't be able to hurt me whatever he says.

Perhaps Herbert was not able to hurt her with the things he said that night, but he was certainly able to irritate her, to plunge her into despair. When he realised that she was actually asking for a divorce, although she only put it on the grounds of not being happy with him, he was furious.

"It's that young Carr," he kept on repeating. "I know what it is. You want to go off with that young Carr."

"Herbert, if only you would listen to me. You can't enjoy living like this, any more than I do."

"You think of nothing but enjoyment. That's your trouble. We're husband and wife, that's what matters. We're husband and wife, and we're going to stick it whether we enjoy it or not. Nobody else shall have you."

Julia was terribly tempted to tell him that somebody else had already had her, but she refrained. Leo's career and her own, these were too precious to be lightly thrown away.

Oh, Leo, he's hopeless, she wrote, *quite hopeless. What are we to do? He has utterly refused to divorce me. He has accused me of wanting to marry you. He is wild with anger and jealousy, and I can't bear anyone but you to be jealous. I want you to be jealous, darling. Isn't that odd, although there is really nothing for you to be jealous of, yet I want you to be. Isn't Miss Lestrange lucky? Frank Bellingham was going to divorce her, and instead he has died, so there won't be any trouble after all. It appears he had some sort of heart disease, though he wasn't ill for more than a few hours. So now she will be able to marry her third husband, and she has had heaps of affairs as well; and all I want is you, my own darling lover. I've been so good always, and Herbert has never been easy. You said to me once, do you remember, "Why did you marry him? Why couldn't you have waited?" Darling, was that a reproach? I've often wondered. I couldn't tell you were coming into my life, could I? Of course, I would have waited if I had known; but one doesn't know things till it's too late. I've just been reading about Lucretia Borgia. It must have been wonderful to have lived then, and been a great lady, and been able to hire bravos to kill people who got in their way. I should have been quite ruthless if I had lived then, and shall I tell you, darling, I believe any woman would. Men aren't nearly as ruthless as we are. You see, darling, when a woman, especially a good woman, loves—I don't mean one who keeps on having affairs, but one who loves just once tremendously—she would do anything for the man she loves. There is no longer any right or wrong for her, except what is good and what is bad for the man she loves, and our love is good for both of us. Tell me you agree with me, darling.*

265

Leo, excited and stimulated by her letter, wrote back that he did.

I had forgotten asking you why you married him, he wrote, *but I expect if I said it it was in a moment of curiosity, not in reproach. It is wonderful to know that you would do anything for me. You say men aren't as ruthless. Does this mean that you think I wouldn't do anything for you? You don't do all the loving, you know.*

Julia had a moment of wondering why it was that no two persons ever remembered quite the same thing, quite the same phrase, quite the same aspect of an hour together. It made the past oddly unreal that this should be so, that only the general effect of the time shared together should be the same to two people. Why, she reflected, two people did not even see the same person. She had Leo in front of her eyes whenever she "thought back," and he had her.

She wrote her thought to him: *not that it matters,* she added, *because you and I are the same, really, aren't we, darling? We're one.*

Yet this feeling of one-ness was very difficult to hold in her mind with Leo in Scotland and herself going back and forward between Saint Clement's Square and George Street.

But we'll be married some day, darling, she wrote, determined not to let even her fits of despair weaken her ambitions. *Of course, they will all have a fit at Two Beresford, but what does that matter? What would they say if they knew I was sitting here writing to my lover? Fancy if I said to them—I've got a lover. Can't you see all their faces? Oh, darling, you will be home again by Christmas. Just imagine if you were coming home to me. If we had a little flat, however small, together. I shall be going to Paris before you are back. It won't be a bit the same. All the time I shall wish you were with me. They don't mind a bit if they know you are just lovers in French hotels. They like it. Isn't it lovely of them? So different from England. Now I must stop. He has gone to bed, and I am sitting by the fire talking to you. It doesn't matter to me that the opposite chair is empty,*

*because you are not sitting in it. You are sitting on the
arm of my chair, darling, with your arm round me, and
I am leaning my head against you. Do say you feel it that
way.*

Thus the dream went on, building itself up in both
their minds.

Julia came back from a few days' successful buying in
Paris and Gipsy was pleased with her, as always. What
Julia had to keep secret was that she had tried to find
out something for herself, something that affected her
personal life; and what she had found out did not encourage her.

Before leaving for Paris she had had a less optimistic
letter from Leo than usual. For the first time she heard
in his letters that note of defeat which her own soul
sounded sometimes in the small hours of the morning.
She remembered—what she had never entirely forgotten
—that he had told her how pretty the girls were in Scotland. Once when they had discussed them, he had told
her that they were "hot stuff" as well. She tortured herself with the thought that perhaps this pessimistic letter
of Leo's meant that he had met some Scotch girl who
attracted him more than she did. She sunk into one of
her moods when she wished she had not done what she
always phrased to herself as "given him everything." She
had always been brought up to believe that once you
gave a man everything, he thought less of you, and
wanted you less ardently. She knew with a certainty of
absolute knowledge, however much she might tell herself to the contrary, that Herbert would not give her a
divorce, and that if she left him for Leo, he would come
and make "scenes" at l'Etrangère's. During the rather
dreary crossing to France, it had occurred to her it
might be possible to get a job in Paris. There must be
some little shops, or some big dressmakers, who wanted
somebody who spoke English perfectly, and yet who
could wear clothes, to talk to the English and American
customers. And, after all, she could deal with the business side of the transaction as well in French as in English. If only she could get a job in Paris, it would not
be too impossibly far for Leo to come on his leaves,
and she could arrange her holidays for the weeks he was
in the Mediterranean. It would be easier to arrange

in Paris, where nobody knew her, to stay at an hotel with Leo whenever he came over, some quiet little hotel in the outskirts of Paris. For the first time she wished ardently that she had not quarrelled with René Imbert. She wished it still more when, having finished in one hectic week all her business for the shop, she started going round on her personal quest. Trade was not so good in Paris that anyone wanted to turn off a Frenchwoman and take an Englishwoman in her place. Besides, the only firms she knew in Paris were the wholesale model-houses, and her business gifts, which were largely personal, would be wasted in a wholesale house. She knew nothing of the little shops, the equivalents of l'Etrangère, and it was impossible to get a position in one of the big dressmakers. They paid you so little, for one thing, expecting you to supplement your income in another manner, and that, for the exalted Julia, was impossible.

So, in spite of Gipsy's praise, it was a depressed Julia who arrived at Saint Clement's Square. She paid off the taxi, and carried up herself the small suitcase containing her personal luggage. She fitted her key into the lock, and went into the hall. The murmur of voices came from the sitting-room. She opened the door and went in. Herbert was seated one side of the fire and Bertha the other. Bertha was obviously not paying an afternoon call. She was bare-headed, and she was busily knitting. Julia stared at her in surprise.

"Hullo Bertha," she said. "Where did you spring from?"

"Bertha's staying with me," said Herbert.

"How nice for you," said Julia. "Prevented you feeling lonely while I was away. Well, I'm back now."

"Herbert has asked me to stay on," said Bertha. "He says, and I quite agree with him, that he gets very little attention, what with your being out at business all day and very often gadding in the evenings. Herbert likes his home, as you always knew," she said.

Julia stared first at her, then at Herbert. "Oh, well, I suppose we can manage for a short time. If you look after your own business, Bertha, I'll look after mine. Where's Bobby, Herbert?"

"I don't know," said Herbert. "In the kitchen with Emily, I suppose. She's as silly about that dog as you are."

Julia went out into the little hall, and closed the sitting-room door behind her. So this is what Herbert had arranged! She knew the workings of his mind so well. As long as Bertha was with them it meant that she would have to have the back bedroom, and that Herbert would have to share the front room with Julia. Oh, it was insufferable, she told herself, putting her hands to her hot cheeks. She pulled off her hat, threw it down on the hall-table, and went into the kitchen.

Emily, who was nursing Bobby, looked up at her anxiously. She knew well enough what was going on in Julia's mind. She helped Bobby down carefully, he was in the middle of one of his attacks of rheumatism, and he limped painfully across to Julia, whining with pleasure and trying to hold his paw up to her. Julia fell on her knees and gathered him gently to her, kissing his satiny rumpled forehead, and talking to him in a low voice.

"Emily," she said suddenly, when Bobby's rapture had subsided, "where does Bobby sleep now?"

"With me," said Emily, "I wasn't going to have him sleep on that nasty oilcloth in the kitchen, and so I told the master."

"He'll have to stay with you, I'm afraid," said Julia, "it's awfully good of you, Emily."

"I like having him," said Emily, "I always was fond of dumb animals. If a person isn't fond of dumb animals, there's something wrong with them, that's what I say."

"What should I do without you, Emily? I've brought you a blouse from Paris, by the way, I think you'll like it. It's navy *crêpe de Chine.*"

"Oh, thank you," said Emily, "I always did say there was nothing like a nice navy. It's sure to be in good taste if you chose it."

Julia's heart warmed a little. Emily's loyalty was a very precious thing to her. Many old servants would have resented the incursion of a young second wife. Emily had taken to Julia from the first. Emily felt that her young mistress gave a little life to the place, and Emily was all for a bit of life, just as she was all for dumb animals and a nice navy.

Then began weeks of misery for Julia. She could not dislodge Bertha. After all, it was Herbert's house, and if he chose to have his sister to live with him, what could she do? Julia fretted and grew thin. She watched anxiously for fresh lines about her eyes. She was getting very little sleep, for Herbert's bulk and his snores made her bed a place of discomfort rather than rest.

Also Herbert, a sort of lazy lust engendered in him by warmth and proximity, began to demand his rights once again. This is partly why he had Bertha here, thought Julia, and determined not to give way to him. One night she told him in her anger that she would never give way to him as long as he had his sister living with them.

"That's why you had her, I know," she said, "so that you would have to sleep with me. Well, that's not the way to get me, Herbert."

Herbert lost his temper, not with Julia, but with Bertha and obscurely with himself.

"She can go," he said, recklessly. "I'll tell her to go, if it means that we can live as husband and wife should. I won't have anyone here, I promise you, Julia. I was desperate. That's why I got her, I don't really want her, I don't want anybody but you."

"That's all very well," said Julia, "but you've got her and she's here."

"Look here," said Herbert, "I swear to you, I'll send her away if you will be nice to me now."

Julia wavered. After all, Herbert was a good deal stronger physically than she was. She couldn't fight him all night, and short of crying for help out of the window, which she had threatened to do, there seemed to be no way but to do what he wanted.

"When will you tell her to go?" she asked.

"Directly she can arrange it."

He caught hold of her and Julia yielded. She put out her hand and turned off the light. "Be gentle, Herbert," she whispered, and to his surprise he found her becoming languid instead of rigid in his hands. Passive she always had been, but this was something softer, more vital, than mere passivity. Herbert was happy, not knowing that the clumsy touches of his hands were being translated by Julia into the light caresses of her lover. She was being unfaithful to her husband in her mind, as thousands of women all over England were probably being unfaithful to their husbands at that moment. He

270

was aware for the first time of her answering pleasure, unaware that in his flesh her lover was betraying him.

Darling, I've had to give way to him, wrote Julia with remorse the next day. *It wasn't possible to go on, but I feel I can't ever give way to him again.* And that was true. Julia hated herself for the pleasure she had felt, because to her it was a betrayal of Leo. She hated herself still more when a few days later Herbert made excuses for not getting rid of Bertha. It was hardly worth while, he pointed out, before Christmas. She would have to come back to them for Christmas anyway, and why the double move and the double railway fare? Julia knew it was no good arguing, and she looked at him with a sick contempt that was half for him and half for herself.

But her surrender was renewed and renewed again. The flame that Leo had lit within her could not go unappeased and Herbert, half fearful of his luck, became more gentle and considerate. She could shut her eyes and imagine Herbert to be Leo, so that it was actually as though Leo was standing by the bed, bending over her with his dark head, and round young neck, and bright glinting eyes, saying softly, with a sort of deep anger of love: "Now I'm going to have you whether you want it or not. . . ." and this dream-Leo transmuted by her imagination into the actuality of her husband's flesh, claimed for hers a toll of pleasure that was in truth her lover's and not her husband's.

Of course, you know what we quarrel about, don't you, darling? she wrote to Leo, *what he wants and what I hate to give him. I can't really give it to anybody but you. In a way I am giving it to you. I can't explain, and yet I hate it. Oh, I'm so tired. It hardly seems worth while holding out any longer.*

Leo wrote back impetuously, almost angrily, and Julia felt that her troubles were almost worth while to rouse Leo to such fullness of expression and such a blaze of jealousy.

Oh, she wrote back, *there's no doubt about it, I love you to be jealous, darling. If you're jealous you'll think and plan how to get me away, for you'll get me away,*

271

won't you? I know you can plan anything if you only think hard enough. I enclose you a very sad bit out of the paper. Two people who loved each other like we do, not as much as us—nobody could do that—but I'm sure they did love each other. His wife would not divorce him, so they decided to kill themselves. It must be a dreadful thing to decide, mustn't it, when you're full of youth and life, and you're driven to it because somebody won't let you go? And you see she died and he didn't, and they're going to try him for murder when he's well enough. I think that's awful when they both decided to die, and he was only doing what he promised when he shot her, before he shot himself. Think how she must have loved him to let him do it. Yes, darling, I think perhaps they did love each other as much as we do after all. I think I could be happy while you were holding the revolver against me, I do really. Do you think all that's very absurd, and exaggerated? Do say you don't, my heart. Do you like that expression—my heart? It seemed just to write itself. I didn't even know I was thinking it. That's what you are, Leo, my heart, and I am yours. Do they give you a revolver in the Air Force? I don't want us to have to do anything dreadful, but I feel I can't go on for ever like this, and I want you to feel it too. Anything would be better than that.

Leo had no intention of killing himself or her. Suicide pacts seemed to him foolishness as, indeed, they did to Julia, except in moments when she luxuriated, with closed eyes, in that imagination of death at Leo's hands. After all, they could always meet somehow, but he couldn't help feeling flattered at Julia's ardour. It was true, he reflected, smiling a little, she would let him shoot her if she knew he was going to follow her. You might say what you like, but a woman like that had got something that a girl like Elsa could never have.

Leo's letters reflected all his moods: his complacency, his jealous anger and his fits of weariness. He was not like Julia. He carried no living image of his love in his mind. Julia knew this only too well. Beside the perpetual fear which the difference in age imposed upon her, the fear of losing him to some young girl—not Elsa, for she had long ceased to be jealous of her, she knew she could outshine Elsa—but some new and beautiful unknown; she had now another fear.

She was terrified that she was going to have a child. Her anger against Herbert rose deep and dark, for go over her dates as she would, there was no doubt that it would be Herbert's child, and not Leo's. To have had Leo's child would have been somehow marvellous. Matters would have been taken out of her hands. The affair would have become too big for the petty rulings of the Starlings and the Beales. There would have to be a divorce, and she would be able to marry Leo. And she would have a child like him, bright-eyed and vigorous, in whom he would see himself when he came back on leave. But to have Herbert's child meant being caught for good. He must have been careless on purpose, she told herself, angrily. He must have meant to catch and keep her this way, once and for all.

Julia bought every kind of patent medicine that urged married ladies to end irregularities and delays now. No Female Pill advertised failed to pass her lips, but beyond making her feel wretchedly ill, achieved nothing. She walked most of the way back from the shop every night, jumped on and off the bus, and ran feverishly with Bobby in Heronscourt Park; but still nothing happened. She was still hoping for the best, but fearing the worst, when Leo came back to London for his Christmas leave. He came determined that he and Julia should seize every opportunity to be lovers, but the fates seemed against them. Herbert seemed suddenly endowed, as Julia declared, with the watchfulness of the "Big Five" rolled into one. Leo's mother always managed to know where he was. The Beale family, without saying it in words, managed to convey that they forgave him for any little neglect at Torquay. Indeed, that they really only blamed Julia.

But again the hard compulsion of the world was upon the lovers, and not only of the world but of their particular class in it. Julia dared not be late home more than once or twice, and swift meals at a tea-shop, rides home on the top of a bus, and large family parties were all they could attain. Julia, for all the urgency of her pulses, was happy merely to be with Leo, to pour out her thoughts as she had never been able to do with Herbert, or indeed to anyone else. That in itself was bliss. Self-expression was hers for the first time, and she was dizzy with it. Much as she longed for his love-making, she could be, and was, happy discussing the little flat that they had planned one day to have together; to be kissed, danger adding to its charm, in a dark corner of Saint Clement's Square. But with Leo this was not enough. Julia, herself, and what she could give him was what he wanted; and now that he was back in London a change of leadership took place. Her letters ceased to influence him, but her physical presence influenced him very much, and he became discontented, moody. Even his quick decisiveness was helpless in the web of circumstances in which they were caught.

Julia had not dared to discuss divorce again with Herbert for fear he would make it impossible for her to see Leo at all; and she did not dare tell Leo of her cowardice. He would have very little sympathy, she knew. Therefore, she had to invent scenes that she had had with Herbert; rages on the part of Herbert.

"I've done all I can, I really have, Leo," she said. "Last night when I got home, you know I was a bit late, he was waiting and was frightfully angry. He guessed I had been with you. Of course, I said I hadn't, but I don't think he believed me. If it were not that we both act so well when we meet with the family, I don't know what would happen. That does put him off. I notice him looking at me in a puzzled way when you are talking to Elsa, and I'm paying no attention to you."

"It's all very well," said Leo, thrusting away his coffeecup—they were having a quiet lunch at Lyons'—"I can't go on like this for ever."

"Nor can I, darling," said Julia, suddenly despairing.

"You'll have to leave him, that's all there is to it."

"Yes, and if I leave him I shan't be able to keep my job, and he won't support me, and you can't."

Leo propped his chin in his hands, and stared at her hungrily. "Risk it," he said. "After all, he can't make more than one or two rows at the shop, they could have him run in."

Julia shook her head. "They'd never stand for it," she said. "It's one thing if one of Miss Lestrange's lovers were to come in and let off a revolver; that might be good for trade. All the customers would come to see where it had been done, and want to talk it over; but it wouldn't be a bit the same thing if Herbert were to come and just make a scene about me. Oh, I'm terrified it will have to be that suicide pact, darling. You can't go on like this, I can't go on like this, but what are we to do? We can't live on air. I'd take ever such a small job abroad if I could just live on it."

"I'd leave the Service if I could get a job," said Leo. "But you can't get jobs nowadays. There are hundreds of good men out of work, and then you've always got to be married. I'd have to really be married, or pretend I was. It may be all right in France, as you say, but it isn't all right in England or the Colonies. They hoof you out of the country in the Colonies if you haven't got a marriage certificate, and so they do in America."

"Oh dear, isn't it absurd," said Julia, laughing, "everybody knows people live in sin, or whatever it's called, and that men have mistresses, and women have lovers, and married couples are unfaithful to each other, and yet unless you are somebody very great and important you are always in danger. Why, Miss Lestrange went to America one year when she was married to Frank Bellingham. He didn't go with her, somebody else did; but it was all right, nobody made any trouble, although they stayed together in hotels everywhere. If you and I did that they'd pinch us. Leo," she leaned forward to him across the table, "would you mind the suicide pact very much, darling? I get so tired, so dreadfully tired, what with working all day and then not having any peace at home, and not being able to see you alone sometimes. I think I'd not mind a bit."

"I'd mind," said Leo, "my God, I'd mind. I want to live, Julia. I want us both to live."

"Still, we can always have it in the back of our minds. It makes me feel less hopeless. Let's give ourselves a time. Let's say if we haven't managed to get free in three years' time. That'll make us work harder. We must think of everything, try everything, Leo."

"Try some weed-killer in his tea," said Leo impatiently. "That'd be the best thing, only they'd be sure to find out."

"Oh, Leo," said Julia, half laughing, "what awful things you say," but even as she spoke her mind lit up with the notion of a woman who would dare all for love. Naturally, she would never really kill anyone, but it would be marvellous to feel that you were what she had read of in books, one of the "great lovers of history." Of course, it was true, she supposed quickly, that Petrarch and Laura, Dante and Beatrice, hadn't killed anyone, but then they didn't really love anyway; and as far as she remembered Paola and Francesca got killed themselves instead of killing anyone; but there were plenty of those mediaeval Italian people who would do anything if they loved enough. She glanced at Leo's face, fallen in the sullen lines she had grown to dread during the Christmas leave.

"I believe," she breathed earnestly, leaning forward, "that I'd do even that for you, Leo." She could almost see herself, glowing and vibrant as she spoke, one of the "great lovers of history."

"Well, don't," said Leo, "or we shall both be in the cart."

"Oh no, weed-killer is silly," said Julia. "I mean one is always hearing about it, and people are always caught. Do you remember I wrote to you and said I wished I had been one of those Italian women in the Renaissance? Just fancy, I could hire people to put Herbert out of the way. I wouldn't let them hurt him, as long as he was sensible and agreed to a divorce. They could just keep him in one room somewhere and go on at him until he agreed."

"You could arrange all that in America, if you had the money," said Leo, "and knew whom to go to."

"Oh," said Julia, half laughing, "America is more civilised than I thought. Even if you do have to have a marriage licence you can hire gunmen!"

Leo laughed a little too, but not for the first time Julia found he could not follow a twist of thought; that he was more amused by the jokes of the Beale family than by her two-edged little social comments. She changed to seriousness at once, quick to fall in with any mood of his; for to him she submitted all her thoughts with joy, and asked for nothing better than to be able to submit her actions.

That evening they went home by train, alighting at Heronscourt Park and walking, not through the Park, for that was closed, but in the quiet by-roads on the way to Saint Clement's Square. For the first time Julia forced herself to tell Leo of her fear. She felt herself blushing with shame and unhappiness as she did so.

"I can't have it, I won't, Leo. Yours would be different. I can't have any but yours."

"Good God," said Leo, "I don't want a kid, and this can't be mine, Julia You say so yourself."

A sort of sick disappointment welled up in Julia.

"No, this isn't yours," she said dully. "I shouldn't be minding if it were. But you must help me somehow, Leo. I've taken everything that I've ever heard of, and there must be something one can do, somewhere one can go to, but I don't know how to begin. I don't know whom to ask. I daresay somebody at the shop knows, but I couldn't ask there, and of course it would be no good asking Mum or Aunt Mildred; and I don't suppose your mother has ever heard of such a thing."

"Christ! no," said Leo. "I say, are you quite sure?"

"Practically, I'm afraid so."

"What about that woman friend of yours who's a doctor?"

"Anne? Oh no, she wouldn't dream of doing a thing like that. She's—she's not that sort," and Julia thought of Anne with a yearning wish to be like her; of her shining integrity; of her enthusiasm in her profession. No; Anne, started in partnership with her father, would be the last person who would even discuss malpractice.

"I can find out, of course," said Leo suddenly, plunging his hands into his pockets, and striding on faster than usual. He caught sight of Julia's face in the light of a street-lamp, and felt sorry for her. She looked much younger suddenly in this fear and misery. Yet, while he was sorry for her, he felt a physical jealousy of what had made this sorrow possible; and somewhere right in the back of his mind a little voice whispered that perhaps Julia wouldn't be able to get out of it; and that perhaps she would have to settle down to being a wife to Herbert, and he himself would be free, if the demands upon his love and loyalty were to become rather extravagant.

"I can find out," he repeated; "several men I know from the ship are in London."

Julia drew a sigh of relief. Once again she was going to be able to leave everything to Leo. He would find out, he would arrange everything. Her spirits rose, and next day she was able to enjoy a movie that they went to—a romantic affair which ended happily after the hero and heroine had surmounted almost insuperable obstacles.

"That's like us, Leo," she said, pressing his hand as they sat together in the warm, heavy darkness, thick with the breath and odours of humanity. "That's like us. We'll make a success still, won't we?"

"You bet we will," said Leo absent-mindedly. To himself he was thinking that everything was becoming rather a worry. This was not the Julia to hold him enthralled, not this dependent, half-frightened creature. The Julia he could not resist was triumphant, clever, with a quality of brilliance that no other woman he knew possessed.

He took her back to Saint Clement's Square, and since it was better not to hide the fact that they had been out together—for no one was sharper at putting two simultaneous absences together than Herbert and Bertha—he entered boldly with her, and drank a whisky and soda while discussing the picture they had seen. Bertha had a headache and, had gone to bed, and Herbert was alone, standing on the hearth-rug, his shoulders hunched to his ears, and his hands clasped behind his back. He hardly spoke to either of them while they kept up a gay conversation with him and with each other. Then he suddenly put his hands in his pockets and took a few steps forward.

"I've had enough of this," he said, ignoring Leo and addressing Julia. "I've had enough of this. It's the last time you go out alone with your fancy-man."

Julia was furious. After all, she and Leo hadn't, as she put it, done anything at all—this leave they hadn't had the chance—and for Herbert to talk like this. . . . Herbert, who had apparently added to her difficulties, that was too much.

"I shall do as I like," she flashed at him.

"You'll do what I tell you, my girl, or I'll know the reason why." Herbert's face was flushed an angry dark red. Leo had seen that look in a man's face before, and he tried to get between Julia and her husband.

"Leave her alone, can't you, Starling? Can't you see you're frightening her?"

"And what business is it of yours?" commented Herbert. "I can do as I like with my own wife, can't I?"

"Not while I'm here," said Leo, and Julia shot him a glance of admiration.

"Oh, can't I?" said Herbert, and taking Julia by both arms he tried to push her out of the room.

"Herbert, you're hurting me, let go," she cried, and indeed she spoke truly, for his fingers seemed to be wringing the flesh of her delicate arms. She screamed again. "Let me go." She tried to wrench herself free. There was a scuffle, she tore herself away and fell against the edge of the heavy mahogany bookcase. She gave a cry of pain, but Herbert, his temper thoroughly beyond control, shook her, so that she knocked up against the edge of the bookcase once again.

Leo caught Herbert on the cheek with a blow from his clenched fist, and Herbert staggered a little, let go Julia and put his hand to his face. They all three stared at each other for a moment.

"You swine," said Leo, "you can't let her go, and you can't treat her right, and you call yourself a man."

"Oh, Leo, please go," said Julia, sobbing, "please go." She saw Herbert's rage was already over, that he was standing looking ashamed, and rather dazed by Leo's blow.

"I can't go and leave you alone with this fellow."

"I'll be all right . . . please . . ." said Julia. "It'll be quite all right. Listen, there's Bertha coming downstairs. Oh, please go."

They all listened and heard a heavy tread beginning to descend.

"You're sure you want me to," said Leo. "I don't like leaving you here. Can't I take you to your mother's, or back to mine?"

Julia laughed bitterly. "I should be welcome in either place, shouldn't I?" she asked. "Go, Leo. It will make it worse if you stop . . . for my sake . . . please."

He went reluctantly enough, and yet half relieved because he saw that she was wise, and Julia, for once unassailably in the right, disposed briefly of both the critical Bertha and the half-angry, half-repentant Herbert.

Herbert had to get into the same bed with her. There was no help for that, but at least she had a good excuse for turning her back on him and lying in silence, while he, for once unable to sleep, lay silent also.

Some sort of peace was patched up, of course. There was the family Christmas party to be thought of. Herbert was really ashamed of himself. Julia was hopeful that his violence would bring about what all her dosing had failed to do, and therefore inclined to forgive him. Besides, the position of the forgiving wife is always a pleasant one.

"No going off into corners, mind, at the party," said Herbert, and Julia answered wearily:

"Of course not. Don't you see you've spoilt everything. I had a beautiful friendship, and you've made it vulgar and horrid."

Herbert grunted disbelievingly. "I dare say," he said, "young Carr won't come. I shouldn't think he would after what's happened."

"I dare say he won't," said Julia. "I know who will come, and that's your sister Bertha. For one thing she's here anyway. You've got to tell her she has to behave herself."

"Who's going to tell Carr he's got to behave himself?"

"Well, I can't if you won't let me see him," said Julia, reasonably.

The question, however, solved itself. Uncle George, who was giving the party, hadn't the smallest notion of letting anybody drop out of it, and he had already had hints from Bertha of the trouble at Saint Clement's Square. Uncle George talked breezily to Leo, as one man of the world to another, and Leo, rather glad of this easy way out, joined in laughing at Herbert and shrugging his shoulders about Julia, and saying that he thought both had had their lesson, and there would be no trouble at the party.

Nevertheless, Christmas was not very happy for anyone in Julia's little world except, perhaps, for Elsa, dimpled and bright in the possession of a new young man. He was in a bank, and hence in a very good position indeed, and he was a pleasant enough young fellow, shy and likeable.

Julia, pale and worried, had lost her illusive, butterfly brilliance, but even had it not been so, she would not have tried to take Elsa's young man from her. There was no spite in Julia's composition, and she was very glad for Elsa's sake, as well as for her own, that this new interest had come along.

The kid couldn't help being insipid, and perhaps it was better to be insipid—it meant she would not get herself into the sort of mess that she herself was in. There never could be anything, thought Julia, half comtemptuously, of the *femme fatale* about Elsa. Therefore, she did not grudge Elsa her little triumph, and sat back as a respectable married lady should, without entering into any competition.

She had few chances, at that Christmas party, for a talk alone with Leo. In the middle of the cracker-pulling, and the adjustment of the paper-caps, he managed to murmur to her:

"I've got an address," and she managed to reply:

"Send it to the shop," and that was all.

She found the address waiting for her when the shop opened again after the holiday. Leo had simply written on a slip of paper—Mrs. Humble, 5, Prospect Villas, Camden Town. Julia stowed the slip of paper away in her bag, feeling utterly miserable. Leo was leaving the next day for the Mediterranean cruise, and she was already tortured with thoughts of charming French, languorous Italian, and complaisant Maltese girls.

They were not very busy at the shop after the holiday, and it was maddening for her to have to stay there. Marian, of course, was away, and Gipsy had gone home early, and Julia had to be faithful to the trust reposed in her—as she had always been as far as l'Etrangère was concerned. She saw to the shutting up of the shop, and then went forth, her heart heavy, and with the sense of misfortune upon her, into the dark evening. Directly she saw Leo waiting for her on the north side of Hanover Square, where they were wont to meet on the few occasions that she allowed this dangerous practice, her heart began to beat more gaily. After all, she was probably making a fuss about nothing. Leo loved her. Why should he bother about her now, when she was frightened, and pale, and anxious if he did not love her? She would write him such marvellous letters all the time he was away, that he would be able to think of no other woman. He was hers, and she would keep him hers.

She slipped her hand under his arm, and together they made their way to Oxford Street into a tea-shop. When tea had been brought they found themselves, for the first time, unable to talk. The free-and-easy interchange of ideas—ideas promulgated by Julia—had somehow ceased to be possible. Did Herbert's hostage stand between them in some queer way, making strangers of them?

"I mustn't be late," said Julia, looking at her wristwatch, "not after that awful row the other night, although I think that deadly Christmas party put them off the scent."

He helped her on with her coat, and still in that strange unnatural silence they went back together on the top of a 73 bus—the night was not cold for the time of year—to Hammersmith Broadway; and then they walked in and out of the bars of light and shade, past the evening shoppers turning over things at the food shops, overtaken every now and again by the roaring, brilliantly-lit tramcars; on and on along the hard pavement until they reached the Square.

A sudden compunction seized Leo as they stood in its darkest corner, under their favourite tree.

"I say, this is good-bye, Julia," he said.

She nodded. Her throat ached intolerably, and she could hardly speak. Suddenly, the remembrance of the passion of the summer, so different from anything he had ever known, invaded Leo's mind and mingled with the deeper sense of frustration which had been his portion this Christmas leave. He pressed her to him fiercely and kissed her again and again. A sweet surge of joy filled her heart—what did anything matter if Leo loved her?

"Darling, it's all right. It'll be all right," she assured him, through her tears which were running down her face as fast as he kissed them away. "I'll go to that address. I'll get rid of it, and we'll have thought of something by the time you come back. You remember what you said to me when you were joking about weed-killer? That wouldn't be any good, of course, but there must be something if he won't give me a divorce. There simply must be something, Leo. You're so clever. You go about everywhere, you must be able to find out. I'd do anything for you, Leo." And for the moment, while she spoke, she believed it. Leo, while he listened, liked to think he believed it too.

They kissed again hungrily, her tears salt between their lips.

"You won't find anyone else who'll do for you what

I will, Leo," she whispered, when he let her go. "No other woman would risk for you what I will. Oh, I must go now, but don't forget I'll write to you, and when you write to me, if you hear of anything, you'll tell me of it, won't you? Don't forget I'll be working for both of us all the time, darling."

By George! I believe she means it, thought Leo, with a certain excited pride.

Julia couldn't have told whether she meant it or not. She only knew that a wonderful weapon had been placed in her hands, a weapon not to attack Herbert, but one with which to grapple Leo and hold him more closely by her side. Their love, which had seemed to be dying of inanition, had found a new, wonderful food by which to live. Danger and risk, even if they were only imaginative, yet gave a thrill when neither of them knew quite what was imagination and what was real.

She broke from him at last on a high note of exaltation, and fled along the Square and up the steps between the smiling lions.

Business was slack for her in the New Year and Julia went again into a trough of depression at Leo's absence. Her fantasy of herself—the great lover who was prepared to risk everything—faded in the chill winter daylight of Hammersmith. She began to think more urgently of the trouble in which she found herself, and the absolute necessity—for she could no longer avoid that fact—of a visit to the address Leo had sent her. She was terrified . . . who would not be? She had heard so much of girls who had died after an adventure such as she was planning. Why, the *News of the World* was full of them every week; but then, that was probably because the girls didn't take sufficient precaution when they got home; didn't keep themselves as spotlessly clean as Julia always did.

Anyway, it was no good going on living with this menace looming over her. Better to gamble everything with the risk of loss of life itself than go on with life as it must be, unless she dared to gamble.

Rather to her surprise, Julia found the name and address were in the telephone-book, and she rang up when alone in the shop, before closing, and asked to speak to Mrs. Humble.

283

"Mrs. Humble speaking," a pleasant though uneducated voice replied.

Julia began to stammer. "I . . . I've been given your address by a friend," she said at last.

"Oh, you want those newspapers," said the voice. "Well, I expect I can get them for you. Let me see, what's the name, I've forgotten?"

"Beale," said Julia frantically. It was the first name she could think of suddenly. Instinct told her not to use her maiden name, or her married name. "Mrs. Beale."

"Mrs. Beale," said the voice. "Well when could you come and get the papers? You know this shop, don't you?"

"No, I mean, of course, yes . . . I mean, I can find it," said Julia.

"To-morrow evening at 7 o'clock," said the voice.

"That's rather late . . ."

"I can't help it," said the voice more sharply. "It wouldn't be convenient earlier."

"Oh, all right, I'll manage somehow. You're sure it'll be all right?"

"I don't know what you mean, Mrs. Beale. You've ordered the papers, and I'll be able to get them for you by to-morrow. We're the little shop just before you get to the railway arch," and there was the sound of the receiver being hung up.

It was easy enough to tell Herbert a story of going out to tea with one of the girls from the shop next evening. Leo having left the country, Herbert was no longer interested in what Julia did—for possessiveness was the mainspring of his emotion towards her. After what he considered his triumph in downing Leo—as evidenced by the complete lack of interest he and Julia showed at the party—he had considered the trouble was at the end. Leo was gone, until Easter this time, and the thing, thanks to the stand he had taken, was finished. . . . Julia was once again his wife, and this time for good. But Julia had refused to let him touch her; not only that, she had told him never again as long as she lived, and there was a new quality in her voice that frightened Herbert. He had blustered, he had argued, at last he had implored, but he might have been talking to a dead woman.

"Look here, I'll get rid of Bertha," he said at last. "I admit I was wrong not to do it before when I promised. It didn't seem worth it, with Christmas so near; but I give you my word I will, I'll tell her to-morrow."

"I don't care," said Julia, "whether you tell her or not, except that I would sooner she went. I want my room to myself again. I'll go mad if I have to go on like this. But I'll never sleep with you again, Bertha or no Bertha."

That had been the night before, and when Julia rang him up to tell him she would be late that evening Herbert took it humbly. He was frightened, and Julia knew it, but she no longer cared.

Julia went on her errand very quietly dressed, with entirely clean underthings—a relic of her early childhood. For her mother had always put her into clean underclothes for a railway journey "in case anything happened," by which Mrs. Almond meant a railway accident. This curious piece of family folk-lore having been subconsciously obeyed, Julia was ready with the pound-notes in her bag for what might befall.

There have been pilgrimages more praiseworthy, but still less courageous than was Julia's that evening. Leo away at sea, Herbert sitting over his supper . . . they were men, and so this thing could never happen to them, although they were both, in a way, responsible for it having happened to Julia. Leo's child, because of the desire he had awakened in her, Herbert's in actual fact; it was nobody's child less than Julia's, whose life had not prepared her for such realities.

She went on in a sort of dream, until she arrived at the little street where she was told Prospect Villas were. It was a dark, irregular street, with dingy little yellow-brick houses that led under a railway arch, and at the corner, just before the arch, stood a newspaper shop, a dingy little shop where postcards and cheap novelettes and cigarettes were sold. Julia went in.

"Is Mrs. Humble in?" she asked brightly to the weedy-looking youth behind the counter, "I'm a friend of hers, she's expecting me."

"What nyme?" said the youth.

"Mrs. Beale."

"Ma," called the youth over his shoulder, "here's a Mrs. Beale to see you."

The door of the parlour at the back of the shop

opened, and a pleasant, mother-looking old woman came out.

"Well, well, it's Mrs. Beale, is it! I shouldn't·have known you, my dear. It must be years since I've seen you—not since you were as high as this counter. And how is your dear mother?"

"She's all right," said Julia, rather startled.

"Well, I've got those papers for her. You must be tired coming all this way. Come in, and give me all the news. Look after the shop, Johnny, Mrs. Beale and me has got lots of things to talk over."

The youth seemed quite uninterested, and merely nodded in reply. Julia gazed in awe at the fat, comfortable Mrs. Humble, who took her through in the little hall and led her upstairs.

"Feeling a bit nervous, I expect, dear, aren't you? Ah, well, it's only natural. Sit down and let's have a look at you."

She turned on the gas-jet, and Julia found herself in a bedroom furnished with yellow-painted deal, with thick, dark red curtains drawn closely over the window. Mrs. Humble shut the door and her manner seemed to change.

"Now," she said, "it's all very well. You say you're from a friend of mine, but how do I know?"

"I don't know," stammered Julia.

"How did you get my nyme?"

"My husband got it . . . he's in the Navy; he got it from one of his friends on board ship."

"Oh, in the Nyvy, is he?"

"Yes, he's in an aircraft-carrier, and he's just left for the Mediterranean cruise." It gave Julia a curious joy to make these statements, and an added confidence— and this added confidence impressed Mrs. Humble, who appraised her shrewdly.

"How long gone do you think it is, dear?"

"About two and a half months—two months, I think," said Julia.

"Oh, well, that oughtn't to be serious, ought it? Cheer up, duckie. Now take off your things and lie down here, and I'll soon tell you."

Julia, feeling sick and outraged, submitted to the ministrations of Mrs. Humble, who, at least, first scrubbed her hands, gnarled but clean-looking hands, with carbolic soap and hot water.

"Well, that oughtn't to be a difficult job, dear. I'll just boil my things up. But first, where's the money? I do all I can to help poor women—God knows they get a bad enough time of it in this world—but I can't do it for nothing, see?"

"That's right, isn't it?" murmured Julia, holding out the ten one-pound notes which Leo had told her would be necessary.

"Yes," said Mrs. Humble, rather discontentedly, "that'll do; but from the looks of you. . . . Oh, well," but her eyes travelled discontentedly over Julia's spotless *crêpe de Chine* underclothes. "Now all you've got to do is to lie still there, and then I'll fix you up all nice and comfortable, see? and by the time you're in bed tonight, you oughtn't to have any more cause to worry. That's the way it'll happen, see?"

Julia lay with her eyes closed, and her teeth ground together, bearing everything. This was degradation indeed. She was thankful it was not Leo's child—but if it had been she would never have been here. No sound passed her lips, but tears of self-pity more than of pain trickled from under her closed lids.

"I can see I don't need to tell you, dear, to take care of yourself. Antiseptics, and all that. I'm careful myself, I've boiled everything, and I expect my patients to be careful, too. It's hard on me when they ain't, see?"

Julia, sobbing by now, was lying with her head pressed against the pillow, her hands over her face.

"I know what'll put you right. You can't go out like that," said Mrs. Humble, with a note of sharpness in her voice. There was a sound of a bottle clinking against a glass, and Julia found herself drinking gin and hot water. It was pleasant and comforting. Slowly, slowly, her sobs subsided.

"That's all right, dearie, take your time. You mustn't go out from here looking as though you've bin crying. That would never do, because of me, see?" said Mrs. Humble.

Julia nodded; and when she had powdered her face and made up her mouth, and dressed herself in her outdoor things, she put on her horn-rimmed spectacles, partly to hide the ravages of her tears and partly to show her the way out of this dark, unfamiliar place.

"That's right, dear," said Mrs. Humble, highly pleased

at this last touch—which she evidently took to be in the nature of a dramatic effect—"that's right. Now which way do you go from here? You'd better not go the same way you came in. I'll take you out the back way. It's quite dark now, and you turn to the left, and you go under the railway arch and keep straight on, then take the first to the right and you'll come to the railway station. You can find your way to anywhere in London from there; only get home quick because your pains will be coming on, and you don't want them to take you half-way home, do you?"

Julia followed Mrs. Humble's instructions. Her body felt wracked and humiliated; but the gin gave her strength and the unaccustomed clearness of the world, owing to her spectacles, gave her decision of movement. She arrived home at about nine o'clock. Her one conscious longing was for a bath. There had been something horrible about the motherliness of Mrs. Humble, though she was, after all, not a bad old woman. She evidently believed she was helping girls out of difficult places, and if she considered the labourer worthy of his hire, why should she not do so? But the weedy youth in the shop . . . he must have known what his mother did; here was a depravity—and, worse, a casual acceptance of depravity that shocked Julia's nerves. There was something dingy about the morality of the place, and at least the Darlings were never dingy. That little newspaper-shop . . . so blatantly innocent . . . seemed more sinister than an ordinary house would have done. It courted publicity, in a way. It said: "See how open and above-board I am." It was all horrible—and never again should Herbert come near her.

In spite of her growing bodily discomfort, she almost ran up the stairs to the door of the flat. She had hardly put her key into the lock when it was opened from within, and to her surprise there stood Herbert. There was a curious look on his face, half frightened and half sorry; a look to which she was unaccustomed. She stared at him.

"Why, whatever is it, Herbert? You weren't worrying about me, were you? I told you I should be late."

"No, no," said Herbert, "it isn't that. I've got something to tell you, Julia. Come into the dining-room—Bertha's in the sitting-room."

"I thought you were going to tell her to go?"

"I did," said Herbert, "that's just it." He followed Julia into the dining-room, and shutting the door, stood looking at her miserably. "I did tell her. I made it quite clear. When I make up my mind, I make up my mind, as you know, Julia. There's no two ways about it. I told her she was coming between man and wife, and she had got to go. She said—if it came to coming between man and wife . . . there was someone else." He stopped.

"Oh, I can guess all that," said Julia.

"Julia, she's done a dreadful thing. She got very angry with me. I don't think she really meant to do it, only she thought she was doing it for the best. But you know what a trouble Bobby has been lately, with his rheumatism. . . ."

Julia's heart seemed to stop. She gazed at him with her mouth open.

". . . yes, hardly able to move," Herbert went on, "and you having to carry him up and down stairs, or my having to when you weren't here. She never liked it. Well, after all, he wasn't my dog, was he . . . ?"

"She hasn't done anything to Bobby! What are you trying to tell me? He's not hurt? Where is he? Bobby! . . . Bobby . . . !" she heard her own voice begin to scream.

"Now stop it. Julia, he isn't hurt. It's quite all right. Bertha wouldn't do a thing like that. She had it done ever so quietly—chloroform. He never knew a thing about it, I swear he didn't. I'm not standing up for her, mind you . . . it wasn't her dog . . . and she had no right to do it; but she was wild with my telling her to go and everything."

"Where is he?" said Julia, to Herbert's relief in a very quiet voice.

"He's at the vet's. She took him in a taxi. When I found out, I made them keep him for you to see. I did my best . . . I did really, Julia. He didn't suffer a bit, the vet told me so. I've just seen him, and the people down below will let us bury him in the garden . . . I've asked them."

Herbert had probably never been seen to such advantage as he was now, but it was too late, as far as Julia was concerned. The utter desolation which fell upon her at the news wiped all fairness for Herbert out of her mind. She turned and pushed him aside and stumbled upstairs to the front room. She managed to get on to the bed, and then was aware of Emily bending over her. Next she was terribly sick, and then what Mrs. Humble had referred to as "the pains" began. A thoroughly frightened Bertha cowered in the parlour while Herbert telephoned frantically for Dr. Ackroyd or Anne. He didn't believe in women doctors himself, but he had a queer sort of faith in Anne.

Anne came and got Herbert out of the room. It was Anne's kind brown eyes that Julia saw before at last she fainted.

The next three days were more or less of a nightmare to Julia. To her intense surprise a nurse appeared at her bedside. She wondered whether she was very ill, whether perhaps she was going to die. She felt too tired and drained of all vitality to care very much.

On the third day, when she was sitting up in bed, Anne, after her usual talk with the nurse, settled herself by Julia's bedside. Julia sat looking at her sullenly, although she felt truly grateful. Anne was going to lecture her, she supposed.

"Julia," said Anne, "there are one or two things I must say to you. I know what you've had done to yourself, of course . . . no, don't bother to interrupt . . . oh yes, I know you've had something done . . . it's my job to know these things. And I suppose it's a relief to you to know it's been successful. Well, I simply told Herbert that you had been going to have a baby, and now it's all over. He jumped to the conclusion that it went wrong because of poor Bobby. It wasn't any business of mine to contradict him, and I didn't."

"Thank you," said Julia meekly.

"I found you hadn't told Herbert anything about it. He was very surprised, and I think he's very disappointed, Julia."

Julia said nothing.

"Oh, Julia, why did you do it?" said Anne.

"It's all very well for you, Anne," Julia said, "but where should I be with a baby? I couldn't go on working. I'd be tied up here with Herbert for the rest of my life. You don't know what it's like."

"It *was* Herbert's, then?" said Anne calmly.

290

"Oh yes, that was the trouble."

Anne looked at her sharply.

"Yes," said Julia—half proudly and half casually as though she had been one of the Darlings—"I've had a lover, and though Herbert's suspected it, he hasn't been sure. I haven't told anybody but you, Anne, but there have been rows about it for months. If it had been *his,* I wouldn't have minded. Herbert would have had to divorce me then."

"You'd like that?"

"Of course I'd like it. Oh, Anne, you'd have to be married to Herbert to know. And then to have known the other thing . . . ! Oh, you may be ever so clever. I know you've done wonderful things—passed all your exams., and walked the hospitals, and the rest of it . . . but you're not married, Anne, and you haven't had a lover."

Anne accepted the perpetual shame of virginity calmly.

"No, I can't know about your affairs as you do, of course," she said, "but you've done a dreadful thing, and a very dangerous thing. You ought to go to hospital now to be tidied up."

Julia shuddered. "No, thank you. I'm over it, and never want to think of it again. There never will be a next time, don't worry, I'll go on as I am."

"Are you what's called 'in love' with this man?" asked Anne.

"Of course I'm in love," said Julia, "terribly in love. I never knew it could be like this."

Anne sat in silence. It was no good preaching to Julia, she knew that. She also knew, only too well, that a doctor with a rich and fashionable practice might not have known the compulsion under which such as Julia lived; the compulsion not only of the bread-earner, but of the outward pressure of a small and rigid society.

It occurred to her, as it had often occurred to her before, that it would be simpler if people could go to bed with each other without making so much fuss about it; but then Herbert, she had to agree, would be the first to make a fuss about it. Julia was not the only sinner in that respect. Each made too much of it in a different way.

Anne gazed thoughtfully at Julia. After all, what did

291

she know of her? Although both had lived in Saint Clement's Square for years, their ways had lain so far apart. Anne's various experiences while she was taking her degree, her life with the other students, her gradually deepening knowledge of the human body and mind; her acquaintanceship, as she went through her various courses, with sick people in hospital, with women in labour, with the mentally afflicted—all these things had made her even more different from Julia than when they had attended school together.

Julia, she felt, in spite of being married and having had a lover—experiences which Julia seemed to think taught her all there was to be known about life—had remained strangely childish. After all, what training had her mind ever had, apart from business at the shop? Her mind had been free all these years to wander unchecked in the fields of imagination. No humble and arduous following of any exact knowledge had taught it discipline. I wonder what she's really like, thought Anne. I don't suppose I really know. I'm only frightfully sorry for her. How much does anyone know about anyone else? Very little . . . at the most one catches certain aspects, gleams, sudden shadows. Niceness . . . everyone is at the mercy of what is called niceness . . . if the little point of contact between two human beings chances to occur in a moment of pleasantness, then the two people think each other nice. A man may meet another, admire his operating, or his painting, or his sculpture, or whatever it is he does, and at once the other man will feel a softening of the heart, a sudden little glow, a sense that here is a nice person. Just as two men may meet, and one be offended at some heartless remark of the other, and quite a different moment will spring to life between them. Yet both moments are true, and both untrue. They are true because the contact is real, untrue because it covers such an infinitesimal point in the soul of each man.

"Knowing" anyone is only the getting together of a collection of these little points, or catching a spark as it flies off the surface of the mind struck at a certain angle for a brief flash.

You saw yourself in a glass, you were terribly isolated with yourself all your life, even in dreams; yet abysses were always opening in yourself before your horrified gaze. In the same way you saw the semblance of other isolated selves walking about, going through all the funny actions with which human beings complicate their lives; but you never saw a whole person, even physically. You couldn't see his back, and his front and the sideways view of him at the same time, although all three existed together. How much less, then, could you see the areas of the personality? The most you could do was to pin down in your memory—which chose them for you quite apart from your own selective volition—certain physical aspects, expressions, here a smile, there a habit of glancing sidelong, and certain reactions that you dubbed "characteristic." How odd it was, by the way, that no one ever said, "How exactly like So-and-so" in a complimentary spirit!

And shy, blind, voiceless, deep down in everyone was a tiny, lonely point of consciousness, that passionately wished for approbation, that was always being wounded by the lack of it.

Julia had gone about the world, as every human being went about it, quite a different person from the one that was seen in snatches by the absorbed consciousness of others. She went about it, from Saint Clement's Square to George Street, to Paris, to the seaside, a loving, passionate creature, greedy of life perhaps, but sure that she deserved, and must have, whatsoever she wanted; that she was misunderstood; that she was really gay, kind, charming. Julia saw Bertha as a crabbed, wicked old woman, but Bertha saw Julia as the wicked woman and herself as a noble character unappreciated.

Anne shook herself out of her thoughts and rose.

"There's one thing I've got to say to you, Julia," she said, "you must stay in bed for eight or ten days. Do you realise that you're not free yet from the danger of septicaemia? If anything were to happen to you now, it's quite likely I might be suspected of having had a hand in it. I'm known to be your friend, and I'm called in when you're taken ill. So don't think you can get up and go to the shop, or do anything like that. You must think of me as well as yourself."

"Oh, I will, indeed, Anne. I wouldn't let anybody think it was you," said Julia truthfully. "You've been wonderful. I don't know what I should have done without you. However did you get Herbert to agree to a nurse? Didn't he say it would be awfully expensive?"

"He did at first, but when I told him what was the matter, he didn't say another word. I've told him you'll be very nervous and very delicate for some time, and he has promised to be very good. He's brought Bobby home and buried him in the garden. I think you'll find he'll be quite all right if only you don't expect too much of him. And, Julia, I ought to warn you—Daddy says that Herbert isn't nearly as strong as he looks. His heart isn't good. You mustn't worry him or yourself. Your rest won't do you any good if you're worrying and fretting the whole time either about Herbert or about the other man. I suppose it's no good asking you whether you can forget him?"

"Never, never never," said Julia. "You don't understand, Anne."

"Well, if you can't, you can't," said Anne practically. "Have you heard any news from the shop?"

"I had a letter this morning frm Mrs. Danvers," answered Julia. "She was awfully nice. She thinks I've got the flu."

"I know," said Anne, "I'm afraid I let her gather that on the telephone."

"Well, anyway, she says I mustn't come back until I feel quite well. I can have ten days or a fortnight."

"Well, take the whole fortnight, Julia. And I'll send you some stuff in a bottle which will stop all this business you're suffering from now. Mind you drink it, or I'll throw up the case."

"All right," said Julia, "I promise to be good." She pulled Anne down to her, and for the first time for years —for neither of them was demonstrative—kissed her.

"You have been good, Anne," she said unsteadily.

"Oh no," said Anne, "my job, that's all. Try and think of *your* job, Julia. You're keen on the shop, I know, and being married to Herbert's a job—although it's turned out all wrong. I must sound an awful prig, but I don't mean it that way. I'll look in to-morrow, and mind you take the tonic."

Julia leaned back against her cushions after Anne had gone, feeling very weak and shaky. Herbert had a bad heart! Perhaps there was hope for her and Leo after all, even if he wouldn't agree to a divorce? Things might have been worse. Anne had found out, of course, but she'd never tell, and, anyway, the great dread was over. It had been worth it. Of Bobby she could not bear to think; that she would never again see him, never fondle his satiny brown head, look into his yellow eyes, hear the high whine of delight, or ease his stiff, rheumaticky old legs down the stairs just once more, all this knowledge was terrible. Tears came to her eyes. She had loved Bobby truly, devotedly, and unselfishly, and he was gone —without even a memory of good-bye between them. She felt no rancour towards Herbert now that her trouble was over. She felt, indeed, very little when she thought of him. She knew he had been kind about Bobby, but when one human being has frayed another's nerves for as many years as Herbert had frayed Julia's a solitary act of kindness seems of small account. Even Leo did not seem very real to her, far away as he was. He would be past Gib. by now, in that blue Mediterranean of which he had told her so often. There would be letters coming to her to the shop. She must do something about them. They mustn't be forwarded to Saint Clement's Square.

A few days later, when the nurse was a thing of the past, she crawled downstairs and rang up Gipsy.

"I'll be coming in a few days to see you, Mrs. Danvers. I'll be quite all right to come back to work in a week or ten days, the doctor says. I'm so terribly sorry to have let you down."

"That's all right, Julia," said Gipsy. "After all, you've been away ten days before now with one of your colds. Is it a bad one this time? Because if so, don't come near the shop. You know what the customers are, if they hear anybody sneezing."

"Well, perhaps I'd better not come for a few days," said Julia, "the doctor's sure it's influenza. I've been very ill, and I was terribly sick . . . and I fainted."

"That sounds very like influenza," agreed Gipsy. "By the way, there are two letters here for you. Shall I send them on?"

Julia was still very weak, and at the thought of the letters her heart began to beat as though it would suffocate her. She longed to say: Yes, yes, send them by special messenger, but she forced herself to reply:

"If you don't mind, Mrs. Danvers, I'd rather you kept

them. I'll be along in a few days to fetch them before I come back to work. I must go out once or twice, anyway, and I may just as well come to the shop."

"Very well. Take care of yourself," said Gipsy.

Julia had already written to Leo to tell him that all was well. *I was horribly ill, darling,* she wrote. *You can't think what it felt like. It's the sort of thing no man can ever imagine. But it's all right now, thank goodness.*

She could only write a short note, as she found any exertion tired her. When she had read Leo's letters she wrote again.

All those things I bought to take weren't any good, though you know I tried any amount. That's why I don't believe you can buy any drugs in England worth anything. So you must help me with something, for the purpose you know.

By the way, I bought myself a bottle of chlorodyne, because I thought it would help me when I got the pain, but I didn't use it because Anne looked after me. He can't bear anybody to be ill but himself, and he has already said he has had an attack of indigestion; so I gave him ever such a lot of the chlorodyne in sherry and told him I had only given him the ordinary dose, but it hasn't done anything except make him sick, although the doctor says he has a very bad heart. I was warned not to worry him. But isn't it cheering, because I've asked him again for the divorce, and told him I won't have anything to do with him again, and he still won't listen to me. Darling, you can't think how I'm longing for your first letter.

She had been to the shop towards the end of the week and collected the two letters. The first, written on the way out to Gibraltar, was full of the ardour and the excitement she had communicated to him in their farewell. The second told more of the bright sunshine and the fact that the Fleet was going to pass some time at Ste. Maxime, one of their favourite Mediterranean ports. He had often told her of it, not a posh place, he said, like Monte Carlo, but they had a ripping time, and everybody turned out to do them proud, from the Mayor downwards.

So Julia, sitting alone in Saint Clement's Square, began to write the first of a stream of letters, with which she was quite sure she could keep Leo attached to her and excited by her. In the days during which she rested, and gathered herself together again, she had very little to do except to dream and think of Leo. She did not ask herself how she could live up to the dream of the letters when he came back. She knew in the back of her mind there could be no living up to it. But this delightful, mad game that she had started to play, this game of writing about Herbert as "him" and "he," referring to him as somebody who could not be allowed to stand in the way of such a wonderful love as theirs —this game was, in itself, absorbing enough to fill the time until Leo should return; and, after all, anything might happen. Accidents happened every day; Herbert might get a shock and his heart give out; he might get run over—anything might happen. She did not visualise to herself the details of any accident. If a magician had appeared before her and offered to have Herbert crushed out of life for her benefit, she would have refused in sick horror; but it was another thing to write about what life would be like if only Herbert were not there. And supposing by any chance "something happened" and she and Leo were free to marry, he would always admire her for the courage she had been ready to show for his sake, had it been necessary. He would look at her always, surely, with something of awe, as one of the great lovers of the world, ready to do anything for his happiness.

That was the thing. They had to be happy together. And happiness was assuming more and more of a domestic shape for Julia. The glow and beauty of those days on the mere, although they were all the love-making that she and Leo had ever had, yet did not represent what she really wanted. The Julia who had made of love a pagan festival was only a very small part of the whole Julia.

Now we will be together always some day, won't we, darling? and don't let it be too far off, will you? Life goes by so terribly quickly. Do you know we have never yet done the thing I want to do most in the world —to go away with you, just for one night if we can't manage any longer, to some place where people will think we are really married. We've had so little really, darling, haven't we—just that time in Essex. I'd love

297

to stay at an hotel—I wouldn't mind how simple it was with you—and sign the book "Mr. and Mrs. Carr." If only you were ever on leave when I was going to Paris, it would be quite simple, but you never are. We could stay the night at some hotel in Dover. It wouldn't be any good in France because they would be sure we weren't married there, even if we were. They'd see how in love we are. I'd like—don't laugh at me, my heart—I'd like to put our shoes outside the door, and be called with early tea in the morning by the chambermaid. It would show us what it would be like when we really belong to each other in the eyes of the world for always. It would show you I could make it just as lovely as the time in Essex.

Thus wrote Julia, forgetting that she had once praised France because there the hotel-keepers were sympathetic towards unmarried lovers. More and more as her imagination became obsessed by pictures of Leo leaving her, her letters were filled with some urgent plea for permanency. It was sometimes in the projection of what life would be like together when they were married, and sometimes she reverted again to the fantastic idea of "doing something to him."

Leo wrote back and played both games with her amused, proud, only faintly uneasy, swaggering a little when he read the letters, and looked at himself in his little shaving-mirror. There must be something about him to make a girl like Julia so wild about him; and, after all, when he got tired of her—one couldn't go on for ever—then he had got the letters. She couldn't make a row when he had got the letters. Of course, he had promised to destroy them, but he would be a silly ass to do that. Oh no, thought Leo, stowing the passionate, eager, foolish letters away in his box, I know a trick worth two of that. I'm keeping those letters, my dear. And Julia, after reading and re-reading Leo's answers, would creep downstairs at night and burn them in the parlour grate after Herbert had gone to bed in the back room.

Of course, her letters were not only about themselves, their happiness, the necessity of "arranging something" if fate did not arrange it for them, or if Herbert still refused the divorce. All this was merely the spice, the sharp and biting flavour which Julia added; but for the rest she spent the time when she was writing to him, and very often the hours when she was going back and forth, in a sort of dream, between the shop and Saint Clement's Square; in building up for him a picture of herself and her life as she felt sure it was. Amusing little stories about the customers, and the work-girls, that showed her humour; little flashes of description, and, above all, accounts of the theatres she went to. Ruby was still the casual, good-natured friend she had always been, and often she took Julia to the theatre if she had been given free seats herself, and was "resting."

The theatre held a glamour for Julia that "the pictures" had never quite succeeded in giving her, and it was difficult to get Herbert to go to the movies, and practically impossible to get him to go to the theatre. For one thing it meant going "up West" again after he had come home from his work, unless he met Julia somewhere and they dined in Town—a thing from which his increasingly thrifty mind revolted.

Neither did Julia like going out with Herbert. She was doing her best, according to a promise given to Anne, to be pleasant to Herbert, and she was succeeding. She had a naturally pleasant temperament, and she loathed ugly words and sharp speech. But here it was Herbert who was the offender. In his family it had always been the prerogative of the man to criticise without cease, and the women were supposed to put up with it. Carping, as Julia called it, was Herbert's chief notion of domestic conversation. She bore with him patiently, however, for at least she had her nights to herself. He had been too alarmed by her illness, and the intensity of her dislike of him now as a lover was too obvious an affront even to his nerves, for him to attempt any violation of her privacy.

He wondered about it, poor Herbert, occasionally. Why had she seemed to like him, and not only him, but liked, as he put it, "the whole box of tricks" just for that autumn? and now why did he feel that never again would she soften towards him in that relationship? Women were odd, he supposed, but she must have been disappointed about the baby—though it was funny she hadn't told him it was on the way. Wanted to make quite sure, he supposed, before she did.

For, though Julia had always insisted that she would

not have a child until she was ready, Herbert was firmly convinced that "it would be all right when it came," and that she would like it when it was there—things which his sister Bertha had impressed upon him. Women were always changing, that was obvious.

For the first year of their married life Julia had been nice to him, although as cold as a fish; then she had begun to quarrel more and more, until at last she had never let him come near her. Then she had had this flirtation with young Carr, and when she had stayed at Torquay, seeing more of him, had suddenly dashed off by herself to Essex. Then for a whole autumn she hadn't minded Herbert's attentions, then she had suddenly refused them; started going to the pictures with young Carr, until he had had to put his foot down; and now she seemed happy in an odd sort of way, although Carr was safely tucked away in the Mediterranean. She wasn't having any letters from him either, though, of course, these might be going to the shop; but Herbert had gone quietly through all Julia's belongings on several occasions, when she was out of the house and hadn't found so much as an empty envelope. And although Carr was gone, she didn't seem to mind, and seemed happy; and yet she wouldn't let her husband near her; although he had got rid of Bertha for her sake. Oh, well, Anne had told him that women take a long time to get over a miscarriage, and Herbert always felt oddly guilty himself in the affair of Bobby. If Bertha hadn't felt she could trust to his support, she would never have dared to do it. He hadn't been fair to Julia about Bertha, and he knew it. But then, as far as he could see, Julia was hardly ever fair to him, except when she started to argue things out; and then, somehow, in some horribly unaccountable manner, she always seemed to be quiet and reasonable and in the right; he felt helpless before her, although he knew it must be he who was "really" in the right. Yet he was reduced to thumping the table and saying: "After all, I am your husband."

Well, that was married life, Herbert supposed. But he was uneasy, occasionally desirous, and always discontented with this new Julia, who seemed enwrapt in a world of her own. She had always been prone to be that by fits and starts, but now it seemed to last most of the time, complain and grumble and nag at her as he would.

He announced, half defiantly to Julia, that he should have Bertha to stay with him as usual when she went over to Paris for the spring collection.

"Certainly, if you like," said Julia, "as long as she isn't here when I am."

"There's Easter, you know," said Herbert, looking away from her, and cracking his nails after a peculiarly unfortunate fashion which had grown upon him of late. "I suppose you couldn't make up your mind to overlook it, Julia, and have Bertha for Easter?"

"No, no!" said Julia sharply.

"All right, it's as you wish. We won't stay here then. We'll go away somewhere together, just you and I. I had thought we would have her, and stop in London for Easter and save a bit of money, and patch things up."

Julia stood thinking. She did not look at him, but stared out at the Square where the pale spring sunlight showed up the naked, dark tracery of the trees. Go away somewhere alone with Herbert . . . that would be dreadful. Leo would be home for his Easter leave, and if she were away she would not be able to see him at all. He only had ten days. Of course, she could refuse to go away with Herbert, and then he wouldn't go away either. If Bertha were with them she would insist on a lot of her brother's company. Bertha's eyes were sharp, of course, and she would be on the watch for anything between Julia and Leo, but Herbert would be on the watch, anyway. It was really better to have the two of them, so that she could have the excuse for going out alone. It seemed somehow a betrayal of Bobby to forgive Bertha for what she had done, and yet . . . and yet . . . if it made things easier, if it made Herbert any less suspicious, if it took up some of his time, if it enabled them to stay in London . . . ? Bobby, poor darling, was gone; it was no good having these fanciful feelings about him.

"I . . . I'll try, Herbert," murmured Julia, dropping her eyes. "It's horribly difficult for me. I can never really forgive her, you know that, even if she is your sister. I'll think about it when I'm in Paris."

Herbert was absurdly grateful. His eyes became quite moist, and he poured out two whiskies and sodas.

It seemed to him, in the optimism engendered after he had drunk his, that perhaps everything would be all right. After all, he didn't ask much—only a little peace and quiet in the home, and to exercise his rights as a husband occasionally. Nobody could call that much; and as to having his own sister staying with him, well, *that* was only natural, too. It was no good being high and mighty about a dead dog, even if Bertha had behaved as she should not; and it was a good thing that Julia saw it at last. He actually did not try to pick a quarrel with Julia for the remaining four or five days before she went to Paris.

A parcel arrived at l'Etrangère's for Julia on the Wednesday of Holy Week. It bore the London postmark, but it had Leo's writing on the label. Julia had learned a great deal of control by now. She put it aside and did not open it until the girls had gone. Then when she untied the thick brown paper, she shook out a heavy grey-blue cloak of a thick smooth cloth. It was quite plain except for silver buckles at the throat. Gipsy, with hat and coat on ready to depart, came into the fitting-room as Julia was trying the cloak on in front of the long glass.

"Oh, Julia," she cried, "how lovely! An Italian officer's cape. Where did you get it?"

"A friend who has been in the Mediterranean sent it to me," said Julia, blushing slightly. "Do you like it?"

"It's lovely. I've always admired those capes, quite apart from capes being so fashionable nowadays. It makes your eyes look quite blue, Julia."

"It's frightfully heavy," said Julia, pouting a little. "I shouldn't like to walk far in it."

"I know, they weigh a tremendous amount. They're frightfully expensive. Just think, it will never go out of fashion, and will always clean as good as new. It does suit you, Julia. Try throwing one side over the other shoulder. . . . Yes, that's it."

Julia did so, and gazed at herself in the glass. Yes, it was very becoming, with the little black helmet hat which came down to her eyebrows . . . and her eyes did look quite blue. When Gipsy had gone, Julia hunted in the parcel and found a note.

This is for you, my beauty, wrote Leo. *I don't pretend I didn't get it second-hand, it would have cost about £10 otherwise; but I didn't get it from another girl, so don't be anxious. Directly I saw it I thought of you. I suppose you'll have to say you got it from a customer,*

*or something. You've probably got it on while you're
reading this note, and I shall be at home at Heronscourt
Park. Do you realise it? I daren't meet you on my first
evening back. You told me in your last letter you would
be staying in London for Easter, but I expect I'll have
to go away with my people just for the holiday. You
know what families are. I wonder if you're going to live
up to the things you've been writing me, Julia, or whether
we shall find we are only friends after all? It might be
easier that way, but I haven't met a girl as good as you
yet. Leo.*

Julia wore the cloak home, trying in its warm folds
to forget the little chill that his letter had given her. It
wasn't an enthusiastic letter, and who could wonder? Just
look what his last leave had been! But she would make
him forget all his caution, all his doubts. She would
manage something this time. She was desperate.

She learned—with apparently a mild interest—that
young Carr was home again and off with his parents and
some friends of theirs, girls, of course, added Herbert,
for the Easter holidays. They wouldn't be back until
the Tuesday; and her heart sank still further. But to
Bertha's watching eyes she presented not the slightest
flicker of emotion.

Elsa, happy with her bank clerk, and successfully
weaned by Julia from her pale blue to the more subtle
shades of that colour, was frankly admiring of the Italian
officer's cloak.

"You are lucky," she said enviously, "the way you get
your clothes cheap."

"D'you think it's lucky to have a bad debt?" said
Julia. "It was from a customer who couldn't pay us.
It's no good to us, of course, and Mrs. Danvers let me
have it. I've paid for it in a way, because I've missed
the commission on the clothes the woman had. It's all
in a day's work, I suppose. You ought to wear this sort
of blue, Elsa, it would suit you."

"Yes," agreed Elsa. "I always did like a nice saxe."

Julia winced, but made no reply. "A nice saxe," indeed! Oh, shades of the little "matcher"!

On Tuesday Leo telephoned her at the shop, a thing
she rarely allowed him to do. She felt her heart beating
with the old sweet suffocation at the sound of his voice.

What did it matter how he behaved, how casual he was, when he had this power to move her? She agreed to meet him at a tea-shop that afternoon. There was no business at the shop, and she knew Gipsy would let her off early.

This was very different from the last meal they had had together. No hostage of Herbert's made a barrier between them now, and it was a triumphant Julia—who had dared pain and danger, and perhaps death, to preserve her integrity for her lover—who met Leo. Julia, moreover, in the excitement of the meeting, was prepared to promise anything to keep up the fairy story of the letters; she'd say anything to make him see that they were not just meeting as friends; that there was still no girl like her, that for him there never could be.

Leo hardly knew her as she sat chattering. A high natural colour burned in her cheeks, her eyes shone under the level brim of the little close-fitting hat; the blue cloak he had sent her covered her shoulders. Julia's invention had never flown faster. She gave a description of how she had begged Herbert again and again for a divorce, and how he still refused. And she told Leo, with that measure of truth which always mingled with her fantasy, that she had kept herself for him, that Herbert had never touched her again. Even now, when, owing to necessity, they were sharing the same bed.

"But he'll try, of course, Leo, he'll try. But I won't let him, whatever happens. Everything is for you."

"That's all very well," said Leo excitedly, all his fears and his caution blown away from him now he saw her in the flesh, "but what are we going to do? Think of that Christmas leave. I can't go on like that again. You know I've always warned you, Julia."

"Oh, I know, I know. I tell you what, Leo, I was going to the theatre with Ruby to-morrow night. I told Herbert about it a week ago. She won't mind if I put her off; she only asked me because she hadn't anyone else. She can always get someone. But where can we go? Leo—can't you find a safe hotel? where they'd think we were married? I'd love that. . . ."

"No, no, that's not possible. We'll have to go to the shop," said Leo. "You must forget all that nonsense you've talked about them trusting you, and the rest of it. It won't hurt the shop, will it? Nobody will know. You've told me yourself that the whole house is empty at night."

And, looking at his eager face, feeling she had re-captured his interest, Julia found that her old arguments no longer held good. Where could they go, if not to the shop?

So the next evening, after a little dinner in Soho, it was to the shop they went. What an exciting adventure it was waiting until the street was darkened and quiet. They did not have to wait very long, for hardly anyone lived in George Street, and Julia slipped her key into the familiar door and crept in with Leo, without turning on the light.

As she made her way before him, through the dark passage, lit only from the Georgian fanlight at the top of the door, she had a sudden recollection of the evening when Herbert had called for her in the war, and kissed her so roughly. It gave added zest to what she was do-ing now. Served Herbert right, although he mustn't know of it.

It was exquisite to feel Leo's arms go round her, even before she had reached the foot of the stairs, and to meet his gentle, burning kisses. Until that moment they had only been able to press each other's hands since his re-turn.

They groped their way up the little narrow stairs, up to the second floor, and Julia led the way into the fitting-room. For a while she stood by the window listening. It was all right; nobody had seen them come in; nobody was going to inform the police of a suspicious entry into l'Etrangère.

Leo gazed about him as the room became visible to his eyes in the soft light from the street lamp which shone through the gold net curtains that allowed him to look out, although it prevented anyone seeing in.

"I can't think what they have that bed for," he whis-pered, "unless it's for this sort of thing." Somehow the effect of the time and the place, and the secrecy, was to make them both whisper.

She took her cloak off, and pulled off her hat, and then he picked her up and laid her down on the divan, while she stayed quiescent with an exquisite submission in his arms. He threw aside the painted doll, which subsided in the corner of the room standing on its shock of red hair, with its skirts falling over its face. He looked down at her, as she had been wont to imagine him when, with

305

closed eyes, she had submitted to Herbert. There was his dark, high-held head; there were his bright eyes staring at her; here were his hands, closing slowly about her body. She lay absolutely relaxed, her outstretched arms lying over the edge of the divan, and the light from the street lamp upon her face. The shadows of the window-bars lay across her as though they were impalpable bands tying her down. She laughed for pure happiness as she looked up at Leo.

"This is better than the punt," she whispered; "we've two or three hours, Leo, and no fear of anyone coming in."

It was the first time they had been absolutely free from the fear of an eavesdropper, and that the hours had been theirs to dally with as they liked.

It was nearly midnight when Julia let herself in at Saint Clement's Square, and Herbert was already asleep on his side of the big bed. Julia slipped in beside him, and turned out the light. She closed her eyes and slept all night, not with her husband, but with her lover.

That was all there was of pleasure. Leo had already had a week's leave, of which he had had to spend the greater part with his parents. There only remained to him two evenings. The evening following the wonderful night at the shop was a repetition of many other evenings —a family reunion to celebrate Elsa's engagement; and Leo now rather surprisingly found himself in the position of the rejected suitor, or so the Beales seemed to think, and had to be present at the party to show there was no ill-will. And, of course, the Starlings had to be there also because they were "the family." They all played "Up Jenkins" and "Consequences," and there was much laughter when, as a result of the latter game, Elsa was proved to have met her fiancé in the bathroom. Julia endured the evening. She was even bright and amusing in a perfectly respectable way, not enough to make Bertha or Herbert eye her suspiciously. She tried to be specially nice to old Mrs. Carr, but old Mrs. Carr had her simple country obstinacies, which she had never lost, and she refused to like Julia, whom she saw as the scarlet woman of the Bible, laying traps for the feet of her good, young son. If an angel from heaven had appeared to Mrs. Carr and told her that Leo dominated Julia's every thought and action, that his had been the first advances, as his had been the threats of making an end of the affair, threats which had always brought her to heel, Mrs. Carr would have refused to believe it. She would have been almost equally indignant with Julia if the latter had not thought Leo attractive and lovable.

She could not argue. She could only feel with the whole of her sturdy, muscular old body; even with her mind she felt rather than thought.

Leo had time for a few angry words to Julia as the Carrs and the Starlings went down Love Lane to their respective homes.

"You must come out with me to-morrow night, Julia, it's my last night. I don't believe anything you said, anything you've written. It was all pretence. I thought it was at the time, and now I'm sure of it . . . if you don't come out to-morrow night."

A perilous moment of reality hung between them. If she once acknowledged to him that he had spoken the truth when he voiced his disbelief in her fairy story, something bright and lovely and shining would be gone for ever.

"Leo, I can't, I daren't," she said hurriedly. "I've arranged with Herbert for ages to go with him to-morrow. There's no getting out of it this time. I can't say any more now. Ring me up at the shop to-morrow lunchtime . . . and don't talk like that, Leo, you'll break my heart."

She pressed his hand feverishly, and hurried on to catch up with Herbert. She was very unhappy. This banal "family" evening had been horrible after the beauty of last night. If only she could have got hold of Leo sooner . . . if only those wretched Easter holidays had not taken him from her . . . if only . . . there she was again. It always came back to the same thing . . . if only . . .

"I can't get out of it, Leo, I can't," she told him urgently on the telephone the next day. "I'll slip out and meet you at tea. I can't do anything else. Herbert takes these tickets every year, and he so seldom takes theatre tickets. It's for an awful dud amateur show that the men in his business put up every year. It'll be dreadful, but I don't see how I can get out of it. Herbert always has to put in an appearance, and I always have to go with

307

him. I've never missed. No, Bertha can't go with him. You know the row there'd be. Why, he has known about this for weeks, long before I said Bertha could come back to the flat. Besides, she's fixed up to go to some old crony of hers for the evening, and nothing makes her alter her plans. I'd give the world to get out of it, you know I would. Look, I can't talk any more now, I'll see you for tea."

She hastily replaced the receiver as she heard the buzzer of the door sound.

She went over and over the argument wearily with Leo at tea-time, wondering where the gentle, ardent lover of two nights ago had gone. This was Leo at his sulkiest, his most bitter. His leave was up, wasn't it? he would have to go back to Portsmouth, and then to Scottish waters for the summer cruise; she had known all that; she knew the routine by now.

"But you knew it all, too, Leo," she pleaded. "Why did you go away for the Easter holiday?"

"Because I had to. Dad and Mum had fixed it all for me. It's all very well, Julia, I couldn't get out of it."

"And I can't get out of this, Leo."

"Well, you don't love me."

"How can you say that, when you know what I've tried to do for you!"

"Oh yes, so you said. Fairy stories! You know that, and I know it. Giving Herbert chlorodyne!"

Again that awful moment of truth hung between them. She felt oddly helpless, her usually quick wits would not come to her aid. Leo went on:

"As though that would hurt a kitten, anyway! Could I get anything to give him! I don't suppose you really even talked to him about divorce."

"Oh, I have, I have, darling," she declared, with truth, "how can you talk to me like this?" She was pale and shaking with misery. The tears rolled down and fell unheeded on her plate.

"Well, I'll believe it when I see something. I'll have to get myself a girl who doesn't let me down, that's all."

"Leo, I can see you to-morrow before you go. I promise I'll manage to see you to-morrow."

"See me!" said Leo scornfully.

They parted miserably, and it was with even less expectation of pleasure than she had thought to have that

308

Julia dressed in a grey evening gown, of which she was not particularly fond, for the amateur show that evening. Nevertheless, she thought, after she was dressed, one must always look one's best. . . . She touched up her cheeks a little, darkened her lashes, and applied her lipstick with a conscientious care which was second nature. Her spirits rose a little as she placed the beautiful cloak about her shoulders, for it made a lovely evening wrap. None of the wives of Herbert's stuffy colleagues would have anything like that!

The show, held in a hall in Baker Street, was boring to her as it had been in preceding years. More so, really, for there actually had been years, before she met Leo, when she had hoped vaguely that she would meet at one of those shows a captain of finance such as she had read of, who had taken, in her romantic imagination, the place of the khaki-clad captains of earlier days. Now, of course, she knew she couldn't meet anyone thrilling at one of Herbert's stuffy "shows."

Herbert was full of importance—pleased to meet the managers of other branches and to show off Julia; but his friends bored her, and so did the amateur warblings and dancing upon the stage. She leaned back in her seat, at last, and yawned at great length, hardly bothering to put up her hand; and Herbert glanced at her reproachfully. He was enjoying himself. What did she want to come over all superior for?

He spoke to her sharply about it when they were on their way back in the Underground train. Julia was too tired and too unhappy to answer back. She merely said: "I'm sorry, Herbert, I'm tired," and they lapsed into silence amid the swingings and rattlings of the train.

It was a dark mild evening, and they walked home, still in silence. How often, she thought drearily, as she walked up the street to Saint Clement's Square, how often had she come this way; how many thousands of times had this pavement echoed to her feet—and all her bright dreams of getting away, of a new and wonderful life with Leo, began to fade into nothingness. And would her feet, growing more and more weary, tap these same echoes into life for years to come?

A sense of darkness and futility weighed upon her. These months without Leo had somehow been so bright with dreams. That evening at l'Etrangère's, though not the pretence of domesticity at an hotel for which she had hoped, had been such an ecstatic culmination, and now something at once solid and shining that she had seemed to have within her grasp, was vanishing into the mist. How could she keep Leo, how could she?

As they entered the Square they heard some footsteps running swiftly up from the road at right angles to them, but she paid no attention, and she and Herbert went on in silence. The footsteps came nearer, and suddenly Leo's voice, thick and blurred with drink, spoke behind them.

"Stop . . . you've got to stop, I say."

"What's that?" said Herbert, startled and half turning round. "Why, what are you doing here?"

"I've come because I'm sick of you, and this way of going on," said Leo. "Get out of the way, Julia, unless you'll come with me now as you are. That's what any decent woman would do."

Yes, he was drunk. If only he had spoken like that when he was sober!

"What are you talking about?" said Herbert. "Julia, what's all this?"

"Oh, Leo," cried Julia, "go away. This isn't any good. Go away."

But Leo was scuffling with Herbert. Herbert's hat fell off, but he got free from Leo's detaining hands and turned his back upon him.

"You can go to hell, Carr," he said, "and stay there," and he stooped down to pick up his hat.

Leo, furious that Herbert was escaping him, gave him a violent blow on the back of his head. Herbert began to crumble up in the knees in a curious way, and fell forward. Beside himself with anger Leo hit him again. Herbert fell upon his face, striking his temple against the kerb. He rolled over the kerb and lay upon his back in the gutter, with his arms flung out. The whole thing only took a few moments, but it seemed to Julia like a slow-motion picture. She screamed from the moment Leo first hit Herbert:

"Stop! stop! stop!" she cried, in an agony of terror. "Oh, do stop, stop! . . ."

But Leo only laughed, a shocking sound in the now silent Square. For a moment he stood and stared down at Herbert as though he were amazed at what his hand had done. Then Julia dropped on her knees beside Herbert

310

and tried to raise his head; but Leo, turning, vanished swiftly into the shadows, his feet beating out a stumbling rhythm, but his footsteps never paused, and the sound they made was swallowed up in the noise of the High Road.

Julia tried to pull Herbert to the pavement, but he was too heavy, and she crouched down holding his head against her breast. She could see that he was bleeding from a wound on his temple. For a few moments she was too frightened to call for help. She hardly knew, so dazed she was, what she feared; but then she screamed, again and again, this time for help. Alone with that stark terror she still tried to pull herself together. There was Dr. Ackroyd, if only she could get to him, but how could she leave Herbert like this? She screamed again, but not this time in panic, but deliberately for help. The sound of footsteps coming towards her beat upon her ears with an accelerated pace. Help was coming. All might yet be well, thought Julia.

But she was wrong. The dream was over. It had fallen away like a great wave and, sharp and hard, one deed remained; a deed that seemed to have nothing to do with the dream, and that yet in some fantastic fashion was the outcome of it. No one would understand the dream, but they would see the deed, standing out black and angry, a pinnacle of dreadful isolation.

BOOK FOUR

"No one can say
That the trial was not fair. The trial was fair,
Painfully fair by every rule of law,
And that it was made not the slightest difference.
The law's our yardstick, and it measures well
Or well enough when there are yards to measure.
Measure a wave with it, measure a fire,
Cut sorrow up in inches, weigh content.
You can weigh John Brown's body well enough,
But how and in what balance weigh John Brown?"
—*John Brown's Body*,
by STEPHEN VINCENT BENET.

1

The Nightmare Begins

Two young men came running up breathlessly, guided by her cries.

"What's the matter?" said one, peering as short-sightedly as Julia herself.

Julia didn't think about her answer. She had planned nothing; she was only hoping, passionately, that Herbert was not seriously hurt, and that nobody would find out about Leo. She had no room even for resentment that Leo had rushed off and left her to deal with the situation which he himself had created. She was fondling Herbert's limp hand, trying to feel a responsive pressure in his fingers, and she answered:

"It's my husband . . . he's ill . . . I think he's had a fit. Please go quickly . . . there's a doctor at the corner of the Square . . . Dr. Ackroyd. Tell him it's Mrs. Starling . . . tell him to hurry. Oh, please be quick."

The short-sighted man still stood staring, but the other started to run quickly towards Dr. Ackroyd's house. Julia sat with Herbert's head against her arm. What had Leo done, what had he done? Why had she always laughed at Herbert's account of his bad heart?

The short-sighted man knelt down on the pavement

beside Julia and tried to feel Herbert's pulse, but, like most laymen, he had very little idea how this should be done, and feeling the pulse in his own thumb, announced hopefully that Herbert's pulse was still beating.

Julia hardly heard him. She crouched there in her evening gown, unaware even of the wet stains that mottled the front of it, and felt she must be in a nightmare. It couldn't be to her, Julia Starling, that this dreadful thing had happened, her husband assaulted, made terribly ill, perhaps dying, and then Leo gone, flying across the Square into the noise and light of the High Road, leaving her there with Herbert a dead weight on her arm and on her soul. It was but a nightmare, till the familiar face of Dr. Ackroyd was bending over her in the light of the street lamp. He lowered Herbert's head gently, and striking a match, looked at his face and felt his pulse. Then he motioned to one of the young men to lead her away. To the other, a keen-faced alert youth, he spoke quickly:

"Fetch a policeman, You'll find a man on point-duty on the corner of the High Road. It's a mortuary case."

"You mean . . ." gasped the young man, shocked, yet filled with that interest in the horrible which moves most human beings, "you mean he's dead?"

"Dead as mutton," said Dr. Ackroyd. "Hurry."

The young man, swift as ever, set off down the street, his Burberry flapping behind him. The short-sighted man was trying to detain Julia, but she broke away from him and came up to the doctor.

"Why has he gone away?" she asked. "Can't they help to carry him in? Look, we're only three doors away from home."

"Go ahead, Julia," said Dr. Ackroyd. "Have you got your key? Right. Open the door."

Julia fumbled in her little evening bag, found the key, and started running towards the lion-guarded house. Her spirits felt better. Dr. Ackroyd was in charge, he would do something—he must do something—all would yet be well. She ran up the steps and with a shaking hand fitted the key into the lock. She heard voices behind her, but paid no attention. She threw open the door and turned on the light which gave upon the stairs leading up to the Starling flat. There was no sound; Bertha slept heavily, and her room was at the back. Julia ran up, unlocked the door of the flat, turned on the light in the hall, came down again and out across the little paved garden and through the gate.

There were five men round Herbert now, making a little crowd, that had swelled with the horrid persistence of flies or of vultures. She started to run towards them, her breath coming short and fast, her heart feeling as though it would knock her to pieces. With a sudden panic she saw that one of the men was a policeman—a policeman . . . why had they called a policeman? She tried to take a pull on herself, and her voice sounded fairly natural as she spoke.

"I've opened the flat, Dr. Ackroyd. Can you bring him up?"

"No, Julia, I'm afraid we can't," said the old doctor.

"Why not?"

"He'll need more immediate care than he can get at home. I'll take you back, Julia."

Julia stared about her. There was the policeman; there were the two young men who had come to her help. There was another man in pyjamas, a man with a bald head and a brown pointed beard and a dark overcoat, who kept repeating: "I heard her cry out, 'Stop! Stop!' I heard her cry out."

Julia stared at him, and wondered what he was doing there.

"I came as quickly at I could," the bald-headed man went on. "But my wife made me put on some things first."

The policeman stood up, oddly immovable, looking more like a statue than a man, the lamplight glinting on his silver buttons and throwing a shadow across his eyes beneath his helmet; and beneath it his ruddy cheeks swelled out like a child's balloon.

"I must use the telephone," he announced in slow, husky accents. "Who has a telephone?"

"I've always wanted a telephone," said the bald-headed man, "but my wife and I should get no rest from business if I were on the telephone at home."

"Why, we've got a telephone," said Julia.

"Of course, yes," said Dr. Ackroyd. "Julia, take the constable to telephone from the flat. We shall want an ambulance."

"Oh, quick," said Julia, "quick. Do hurry."

317

Did policemen ever hurry? she reflected bitterly as the heavy, even steps followed her fleeting feet along the pavement.

The constable rang up the police station. "Station officer, please," said the policeman in his thick, husky voice, and then after a moment: "Ambulance wanted, sir, Saint Clement's Square. Got a body to take to the mortuary."

Julia gave a scream, and once she had screamed she found she couldn't stop. She screamed, and screamed again, till the sound was so horrid in her own ears that she had to hold her hands over her mouth, and still the screams went on behind her hands, forcing their way past them like animals forcing their way through a fence.

There was a sound of a door opening, and Bertha, wrapped in her dark red woollen dressing-gown, appeared at the end of the passage.

"What's the matter? What's all this noise, Julia? Has there been an accident? What's the policeman doing here?"

"Gentleman fallen dead on the corner of the Square," said the constable.

He looked at Julia, as though to ask who Bertha might be, but Julia paid no heed to him. She sat down suddenly on the hall chair, and the blood seemed to have left her legs, which were suddenly full of pins and needles instead. She clutched the arms of the chair and wondered whether she were going to faint. Why had it to happen like this? Why had Leo had to hit Herbert? Why couldn't he have died without?

She heard the voices of Bertha and the constable beating about her like dark birds. Then the flat seemed to become full of people; the policeman began to take down names and addresses in his book—that of the short-sighted man, of the keen-faced man, of the bald-headed, bearded man, of Dr. Ackroyd, and Bertha herself, and there were other people there, too—the person called the station officer, to whom the constable had telephoned, and who had by now arrived.

Julia, her legs still feeling very weak, went out through to the balcony and saw that men were lifting Herbert's body into the ambulance. "A heart attack, I think," she heard Dr. Ackroyd saying from the hall, "and in falling

318

he seems to have caught the edge of the kerb. He's bleeding slightly from the temple."

Julia breathed a deep sigh of relief from her troubled heart. She had always heard you died if you were hit on the temple. Leo's blows had been on the back of Herbert's head.

"If he fell," it was Bertha's voice speaking now, strident with anger as well as grief, "I believe she had a hand in it."

"I didn't," said Julia, "I never touched him. He just fell down; I think he was feeling ill."

Everybody turned towards her. The light clicked on, and she realised she had been speaking from the dark drawing-room to the little crowd in the lighted hall.

"I swear my brother hasn't died naturally," said Bertha. "Look at him again . . . look at him again."

"I saw nothing except a slight wound on his temple, where he had evidently hit the herb. There's blood on the kerb as well," said Dr. Ackroyd.

The station officer looked at him. "Better have another look, doctor, before the ambulance goes off."

Julia heard their feet going down the stairs, then down the steps across the little garden. She sat, her throat dry and constricted, for what seemed hours, but what she realised was probably only about ten minutes. Presently the two men came back.

"I'll have to ask you to come to the station, Mrs. Starling," said the officer. "And you—Miss Starling, isn't it? We have the names and addresses of everybody else. Get a taxi."

A taxi that sounded like an antiquated sewing-machine presently came chug-chugging slowly up to the front door, and Julia climbed into it, and had to sit next to Bertha—a hated contact that made her shrink up into herself. Dr. Ackroyd did not come with them. His name and address were known. Another doctor had arrived on the scene, somebody called the divisional surgeon. He appeared mysteriously in the chug-chugging taxi. Julia vaguely remembered there had been some telephoning in the interval.

For the first quarter of an hour Julia would not have known that she was in a police station. She might, as far as the look of things went, have been in a Tube station. The walls were covered with brown glazed tiles half-way up, then cream-washed. Everywhere there was shiny wood, and doors and benches. Behind a desk sat a man taking down particulars. She sat on a bench feeling utterly limp, and then she was taken into another room, and a man began to question her, all sorts of questions that she didn't know how to answer.

Was she sure that her husband had fallen down?

"Quite, quite sure," said Julia. "He just gave a sort of cry, and seemed to stumble, and fell down."

"Did he fall forwards or backwards?"

Julia tried hard to think. Yes, he'd fallen forward, she remembered. "He fell forwards, but then he rolled over the edge of the pavement on to his back."

"And what did you do?"

"I called for help. I could see he was very ill. I thought he must have hit his head."

"Why did you think he had hit his head?"

"There was blood on the pavement."

"There's blood on your dress now. How did it get there?"

"I tried to sit him up, and held him against me while I was calling for help."

"Did people come?"

"Yes, two young men. I sent one for Dr. Ackroyd, and then the policeman telephoned . . . and the ambulance came."

"You're quite sure that's how it all happened?"

"Yes," said Julia, gaining confidence. "I think I am, but I was very dazed."

"You were dazed? Why were you dazed?"

"I was so frightened. It all happened so quickly. You are frightened when anybody falls down suddenly."

"Well, then, you say you were walking home together. Where had you been?"

Julia told him wearily, and described the route they had taken home.

"And then your husband suddenly cried out and fell down?"

"He knocked up against me first, and I tried to hold him up."

"There was nobody else there?"

"Oh no, nobody," said Julia quickly.

"You know somebody called Leonard Carr, don't you?" said the officer suddenly.

320

What had Bertha been telling them?

"Yes."

"Tell us about him, Mrs. Starling."

"There isn't much to tell, really. He's on an aircraft-carrier. When he comes home he stays with his people."

"He sees a good bit of you when he comes home, doesn't he?"

"Yes, at least, I don't know."

"Come now, Mrs. Starling, does he see a great deal of you or does he not?"

"Not always."

"Does he see you whenever he can?"

"Not always," said Julia, with sudden bitterness.

"Anyway, you see each other, shall we say, once a week?"

"Yes, I suppose so."

"Wouldn't it be oftener than that—two or three times a week?"

"I don't know . . . sometimes."

"Hadn't he and your husband had a quarrel?"

"They had once."

"Why?"

"My husband was jealous."

"Oh, your husband was jealous, was he? He didn't approve of your friendship with Leonard Carr?"

"It wasn't that so much. He was jealous of everything —always."

"He was jealous of Leonard Carr in particular, wasn't he?"

"Yes, I suppose he was."

"What was the quarrel about?"

"It was nothing really—it was very silly."

"Never mind it being silly, tell us what it was about, Mrs. Starling."

"We had been to the pictures—Mr. Carr and I, I mean—and when we got home I asked him up to have a whisky and soda with my husband."

"So you didn't keep your friendship secret from your husband?"

"Oh no," said Julia eagerly. "He knew about it, that's why he was jealous."

"I see. And what happened on this particular evening?"

"My husband began storming at us both—I forget what he said. Anyway, he got hold of me and threw me against the bookcase and hurt my arm, and Mr. Carr was very angry."

"Your sister-in-law came down the stairs, didn't she?"

"Yes, but I had got Mr. Carr to go then."

"When did all this happen, Mrs. Starling?"

"On his last leave—his Christmas leave. It would be four days before Christmas, the twenty-first."

So it went on, stupid questions and answers. Julia felt if she could have seen the men's faces she could have answered better. She had her distance glasses in her evening bag; she had been using them at the theatre. But how could she take them out and put them on? She wouldn't look pretty, and helpless, and young any longer. She would look cautious, clever. She mustn't look that whatever she did.

What was the man steated opposite to her saying now?

"I expect you would like to sign all that, Mrs. Starling?"

"Well—yes—if you like," said Julia nervously.

A man who had been busy writing read aloud everything Julia had said, but all in one piece, as though it had come out of a book. Then this statement was read over to her. Yes, it was just as she had said, but it ended: *It is voluntary, and it is true.* She signed it. Then a policeman took her to the matron's room, and told her she would have to spend the night at the police station. She stared aghast. For the first time the knowledge that she was no longer free pressed itself upon her.

The matron appeared—a cosy, pleasant-looking woman, with a quiet manner, who made her up a bed with blankets on a couch. It was horrible not to be able to undress—not to have sheets. Julia lay watching the dimmed light, unable to sleep, her pulses ticking all over her, as though she were a vast conglomeration of city clocks, all signalling the one to the other. Once or twice the matron came in and looked at her, and Julia closed her eyes and pretended to be asleep. Towards dawn she fell into an uneasy doze, but after she had slept for about half an hour, noises of cleaning and of doors opening and shutting waked her. The life of the police station had begun.

She was given tea and bread and butter. She washed her hands and tried to repair her face with the materials

322

in her bag. Couldn't she, she asked the matron, go home and change her clothes? The matron shook her head.

"No, you can't do that," she said, kindly enough, "but we will send and ask your sister to pack any clothes you want in a suitcase."

"She's not my sister," flared Julia, "she's my husband's sister."

"Well, anyway," said the matron pacifically, "you make out a list of what you want and I'll have to go through the things when they come, just to see there is nothing you shouldn't have, you know."

"I shall want some face creams, and things," said Julia, anxiously.

"Oh, well, I'll take a look at them and see the powder, too. I'm sure you'll want that. I'll do the best I can for you."

Julia made out a list of the things she wanted. She hated changing her evening clothes for those of every day without her bath, and asked the matron if she couldn't have a larger jug of hot water, which was at once brought to her. She washed as best she could, and when her suitcase came, and it had been examined, she changed to the little dark-blue suit of every day, and made up her face.

Then she was told she must come along to the C.I.D. office and she followed the matron. Her way led past a room where the door was open. Somebody was saying: "Well, Carr, you might just as well tell the truth . . ." and suddenly she stopped and stared into the room. There was Leo. . . . Leo, in his grey felt hat with the dented crown, his under-lip thrust out as she had so often seen it, his hands thrust deep into his overcoat-pockets. She gave a wild cry and burst into tears. She was not allowed to stop, but hurried along into the office.

Somebody was saying to her: "Would you like to make a new statement, Mrs. Starling?" She tried to control herself, to think what she could say for the best.

"Do you still persist in saying that nobody touched your husband last night before he fell down?"

"Leo did."

"Leo?"

"Leonard Carr. I can't remember, I didn't see it very clearly. I'm very short-sighted."

"You recognised Carr in that room when you passed just now, Mrs. Starling."

"I can always recognise people I know very well," explained Julia, truthfully. "If you don't wear your glasses always, your eye gets used to recognising people just from the rough shape they make. I can't explain it, but it's quite true."

"Did you know, Mrs. Starling, that your husband had had a severe blow at the back of his head, and his skull was fractured before he fell down?"

"I . . . no, I didn't, it was all so quick."

"You saw no weapon in Carr's hand?"

"No," said Julia, truthfully. She had imagined Leo had merely hit him with his fist.

"He was hit with something pretty heavy, you know, Mrs. Starling. We've found the weapon. It was thrown away inside the Square railings."

"I didn't know," said Julia.

"So you did know then, last night, that it was Leonard Carr who hit your husband? You saw well enough for that?"

"Yes, he seemed to be having a tussle with my husband, and then he ran away. He was wearing the hat and coat he's wearing now."

"Why didn't you tell us this last night?"

"I didn't think it had anything to do with my husband dying. I knew he must have hit his head when he fell down."

"Well, what you now say is that you approached Saint Clement's Square, where your husband's body was found, and Leonard Carr ran up?"

"Yes."

"And there was some sort of a scuffle, and then he ran away?"

"Yes."

Then Leo was brought into the room, and the nightmare deepened in horror. They were both charged with murder . . . she and Leo . . . with having murdered Herbert. A terribly impersonal voice was saying: "Do you wish to say anything in answer to the charge? You are not obliged to say anything unless you wish to do so, but whatever you say will be taken down in writing and may be given in evidence."

Why, those words sounded horribly familiar to her.

She had read them often in newspapers. What a nightmare to hear them being used to her!

Leo did not seem to mind so much. He held up his head and said:

"Yes, I do wish to make a statement," and he made one; and then she made one, a much shorter one this time. She said as little as she could—merely that Leo had rushed up, and that she had seen him scuffling with her husband, but that she had been knocked aside and was half dazed, that Leo ran away. He was wearing the same hat and coat that he was wearing now.

Then she and Leo were separated and she was put into a cell in the police court. Oh, it must be a nightmare. Things like this only happened in newspapers. This could not happen to her! It wasn't possible . . . it simply wasn't possible!

That strange incredulity still held Julia in its grasp. It couldn't, of course, be she, Julia Starling, who was going to appear in a police court, and who was going there in that strange thing which she had often got glimpses of in her childhood, called a "Black Maria." Once, when she had been a very little girl riding on the top of an omnibus —there were still horse omnibuses in those days—a "Black Maria" had been driven just in front of the omnibus. It couldn't be possible that she herself was now going in one of those things. They were motors now, of course, but the old sick horror of them was unchanged.

Julia did the best she could for her face, pulled her hair forwards in a curve over each cheek, adjusted her little hat, and wrapped the blue Italian officer's cape about her. She thought she would die of a sort of sick shame as she mounted the steps at the back of the prison van, and went into the little compartment, which was promptly locked upon her. Oh no, it was a nightmare, it must be.

She heard London all about her; the noise of the motor-buses, the sound of horns, the rarer clop, clop of hoofs, the trill of a bicycle bell, and here she was being jolted along, hidden in this shameful conveyance.

It came to a standstill. The motor went into reverse, and she felt the van being backed through a wide gateway, which she heard closing behind it. Her door was unlocked—it seemed to her already that for years she had heard nothing but the locking and unlocking of doors—it was odd how all her life she had never noticed the opening and shutting of a door until now, and, blinded by the bright cold sunlight, she felt her short-sighted way down the steps into the yard of the police court. It was very like a police station, was her first thought, the same brown and white walls.

The matron took her along a corridor and showed her into a little cell. She was shut in again. There was the sound of a key turning in the lock, and she was by herself. The cell was very tiny. It had one chair, and in the corner there was a water-closet with a seat of scrubbed wood.

Julia looked at it in horror. How could one use that when there was a large square opening cut in the door, through which a policeman might look at any moment? Nevertheless, she had to use it during the hour that followed; an agonising hour of waiting, during which her entrails seemed turned to water. The matron walked up and down outside, and no man looked in through the door.

Then again there came the turning of the key, and she was taken to another room where stood an elderly gentleman who had what Julia would have called a clever face. He shook hands with her.

"Mrs. Starling," he said, "I'm a solicitor. My name is Henry Withers. Apparently, your mother rang up Mrs. Danvers last night. I have known Mrs. Danvers nearly all her life, and she at once telephoned to me and asked me to come here. You must have a solicitor, you know. I wish I could have seen you last night at the police station, but that can't be helped. Now, I want you to say as little as possible. Just plead 'Not Guilty' and reserve your defence. You must leave everything to me."

"Oh, but I want to tell them . . ." began Julia.

"Don't tell them anything. Believe me, what I say is for the best, Mrs. Starling. I can't act for you unless you trust unreservedly to me. I assure you I'm a very good solicitor, and there's absolutely nothing for you to worry about. Do you understand?"

"Oh yes," said Julia, "thank you very much. How sweet of Mrs. Danvers."

"She has," said Mr. Withers, "a heart of gold, and she's

very fond of you. Now you've got to go into the court. Don't be frightened, there's absolutely nothing to alarm you."

She was taken along rather a dark passage and a door of ingrained yellow wood was thrown open, and she found herself suddenly in the white light of the police court. The roof was of glass, and through it the light seemed to beat down and make her blink. Straight in front of her was a little pen, surrounded by an iron railing. She was told to go into it, and stumbled up two steps, and going along to the far end, sank upon the polished wooden seat.

Leo was already there, looking spruce and confident, as usual. He stood very upright, his hands in his pockets, beside her. She could hear a whispering and a buzzing from behind her, and turned her head. A long seat ran behind the dock, and on it she could see Leo's mother, pale, with red-rimmed eyes, a black bonnet stuck on anyhow, and there was her own mother, and Aunt Mildred, looking grim, and Elsa, looking somehow excited and important, and there was Bertha—Bertha looking far grimmer than Aunt Mildred—looking dreadful.

Behind her was a wooden fencing of the same light ingrained wood as everything else in the court, and behind this fencing was a strange many-headed beast that surged and muttered and stared at her.

Julia turned her head back very quickly and stared in front of her. That was the magistrate, that ordinary pleasant-looking man, in a morning coat, sitting at a desk. He had above his head a carved wooden canopy with the Lion and the Unicorn striving eternally to get at each other on either side of a shield. Dark red curtains hung down straightly against the wall on either side of the canopy.

For the first time Julia felt caught and trapped, far more than she had at the police station, or even in the cell at the police court that morning. Here she was in the middle of this large, light, airy room, with its white-washed walls, its glass roof, its ingrained woodwork and maroon curtains, and she couldn't get out of it. Beyond the narrow little opening of the dock were policemen. In front of her was the magistrate, behind her were people who wished her ill. To the left of her, over the door

327

opposite that by which she had come in, was a great moon-faced clock, a clock that was ticking out relentlessly the minutes that were henceforth to be ordered for her.

2

Remand

LEO had gone, still with that high head, and pouting under-lip—that swagger for which she had loved him! She felt she didn't even know what it meant now, or what it had ever meant, for she was being taken to prison; not even back to the police station, but to prison. "On remand" they called it. She had not been found guilty—magistrates couldn't do that—but they told her she had been sent for trial.

She was given a good midday dinner at the police court, a dinner that was sent out for, but in the afternoon came again the hideous degradation of the prison van, but a long drive this time, right across London. She said to herself—now it must be passing close to George Street. They have just begun to get going at the shop. It was the day for Lady Evelyn's fitting, and she wanted more passionately than she had ever wanted anything in her life to be in the fitting-room at l'Etrangère's; to be pointing out where the frock needed altering, to be coaxing even the most difficult and unpleasant customer into acquiescence.

The van went on and on, and it seemed to Julia that even the sound of London changed and grew less pleasant. Then she heard what was to her the familiar sound of tramcars, the rhythmic scream, the grinding, the jolting, the clanging of the bell. The van took a sharp turn and stopped. Again came the opening of great gates, the van went in, and turned to the right so suddenly that Julia was thrown against the wall of her little compartment. Then the van stopped, and again she got out.

She was sick with exhaustion by now. She had been unable to eat her lunch, and she was helped down the steps, and stood blinking in front of a brown doorway. She was in a wide space that was half yard and half garden, and there seemed to be grey walls enclosing the buildings all about her. She went in through the brown door and into a little room on the right. How odd that there should be such cheerful-faced women there in dark blue uniforms; women who took down all her particulars as though it were all in the day's work—as, of course, it was.

She saw, with a shiver of repulsion, that on the bare, polished table lay the clothes of a woman who must have come in just before her. A pair of dirty, artificial-silk stockings, and a still dirtier suspender-belt, that had once been pink, but whose frilled edges were now dark grey.

She was told to go behind a screen and strip to her last garment, which was a little yellow chemise that Leo had given her. She was weighed and measured, given a wrapper and some washable heel-less slippers. Then she was led to a bath. It was all clean, spotlessly clean, but her flesh seemed to crawl. She could not get the thought of that dirty suspender-belt out of her mind. She washed herself with the soap in the bath, and dried with the coarse towel. Then her own clothes were given back to her—clothes that she had brought in a suitcase, and when she had dressed, one of the pleasant-faced women said briskly: "Now, come across to the infirmary. I expect you feel you could eat something by now."

Julia felt she could never eat again, but part of this horrible new life was that you had to do everything you were told. She had to walk across that yard, and in at the door of the hospital, which was unlocked for her entry, and locked again behind her. Otherwise, she thought, you wouldn't have known it was a prison. It looked just like any other hospital. The walls were painted green half-way up, with a darker green at the top of the dado, and white paint above. She was taken up white stone steps and into a ward with about a dozen other women in it. How frightful—and she had always wanted her room to herself.

Julia sank upon her bed hardly noticing its hardness. She felt her feet lifted up, then her head was propped forward; a glass of sal volatile was held to her lips. She drank it, almost choked, and felt a little better.

"That's all right," said someone cheerfully. "Now do you think you could manage to eat some tea?" And, oddly enough, Julia suddenly felt she could. She felt hungry, almost horribly hungry. She nodded, a little shakily, and sat up.

When the tea came in she attacked it ravenously, but soon found that, after all, she couldn't eat. The tea was Ceylon tea, and after a few mouthfuls she put down her cup. She felt curiously light-headed; perhaps that was the sal volatile—light-headed and yet very clear—she was noticing everything. There were the initials "G.R." on the plate and on the cup of tea that they brought her. "G.R.": what was that? Georgius Rex, of course. How did the King like having his initials on all the crockery of this dreadful place? There had been a joke in the war, she remembered, about all the old buffers in uniform, "gorgeous wrecks," somebody had called them. She pushed the plate away. It wasn't any good, and the tea was hateful, strong, Ceylon tea.

But worst was yet to come, she wasn't to be left alone. Not only were these other women—who most of them seemed half-witted—to be with her, but there were always attendants, always someone watching. One of the brighter patients told her it was the Observation Ward. She was going to be watched perpetually. She was asked if she would like a book, and she tried to read; but for the first time in her life could not make sense of the printed page, though she read one over five times.

The doctor, a big-boned Scot, with eyes that were oddly gentle considering how keen and searching they were, came and looked at her and talked to her; asked her a lot of questions. Tea-time came, with more of that horrible strong tea, and more bread and margarine. Supper-time came, and she was asked what she would like.

Would she like milk or bovril? She stared, she didn't know. What she would have liked would have been a stiff whisky and soda, but if she felt faint they only gave her sal volatile.

She was told it was time to go to bed. She was escorted to the lavatory. It had no lock on the inside. When she came out the female officer was waiting for her, and went back with her. She washed and got into her nightgown, and into bed. The sheets were unbleached calico, and rasped her skin. Lights weren't lowered till nine, and an officer asked her if she would like a book. They seemed to think, she thought, that she always wanted to be reading, and the funny thing was she always had wanted to be reading, and now she didn't want to any more. If only she could be alone!

At ten o'clock, an hour after the whole prison seemed to have gone to bed, she sat up and began to scream. The nurse pressed a bell, and presently the doctor was there again. She was given something to drink out of a little glass and told it would send her to sleep, but it didn't. She lay awake all night until the white light of dawn came in through the clouded window, and the gas was turned out.

The days went on, one very much like the other. She was allowed visitors every day between ten and eleven in the morning, and two and three in the afternoon; but except for her solicitor she did not really care about visitors. Who was there to come and see her? Mum, Uncle George, Aunt Mildred, Elsa . . . what comfort was there in these? Gipsy came every week, sometimes two and three times a week. Gipsy kept on telling her that she and Miss Lestrange were doing all they could, that they were getting a fund together for the defence. Gipsy would sit and talk to her easily, and try and cheer her up. Oddly enough Julia only wanted to know what was going on at the shop. Gipsy soon found this out and told her everything that was of interest. What had happened to Lady Evelyn's fitting; what had happened with the Richborough woman, the Manton woman, and the rest of the more or less faithful customers.

Marian came once, graceful, smart, delicately made-up, but she never came again. Ruby came once, but the Governor did not prove very amenable to the charms of Ruby. Anne came as often as she could, and so did

Dr. Ackroyd; but the message of Gipsy, Anne and Dr. Ackroyd was the same—Don't get depressed, Julia, it'll be all right. How did they know, Julia thought!

And yet, after the first five or six days, during which she lived as one half-conscious, she began to feel confident herself. Of course, everything would be all right. After all, although Leo had done this dreadful thing, although he had done the far worse thing of keeping her letters, she hadn't had the slightest idea that he was going to meet her and Herbert in the Square that night, or that he was going to attack Herbert. Of course, everything would be all right.

The solicitor came very often and went over every detail of the case with her. He suggested points of view that Julia had never known existed. He was kind, and believed she hadn't known that Leo was coming to the Square that night. Yet he seemed anxious. Above all he was anxious that Julia should not do what he called "go into the box"—that meant the witness-box.

"You can't go and tell your own story yourself," he said.

"But why shouldn't I?" asked Julia. "I can tell it better than anybody."

He looked at her for a moment or two in the little green-panelled room where he always saw her. They were always alone together, with an officer outside the glass doors, and they could talk freely.

"Mrs. Starling," he said, "you have never been subject to the ordeal of the box. You have no notion what it's like. You are, I believe, a very successful business woman. You have always managed to—how can I express it? —to put it over. You won't be able to in the box."

Julia could not believe him. She had always been able to make men believe what she said. Why should this be different, especially when she knew she was telling the truth?

"But I shall be telling the truth," she pointed out.

"About that night in Saint Clement's Square? I don't doubt it—but how will you be able to explain about the letters? As a matter of fact Sir Oswald Pelham is most anxious that you should not go into the box."

Julia shut her mouth stubbornly. "Of course, I'll go into the box."

"Sir Oswald may throw up his brief if you insist."

"Oh, all right," said Julia, wearily, "there'll be some-body else."

"My dear Mrs. Starling, it creates a very bad impression if one of the best-known counsel at the criminal bar throws up his brief. You can't swop horses while crossing the stream."

"I'm going into the box," said Julia stubbornly.

Her solicitor, who knew Sir Oswald was not going to throw up his brief, because he believed—at the least—in his client's technical innocence, made a little gesture of acquiescence. After that he confined himself to going over the various details of the case with Julia, trying to impress on her what she must say, and what she must not say.

The prison life went on regularly, just like a clock. The chaplain, Mr. Davidson, a thin man, burned up with the love of his fellow humans, in a state of perpetual distress because he could do so little for them, visited her every morning; but Julia had very little to say to him. He found, not very much to his surprise, that she was completely without the elements of religion; that a child in any well-run Sunday school would have known more than she did. Neither the Bible nor the Sacraments meant anything to her, because she knew absolutely nothing about them. The medical officer—a Scotsman, Dr. Ogilvie—visited her every day, and to him she talked free-ly, because in her eyes a doctor was more of a man than a parson could be—especially an unmarried parson such as Dr. Davidson.

The Lady Superintendent she liked because she had some of the qualities of Gipsy; a warmth, a genuine kindliness, which even the strict discipline she enforced could not hide. But after all, what good was a Lady Superintendent to Julia? The Governor was kind; but, felt Julia uneasily, he was somehow too clever; he understood her better than she wished to be understood. Just as she was beginning to tell him about herself, he would turn the conversation and say: "The Lady Superintendent is the best person to listen to all that." Yet he was not the sort of man you would have expected to know about women. He was, in appearance, the ideal soldier that she had day-dreamed about in the war. Very tall, upright, thin and brown, with a little close-cropped moustache.

Daily she exercised with the other women on remand, in a garden where there was a circular path of asphalt round a grass centre. There were some flowers growing in some beds and some glass-frame houses on one side, with little plants budding in them. There was a seat on which she could sit when she was tired.

The other women looked at her, and she could feel something of awe and admiration in their gaze, and she would hold her head up, and for a moment feel Julia Starling again, the real Julia Starling, not this creature caught in a nightmare.

At the far end of the exercise ground was a high wall, of the same dark, yellowish-grey brick as most of the prison, and beyond it she could see the roofs and chimneys of the houses where free people lived—only the other side of that wall. That very smoke that curled up out of the chimneys seemed to have a quality of freedom in its vagrant eddies.

She had begun to get books from the library by now. Anything to help pass the long days, and she tried, listlessly, to play draughts and patience; but the days dragged dreadfully. There were the visits from Mum, and even from Uncle George, Aunt Mildred and Elsa, strained little visits, when she felt that they were ashamed of her; and yet were aware of a certain importance which she had bestowed on them. There were visits from the Governor and the doctor and the Lady Superintendent, and visits from her solicitor, whom she saw alone in a little green-panelled room.

Sometimes it seemed to her that the day of the trial was approaching horribly quickly; sometimes it seemed to her that it would never come.

3

Trial

THE day came at last, and Julia, under the prim, but not
unkindly, eyes of the officer, made-up her face. Thank
God she was allowed her own things, she thought; if the
light at the Old Bailey was anything like the light at the
police court, she'd need all the help she could get. She
adjusted her little black hat carefully, swung the blue-
grey cape round her shoulders, picked up her bag, and
was ready. Down the stone stairs, people peering at her
from the closed doors of the wards. She was Julia Starling, everyone knew about her, she was a figure of importance. This time she had a real car—you wouldn't
have known it from a private one, and it added to her
feeling that soon she would be free again. It would be
terrible, this ordeal she had to go through, but soon she
would be free. She heard the screaming of the trams. She
thought: soon I'll be riding on a tram again, on the top
of the tram, sitting in front as though I were in the prow
of a ship; and as she thought of a ship, she thought of
Leo, who had brought her to this pass.

It was because of Leo she was riding to the Old Bailey.
It was right that Leo should be punished for what he had
done to her, as well as for what he had done to Herbert.

But then she thought, with a sudden ache, of his curly head that she had held to her bosom, and of his long, deep kisses. She didn't love him now. How could she love anyone who had done to her what he had done?

What she had called love, that high, romantic thing she had lived for, now seemed unreal; it no longer existed. More than that, it never had existed. For this hideousness in which she was now caught was reality. Beside this, nothing was real. These walls, these floors, these people, this dread . . . this whole nightmare was real as she had never known reality till now.

At night in that dreadful ward, with its perpetual vigilance, even when she slept, neither dreaming mind nor reminiscent pulses wanted Leo any longer, though in sleep one was defenceless, at the mercy of mind and body. In the daylight, with reality driving her into the corner of each moment, there was no place for Leo.

The car stopped and she got out, this time with her head held high. She was here to fight, and she was going to fight. She was no longer going to be the dazed human being who had lived through these terrible weeks since Herbert had died.

Julia was dimly aware of grey walls going up into the grey air round about her, and a door through which she was hustled. She was so determined on still being herself, still being Julia Starling, that she hardly noticed the things around her.

There was a long counter to her left, and a man in uniform sat behind it. She did wonder for a moment, as she was checked in, whether Leo was there already or not; she was too intent on holding on to herself to think of much else. She was taken through a door made of iron bars—again that dreadful locking and unlocking— and down a flight of stone steps, and she wondered vaguely why it seemed to her that she was in the Tube. Then she realised that it was exactly like the Tube. There was the same artificial air, full of artificial ozone, the same shining washable tiles on the walls, the same long echoing corridors. Brown shiny tiles below, white shiny tiles above. Dry, cold Tube air—what wouldn't she give for it to be all true? To be going up to one of the wholesale places in the city, her cloak blown about her by those strange blasts that met you at the corners of the passages.

"In here, please," said the constable, briskly, and she was taken into a little room, one of a row all exactly alike, on her right. It was very like the cell in the police station, but a bit larger, and it had one chair, a little table, but no water-closet; and the square cut in the door was filled in with glass.

She sat down, her heart beginning to beat thickly and heavily, in spite of herself. Everything had begun by now to seem very much the same to her—police court, prison, and now the Old Bailey; turnings of keys, brown and white walls, perpetual spy-holes, long corridors, jolting, uncomfortable drives, checkings in—all the rest of the paraphernalia of this strange life, which apparently had existed always for so many people, but of which she had never thought.

As she had been taken to her cell she had passed one or two with strange, anxious faces pressed against the glass in the doors; faces whose chief characteristic seemed to be a corrugated brow; faces that looked like something at the Zoo, and now here she was herself, like something in the Zoo, but at least she wouldn't go and press her face against the pane of glass. She even welcomed this time spent in the little cell, because at last she was alone. The officer, Miss Bendon, who by now seemed almost a friend, was waiting outside in the corridor.

For the first ten minutes Julia sat on the one little chair, her eyes closed, thankful to be alone. Miss Bendon wasn't even looking in. Once or twice Julia glanced up and saw the back of her neatly-trimmed head, the straight line of her averted cheek, tinged with a smooth russet. It was decent of her not to be staring in.

Then, after the first ten minutes, panic suddenly seized Julia. The four walls, already so close together, seemed to draw nearer, and press round about her. Even standing on the chair she couldn't look out of the little high window. She ran to the door and pressed her face to the pane of glass; and then feeling that she too must be looking like something from the Zoo, wrinkled and anxious, she drew back, and forced herself to sit on the chair again, and went on waiting, her throat dry and constricted. Once or twice Miss Bendon glanced in at her and looked away again. Then the door was unlocked, and there were two police officers besides Miss Bendon.

Julia was being told to go along, and there in front of her as she turned to go along the passage was Leo. She couldn't mistake the back of his dark, curly head, the set of his shoulders, even with her short sight; she knew them too well. He turned to go up a flight of stairs, and she saw he was holding his head up, and she remembered that she too must hold hers high.

She began to follow him up the stairs, that curved into a sort of pen. Coming into the pen was like coming up to the surface after being in a mine, for the bright white light seemed to fill it like a sudden tide of clear water after a dark night.

It was a big pen, this. Everything here, as it had been below, was brown and white, save for the green leather of the seats and backs of chairs; but it was a different brown and white, all suggestion of the Tube had vanished. Here everything was light-brown polished oak, pens, benches, boxes, and even the panelling of the walls —and white curves went up to meet the white glass roof. Light, light, light—cruel and cold. Light in which one drowned. Light that welled upon one like water, and in which the countless creatures' eyes stared, apparently magnified, like the eyes of fishes in an aquarium. Everywhere there were eyes; eyes looking down at her from a gallery high up on the right, looking at her from serried ranks of seats, boring into the small of her back from fows of seats behind; looking up at her from the solicitors' table below, looking at her from the angle of the jury-box, looking at her from everywhere. Before her, a blot of scarlet told her of the presence of the lord of life and death. By screwing up her eyes she could see the grey fuzz that his wig made above his reddish clean-shaven face.

Julia felt something arise within her to meet this battery. She held her head up. She didn't look at Leo, except with that first glance, which had given her a curious choking sensation. For that glance had revealed to her that they were strangers, such strangers that it was an indecency that they who had been together in a bed should be together in this pen. Together in their trouble, they yet seemed to look at each other across a vast desert of amazement. His eyes said to her the same thing that hers said to him. *How has it happened that we're here? It wasn't worth it. It was none of it real.*

That was true, thought Julia, it was none of it real. This couldn't be real. It was just something she must get through as best she might, and then the whole hideous nightmare would be over.

Vaguely, not only because of her short-sighted eyes, but because of the mist in her mind, Julia heard a little man gabbling something to the jury, and the jury, also gabbling something in turn, answered. The jury . . . it was with them that her fate lay. She screwed up her eyes and studied them. Two women and ten men . . . they looked the sort of people she was used to dealing with in her life behind the scenes at l'Etrangère. The foreman was just such a one as Mr. Coppinger; the women might have been a couple of Mrs. Santleys. The rest of the men looked like buyers or travellers. She noticed that her hands were trembling oddly, and Miss Bendon passed her a glass of water. She took a few sips with difficulty. There seemed to be an iron bar across her throat which prevented her swallowing. She held her hands firmly clasped together in her lap.

Her counsel was saying something about an objection and the judge said the jury would retire. The jury did retire, with a scraping and shuffling of feet.

More people were talking now, arguing about letters, her letters to Leo. There was her counsel, arguing, as far as she could follow, that the letters were not what he called admissible.

The judge seemed to be arguing that they could prove there was a conspiracy—Oh, thought Julia, desperately, I've got a good business brain, I know I have. Why can't I follow this?

But fear had invaded her, invaded all her brain and all her body, and she was almost numbed with it. Instead of being alert, following every argument, she sat like a woman in a dream. Anyway, what was all this about accessories before the fact and principals in the second degree? Her solicitor had tried to explain it to her at the prison, but she had not understood much of it then.

The man who was against her, the man who was for what they called the Crown, was arguing also about principals in the second degree, and about something called incitement. She hardly followed the remarks of the judge, except that he used the word "admissible" again. So she supposed that the letters, her precious, private letters, that Leo had kept in spite of their agreement, were going to be read in this dreadful place.

The jury shuffled back with the same scraping of feet, and again the man who was against her stood up to talk. Funny, thought Julia, staring at him, holding her hands tightly together in her lap, he didn't look like a man at all. He seemed something quite impersonal, and yet, under those robes, he must have all the funny clothes men wore, and in which they looked so undignified; braces and pants, and socks and a vest, and a shirt, all the funny clothes that seemed to a woman's eye to be cut up into all the wrong proportions.

She had thought that before at St. Michael and All Angels, when she had gone with Miss Tracey to what Miss Tracey called "High Mass." There was the priest at the altar, stiff in brocade and gold, and as his head bowed low, she had seen the ends of his trousers below his cassock and alb, and suddenly had a vision of him with those funny clothes men wore. Now the barristers and judge were the same. It was as though they had to dress themselves up to look anything at all. Why, if all the clothes in that court were suddenly whipped away by the hand of a fiery angel, and everyone found himself or herself naked, the trial would come to an end. People with hair on their chests, and all the funny little incidents of the human body displayed all over them, couldn't have conducted a trial; and yet that was what they all were—just tiny little people with hair in odd places, and toe-nails that needed cutting, and tiny, bewildered hurt souls inside of all of them. They only got on with their business at all, or with any business, by dressing it all up.

And this wasn't her life that the man who was against her was describing. It couldn't be. She and Herbert had never been happy together. Leo hadn't broken into a happy marriage in the way this man was saying. She had been profoundly unhappy all the time, and she and Leo had just known when they met each other that they could have been happy if only they had been together. How ordinary this man made her life sound, ordinary and yet dreadful. Why, he was even quoting the letter she had written to Leo after they had had tea together— that time when it had first occurred to her it would be marvellous and splendid to be one of the great lovers of the world. Another letter, the one in which she had said that she was having to give Herbert the "love" which she could only bear to give Leo. . . . Well, that had been true. That didn't prove you wanted to murder anyone. She had given it to Herbert, anyway, or at least Herbert had thought so—although in her own mind she had known that she was really enjoying Leo.

Letter after letter. Why, here was that silly chlorodyne letter now, as though chlorodyne would hurt anybody; and all the letters she had written Leo about their meetings and about when he was coming back. Why, he was even reading one that she had written after she had managed to get rid of the baby.

Julia came out of her dream, and leaned forward. How horrible. He was making it sound as though it referred to getting rid of Herbert. What was he reading now?— *My heart. I always think of you as my heart.* How horrible, to hear that sort of thing read aloud in that dreadful place. What was he saying now . . . something about a meeting between Mrs. Starling and Leo on the afternoon of the crime, a meeting at which they had planned the crime.

But she hadn't known she was going to see Leo that night. They had quarrelled about it. Oh, why hadn't she written to him that last day, instead of just talking to him on the telephone? Then everyone would know she had made no arrangement to meet him.

She sat back in her chair exhausted by the time the man who was against her sat down. She hardly listened to the first few witnesses. A policeman—the policeman whose cheeks were like a child's balloon—had made a plan of which he was evidently very proud. Everybody looked at the plan. It was handed up to the judge, it was handed to the jury. As though it mattered how wide the pavement was, and how wide the road was, and how big the Square was.

Why, this must be one of the young men who had come to help her. He was saying that she had said: "Oh, help! help! my husband's ill." She relaxed slightly. The other young man said much the same thing and added that she asked him to go for a doctor. Well, all that was true. Didn't it show that she hadn't known anything about it?

The bearded man, who hadn't a telephone. . . . There he was, saying how he had heard her crying out: "Stop! stop! stop!" That was true, too. Of course, they couldn't say that she had anything to do with it.

Then came Dr. Ackroyd. He did not look towards her, but he was very quiet, and she felt more confident, happier, when she heard his voice. Yes, he had found Herbert dead. The deceased was lying on his back in the gutter, and he did not wish to disturb him until the police came, because he had discovered at once that he was dead. The only wound he had been able to see was a contused wound on the inner angle of the left eye, and on the left cheek-bone. The bone had not been fractured in either wound. Deceased had . . . and here Dr. Ackroyd went off into technicalities about Herbert's heart which Julia did not understand.

Now Julia's man was on his feet.

"Yes," agreed Dr. Ackroyd, "Mrs. Starling was terribly upset, hysterical." His first object was to get her away. No, the notion of foul play had not occurred to him. It still did not, as regarded Mrs. Starling. He had known her ever since she was a child. Yes, she was romantic, indulged in day-dreams. No, he could not be mistaken, she was genuinely upset. She kept on begging him to let her take her husband home and nurse him. She didn't know that he was dead.

Here was somebody in a uniform who said he was the station officer. She didn't know him well enough to be able to recognise his face from here, but she recognised the voice. He was the man who said she must go to the police station.

And now the nightmare became deeper and darker, for here was Bertha. Bertha was hating her more than ever, she felt that: and although she could only answer the questions that were put to her, about what had happened when she had first heard the news of the flat, she gave the impression that Julia's agitation was all "put on."

Julia's counsel was talking to her now, only one question, asking her about Herbert's health. Bertha was admitting Herbert had told her he was suffering from a bad heart and indigestion often made him giddy. If he had been as bad as that, thought Julia, drearily, why hadn't she known? Of course, she had only thought it

343

was Herbert fussing about himself as usual. Why, he might have died, anyway, in a year or two.

Here was the police surgeon telling in horrible detail what he had found. There had been a contused wound on the back of the head in the occipital region, the skull had been fractured. That blow could have been inflicted with the spanner that had been picked up in Saint Clement's Square, and would have caused death. There had also been a second blow on the shoulder. The deceased's clothing had not been cut, but the markings of the blow were very evident on the body. The first wound was the fatal wound; the blow on the shoulder would not have been fatal.

Leo's counsel now stood up, and there was much talk about the wound on the temple. How could it possibly be said that the wound on the back of the head had proved fatal? Leo's man "suggested" or "put it" to the witness—what funny expressions they used, thought Julia—that striking the edge of the kerb with his temple had killed the deceased. The police surgeon said this could not possibly have been so, since there had been no fracture of the bone, save in the occipital region. That blow must have been fatal. Leo's man had to sit down again.

For the first time Julia looked, with only a vague curiosity, at Leo, who was sitting with his arms folded and his head held high. He didn't seem to mind. He seemed to be following everything with his bright, darting eyes.

Now he picked up a bit of paper from the ledge in front of him where blotting-paper, ink, and a lot of slips of paper were arranged. He looked at the ink dubiously, and the officer with the genial face who was sitting in the corner of the dock, leaned forward and handed him a pencil. Leo began to write busily, and then looked at the point of the pencil dubiously. He turned his head towards the officer and away from Julia. She could tell that he was smiling by the sudden outward curve of his cheek—that charming smile that she had seen so often. He was holding out the pencil to the man. The constable felt in his pocket and took out a pen-knife and sharpened the pencil and handed it back to Leo. He wrote busily, and the constable took the slip and leaned over the edge of the dock and, catching the eye of Leo's counsel, handed the slip down to him. After that Leo was always writing. What on earth was he writing for. . . ? Sometimes the policeman tried to attract the attention of counsel, but none of them was looking up. The constable would throw the slip, or a man in ordinary clothes seated behind counsel touched one on the arm and then counsel stood up and took the note, read it and passed it to the counsel next him. Julia didn't look much at Leo after that, but she wondered vaguely what he found to write about.

He stopped writing when his father came into the box and described how Leo had stayed at home the evening of the tragedy, and about eleven o'clock said he would go out for a breath of fresh air; his mother had gone to bed by then. No, witness could not say where his son went. Yes, Saint Clement's Square was quite near. Yes, his son often went there. And then Leo's counsel got up and made everything sound quite different. Mr. Carr said in answer to Leo's counsel that his son had seemed quite as usual that evening. No, he did not seem as though he had anything on his mind. The witness had certainly not received the impression that he was going out to keep an appointment. Mr. Carr left the box. Nothing had been said by counsel on either side about what Leo had had to drink. Julia's solicitor had explained this to her. He said it would not help either side, whatever he meant by that.

Then to her intense surprise Marian came into the box. I should have thought she would have been called *for* me, thought Julia, not against me. Marian hadn't much to say—just that once or twice she had seen Mrs. Starling with the prisoner Carr outside the shop. Fancy . . . you wouldn't have thought Marian noticed so much about people!

Here was Gipsy. Julia could tell from the direction of her face that she was looking towards her. She knew Gipsy well enough to know that she was smiling at her. Yes, Mrs. Starling had been telephoning during that last day at work. She had asked whether she could go out to tea.

Now Julia's man was on his feet talking to Gipsy. Gipsy in her warm, kind voice was saying how good Julia had always been at her work, how conscientious, how trustworthy. Julia relaxed again a little.

345

So much . . . so many people . . . all talking about the thing that she and Leo had tried to keep to themselves, being listened to by people who knew nothing about her and Leo; who wouldn't understand what they were like. All this long day it had gone on in this bright, light court. Julia's eyes were aching under her brimless hat.

At some time during the day there was an interval for lunch. She was told she could have anything she wanted, but she really didn't want anything much. The interval seemed to make no break in this nightmare of a day. She had left what dazed mind she still had in the court. All day long people had gone into the box. All day long first one man in black, her man or Leo's, or the man who was against them, had been getting up. All day long that other man in red, seated opposite her, had been making remarks. He talked often about adultery. How odd and strange it sounded—as though that was what she and Leo had had together! Even now, when she was bitterly resenting him, when she wished nothing had taken place—because nothing was worth this terror— still she never thought of it just as adultery. That was only a thing you read about in the Sunday paper. You didn't think about it in your daily life.

Tired, and with a pain that seemed to constrict her temples, and with swimming eyes from being so long without her glasses, Julia stumbled down the steps and was again put into that shameful van and jolted once more across London.

That was the rhythm of her days now . . . different from the blank, white rhythm of the prison days and nights. More tiring, more terrifying, and yet somehow, as she lay in her little bed, with her eyes closed, she thought if only she could concentrate more . . . if only she didn't feel as though she were in some curious sort of nightmare, these new days would be less awful than the days of waiting. The truth was bound to come out. She herself was going into the box to tell them just how it had all happened. Silly she had been, perhaps, but nothing worse. She must try and pull herself together before she went into the box.

The second day was like the first. Getting out of the car in the yard of the Old Bailey, passing the man at the counter, going down the stairs, waiting in the cell, talking to her solicitor, going up again into that awful dock, into that place of light and staring eyes, and strange voices, saying such strange things—things they evidently believed and that yet were not the truth at all, as Julia knew it.

Why, here was the woman who had kept the tea-shop where they had had tea on that last day, saying how she had seen her and Leo together. Well, she had never denied that they had had tea together. Of course they had. She had had to tell Leo she could not come out with him that evening . . . that she couldn't get out of her engagement with Herbert . . . that was when Leo had been so furious.

Here was another policeman, one she didn't know. He said he was a detective-inspector. He had been to Leo's home, and taken charge of a locked tin box. That was what all her letters had been found in, and her photographs. Oh, why, why had Leo kept them?

Here was another detective who had gone all over the flat at Saint Clement's Square. Why, he was holding up her silly little bottle of chlorodyne, and the spanner which, apparently, he had found thrown over the railings into the Square—half hidden by the bushes.

Oh dear, here was another inspector. Why, she remembered this one. He was the one who had first talked to her at the police station. He was reading her statement —they called it a voluntary statement. As though anything you did when you were in a state of nightmare was voluntary! It was the one in which she had said that there had been nobody there when Herbert staggered and fell down. Oh, why had she thought of nothing but shielding Leo? Why hadn't she told at once what he had done? Now the inspector was describing how he had taken her past the room where Leo was. How she had looked in and seen him; and how she had made another voluntary statement saying that Leo had quarrelled with Herbert and ran away. Now he was reading Leo's statement. She sat up and listened more intently. He had behaved as she had, of course. He had said that he had never been to Saint Clement's Square that evening.

The dreadful man in the box was repeating what he had said to Leo—"I am going to charge you and Mrs. Starling with the wilful murder of Herbert Starling." Leo had said: "Why drag *her* in? She knows absolutely nothing about it." Well, it was true that Leo had said that, and what was more, it was the truth.

Then he read Leo's second voluntary statement . . . how he had tried to fight Herbert, and Herbert wouldn't fight him . . . and how he had hit him, and thrown the spanner into the Square and ran away. Now he was talking about the tin box and the letters. Oh, those letters . . . those letters. Why had Leo kept them?

Now there was a man from the aircraft-carrier. Yes, he was Flight-Officer Smythe. He was the Stores Officer in H.M.S. *Thunderous*. She heard him identify something which was called Exhibit No. 1. He was saying he could identify it by the markings on it as an eight-inch spanner of the R.A.F. Yes, a leading aircraftsman would be issued such a spanner.

Julia was feeling relaxed again, even more in a dream than she had been the first day. What had it got to do with her that Leo had attacked Herbert with a spanner, and thrown it over the railings into the Square? She hadn't known he was going to do these things.

The next witness again caused her to sit up with that strained, eager attention which alternated with her fits of dreaming. Through both phases she was aware of Leo perpetually smiling, perpetually writing notes; very practical, living in the present . . . Leo as, she realised now, he had always been, and not the Leo of her imagination. He sat forward and examined the next witness eagerly, and this action brought his face slightly round towards Julia. He had no look for her. Those bright intent eyes were fixed on the witness in the box, somebody who said he was the senior official analyst of the Home Office. He had found blood on the right sleeve of Leo's coat. He had examined Herbert's internal organs. How odd . . . for years she had heard from Herbert's own mouth of his internal organs, of the trouble that they gave him, and now she was listening to somebody else talking about them; somebody who had received them in a jar. There had been no traces of poison in Herbert's liver and kidneys. Why, indeed, thought Julia, frantically, should there be? The only serious way in which she had thought of liver and kidneys in connection with Herbert was his passion for eating them for supper. He had always been fond of what, in the war, was called offal, which she had always disliked. It seemed too absurd that a human being had liver and kidneys just the same as you bought from Palmer's Stores. That they should be the cause of serious argument in a court of law!

Another man was in the box now, a pathologist. He described Herbert's wounds. He was asked whether he had found any trace of poisoning, and replied in the negative. Julia's own counsel cross-examined him at length on this point, and Julia again was able to relax.

When the man who was against her—for the matter of that against them both—stood up and remarked: "That is the case for the Crown"—Julia was still relaxed. After all, it hadn't been so dreadful, she thought.

Leo's counsel was telling him to go into the box; and head up, hands in pockets, with a slightly swaggering gait, he walked past her out of the dock and made his way towards the witness-box. Again she listened to so much that she knew. Yes, he had known Mrs. Starling since she was a girl at school. Yes, his family had always known her family. Yes, he had had a quarrel on December 21st with Herbert Starling because they had come in together after going to a cinema and Starling had knocked his wife about. Had he been in love with Mrs. Starling? Well . . . yes . . . certainly. Julia bent her head, and gazed at her hands still lying in her lap. In love? What in heaven's name did it mean? In a dream of the past she missed a good many questions and answers. There was, it seemed to her, a ghost of many conversations going on, as though this examination had power to raise the dead. Leo was telling his counsel about the times that Herbert had been asked for a divorce—a divorce . . . as though any of that mattered now. He was telling of the suicide pact, of their plans for going away together, of the time limit they had set themselves, of how he had told her to be patient. He wasn't she thought bitterly, recounting the times he had threatened to leave her if she would not make it possible for him to make love to her.

"These letters," said Leo's counsel, leaning forward and speaking impressively, "these strange letters that she wrote you, did they incite you in any way to raise your hand against Herbert Starling?"

"Not in any way," said Leo.

"Nothing that was written to you made you feel that

you must get hold of some poison that could be used in a deadly manner against Herbert Starling?"

"Nothing."

"These letters never made you consider doing anything you should not do against Mr. Starling . . . they did not affect you in any way?"

Leo almost laughed. "Oh no. I never took them seriously," he said.

The next day there he was again in the box detailing that last Easter leave. How he had come home . . . how he hadn't even seen Mrs. Starling . . . how he had gone away the Easter holiday with his father and mother. And then, not mentioning at all that night of love at the shop, he went on to describe how he had tea on the last day with Mrs. Starling, who had come out to meet him.

Yes, she had told him she was going to the special amateur show that her husband's firm put on every year, and she couldn't do a show with him. Had he been angry? No, not particularly, only disappointed, and only wondering what he could do to help her because he knew she was very unhappy. He had spent the evening at home with his father and mother. Had he had it in his mind then to go and intercept Mr. and Mrs. Starling on their way home? Nothing had been further from his mind. He had said to his father that he would go out for a breath of air. That was true, too . . . he had done so, and he had met Miss Elsa Beale and her fiancé on their way back from a theatre to Miss Beale's home. They had stopped and talked. They all lived quite close to each other, but still he had had no idea of intercepting Mr. and Mrs. Starling; but after he had left Miss Beale and her fiancé, he had thought he would make one last effort to try and make Mr. Starling be more decent towards his wife, and he had walked across the road and into Saint Clement's Square. Mrs. Starling had known nothing about it—in fact, he had just gone up to Mr. Starling and said to him that he couldn't go on as they were; that he must let his wife go; and Mr. Starling made a movement towards him. He thought he was going to hit him. He was so sure of it that instinctively he had taken the spanner out of his pocket and hit back. Then he found himself with the spanner in his hand, and he supposed he ran away. It had all seemed so hopeless, he hadn't known what to do. He was taken to the police station early next morning, where they had told him that Mr. Starling was dead. He simply couldn't believe it.

Yes, he made his first statement. He did it to oblige the superintendent, who told him Mrs. Starling had been in the police station all night, and he wanted to help her to get out because she had nothing to do with it.

Leo's counsel sat down and the man who was against them both got up and asked him many questions about that thing called "love," about which Julia had once thought she knew so much. The suicide pact came in again . . . the game of the letters . . . how he had never imagined anything except that she was trying to show him how much she cared for him.

So it went on, question and answer, all more or less true, and yet not in the least like what their life had been.

"Why did you change your statement?"

"Because," said Leo, "I was told that Mrs. Starling would be allowed to go home if I did."

Again Leo reiterated that Mrs. Starling had not known he was going to meet her in the Square that night, that she hadn't known he was going to make a last appeal to her husband. He maintained that they hadn't discussed any desperate remedies at tea in the tea-shop.

Well, that was perfectly true. Couldn't everybody see, thought Julia, with anguish, that it was perfectly true? Why, he had been very cross with her at tea that day.

His own counsel re-examined him, and Leo reiterated that he never believed in the fantastic suggestion of the letters. His counsel, as the man against them had done before, remarked: "That is our case."

Leo left the box. Oh, he had made a wonderful impression, Julia told herself bitterly. Even through her misery she could see that, but what sort of impression had it been? It had been that of the gallant young man who refused to incriminate a woman, and by so refusing he had made himself more of a hero, and herself, in some queer way, more responsible than if he had blamed her.

She could hear a stir and rustle at the back of the court as he came back to the dock, still with his head held high. She felt that there was not a woman in the court who was not sorry for Leo, and who was not blaming her.

Only two witnesses were called for Leo, although his father, who had, so Julia gathered through the mist that surrounded her, been called for the prosecution, had somehow seemed a witness for the defence.

Now Leo's mother came into the box, her voice filled with tears, and yet very calm and self-controlled. She had not lost dignity even at this pass. If Julia had been capable of feeling sorry for anyone but herself just then, she would have felt sorry for Leo's mother.

"There had never," said the old country woman, "been a better son," but unfortunately that was about all she had to say. She had gone to bed when he went out that night. He hadn't seemed in the least as though he were going to keep an appointment. She was sure she would have known if he had been, because it would have meant his coming in very late; and he was always thoughtful of her, always kind . . . her boy couldn't be unkind.

She was not cross-examined, and she left the box in a hush that seemed to hold the court-room, so that her old boots, not shuffling, but still unfaltering, made the only sound that broke the stillness.

She was followed by somebody called Flight-Commander Ridgeway. He was reading from Service documents, explaining that they could not be handed up even to the judge; that the R.A.F. regulations did not permit that; but he read aloud where Leo had served; how he had always been marked as V.G. for conduct—that, of course, meant Very Good, as it did at school. Leo's man asked him whether there was any record of Leo having been charged during the whole of his service with any offence as a consequence of shore leave, and the Flight-Commander said: "No, never. He was one of the most dependable men I had."

And now, with a knowledge that Leo had made a favourable but somehow wrong impression fraying her nerves, it was Julia's turn to go into the box. She took a last drink of water, settled the blue cloak about her shoulders, and fumbling a little at the steps went up into the witness-box. She, at last, would tell them the truth . . . everything would be all right now. How silly her solicitor and counsel had been, begging her not to go into

352

the box. She could tell the truth, if others couldn't—and, besides, she had always been able to make men believe her. Why shouldn't she be able to do so now?

It started all right, and her spirits rose. Everything was going to be perfectly splendid. Her counsel led her on to describe her life with Herbert . . . how it had never been really happy. How she had never attempted Herbert's life in the slightest way. Both these things were true. He read out to her passages from her letters . . . passages that she was able to explain truthfully. They had, indeed, referred to the suicide pact . . . to the trying to start a new life somewhere with Leo. Even some of the letters when she had been urging Leo—though she didn't mean it—to bring "something home" so that she could "try it." This she could explain away . . . it was perfectly simple.

It was true her counsel was helping her now, but again she thought: Oh, how foolish he had been to warn her not to go into the box. Even the judge, whom she hadn't liked up to now, hadn't interrupted her. She explained about the chlorodyne . . . she had bought it for herself because she had been ill, and she had never really given it to Herbert at all. She had only told Leo that she had. Well, that was perfectly true, too. If it came to that, she had never taken any of it herself. Her counsel read out more and more of her letters. Why, there was even that old one about the work-girls spitting out orange-pips! Her counsel went on to explain how everything she had written about poison had been because she wanted Leo to feel that she was willing to do anything for him, that that was absolutely all.

"Did you arrange with Carr to do nothing for three years?"

"Yes," said Julia. "We were going to wait until I had got a good job, or until my husband would divorce me."

The judge leaned slightly forward towards her now, and his voice was acid.

"The other witness," he remarked, "said that they had agreed to put off committing suicide for three years. It's the only sensible remark I've heard made yet," and he leaned back against his crimson velvet cushion.

Julia felt momentarily stunned at this incursion of something inimical into her pleasant story that was going so well; but she agreed with her counsel that she had suggested they should kill themselves, and that she had agreed to put it off for three years.

The tea-room, that awful tea-room—if she had only known what a lot of talk there was going to be about that tea-room, she would have spoken to Leo on the telephone that day—was now under discussion again. Yes, she had met Mr. Carr and told him that she could not go out with him that evening. It was an old engagement with her husband; this amateur dramatic performance was something they went to every year, and she could not possibly get out of going. No, she had had no idea that she was going to see Leo again that night. She knew he was spending the evening at home. She had not thought of him again until a man rushed up to them in Saint Clement's Square and she had seen who it was. Yes, she had seen Mr. Carr hit her husband, but she had no idea he had a weapon or that he had killed him. But she had called out to Mr. Carr to stop, and when her husband fell down to the pavement, and Mr. Carr ran away, she called and called for help. When the two young men came, she had sent one for Dr. Ackroyd. When the policeman came she had taken him home to telephone. She had still no idea that her husband was dead. Even when she knew he was dead, she had no idea it was because of a blow from Mr. Carr. She thought he had hit his head on the edge of the pavement, because there was a little blood there. She had made her statement because she did not want to get Mr. Carr into trouble, although it was true she had recognised him.

After she saw him at the police station she made her second statement, because the inspector had told her—what was the good of saying that he didn't do it, when he has told them that he did? Then she thought it was no good trying to shield Mr. Carr any longer, and so she had told the truth. Her counsel leaned forward towards her impressively:

"You had no idea, had you, Mrs. Starling, that Mr. Carr, or anyone else, was going to attack your husband on your way home that night?"

"Oh, none, none," said Julia truthfully, and with a great sigh of relief. She had told her story, and it was all of it true. Surely they must believe her now?

But here was the other man, the man who was against them, standing up, and, at once, she became confused.

354

He kept on asking her about her statement . . . about the first one being untrue—as though she had not already admitted that it was! He kept on and on until she could only say: "I don't remember. I can't remember. I didn't notice, I was too upset."

Now he was talking about the wretched letters again. Did she really maintain that such and such a sentence merely referred to a suicide pact? That three years merely referred to some fortunate future when they would have enough money to be able to go away together?

She said that her husband had threatened to make scenes at the shop where she worked.

Had he ever done so?

"No," said Julia, "but he had always threatened to."

"Quite . . . he threatened to, but he never actually did it, did he?"

"No," she had to reply.

Then was read out the passage referring to what she had had done in Camden Town. They had warned her that she must not tell the truth about this. An English jury might think an illegal operation quite as bad as adultery—and adultery, apparently, was quite as bad as murder! It was awkward, because the letter, as this man read it, sounded just as though it referred to poisoning Herbert, as some of the other letters actually referred to poisoning him. They were right at it now, right in the middle of the letters.

"I never meant any of it," she reiterated, "never. I was older than Mr. Carr—seven years older—and I was afraid of losing him. I thought . . ."—she stumbled and began again—"I thought if he realised I would do anything for him, he would never get tired of me."

"Now, come, Mrs. Starling, can you really put that forward as a truthful explanation?"

"Absolutely. It is the truth."

"But, Mrs. Starling, reflect—I do not wish to hurry you in any way—upon the letters that have been read out in court. You suggested to Carr that he should bring something . . . that you should give your husband something."

"Yes, I know I did, but I didn't mean it. I didn't mean any of it."

He went on with his terrible questions until she contradicted herself, until she hardly knew what she was saying, until, at last, he had cornered her into an admission that perhaps she had been willing to make her husband ill, just a little ill.

Why did I say that, thought Julia desperately. I never even tried that; but looking back carefully as she could upon the cross-examination, she could not see the point at which she had taken the wrong turning, at which it had become possible for the man to trap her into such an admission. She was still muddled and alarmed, the encouraging effect of the examination by her man entirely forgotten, when the court rose for the day.

The next morning, there he was at it again. All her letters, her precious, beautiful letters, building up the future, her future life with Leo—which she realised now she had always known at the back of her mind would never be an actuality—all these precious letters, the spun web of her fancy with which she had tried to enmesh him while he was miles away, continued to be read out in this blind, white place.

At last, after, it seemed, many hours, it was over, and her man was standing up again asking her if she had always done everything she could for Herbert, and she replied that she had. And then she was being told that she could leave the box. For a moment she stood, her hands gripping its ledge. Surely her part could not be all over? Surely there was more she could say, things that she could have put better? They didn't seem to understand. But she was being led out; she was fumbling for the steps again, and she was back in the dock.

She hardly realised that now the witnesses on her side were being called. It all seemed to her to make very little difference.

She heard Emily talking in the box, saying what a good wife she had been; how she had done everything possible for Mr. Starling, and how she, Emily, had said: "What d'you want with that horrid stuff?" and Mrs. Starling had said: "Oh, I got it when I was so ill, but I didn't need it, after all." There had been no suggestion of Mr. Starling taking it. Mrs. Starling had never mentioned such a thing, and she, Emily, had said: "I don't believe in such nasty things, anyway; you're better without them," and had put it in the back of the medicine-cupboard in the bathroom behind the Eno's Fruit Salts.

"Then," said Julia's counsel, "there's no truth at all in Mrs. Starling's letters to Mr. Carr that she had given some of the chlorodyne to Mr. Starling, and that it had made him sick?"

"None at all," said Emily stolidly. "She didn't give him none of it, and Mr. Starling was never sick. I'd have known about it if he was. He made such a fuss if his little finger ached."

There was a thin ripple of amusement in the court, and people eased themselves a little on their hard seats.

"It was, then, a sort of fairy story on Mrs. Starling's part? She just 'made it up,' as the children say?"

"She must have," said Emily. "She was a great one at being amusing, and telling stories. She didn't expect you to think they were true; she just did it to be amusing. She'd always come into the kitchen and cheer me up with something."

Good old Emily! thought Julia, with a faint glow of gratitude. She had somehow produced an element of humanity that had been missing since Gipsy had been in the box; and Emily's was the sort of humanity that these people would recognise more easily than they did Gipsy's.

Elsa came next, and Elsa did her best, although not, perhaps, without some slight pleasure in her own importance. Yes, she and her fiancé had met Mr. Carr as they were going home from the theatre that night. He had seemed quite undecided what to do. He had said: "You're lucky, you two; some people have all the luck. Others can't get fixed up anyhow." No, he hadn't said he was going to Saint Clement's Square. She had said to him: "Well, you had better go back to bed, you've got to join your ship to-morrow," and he said: "Yes, I think I will; that's good advice. I'll just walk round for a bit and try and get sleepy," and he said good night, and that was all she had seen of him.

Her fiancé followed her and gave the same account of the meeting.

Mrs. Almond came next. Her voice was so faint, she could hardly be heard. She didn't look towards Julia. She trembled very much, and was allowed to sit down. She had very little to say beyond the fact that she had let Miss Beale in that night, and had exchanged a few words with Mr. Carr, who was standing on the steps with

357

Miss Beale's fiancé. He had certainly not mentioned seeing her daughter that night. He seemed very hesitating and undecided what to do. Her daughter had always been a very good daughter to her. She had always worked hard and helped to support her mother, and since her marriage had taken her away on holidays.

"Nobody," said Mrs. Almond, gulping, "could have had a better daughter." It was the first time she had thought so in her life, but she was convinced of it now. She was not cross-examined any more than Leo's mother had been.

A very pink-faced man, whom Julia remembered having met at the amateur show, was the next witness. Yes, he had known Mr. and Mrs. Starling for several years. He had always looked on Mrs. Starling as a very devoted wife. She had seemed perfectly happy that night, not at all as though she had anything on her mind. He also was not cross-examined, and Julia's counsel remarked: "That is the case for Mrs. Starling," and gathered his robe about him and sat down.

This was Leo's man standing up, and Julia, exhausted as she was, forced herself to listen. Leo's man did not deny that Leo had killed Herbert—how, indeed, could he?—but pointed out that he hadn't questioned Julia, although he might have done so, as his instructions from Carr had been that nothing was to be done that would in any way tell against Mrs. Starling. His client himself had had to go through the torture of being cross-examined. Again the impression of Leo's nobility was disseminated throughout the court. He was being splendid, Julia supposed, but somehow this way of putting it seemed to help Leo and not help her, just as Leo's whole attitude had done; but Leo's man also insisted that what Leo and Julia had said was true—that there was no arrangement between them to meet that night. He went on and on about that, Julia noted thankfully. Then Julia was dropped out of the argument, and the counsel explained how Leo had thought he was going to be hit by Starling, and began to attack him. That, of course, thought Julia, is not true, but one couldn't blame Leo for having said it.

Leo's man spoke beautifully, but Julia was getting oddly sleepy towards the end. She was so tired that words seemed to mean very little to her any longer. Even when her own counsel got up and began to talk, she found it very difficult to brace herself to the necessary attention. She couldn't understand all the first part of the speech. Apparently, she was being tried, as her counsel put it, "on one of two indictments," but the prosecution had only "proceeded upon the first." What curious phraseology these people used! The second indictment had "five counts," whatever that might mean.

The judge was taking a hand again now. They were back at "accessory before the fact." That meant, she knew, whether she had known that Leo was going to Saint Clement's Square that night. Of course, she had not known it. She yawned a little, and found herself wishing she were back even in that dreadful cell, with the two women always looking at her.

Then a phrase in her counsel's speech caught her ear. Now he was saying the sort of thing she could understand. He was pointing out how absurd it was to imagine, supposing she had wanted Herbert to be murdered, that she would have arranged it to be when she was walking with him, and when she was going to be left alone with him dying on her hands. Well, thought Julia, surely they will believe that! Anybody could see that was sense. And now he was talking about her in much the most truthful way that anybody had talked about her yet. He was describing her as somebody who had always lived in dreams, and in her imagination, in theatres, in books and in her letters. That was true—but she alone knew *how* true! That is what she had been trying to explain to her lawyer all this time, and this man understood it. There, now he was saying:

"This isn't an ordinary woman. She is one of those amazing personalities only met with once in a generation. You cannot judge her as an ordinary woman."

That was what she had always felt about herself. If only these people could understand it! But they looked so dreadfully ordinary themselves as they gazed intently at her counsel. How could they understand? Those two women looked as though they had never had a lover in their lives. Those ten men looked as though they had never been lovers. She supposed they had gone to bed with people, but after all, as she knew from Herbert, that was not the same thing at all. Now he was saying that of course she would not have planned to have

359

Herbert murdered that night, when a short time before she had been writing about only having three years more to decide in.

That was obvious, too. And the suicide pact. He was pointing out that people who made suicide pacts did not kill somebody else; that had to do with killing themselves.

She began to get sleepy again, and kept on yawning. She drank some water; it was maddening to feel so sleepy, when she wanted to listen to every word. She closed her eyes to rest them for a few moments and actually did drift off into a little sleep. Her head fell forward, and she woke up with a jerk.

Her counsel was talking about poison. He was pointing out that no traces of poison were found in Herbert's body. There was no proof that she had ever had poison. Even the bottle of chlorodyne that she had bought for herself and remained unopened. All she had written every word of it—and there were many phrases which she should not have written, and which were wicked phrases—had been a great game of make-believe to keep Carr in love with her. That was a very different thing, even playing such a shocking game as this, from taking the first step towards making the game a reality.

That was well put, thought Julia, more awake now. Soon everybody would believe him, they must.

But the judge had looked at the clock. The fourth day had drawn to an end. Julia could have cried aloud. To stop it just when things were going so beautifully! And, worse than that, the judge was speaking. He was speaking to the jury:

"I feel I must offer you, members of the jury, some advice, though, of course, you will not make up your minds until you have heard the whole of the case; but the advice is this: You have heard so much during these four days about this exceptional woman, about this being a story, a fairy story, about this wonderful love, which is, indeed, a very commonplace and ordinary and sordid case of adultery, you may find yourselves in the danger of thinking you are listening to some romance, or watching some play in which you have no part, and from which, when it is over, you can go home and say: 'That was very interesting, but our lives are not like that, thank goodness.' What I want you to remember, members of the jury, is that you are not reading a novel, that you are not watching a play, but that you are in a court of justice to try, to the utmost of your ability, a sordid and commonplace crime. When you are thinking about it, think about it as just that, and nothing more."

Everything seemed terribly ordinary the next morning. Julia was more tired than ever. She had only had little snatches of sleep during the night, and she could not recapture the rhythm which her counsel's speech had held for her until the judge's remark. But when Sir Oswald first rose on this fifth day, he seemed unperturbed. His deep voice had the same conviction, the same ringing notes. Again he talked about her love for Leo. He read passages from her letters to prove it, and other passages saying that all she really wished was to go away with him—where, she cared not. A job in the South of France. Yes, she remembered that letter; she had written it, but she hadn't much hope that Leo would get her a job.

"Is it likely," said Sir Oswald, "that this woman would be writing asking Carr to get her a job in the South of France when all the time she had murder in her heart? Which is likely to be the real part of her letters, the stories about attempts of poisoning—of which there is absolutely no proof—or the real practical parts discussing divorce, discussing ways and means of living, either by another job in England or a job in the South of France, of the truth of which there is plenty of proof? You are men and women of the world . . . I think you will realise that a practical business woman like Mrs. Starling, whose capabilities have been attested to in this court, would naturally turn her thoughts to continuing elsewhere the same sort of work in which she had been so successful in England; and you see by her letters that this idea had occurred to her not once, but several times, that she is insistent about it. 'Get me a job, just enough to live on, so that I won't be a burden to you, and I'll come anywhere, my heart, wherever I can see most of you, either Scotland or the Mediterranean.' Is that what a murderer writes? No, that is what a practical woman, who is also in love, writes. A woman who wishes to go on working, a woman who doesn't wish to burden her lover, but who has no really serious thought in her head except that of making her life anew somewhere else where she can see her lover, and not be troubled by her husband. This is not a court of morals, and it is most important that you should remember this. I am not holding a brief for adultery, as my learned friend has sometimes seemed to think. Probably there is no human being in this court who has not done something which he or she regrets, or, anyway, something which is not in strict accordance with one or other in the Ten Commandments. This woman has broken the Seventh Commandment, but what she does deny is that she has broken the Sixth Commandment. Do you believe it possible that this woman, highly strung, imaginative, as you have seen for yourselves, could have sat placidly with her husband through that theatrical entertainment if she had known all the time that a murderer, who was there by arrangement with her, was awaiting them on their return home? There is no evidence to prove that she had any such idea. The crime took place in a well-lighted Square. She could have made some excuse to take her husband home by a darker way if she had wanted this thing to happen. She could have called in at her mother's house, and then led him down that little dark lane—Love Lane. But no, they go straight home from the station, from Stamford Brook Station, down the Goldhawk Road, with the lighted trains passing them. They cross the main road, and they go into Saint Clement's Square, straight on their way home. You have heard witnesses describe how Carr seemed vague and undecided that evening. He himself hadn't made up his mind what to do. How, in the light of this evidence, can you say that there was a plot between these two people? That she knew what was going to happen? That she led her husband to some pre-arranged spot? Her husband and she simply went home by the most direct route. I suggest to you that Carr's unhappiness suddenly came to a head, that his indecision suddenly came to an end, that he decided he must see Starling that night, must talk to him, must get him to consent to the divorce which, so far, he had always refused to his wife.

Oh, all that's marvellous, thought Julia, and it's actually true, all of it. A great feeling of rest came over her. She hardly heard her counsel describing the murder, her behaviour at the police court, except that he seemed to think it very noble of her to have tried to protect

362

Leo as, of course, it had been. Why, Leo himself, her counsel was just pointing it out, had maintained steadily that she had nothing to do with it. Of course, everything was going to be all right. What a fool she'd been to be so frightened, to have lived these weeks in torment!

Why, her counsel was finishing now. Wasn't there anything more that he could say? She supposed not, but she had had that same feeling when she had left the witness-box. He was sitting down now, and that terrible man, the man who was against her, was on his feet.

How odd it seemed—he was addressing hers and Leo's counsel, and being so polite to them. Perhaps they had persuaded him of the real truth? . . . but no . . . he seemed to be changing now . . . he seemed to be criticising them. He had only just said that at the beginning, to be polite. He was talking now about the case being commonplace and ordinary. He was saying that it must be a case of murder, that Leo had hit several blows when Herbert's back was turned "Well, of course, that was true! But it had nothing to do with her. And then the terrible leap of the heart that almost choked her . . . she heard him going on to say that undoubtedly she must have known about Leo coming there that night; and that even if she hadn't, she had been inciting him, and if, in consequence, Leo had killed Herbert, she was equally guilty.

How could she be equally guilty? She knew, none better, alas! that Leo had never really believed in her picture of herself as a great lover willing to dare everything. He had taunted her that day.

He was sounding so dreadfully fair, this man, that was the worst of it. He kept on saying things like that. "If you think there is no real connection between the letters and the murder, then, of course, there is no case against Mrs. Starling." Then he would go on to prove that, of course, the letters and the murder were connected. Could nobody stop him, this dreadful man, who went on and on? He was reading bits of her letters now. Why had she written them! Nobody stopped him, he went on and on. And when he had finished it seemed to Julia that although everything he had said—except, of course, the things about Leo—were not true, yet people would be bound to believe him. He had not been

363

quite right even about Leo, because he maintained that Leo believed her letters, and she knew that he hadn't.

Now the judge was going to speak. She was handed a glass of water, but her hands shook so that she could hardly hold it and swallow. She was not a bit sleepy now. Everything except the jury had been driven out of her consciousness. The judge was explaining things to the jury very carefully, putting both sides to them; but there again he kept on using the words "adultery" and "adulterer." He was sure that the jury were good citizens, and right-minded persons, and would pay no attention to such nonsense as had been read to them about love from the letters. Why, thought Julia frantically, should the parts about love be nonsense, and the parts that she knew were nonsense be true? The judge was talking now about common sense. There was no moment in all the past years that she could not have told truthfully what was common sense, and what was not. She had always known at the back of her mind what was day-dreaming and what was fact; but these people—hot could they tell? It hadn't been *their* day-dream.

The judge went on and on. He talked about their love, which he called adultery—had he never gone to bed with anyone but his wife? What about when *he* was a young man? He talked about the finding of the spanner; he talked about their last tea together; he talked about their letters; he talked about their statements; he talked about everything that she had heard talked of before; and always with, apparently, that terrible fairness, but using words that to Julia seemed to make the thing appear quite different from what, in truth, it had been.

He was talking about Leo's story now, that idiotic story. She could see herself that that was idiotic—the story that he had thought Herbert was going to attack him. What was the good of saying things like that, when the blows were on the back of Herbert's head? Ah, now he was mentioning the bearded man, the man who had heard her cry: "Oh, stop! stop! stop!" Why, he was making nothing of it . . . she had been frantic with fear. She had called for help. She had begged for a doctor, and before any of that, she had screamed and implored Leo to stop it, and the bearded man had said so . . . and repeated it with great conviction in that box . . . and here was the judge just dismissing it in a sentence.

364

The judge cleared his throat and stopped. Was that the end of it? No, they were only adjourning for a short time, and Julia was taken downstairs once again to wait. She was given something to eat and drink, but she wasn't really aware of any interval. It seemed to her when she was back in the dock as if the judge had been going on steadily, though now he was talking about her more than about Leo. Again she heard it all . . . that word "accessory"; again she heard about her tea with Leo; that she had known Leo was going to be there; that she wasn't surprised to see him; that she knew he was going to commit murder; and so she was guilty of the murder, too.

But she hadn't known . . . she hadn't known a thing about it. She had been miserably unhappy . . . she thought she had lost Leo for good. She had been thinking of nothing else the whole evening. Only now she knew that losing Leo didn't matter a bit; it wasn't *real*.

The afternoon drew on and she sat there listening to extracts out of her letters, those about killing Herbert, which she knew were not true, and those about love which the judge dismissed as silly and vulgar. Now he was talking about her concealing the truth. Of course, she had concealed the truth . . . her counsel had thought it very noble of her to do it.

Why, it couldn't be over as quickly as this? He couldn't be going to say nothing more in her favour? He was telling the jury to retire and consider their verdict. He was rising, and walking with his dignified gait towards the door through which he always disappeared.

Everybody was on their feet in the court-room, with that scraping sound to which she was now so accustomed.

One hour . . . two hours . . . three hours . . . and she was called back; three hours during which she had swung from a certainty that all would be well to a knowledge of utter despair.

"I think it's all right," she said to Miss Bendon. "It must be all right, they've been so long. If they had thought I was guilty, they would have thought it at once, wouldn't they?"

She saw a queer look of pity on Miss Bendon's face, but she refused to acknowledge it even to herself. She went up for the last time into the dock. The foreman, who was so like Mr. Coppinger, was very pale. None of the jury looked in her direction. The man whom she had been told was the clerk of the court was on his feet.

"Members of the jury, have you agreed upon your verdict?"

The man like Mr. Coppinger answered in a low voice: "We have."

"Do you find the prisoner Leonard Carr guilty or not guilty of the murder of Herbert Starling?"

"Guilty."

"Do you find the prisoner Julia Starling guilty or not guilty of the murder of Herbert Starling?"

"Guilty," said the man in a stronger voice.

The clerk of the court went on almost conversationally:

"You say they are severally guilty, and that is the verdict of you all?"

The man nodded.

"Leonard Carr and Julia Starling, you severally stand convicted of murder. Have you, or either of you, anything to say why the court should not give you judgment of death according to the law?"

Leonard threw up his head. It was his last swaggering moment, and he took it.

"The verdict's wrong," he said clearly. "Mrs. Starling's not guilty. I acted in self-defence . . . Mrs. Starling knew nothing about it."

Julia was silent save for a whimpering like that of a shot animal. She could not speak. She vaguely heard the judge say to her counsel: "Is there any question of law as to the sentence I have to pronounce?" and the woman sitting beside her leaned forward and whispered to her. It was something about—if she was going to have a baby, could she say so now, and everything would be all right. Julia gave a sharp cry; this was the last irony. If she had not got rid of Herbert's child, she would have been safe now. . . . She heard her counsel saying: "No, my lord." He must have known beforehand then . . . he must have asked them at the prison!

A clergyman had placed a queer-looking square of black cloth upon the judge's head. The judge spoke in the same calm, unemotional tone he had used throughout.

"You shall be taken to the place from whence you came, and thence to a place of lawful execution, and

366

there you shall be hanged by the neck until you be dead, and afterwards your body shall be buried in a common grave within the precincts of the prison wherein you were last confined before your execution; and may the Lord have mercy on your soul."

"Amen," said the chaplain.

Julia heard her own voice screaming: *"But I didn't know. I didn't know!"* and then the people closed about her and she was taken away.

4

Last Weeks

It was over. Her screams had died. She was being helped along the Tube passage, she was again in a cell. This was a different sort of cell. It had a big table and a bench that ran round the walls. Miss Bendon and another woman were with her. She was being given brandy and water. There seemed a stir in the passage beyond the door. She heard a strange noise, like an animal in pain, that echoed down the Tube passage, and realised that she had finished gulping the brandy. It was she herself who was making that noise. When she realised that the noise stopped.

A sudden cold reality seized hold of her like a grip of frost. She realised with a dreadful exactitude what had happened. She was somehow different. Even this different cell was a sign of what she was henceforth to be put in—places that might look the same, but that bore a different significance—the places where the guilty found themselves. She was guilty: they had found her guilty. Of course, it was all a mistake, a hideous mistake. Somebody would come along and put it right, because mistakes like that simply didn't happen; but, nevertheless, for a time she must put up with it.

She was asked if she felt better. She nodded, and then there came upon her again the brown and white Tube corridors, the odd artificial air, the stone stairs, the iron-barred door; the outer door, but not the door to freedom. Overhead in the yard the sky held the lilac colour of spring; within the yard a taxi, an ordinary taxi, such as she had always been conveyed in back to prison, was waiting. She was half pushed, half lifted in. The officers got in with her and the taxi set off, the noises of London all about it, taking her back to prison and its sour smell. That sour smell of prison. She'd never get it out of her nostrils, even when she was free again. It was like the smell of a very old person. The old person might be spotlessly clean—but still that sour smell clung to them both. It seemed to have become part of the membrane of her nostrils.

The taxi jolted on. Next time, so her solicitor had told her, she might come out to her appeal. All hope wasn't lost yet, so he had told her. Hope—what did he mean by hope? Of course, nothing could be going to happen to her. Life couldn't be like that. This nightmare couldn't be true. She felt very weak, and fell about against the walls of her little compartment. Vaguely she heard the sound of the trams, and knew they were back at the prison. She heard the unlocking of the great gates and the taxi started again, then stopped.

Ridiculous, but she seemed to have no legs. She had to be lifted out.

This was the same prison, but it was a different part of the prison. She was guilty now. It was the infirmary, but the infirmary of the convicted instead of that of the technically innocent. Well, it was very much the same to her. It had to be unlocked and locked behind her, and as Miss Bendon took her by the arm to help her along the corridor, she heard a sound of laughter; and so strange did it seem in that place that it penetrated even to her numbed consciousness. A baby about two years old, looking like a little clown in a pink knitted wool suit, was stumbling down the corridor toward her, his face thrown back, his mouth open with laughter, his hands outflung. A prison officer and his mother were pursuing him smilingly. He was going too fast to stop, and ran against Julia's knees. She stood, frozen, while the officer picked him up and dropped him into his mother's arms. Two other mothers came along, their babies in their arms, looking as pleased and proud as any ordinary mothers might have done. They had been taking the babies for an airing.

Miss Bendon's grip tightened on her arm: somebody came on the other side of her. She was helped up a flight of stairs, and taken into a bare little cell painted green and white. Thank God they weren't putting her into a ward full of dreadful women. There was a narrow little iron bedstead, three hard wooden chairs, a table, and, high up in the wall, a tiny window of thick-ribbed glass criss-crossed into panes.

She was put to bed. As in a dream she felt them taking the clothes off her. It wasn't her own nightgown they put on, but a strange night-gown, a prison night-gown that the other women wore. She was guilty.

She lay back on her hard pillow and looked around at the white little room. All she could see was the grey line of a near-by roof, wet and gleaming like a piegon's breast from a passing shower. Two women came in, in dark blue uniforms, two women she hadn't seen before.

Miss Bendon whispered something to them, and left. One of the women said, "Wouldn't she like a nice cup of tea?" Julia shook her head. She couldn't bear their tea. There came the usual question, Would she like some milk or some bovril? She shook her head. But the milk appeared, and she drank it for the sake of peace.

Life went on again with her much the same as it had before, except that now she was more frightened. Also the days had assumed a very regular measure. Dr. Ogilvie came every morning and asked what she would like to eat and drink. She remembered that sometimes, when she had been ill, she had been ordered red wine, but she felt that wouldn't be much good to her now; so she just asked for whiskies and sodas with her meals, and for some help to make her sleep at nights. For sleep was becoming more and more difficult.

Dr. Ogilvie would look at her and ask her the usual questions that doctors always asked, but the terrible part of these questions was that it seemed they were being asked about a dead body instead of about a living one. He would look at the report: "A little constipated . . .

we'll see to that. You shall have something to put that right. It's a fine day—sit out until your dinner-time."

Her solicitor came, of course, and she signed something called "The Appeal Papers," and after she had signed them her spirits rose again: but not as they had risen before the trial. The appeal stood between her and the terror of which she dared not think.

Now there were always two women with her, night and day. She had six officers in all. She grew to know them all by name, to know their different personalities. Only one was a married woman, Mrs. Cartwright, and she, oddly enough, looked the least married of the lot—a thin, dry, pinched woman, whose flesh seemed to have withered. Then with her was Miss Pither, gruff, kindly, chubby-cheeked, inarticulate, whose main idea of life seemed to be to suggest a game of draughts. She said it passed the time so nicely, as though the time were not passing much too fast. She had glossy brown hair, the colour of a horse-chestnut, and her eyes were shy, and somehow ashamed behind her gold-rimmed glasses. Julia felt she would have liked to help her, but didn't know how. She and Mrs. Cartwright were with her from five until ten o'clock at night. Then came Miss Paramore and Miss Quint. Miss Paramore had been a school-mistress, and still carried the tones of brisk authority in her voice. She tried to take Julia out of herself, to talk to her about books. Miss Quint was small and grey. She seemed almost mouse-like, and yet she had immense authority of a quiet sort—much more than Miss Paramore. Julia always felt she had to take her bovril, or her milk, or her whisky and soda, or her medicine when Miss Quint presented it, almost shyly. Miss Quint was the only one who Julia felt really knew what she was feeling; the fright that was gnawing at her heart the whole time.

At six-thirty in the morning Miss Paramore and Miss Quint were replaced by Miss Harper and Miss Purvis. Miss Harper was fat to overflowing. She had to have her uniforms specially made for her. She looked as though she had been the mother of at least ten children. Her consolations were frequent, but they sounded like balls rolled along a groove. She was much more comfortable than Miss Quint, but nothing like as real, somehow. Julia felt that Miss Harper would go away and be jolly,

371

but that Miss Quint would always be thinking of her and wishing she could help her. Nothing within Miss Harper was hurt, as something within Miss Quint was hurt. Miss Purvis was brisk and very bright. She was intensely religious, with a cut-and-dried religion, in whose efficacy she entirely believed. She had burning eyes and a pale face, and she seemed consumed with an intense inner happiness that tried to enwrap even Julia. But Julia felt this was a fire which gave light without warmth, and she shivered in its white rays.

Always a pair of these women were with her, always the light burned in the cell, though she was allowed to tie a dark handkerchief over her eyes when she slept; for light had always waked Julia even more easily than noise. Always there was the offer of books, of milk, of bovril, of a walk—she now walked in a different garden from the first one, and alone, save for the officers; a garden from which she could see still more clearly the roofs of free and ordinary houses. She felt it would be something if she could just go back and walk as she had done before, with the other remand women, in the garden with the circular path and glass-houses; but now, in an irregularly shaped garden with a railing she wandered aimlessly about and about, on a fine day.

There were beautiful pigeons that flew about and came down to strut over the earth beside her. They were free, fat and tame. They preened themselves and looked sharply this way and that, so that the light reflected from their beautiful iridescent necks. Julia would watch them walking about, pecking at the grass, eating the bread that she was encouraged to save up for them. She soon gave up this occupation because of the anguish that was hers when the pigeons, with a whirring of wings, rose into the air and were gone. The pigeons might go, but there was something that could not; and that was the view always before her eyes when she exercised—the roofs of houses quite close to her just beyond the prison wall. The roofs of real houses . . . the devilish cruelty of that glimpse of roofs. It oughtn't to be possible to see smoke coming up from the chimneys of homes. There were people in those houses, people who ate and slept and took baths and clothed themselves after their fancy, who went in and out as they chose, who were so used to seeing the prison as they looked out of their back windows that they thought nothing of it. They might have an increased interest now, as they looked at those grim walls and thought: Julia Starling is in there. She hasn't got much longer.

There were people there whose children went to school, whose husbands came home from work; people who made their laundry-lists, who did their shopping, who went to the pictures. Oh, Christ! if only she could be one of them, she wouldn't want a lover, she wouldn't want anything but to go in and out of an ordinary house and do ordinary things.

Every day, when she waked, the roofs of those houses, and the thin spirals from their hearths, hurt her as nothing else hurt her. From the first moment in the morning when she was wakened at half-past six till the last moment at night when she tied the dark handkerchief over her eyes and tried to sleep, after the salty dose of bromide that helped her so little. The night would go in a succession of dozes and nightmares; of patches of bare, bald watchfulness. There would be the change of officers, the pint of tea, the porridge and bread and margarine. Did she want anything extra? Would she like jam, would she like marmalade, or an egg? Anything she wanted, that was the cry. She was allowed whisky and soda with her meals, as many cigarettes as she liked, and a sleeping-draught at night. She could have anything she wanted to nourish and soothe the body they were going to destroy. It was too absurd. Prayers in the chapel . . . nobody had to go to unless they wanted to, and Julia didn't want to.

Then each morning the Lady Superintendent, dignified, quiet, her brown hair heavily streaked with grey, her eyes kind and sorry, would come and talk to Julia. An ordinary conversation . . . how had she slept? . . . how was she feeling? Good, good. And always Julia knew—for prison routine becomes known by some strange added sense to the people within prison walls—that the Lady Superintendent had come from seeing those women discharged who had served their sentences. Always there lurked in Julia's mind the memory of that soiled pink suspender-belt. That would have been cleaned and ironed, as all the clothes would have been cleaned and ironed of the women to whom they belonged, and one morning she would be seen off at the great gates by the Lady Superintendent.

Every day women went through these great gates, clean from top to toe, made new, except for that strange inner thing called the soul, which went out exactly as it had come in. But the women went out—that was all that mattered. They went out . . . they could walk in their clean artificial silk stockings down the road; they could board a tram, pay a fare out of the purse that had been restored to them; go to their homes or back to the gangs of which they had been members.

It was nothing that these women could go out free to love—love mattered nothing to Julia. What mattered was that they went out free to eat when and what they chose, to sleep where they chose. Free to go to the lavatory without having to ask the officer. They went out into a world that was free; a world of trams and eating-houses and small homes, and business legal and illegal, and casual contacts and chance encounters, and relationships renewed. The thought of this free world beat like a great bird about Julia's mind each morning as she met the eyes of the Lady Superintendent, and the thought of those unknown women who had gone free some quarter of an hour before, were more real than the Lady Superintendent's presence.

Then the walk if it were fine, the attempt at needlework or a game, or sewing if it were not. Perhaps a visit from her solicitor, then dinner, the perpetual meat and two vegetables—perhaps she would like a little custard? —and after, would she like to sleep a little, or would she like to change her book, or would she like to sew, or would she like a game of draughts? Then tea, the dreadful tea, the light lit: and would she like to sew, or would she like to play draughts, or would she like another book, or had she a letter to write? And supper: would she like milk and bread and butter, or bovril, and would she like to change her book? Sometimes she did change her book, and instead of tying the dark handkerchief over her eyes she would sit up and try to read through the endless light white night, that was like the northern nights she had read of in novels. Nights where the sun never set; could anything be more dreadful? Then they would bring her salty bromide, and again would come the thin, drifting sleeps, the waking to the same round again, again.

The rhythm of the white days and white nights beat itself out, slow, slow, slow, yet quickening almost unnoticed to a dread velocity; day, night, day, night, a week —Sunday, chapel? No, she'd rather not. She had been there once when she was on remand, but she felt differently now.

Indeed, she felt differently about everything. Ill with sleeplessness, in spite of the kindly drugs, ill with fear, ill with bewilderment, she was, to look at—as she could see for herself—quite a different person from the confident Julia who had gone to her trial. When her solicitor told her it would be better if she did not attend her appeal, that there was nothing to be gained by it, she agreed almost listlessly. For the attack of her personal presence, on which she had counted all her life, had failed her. It had failed her utterly in the box. It had proved a thing as brittle as spun glass. She had no confidence now with which to meet men. Living in her endless white light of days and nights, it seemed simpler to her to stay where she was and let the appeal be heard without her.

About five days after that there came the worst day of all. The appeal had failed. The Governor came in to see her. At first she could not understand what he was telling her. He told her very simply, very clearly, and as kindly as he could.

Julia stared and stared at him, and then she began to scream. She screamed and cried, she threw herself on the bed. She listened to nothing that the wardresses tried to tell her; she could not listen to the Lady Superintendent; she could not listen to anyone, and the Governor had gone. Now and then she fell almost unconscious upon her bed, but when nature had restored itself slightly by this relaxation she began to cry out again; to beat against the wall; to claw at it with her fingers, so that her nails became filled with plaster and broke. Then the doctor came, and a nurse. The nurse rubbed something on her arm, while the doctor spoke to her soothingly. Then she felt the prick of a needle. Still she went on crying hopelessly; but her limbs began to feel more and more heavy, her head began to nod. One of the women came in and slipped the dark handkerchief over her eyes, and presently she was asleep.

The next day the chaplain came and talked to her of the love of God, but that meant nothing to Julia. The love of God, said his tongue, but Oh, God! have pity on helpless human beings, said his eyes, as they looked at her.

One day her mother came to see her. She had not wanted to see anybody else, not even Gipsy. She had not really wanted to see her mother. They were left alone together. Mrs. Almond stared at her daughter hopelessly.

"Oh, Julia, Julia," was all she could say.

"Don't, Mum," said Julia.

"If your Dad could only see you now," said Mrs. Almond helplessly.

"He would have been no good," said Julia. "He never was any good. Nobody's any good."

"Oh, Julia," said Mrs. Almond again.

Then they talked a little about quite stupid things, about how the Beales were behaving, about the messages they had sent, about what the sycamores were looking like in Love Lane. Neither of them mentioned Saint Clement's Square.

"It may still be all right, Julia," said Mrs. Almond.

"Oh . . . oh . . . yes . . . yes . . ." said Julia. "Sorry . . . I wasn't thinking, Mum."

Mrs. Almond thought: She's not taking it to heart. She never had much heart. I suppose it's a good thing. She did not recognise the signs of complete mental exhaustion when she saw them.

Then the officers were in the room again, and it was time for Mrs. Almond to go. And at that last moment all the maternal feeling which she had never, as far as she knew, even felt, much less shown, welled up in Mrs. Almond. This was her child, her only child. She caught Julia in her arms and cried helplessly. Julia stood, without moving, except that she put her arms around her mother and leaned her head against her dress.

"It's all right, Mum," she said dully, and then she, too, began to cry, and Mrs. Almond was taken away.

The whole rhythm of life throughout the prison seemed to alter since her conviction. Hours and rules

376

were the same, but the human mind is only too terribly free of time. The consciousness of a fellow-human condemned to death oppressed all the bright, brisk officers, the nurses, the prisoners whose minds were sufficiently developed to allow of imagination. Every prisoner, except the borderline cases and those actually mentally deficient, was oppressed with a sense of cruelty and sadness. Somebody was going to be killed. It might have been any one of them. There was a great machine, bigger and stronger than any of them that could catch any one of them and do this thing. Every prisoner bore a tiny portion of Julia's burden in her consciousness, and still there was the dreadful excitement, almost an exhilaration in the place at the same time as the depression.

It was odd, that mixture, thought the Lady Superintendent as she sat in her own bright sitting-room, surrounded by the snapshots of her nephews, complete with buckets and spades, taken at Littlehampton last summer. Was time going faster than usual, or more slowly? Was there an intenser sense of life, or a deepened sense of death? She couldn't worry it out, even to herself. She only knew that something was terribly wrong somewhere, so that she rather hated the world, the law that she had served all her life, the great and good work to which she had devoted herself.

Of course, it was a dreadful thing to kill your husband—if this creature had killed her husband—but on the other hand, husbands themselves could be pretty dreadful propositions, if everything the prisoners had told her was true. She only wondered that they hadn't all killed their husbands, for very few of them seemed to have good ones. If everyone were to be hanged who wished her husband dead, they'd have to pull down the prison and turn the whole eleven acres into a graveyard, reflected the Lady Superintendent, with a wry smile.

Some of the men were good, of course. Sad, ashamed young men, who came at visiting-hours and sat the other side of glass and wire-netting and said that little Bert was going on fine, and that the teacher was pleased with Alf, and that May, or Alice, or whatever her name might be, wasn't to worry, because all was going on fine at home, except that they missed her.

There was old Mrs. Humble. She's got a good husband, though he must have known what she'd been up to. What was wrong, and what was right? In what did sin consist? Mrs. Humble, cosy, pleasant-faced old lady, certainly didn't look on herself as a criminal. Last time the Lady Superintendent had seen her, she had shown her with pride long letters she had written to "me husban'," to Mrs. Clarkson, "That's me married daughter"; to Joe Humble: "That's me son," and the Lady Superintendent had enquired solicitously as to whether the spectacles that her husband had sent her suited her, and on hearing that they didn't—which was not remarkable, considering that Mrs. Humble's eyes were entirely different from her husband's—had promised her a visit from the oculist, and a new pair of spectacles. Mrs. Humble had been ever so pleased. Her motherly face had beamed all over, and she had produced a photograph of her latest grandchild for the Lady Superintendent's admiration. Yet Mrs. Humble was doing ten years' for an abortion . . . Mrs. Humble, whose husband only kept a tiny newspaper-shop, and whose son was out of work, had nearly two thousand pounds laid by in the Savings Bank, and it had all been obtained by the pursuit of a profession which Mrs. Humble genuinely believed to be a philanthropic one. What, after all, had she done but help poor girls out of a trouble which civilisation would not permit to be anything else? Wasn't it, except in very rare cases, always economic pressure that had brought everyone into the prison? Not merely women who were in for debt because they couldn't pay their rates—some of whom came in regularly year after year, worked off their debt, so to speak, and went off to their homes again having cost those citizens who did pay their rates quite a lot of money—but all the other women also, the street-walkers; the shoplifters; the members of thieves' gangs; the abortionists. They had all done what they had done because they hadn't any money; and the Mrs. Humbles could even think that they had been doing a good work as well. It was all very difficult, and the only thing to hang on to was that society must be protected. That was the only thing, considered the Lady Superintendent, for she was only too miserably conscious that she herself might have been anything, and done anything, had her circumstances only been different. "There, but for the grace of God . . ." the chaplain had quoted to her once, and it had stuck in her mind ever since.

She hated to visit Starling—she hated her own bright, kind manner as she went into the cell. She hated the futility of her own utterances, but she couldn't think of anything better to say. What could she say? What, indeed, could anybody say? But Starling herself didn't seem to want to say anything beyond the ordinary banalities. She seemed oddly like a woman in a dream. Then the Governor came to tell her there was no reprieve—he had received a letter from the Secretary of State. He read it to her. She didn't seem to mind as she had at the failure of the appeal. She sat quietly.

The door was kept open, as always. A mockery of freedom. It seemed to Julia worse than if it had been locked.

The day dragged endlessly—not that she wanted it to go fast, and yet why didn't she want it to go fast? It wasn't really her last day. She didn't, she couldn't believe that. Yet the day did seem somehow different and odd. Perhaps because they kept on giving her bromide, just as they had done yesterday, and she felt stupid with it.

The doctor came in two or three times, the chaplain came and talked with her. She couldn't speak at all herself. She sat and looked at them with her short-sighted eyes wide open, not screwing them up as usual to try and see better. Miss Quint and Miss Paramore came on as usual in the evening. Miss Quint took her hand and pressed it. Julia let her hand lie limp. The whole thing was, somehow, embarrassing. How could anybody expect her to speak or listen when they must know that all the time she was waiting for the news to come—the news of the last-minute reprieve. She was pinning all her hopes on that—that thing you read about in books, that arrived at the last moment that always saved you.

She thought it had come, about nine. She had been told not to go to bed. She wondered why, rather dully. She didn't want to go to bed, but when the Lady Superintendent came in she jumped up, sure that the news had come at last. But it was something quite different. They were going to move her room, explained the Lady

Superintendent, there was nothing to be frightened about. She would have a nice bed. They would give her something to make her sleep—they would give it her now. It was just that they were going to move her room.

The little procession started out—the Lady Superintendent, Miss Quint, Miss Paramore and a nurse. They went along a corridor and up a flight of stairs. Julia walked slowly and draggingly; her mind, mercifully numb, hadn't told her the reason for this change. Suddenly she realised that she was in the prison itself; the real prison as distinct from the hospital. The corridors seemed to branch out like the spokes of a fan in every direction, the walls were painted a pretty green, all the ironwork of balustrades, the wire netting stretched from floor to floor, the spiral staircases, woodwork, and cell doors, everything was painted this pretty, soft green. It really looked quite pretty in the soft gas-light, and yet the whole place felt, in its silence, like a tomb. There wasn't a sound, save the footfalls of the little procession. They went past cell doors, all locked, to the far end of a long corridor, and in at a green-painted door.

Julia looked about her. There were the usual chairs, the little table. To the right as she came in was the incandescent gas-bracket; opposite, against the wall, was a little bed, neatly made up. It had two windows, filled with small panes of opaque, ribbed glass, of which two or three were missing to allow of air. The night was very blue and still outside. Julia looked about her cell with a dull sort of surprise. Then she saw at the far end of the cell another door, a small, arched door, painted green, and in a flash it came upon her where she was. It was through that door that she would have to pass to-morrow morning, twelve hours from now . . . only twelve hours from now.

Then she screamed and fought, and went mad, and tried to climb up the green wall, scrabbling at it with her nails, but she felt arms all about her, holding her down. She went on screaming; somebody had shut the cell door, and it seemed full of people. Then there came the prick in her arm, and fight and scream as she would, she felt a dullness coming over her legs and arms, and her head fell forward.

They laid her on the bed, and arranged the blankets

380

over her. She mustn't go to sleep—she mustn't. She was losing precious time. She must talk to them, explain how it had all happened. Surely she could show them that they mustn't do this dreadful thing?

NIGHT PIECE TO JULIA

ALL over the prison, and in the homes of those to do with the prison, the uneasy consciousness of Julia Starling, and of the approach of nine o'clock next morning, seemed to hold the very air, gripping it as a frost grips it. The prisoners turned uneasily in their beds, some shouted and cried out, one woman tore her blanket to shreds. The officers wished to God that the next twenty-four hours, the next week, or even month, lay already in the past. It wasn't only that such an event made all the prisoners refractory and difficult, it was also that you felt awful, in some odd way guilty, when you'd known the prisoner herself, tended her in the infirmary, or sat with her in that last awful room where the light burned all night. You couldn't face with equanimity what was to take place at nine. Nine, when so many thousands and thousands of people would be sitting down to their eggs and bacon, when many more thousands would already be on their way to work. And nearly every one of them thinking. . . . Is it over yet? Not liking to look at watch or clock lest it should be the actual minute. Not wanting to look until the hands stood at five minutes past, when they could draw a deep breath and say more comfortably: "Well, it's all over now, anyway."

The Beale family had gone out to the pictures. "No good doing nothing but think," George had said, and Mrs. Almond sat idly listening to the kindly efforts of the woman next door to distract her thoughts. Did some little voice whisper to that kind neighbour that for the rest of her life it would be something to remember, something to say: "I sat up all night with poor Julia Starling's mother. The awful time I had . . . too dreadful it was!" Yet at the same time it didn't seem so very dreadful, only oddly boring, and somehow strange. The neighbour didn't realise it herself all the time; her thoughts would drift off to her own married daughter, who was "expecting" next month; to that new hat of hers with the scarlet flowers in it. She'd have to take them out now; it wouldn't seem quite nice to come and go at One Beresford flaunting scarlet. . . .

"Drink this hot cup of tea, love. . . . It'll do you good," and Mrs. Almond would drink it. And Mrs. Almond's thoughts also wandered. They weren't on Julia the whole of that night. They were often on herself, on the disgrace Julia had brought on her, though she supposed she oughtn't to think of that now; but how could she help it? They'd have to move now, just as she thought she was settled. People blamed her for agreeing to sell that blue Italian officer's cape to the waxwork people, but fifty pounds was fifty pounds when you'd had so much expense and didn't know where to turn for money.

Mr. Carr sat steadily dosing himself with whisky after whisky. Mrs. Carr lay wrapped in a flame of agony. For her no nice hot cups of tea, no thoughts of how she was to live, nothing but the pain that seemed to tear at her womb. Over and over again she remembered Leonard's birth, the agony, her own screams echoing in her ears, the smug face of the doctor who didn't believe in chloroform for women in childbirth; it was more natural for them to help themselves. . . . Would he have believed in chloroform for this agony? She pressed her old knotted hands against her belly; she wished that she were dead, that she could die instead of him, or at least that she could die. Such a boy as he'd always been till he met that woman . . . the way he looked at you and laughed brought out some present or other. That last box of dates hadn't been opened yet.

Gipsy, who had not the habit of prayer, spent most of the hours upon her knees. She couldn't say anything more definite than: "Oh, God, if You exist . . . if You are anywhere . . . please stop it," but she said it over and over again.

Marian was not with her. Marian was dining out with her latest husband-to-be.

Ruby, with her newest lover, a very rich man indeed called Maurice, in the intervals of sipping champagne, sobbed up on his shoulder. Eventually he had to promise her a new necklace and take her to a night club to dance the hours away. When the time for bacon and eggs arrived she was sufficiently recovered to tell him of her childhood struggles in the cause of her art.

Dr. Ackroyd and Anne faced each other miserably in their drawing-room in Saint Clement's Square. If only, thought Anne, they had had a couple of baby cases that night, that would have taken their thoughts off. . . . There wasn't even any influenza.

Anne sat trying to read, but really listening to her father walking up and down the room.

"She'd have been all right," he said suddenly, "if nothing overwhelming had come into her life."

"I shouldn't have thought," said Anne, putting down her book, "that Leonard Carr, would have been overwhelming."

"No, you wouldn't: but after all, he was only the peg to hang her emotions on. She wanted something that she could dress up, and pretend to herself was overwhelming. Why, for God's sake, don't women clear their minds of this 'in love' cant, and simply use a man as most men use women?"

"They want something else," said Anne, "even I should. It was just that something else that Julia always wanted—even when we were at school. She lived on—I don't quite know how to put it—that romantic assumption that there was something wonderful and golden, something complete and round; that was what she wanted."

"Exactly. That's what all women want, and when they

find it doesn't exist they invent it, and dress it up. Oh, Lord, the longer I live the more I agree with Walt Whitman: 'Sometimes I turn and look at the animals. . . .' "

"She wanted what she called love," said Anne.

"Oh, well, it's no good arguing about that, because we should first have to decide what love is. The simple classification of 'sacred and profane love' is not for this generation. I believe that if people were only content with what they describe as 'purely physical,' it would be a much better thing. Instead of simply going to bed with each other, and getting that particular desire out of the system, our modern civilisation makes them dress it up, makes them pretend they're the sort of people they're not, so as to be able to call the thing 'love.' That's what's happened to Julia. Carr would have been content with the decent, honest side of the business—ephemeral, I admit, but none the less exciting and interesting while it lasts. But that wasn't good enough for her. It had to be translated into terms of eternity, or at the least of permanence. And he kept her letters! If only people would keep their mouths shut and their bowels open, what a different world it would be. But this affair of Julia's . . . what waste . . . what sickening waste."

"Yes," said Anne miserably, "what sickening waste. If only she hadn't procured that abortion I believe she would have been a happy woman, although it was Herbert's. She was just the sort of woman to pour herself into motherhood. All she wanted was a vessel to pour herself into." And then she stopped, realising with horror that she was speaking of Julia in the past tense: and she began to cry.

"After all, Anne," said Dr. Ackroyd, putting his hand on her shoulder, "we've all got to die. We're all dying from our early twenties. We all start to go down-hill from then, although we feel so lusty and confident. Old age isn't beautiful, my dear. In another ten years—if I live as long—you'll wish to goodness I were out of it, for your own sake as well as for mine. Old age isn't lovely . . . we grow old and we become a burden, and we think how foolish the young are . . . and we die. . . . And that's all there is to be said of each generation. There are very few dying words worth saying, as you know—being a doctor. Most of us are dead for a considerable time before the undertaker can be called in.

The Ancients knew a thing or two, and they thought that those whom the gods love . . ."

"I know, I know," said Anne. "But not this way, not this way . . ." and to that her father had no answer.

Sir Oswald tried to read, but he kept on finding he had to go back and read the page over again because he had not consciously noted a line of it. At last he gave up the effort and returned to the thought that was always torturing him. Could he have done more? If he had threatened more forcibly to throw up his brief when she insisted on going into the box . . . ? He felt he could have almost certainly saved her if only she had kept her mouth shut, but she would not. And she had lied, contradicted herself, and told the truth, so that a bewildered jury had come to the conclusion that all her evidence was a web of lies. If he had boldly admitted that particular letter which had referred to procuring an abortion . . . ? But then an English jury was likely to hang you for adultery, and still more for abortion.

He listened every day to the casual comments of the streets, and to those of his own charwoman at his chambers. She and the other women of her sort thought that that poor young Carr was a fine fellow, and Julia a wicked woman to have "carried on" like that with a mere boy, because youth and swagger had imposed upon them; and never would they change their minds. And women who were more educated, like Mrs. Danvers, who had understood, had not been powerful enough to stop the process of the law's revenge. How, the Home Office asked, could they reprieve a man who had killed another by attacking him from behind, and how—she being seven years older—could the boy hang, and she be saved? Yet there was something wrong with the machinery of justice that one crime should produce another such as this. . . . Lack of imagination? But then it would never do to introduce imagination into the law. And yet—that a woman should hang because she had slept with a man not her husband, and that man younger than herself; that thousands of other women should be against her, incapable of thinking clearly, and, urged on by some ignoble and unrealised jealousy, sit smugly and allow this thing to take place at nine o'clock. . . . Sir Oswald tried to read again.

Dr. Ogilvie was wakeful, partly because he hated a hanging, partly because he might be needed any moment. Doubtless Davidson was feeling worse, being a parson and not so much used to the brutalities of life; but Ogilvie, smoking his pipe, sipping at a whisky and soda, could not sleep. A hanging was a beastly business, look at it how you would. He would fill the wretched woman up with morphia, but he didn't dare give her too much. She would know what was happening, though the sharp edge would be taken off her apprehension. He wished that some strain of altruism in his nature hadn't made him want to be a prison doctor. Something was wrong with society, something was wrong everywhere, particularly with education. What had been the downfall of this Starling woman? That she'd never been taught anything of her own being, and how to cope with it. He'd had dozens of women like her through his hands, and he had told them some home truths; but it was too late to tell *her* anything. Bit by bit he had pieced her life together as she had poured it out at him, begging him for help; tried to explain herself; gone on lying because she had the habit of it, but unable to prevent his accustomed eyes from seeing the truth.

He saw how completely at the mercy of her imagination and her body such a girl must have been; a girl whose mind had never been trained to look for truth, had never learned any thrift of thought. What guide could such a one have had but her own desires, which were not, after all, ignoble? Her desire for beauty, for something finer than the ugliness which was all that lay within her grasp? Her desire for physical pleasure, the only ecstasy that could be hers? Body and mind—or soul, as he supposed Davidson would call it—how badly adjusted they were to each other, and how carefully they needed training to chime together as they should. How many people realised that body and mind were two separate entities that had to be reconciled, enemies that had to learn how to come to terms, lovers that could not exist without each other? Yet that was the truth. People talk of marriage . . . of the necessity of "giving and taking"—no two human beings had such a difficult task of mutual adjustment as the two component parts of one human being, that the unthinking called "I," as though that symbol stood for something unified and at peace.

The pain of the body, of which he had seen so much, sometimes it grew as with a strange and horrible life of its own, till nothing seemed to exist save the pain, lying like a burden upon the shoulders of the mind. Sometimes the mind triumphed over that burden in the most amazing way: he had often seen that, too. Always the struggle between the two, varied by times of accord, when the body was so healthy or so satisfied that the mind was only aware of it as something light and enjoyable. For there was a gift of pleasure, pleasure in the sweet uses of the flesh, that had been slipped within all its tissues, that knitted body to mind if it were rightly understood. . . . The mind could triumph over the body's pains, could exult in its pleasures, or could be almost overthrown by its pains, in this perpetual marriage that was everyone's from birth to death.

Death—that was the dissolution of the partnership, of the only marriage that ever really mattered in the long run. That wretched creature in her cell at the present moment wasn't, he was prepared to swear, thinking of her lover, except perhaps with anger. Her relationship with her husband and her lover, and any other man she'd had, would seem extraordinarily unimportant. It was the divorce of the marriage within herself, that marriage which neither her body nor her mind had ever been taught anything about, which was worrying her now.

Two things were hanging Julia Starling—her birth-certificate, and her place in the social scale. If only she had not been seven years older than Carr, and if only she had been higher or lower in the world! In the class above hers the idea of divorce would not have shocked, and a private income would even have allowed her and Carr to live together without divorce, and no one would have been unduly outraged. Had their walk in life been the lowest, had they been tramps or part of the floating population of the docks down London River, they could have set up in one room together, and no one thought twice about it, as long as the husband wasn't a big strong man who made a row and tried to do them in.

Starling's two gifts had undoubtedly been her business capacity and the finely attuned orchestra of her body—

391

if only she had combined the two, the most sensible thing to do! But he supposed that was immoral. Why, many people would have thought the worse of her if they knew even that her body was a source of pleasure to her. If she actually marketed that talent, she would be lost indeed. What had there been for her but escape? And such was the compulsion of circumstances, it was only into a world that she had dreamed for herself that she could escape. And a dangerous world it had of necessity proved, but surely not the vulgar world that a vulgar-minded judge had called it?

It was bad luck, all of it. Bad luck for her, bad luck for the stupid husband—who had as good a right to live, poor devil, as anybody else, and bad luck for that other poor devil, who also had to toe the line that morning. And bad luck for himself, and the rest of the poor devils who had to assist at the beastly business in both places. In both prisons the prisoners would be unmanageable and gloomy, and officers would feel like criminals. Here he would have the job of testing the heart that had been stilled for ever, of noting at which cervical the fracture had occurred, even of noting the haemorrhage that might burst forth.

And why, in spite of all logic and reason, did the idea persist, even in his well-balanced mind, that it was somehow worse to hang a woman than a man? The dark consciousness of the womb was present with every man who had to do with the business, of the womb that was the holder of life, from which every living soul had issued in squalor and pain. Some deep awareness of the mother, the source of life, worked in the mind of every man. Perhaps, too, they felt that such a job should be left to another woman to carry through; but then women wouldn't carry it through. Women, as this poor creature had been, were rather the instigators of deeds than the performers.

They were borrowing a couple of warders from the men's prison for to-morrow's performance, the female officers wouldn't go to the scaffold, except the unfortunate Lady Superintendent, whose duty obliged her to do so.

This Julia Starling had evaded the womb's responsibilities, while partaking of its pleasures; but, nevertheless, that dark consciousness of it as the medium by

392

which each one of them had come into the world, would be present to every man at the execution. Ogilvie agreed that if a guilty man were hanged, a guilty woman should meet the same fate, but even with him persisted that dark awareness of the womb.

At that other prison nature would take her last ironic revenge in the body of the man who had killed for what he had called love, making a final gesture, lewd as a sneer. The very officers, the doctor who examined his body afterwards, would feel an almost superstitious dread of that impudent and useless jibe of nature's. And, God knew, hanging a man was a bad enough business, even without that wretched commentary on love which the hanged man presented despite himself.

Davidson made no attempt at sleep. He prayed, and when he could pray no more he tried to read. Then he would make himself some black coffee, lest sleep should come over him. For he had a curious idea that little as he had been able to do for her, he would be doing still less if he let his mind slip into unconsciousness; that perhaps the intensity of his thoughts and his prayers would be permitted to be of some slight help to her in her extremity. Irresistible as temptation's self, sleep came over him at about three in the morning, but he forced it back, drank more coffee, and went on wrestling with the dark angel. A phrase began to repeat itself again and again in his head. *Whom God hath joined together let no man put asunder* . . . That was out of the marriage service . . . he'd repeated it hundreds of times. What was it that Ogilvie had been theorising about . . . something about everyone alive being a marriage, generally an ill-assorted one, between body and mind? If that were so, he was going to assist next morning at the forcible sundering of a marriage.

He was tortured by the knowledge that he had been of very little help to Julia Starling. The thing that he had tried to appeal to was not there—that sense of spiritual awareness which had made his own life; this was lacking in Starling. Armed as he was with the authority of voluntary celibacy, with the fervour of intense conviction: burning as he was with the love of souls, he had not succeeded in finding hers—much less in awakening it.

During the last few weeks he had been reading, not

for the first time, the reminiscences of the Abbé Pirot, who had attended that most notorious and cold-blooded of poisoners, Marie-Madeleine de Brinvilliers. He had been turning over and over the pages of these portentous tomes, which somehow gained instead of losing by their naïve repetitions. The classic beauty of style might have been lost, but the passion survived just because the Abbé Pirot hadn't troubled over-much over the niceties of fine writing, because he had simply poured out on paper, day by day, every little thing that this penitent had said or done. That last day, that terrible last day, he had recorded moment by moment. Pirot had succeeded in obtaining remorse, not a mere regret, from his penitent, but he, Davidson, had failed. He was not, he admitted humbly, a Pirot. But then, on the other hand, poor Julia Starling, whatever the measure of her guilt, had not attained to those horrible peaks of depravity of the Brinvilliers. Perhaps the times were out of joint. Starling could not care enough about her immortal soul, she was too occupied with the thought of her mortal body. Who was not nowadays? And, not for the first time in his life, Davidson found himself regretting bitterly that he hadn't been able, as he expressed it to himself, to "go the whole way." If he had had the authority of Rome behind him; if instead of trying to impress upon Starling his belief of the necessity of the Sacraments he had had behind that belief the whole authority of his church, instead of, as he knew only too well, a mere mass of conflicting opinions!

But then, even so, and even admitting that he could have obtained an emotional response from Starling, how much would she really have known, or cared or understood? She was thinking of nothing but the injustice that was to be meted out to her; of nothing but the terrifying death of her body. Of her soul she knew nothing, and cared less. In the days of the Brinvilliers there had been more crime, and more cruelty; but nevertheless everybody believed. There had been no initial difficulty of a complete lack of interest to be overcome; and so the Marquise de Brinvilliers, with murder thick upon her conscience, had made the most edifying end, and the Abbé Pirot, having wrestled with the dark angels for her soul until he was almost as exhausted as his penitent, was convinced of her ultimate salvation.

None of these words would convey anything to Julia Starling, or to those of her generation brought up as she had been. The Brinvilliers had been able to say: "But are there any sins that by their gravity, or their number, cannot be forgiven, even by the Church?" and Pirot, conscious that the voice of centuries spoke through his mouth, to one who listened with ears which the centuries had not yet dulled, was able to reply: "Madame, there are no sins which cannot be expiated." And with his ardour, his faith, he had succeeded in assuring the cold-blooded woman, who had poisoned for profit from her youth, that there was a gate, straight and narrow indeed, through which she could pass to a remission of her sins.

Why, the very word "sin" meant nothing to Julia Starling. The Brinvilliers, had hours when she lapsed from grace, when the tigress in her had shown itself, when her anger at humanity had been too strong for her new-found grace—hours such as that dread one after her torture when once again she was the jungle animal who hated all humanity—and yet Pirot, endlessly patient, had once again brought her to the foot of the cross. What could Davidson offer? Only a belief as passionate, an ardour as intense, a pity as deep as Pirot's, but without Pirot's conviction and authority. More important still, what could Julia receive? Nothing. What she must be suffering now, unless God were good and sent her sleep. And even so there would be the awakening . . .

He told himself that the actual business would be over very quickly, everyone assured him of that. But what did "quickly" mean? Who could say how long that moment of dropping seemed? Time was relative, an hour of happiness could whip through a man's mind like the flaunt of a blown banner. In misery, five minutes could seem hours. In sleep a lifetime could be lived through in the space of time taken to lift the latch of a door. Who could say how long those few moments seemed to the prisoner, those moments that the authorities flattered themselves were over so swiftly? There was a theory that a man's whole life flashed before him in the moment of drowning. What was time, as the clock knew it, in the face of such tricks as these? One didn't even know to what one was condemning the victim, that was what it worked out at . . . "A thousand years in Thy sight are but as yesterday" . . . easy for Him if that was how He was able to look at it, seeing Time all in one piece. Not easy for man, to whom the next moment is the horizon which, like the sea's horizon, always advances with his own advance, so that never is he able to peer over the rim.

At the other prison men turned uneasily, or paced their cells, or broke up the furniture in the cell, head in hands, wishing the hours would go more quickly. All excepting Leo, who wished they would go more slowly. He still had so much to do—another letter to his mother, one to his shipmates. He was getting sleepy by the time he'd finished them. Might as well take a rest. Christ Almighty! what a fool he'd been. Well, it was no good crying over spilt milk. Anyway, he'd show them he wasn't afraid. When his shipmates heard of him, they'd know he'd met it all right. No brandy for him, he'd leave that for the others—they'd want it. He slept—so peacefully, that the officers looked at him and then at each other. Poor devil . . . let him sleep. What a pity he couldn't go off in his sleep, like you did to sick dogs and cats. He'd never know anything about it then.

One of the officers wished, rather uneasily, that the hangman hadn't altered the drop that evening. It wasn't a good thing to experiment with drops at the last moment. It was bad enough, of course, if the man's head were torn off. You had to go down below and clean up the mess; but at least the man himself knew nothing of it. But suppose the drop were wrong the other way about. . . ? Then the poor devil just thrashed about, kicking with his pinioned legs against the brick sides of the pit, so that you had to rush down and hang on to his feet, as in the days of hanging by strangulation. Nothing like that, he hoped, would happen to this nice young chap. A damned shame that a woman should have brought him to this. A decent young chap, who didn't make the warders' job any harder for them than needs be. You'd have thought something better could have been found to put out the light of a fine young chap with such guts, and such a lot of good in him.

Julia tried to lie quietly, even tried to keep her eyes shut. But what was the good? She opened her eyes and saw the shadows of the watching women like great birds against the green and white wall. She shut her eyes again, so as to be able to try and pretend she was alone.

She was very tired, and it seemed to her for a while that she suffered very little. Her nerves, aided by the bromide, were more relaxed than they had been for days past. She had been a fool to be so frightened, of course they didn't mean to do that dreadful nightmare thing to her. Things like that couldn't happen. Her imagination had always been her curse, everyone on both sides had said so at the trial . . . it had actually led her into believing the Governor when he had told her that the appeal was turned down. She had screamed and fought then, and tried to climb up the bare wall, and they had given her all that bromide and it hadn't done her any good, because she was so frightened. But now she saw that she had been a fool to believe it. They were only doing it to frighten her, that was it. Perhaps she did deserve a little punishment, and this was how it was being given to her. They were letting her own imagination give it to her on this night that they pretended was to be her last. But it couldn't really be so, because this sort of thing didn't happen to people who were in perfect health. Only dying people knew for a certainty that their last night had come. When healthy people died suddenly it was by an accident, not by a set and certain catastrophe. That would be too arbitrary and silly, it just couldn't happen. She relaxed still more in that blessed certainty.

She was in a big shop, it was important she should finish buying what she wanted before the shop closed, and it was going to close any moment now. The stocking department was on the top floor, she must hurry or it would be too late, and she would not be allowed to go up to it. Already the shop assistants were leaving. There was the lift, one of those terrifying lifts one worked oneself; she got in, pulled the iron gates across, and pressed the button.

She had made an awful mistake, it was a lift that went down, not up, she'd been on the top floor and not known it. And the lift was out of order, she couldn't stop it, it was falling . . . falling. With a thin scream she awoke and sat up, wet with sweat. For a moment it was a relief to be awake, to realise that that falling lift had been a dream . . . but the next moment full realisation of everything had flooded in upon her. All relaxation of the nerves had gone, she knew what the Governor had told her was the truth, that it wasn't impossible that they should do that dreadful thing to her next morning. These were her last hours of life; never after to-night would she see shadows on a wall, feel the prickle of a blanket against her cheek, draw her finger down the flesh of her inner arm. Not much to want—to see shadows, to touch your own flesh, rub your skin against a blanket, yet they were going to take it from her. Everything was to be taken from her, and yet she'd never asked or wanted much. Was it her fault that she'd married Herbert when she was too young to know what she was doing? Had it been her fault that she'd thought she'd loved Leo? Who wouldn't have thought they loved almost anybody who came along and was nice, leading the dreary sort of life she'd had to lead? Leo . . . a faint thought of him, perhaps also lying awake in that other dread place not far away, brushed across the surface of her mind like a moth's wing, and was gone. She'd always worked hard and worked well. Mr. Coppinger and Gipsy had always said so. She'd never had the chance to do all she could have with her gifts; life had always been against her. Naturally she'd tried to make a dream world where she had all she wanted, where she was admired and beloved; naturally she'd snatched at any love and admiration that came her way in actuality. Who wouldn't have, who didn't? Everyone tried to get what they wanted, and it didn't go wrong for all of them. Just because in spite of the dreariness of her life, she had been able to create a sort of fairy story that ran alongside the drab reality, was she to be punished in this dreadful fashion? As though she'd intended the fairy story to be real! Leo ought to have known she hadn't meant it to be real; it was all his fault. Just because she was seven years older than he—that seven years which, she had once heard, saw the changing of the whole fabric of the body—people seemed to think that she was responsible for what Leo had done.

She had always been aware of time, and afraid of it. Leo's fewer years had set his whole life at a different place in time from hers, and she had endeavoured, by setting a term for things—such as three years till she got her freedom—to make them match. Life was only time slipping past you; you tried to grab at it, but it went on from between your fingers. Leo had never been aware of any time but the present; he'd never seen that the present was always becoming the past, just as the future was always becoming the present.

There he was again, right in her mind now, but not as himself; it was not for what he also might be feeling that she agonised. She thought of him with a deep and bitter resentment. It was his stupidity that had lost her; she saw him as her executioner. . . . As the awful word struck into her mind, her heart seemed to leap and almost stop, then went on thudding slowly, angrily.

After all, she had not had so very much to do with Leo in reality; he was more terribly real to her now in this aspect than he had often been in real life. It wasn't fair. Why, even the love that she and he had had—how rare it had been, what with the difficulties of meeting, and his voyages. Only those few days in Essex, and once at the shop. More often than not she had only possessed him through her husband's flesh, or in the fastnesses of her own mind and body, lying on her bed alone.

Now that imaginary Leo and the actual Leo of such physical contacts as had been theirs, had fused into the agent of her destruction. It was as though Leo's hands were going to close about her throat. What did that remind her of? Some song . . . long ago, at school; she'd thought it beautiful then . . . something about sooner feeling your lover's hands closing about your throat, choking out life, than bidding you farewe—hell. . . . Rotten nonsense. Nothing mattered but life. Not to have life choked out . . . that was all that mattered.

Leo ought to have known that, would have known it if he hadn't been drunk. He ought to have known she hadn't meant it . . . not to that point. Nobody could. Life was what mattered, life. Not to be going to suffer such a horror. Oh, to be alone, unmarried, old, ugly, poor, sleeping in some doorway, dirty, cold, starving, for no one to be interested in one . . . but to be alive . . . just to be alive. How could people take that away from one? Stop all that that meant? They were killing everything: the trams down Chiswick High Road, the young trees in leaf, the bright winking faces of the shops, the clanging of the bells, all the sparkle and the glitter and the music.

The papers said that Mrs. Starling was to be hanged on Tuesday, but that wasn't really what was happening. Mrs. Starling was a romantic figure, who wrote passionate love-letters, a figure in an Italian officer's blue cape and a helmet hat; a figure that had never really existed except as a pretence. They weren't hanging that Mrs. Starling, they were hanging Julia, who cleaned her teeth night and morning, who went to the lavatory—who would have to even on this Tuesday morning—who ate and drank, and smoked, and dressed, and sent clothes to the wash; whose hair grew greasy and lost its wave, whose nails needed cleaning and filing, whose head sometimes ached, and whose feet always ached at the end of a long day; who kept count of her money in a shabby little leather purse, whose back hurt her every month so that she could hardly go to business, who stopped outside the cinema when the programme was changed twice weekly to look at the new posters. . . . That was what they were killing. . . . What had a person like that, a person just like the rest of them, done to be killed? You couldn't kill a person who cleaned her teeth and went to the lavatory; you only killed romantic people. And no one was really a romantic person, no one. It was not worth this stark reality.

True, Herbert had been killed, but that had really been an accident. He hadn't had to know about it beforehand, hadn't dreaded it. They hadn't waked him at the chill hour of morning and told him that now—now—he had to dress, make use of the conduits of his body for the last time, go through the farce of putting something into his stomach that he and everyone else knew would never nourish him. People hadn't looked at him with a dread apology in their sick eyes. . . .

What was it the chaplain had told her? That we are all under sentence of death. . . . The sort of thing that sounds clever and isn't a bit true. If you didn't know when or how it was going to overtake you, what did it matter? It was this relentless knowledge that was so cruel; she wouldn't have inflicted that upon her worst enemy. "Her own worst enemy" . . . wasn't that an expression she had heard? Probably it was true, but it hadn't been her fault. Everyone spoke of her, especially Herbert's relations, as though she'd been a sort of spoiled darling, but that wasn't true. She'd never had a chance of anything she really wanted. That was why she'd always pretended. She'd only pretended Herbert's death, and it had suddenly come alive in spite of her. Now her own death was here, and she couldn't pretend any more. If, when morning came, she were to stay lying on her bed, pretending something quite different, they'd pull her up; they'd make her stand on her feet, they wouldn't let her go on pretending. She had come to that place where dreams fail.

She struggled to her feet and the two women moved towards her anxiously. She needed their support, her legs failed her; it was as though they were made of straw. She began to moan and cry as they laid her back on the bed. She caught the hard, firm hand of one of them, held on to it desperately. *Don't let them do it, don't let them do it . . . promise you won't let them do it. . . .* They soothed her, gave her more bromide, but she was not deceived. She lay biting her pillow, beating her hands beside her head.

Oh, to sleep, to sleep. . . . But if she slept It would be upon her all the sooner, she mustn't sleep. She must grab back the minutes and the hours. She sat up and held her hands to that unwinking light; she stared at those hands she knew by heart as though she had never seen them before. They were real and alive, there was the shiny oval nail of her left thumb, that had never given her any trouble, and there was the squat nail of the right thumb, with its unchanging ribbed band. . . . She spread out her fingers, held them higher towards the light, while the women watched her anxiously. The blood informed those fingers, she could see the rosy web of skin between them against the light.

To-morrow people would use their hands for all sorts of things; for dressing, and opening train doors, and writing and eating, and doing accounts, and for snatched love too, if they were lucky. They would use their hands for hanging her . . . hanging her . . . hanging her. Because of their hands her own, with their long capable fingers, her thumbs with the smooth nail and the ribbed, would be lying inert; the processes of decay already invisibly begun. No, no, it wasn't possible that people would deliberately cause those hands, so alive and well and strong for years to come, to be dead and useless to-morrow. No one could do a thing like that. They would

401

come and tell her of a last-minute reprieve in the morning, that was what always happened.

Back she was at it again, hope—nay more, almost certainty, giving her the relief of relaxation for a brief minute. Hands, she thought childishly, were very dangerous; people oughtn't to have them. If Leo hadn't had hands he couldn't have killed Herbert, she couldn't have written those letters. But without hands she wouldn't be able to hold on right up in this big plane-tree where she was, so high that it made her giddy to look down, and the tree shook so, too. . . . Even with hands she couldn't hold on, she was going to fall. . . .

She fell, screaming, and again the cell rushed up to meet her, the unwinking light and the unwinking pitiful eyes. Oh, it was true, it was true, they were going to hang her; she was going to fall just like that, with that awful sickening empty feeling, she was going to fall.

It was true, it was true. She saw one of the women— Mrs. Horner, with the pale rigid face that looked paler than ever, look surreptitiously at her watch. That watch would go on ticking after she, Julia, had ceased to exist; after her pulses were still. There was more life in that watch than there was in her, because of the certainty that it would go on ticking. She was dead already, because she had to die at nine next morning. Or was it this morning by now? Was that why Mrs. Horner had looked at her watch? The doctor was here now, and again she felt the needle thrust into her arm, and again she fell into a heavy sleep.

The time, slowly for some, fast for others, continued to exist, and nine o'clock struck.

Morning was fine for those who went to work and for those preparing for Ascot. The trees stood up into the sunlight, their full foliage still a deep untarnished green. Everywhere was the life of sunshine—flickering shadows and bright reflections. Soon the tinted wind-blown posters of the evening papers burgeoned along the streets. For it was ten o'clock, and the "noon" edition, playing its strange trick of forcing Time ahead, was on sale. The posters bore the legend: "Carr and Starling Hanged," or "Double Hanging. Special," but only the stop-press gave a bare statement, the papers themselves gave the latest betting and racing advice. The Lunch edition, on sale long before lunch, reported on its front page that: "Leonard Carr and Julia Starling were executed this morning for the murder of the latter's husband, Herbert Starling. Death was instantaneous in each case. The usual notices were posted on the prison gates, where small crowds had collected." But already the posters had dropped the stale news and replaced it by "Noon Wire and Double." When, after lunch, the 6.30 edition was on sale, the first Ascot winners held pride of place. And when working London had finished brewing its tea in thousands of offices, the Late Extra was pored over by office-boys and heads of departments alike, it was the racing news that was read. Two lines in a column headed "News from Everywhere" and tucked away on an inconspicuous page, recorded the fact of a successful double execution. This item was sandwiched between two others; one saying that sixty police summonses for road traffic offences had been granted at Lambeth that day, the other recording that a Mr. and Mrs. Merritt, of Croydon, had celebrated their Golden Wedding. Mr. Merritt, though now retired, had been for thirty years in the service of the Metropolitan Water Board.

The gleaming cars rolled back from Ascot, the workers of London went homewards in the towering scarlet buses, or the swaying trains. And, after supper, in the extra hour of sunlight man had re-parcelled from his older system, young people played tennis in leafy Greater London, and the older men worked in their gardens.